HANDCUFFS, TRUNCHEON
AND A
POLYESTER THONG

HANDCUFFS, TRUNCHEON
AND A
POLYESTER THONG

BY
GINA KIRKHAM

urbanepublications.com

First published in Great Britain in 2017 by Urbane Publications Ltd
Suite 3, Brown Europe House, 33/34 Gleaming Wood Drive, Chatham, Kent ME5 8RZ
Copyright ©Gina Kirkham, 2017

The moral right of Gina Kirkham to be identified as the author of this work has been asserted in accordance with the Copyright, Designs and Patents Act of 1988.

A CIP catalogue record for this book is available from the British Library.

ISBN 978-1-911331-71-1
MOBI 978-1-911331-73-5
EPUB 978-1-911331-72-8

Design and Typeset by Julie Martin
Cover by The Invisible Man
Cover illustration by David Hallangen
www.behance.net/hallangenart

Printed and bound by CPI Group (UK) Ltd, Croydon, CR0 4YY

urbanepublications.com

MIX
Paper from
responsible sources
FSC® C013604

The publisher supports the Forest Stewardship Council® (FSC®), the leading international forest-certification organisation. This book is made from acid-free paper from an FSC®-certified provider. FSC is the only forest-certification scheme supported by the leading environmental organisations, including Greenpeace.

For my beautiful Mum

In lieu of not being able to get you a proper
'squiffy' Mum, this is for you...
with my love and undying admiration

Sheila Jane Radestock
1937 – 2006

HANDCUFFS, TRUNCHEON AND A POLYESTER THONG

"Oh feckin' hell Miss, don't let go, I'll get some help..."

As Moggie Benson's dulcet tones resonated around the vast warehouse, I quickly reached the conclusion that letting go hadn't actually crossed my mind. What had more than tentatively swept through it however, was how I'd got into this predicament in the first place?

Here I am, 35 feet up, swinging precariously from a rusty old girder by my fingertips listening to the echoing clang of metal hitting the ground below.

Let go or cling on for dear life?

No contest really. Fear has locked my fingers around it like a vice. I'm now glued to it like our local drug dealer Jerome Mills usually is to a bag of cannabis.

I don't know why running across the rooftop of the local scrapyard after Billy 'The Mog' Benson had seemed like a good idea. Moggie's a good commercial burglar, renowned for his cat-like agility and he was seriously living up to his nickname tonight. He'd made it easily over the top and across the back section, landing feet first on the flat roof below.

I hadn't.

The old corrugated iron roof had given way under my sylph-like footsteps in my size 4 SWAT boots, leaving me dangling helplessly like my next door neighbour's onesie on a washing line.

Looking down I try to adjust my eyes but I can only see

momentary glints of moonlight flashing off the stacked metal, giving a strange eerie glow from beneath. If I could sigh at my stupidity I would, but the realisation I might not get out of this particular predicament alive has already started to choke what little breath I have left.

So, whilst I'm dangling here with nothing between me and the jagged scrap metal below, feeling the breeze whistle through my combat pants (which in turn is making me wish I'd worn a pair of thermal knickers rather than a polyester thong with a bow on the front), let me introduce myself.

I am Mavis Upton.

Constable 1261 Mavis Upton to be precise. Ace police driver and apprehender of naughty people; lover of crisps (any flavour); hater of big knickers, which if I survive this, I'll tell you all about later; daughter to Mrs Josie Upton, sister to Connie and Michael and Mum to a rather headstrong young lady called Ella...

... and a woman with one failed marriage under her belt and a totally reckless disregard for danger, as evidenced by the aforementioned crisis I'm currently experiencing.

I start to inch myself along to see if I can swing my legs over the next girder.

"Nooooo Miss, don't do that!"

The frantic voice that screams out from the near darkness below makes my heart jump so much I almost lose my grip.

"Jeez Moggie give us a bit of a warning before you yell will you?" I let a small hiccup escape as I try to focus on the task in hand whilst I weigh up my options.

I could stay here as I am until help arrives, make some futile attempt to save myself or wait for the inevitable drop and get it over and done with. My numb fingers begin to make the decision for me as they start to peel themselves away from the cold metal of the girder.

Option number two suddenly seems like a good choice but nothing is close enough for me to reach. I couldn't be further away from any saving grace if I tried.

"AR21, AR21 what is your exact location Mavis, patrols are on their way?"

The crackle of the radio jolts me more than Moggie's shouting, sending my heart into a fury as it thumps against my ribcage. I manage to cling on, gently swaying.

A forceful gust of wind blows across the scrapyard. It catches my back, pushing me forward so my forearms scrape painfully on the bottom section of the girder. I have to resist my natural instinct to answer Heidi in the Control Room. Every fibre is screaming for me to press the button and shout up for urgent assistance but I know I'll never be able to hang on with one hand.

I feel sick.

My life proverbially flashes before my eyes as I look down into the waiting darkness. I'm going to die without even being given the chance to replenish my legendary Coral Blush lipstick or enjoy the salt 'n pepper chips I'd ordered from Mrs Wong's Chippy on Martins Lane for my scoff break.

Suddenly I don't feel so brave anymore.

"Miss, Miss, don't panic, I've found something, you just keep hanging on Miss."

Moggie's voice echoes from somewhere on the far side of the scrapyard amid the sounds of metal being smashed. My brain is going as numb as my fingers.

"You'd better bloody hurry up Moggie, I can't last much longer."

"Just hang on Miss!"

I want to cry but fear won't let me, a whimper catches in my throat. As the rust and metal began to bite into my fingers, they start to lose their grip.

One – Two – Three -

My left hand slips away from the girder leaving me clinging by my right hand. The muscles in my arm are burning; pain is tearing into my shoulder, making it feel as though it's being slowly ripped away from the socket.

"Moggie, Moggie...for fuck's sake Moggie!"

Now I am crying. The salty tears roll down my cheeks. I think I'm screaming too, but I can't hear it. Maybe it's only in my head. This time I'm not going to make it. This time I've taken one chance too many.

I'm oblivious to the deep rumbling sound from below and the smell of diesel wafting up towards me as my remaining fingers begin to slip away from the girder in slow motion

And I'm falling.

Falling into the blackness...

... for about two feet.

I land in a heap in the outstretched arms of Moggie, painfully smacking my shins against some sort of metal frame.

"Fuck, Miss, that was close," he guffawed, more in shock than humour.

"No shit Sherlock, you can say that again." I give him a sideways glance as I wipe away the cold sweat that's trickling down from beneath my fringe. Shaking the feeling back into my painful fingers, I let that comment sink in. "No, on second thoughts don't, just put me down please, you've still got your hand on my butt and that will never do."

Moggie hastily drops me down into the cage of the cherry picker, that by some miracle he had found in the corner of the warehouse. As the machinery whirred and whined taking us back down to ground level, I couldn't help but feel some sense of gratitude and a touch of admiration for Moggie.

He could have carried on with his escape and disappeared into the night with his spoils but he hadn't. He had stayed to save my life.

As the cage clunks onto the concrete floor amid mangled metal, I turn to him and put my hand on his shoulder.

"Thanks Moggie, I owe you one."

"That's okay Miss, always been sorta fond of youse like." He blushed and scrutinised the toes of his trainers.

"That's good mate, that's nice to hear. Right let's get down to business, you do not have to say anything, but it may harm your defence if you do not mention when questioned…"

As the sound of klaxons blared on the breeze and the blue lights bounced from the stocks of metal and glass stored in the warehouse signalling my back up had arrived, he grinned and winked. "Arrr hey Miss that's proper shady that; not even a freebie graft for saving yer life?"

"No Moggie sorry, not even a freebie. You shouldn't have been thieving in the first place but I'll write you up for Court, they might even award you a fiver."

A smile breaks across the face of this career criminal. "Thanks Miss."

And I smile too as I click the handcuffs into place.

HANDCUFFS, TRUNCHEON AND A POLYESTER THONG

Welcome to my life as a police officer. Proud and sometimes loud, with a very wicked sense of humour!

AN EPIPHANY

"I don't know how many lives you think you've got left Mavis, but even the station cat is getting jealous." Bill Lawrence screwed up a sheet of paper he had been making notes on and aimed for the bin in the corner. He missed.

"I know Sarge, it was a serious lapse of judgement, but it turned out okay. I'm alive and Moggie will get three months minimum."

I tried to sound optimistic whilst discreetly examining the hairs in Bill's left ear. What was it with men? As soon as they lost the ability to retain hair on their heads they would make up for it with copious amounts in their nostrils and ears. Bill squirmed in the swivel chair, picked up a pen and plunged the end into his right ear, giving it a little jiggle. I grimaced.

"Here you go, sign at the bottom of this." He thrust the Incident Form towards me, offering the pen he had just used to excavate something disgusting out of his auditory orifice.

"Err it's okay Sarge, I've got my own thanks."

I left him examining the end of his biro and went to make myself a cup of tea in the night kitchen.

"Are you okay chick, heard you had a bit of a close shave tonight?"

I stopped stirring my tea and quietly acknowledged Marion's presence with a nod.

She plonked herself down at the table. "Milk no sugar for me lovely."

I obliged, using one of the better, less chipped mugs.

Marion was nearing retirement and had taken up a post in the Divisional Control Room. Larger than life in personality as well as size, with her dark curly hair scraped back into a ponytail, she could pass for younger than her 54 years.

"The fact that I now owe my continued existence into another millennium to Moggie Benson has somehow made me a little reflective Marion..." I laughed and took a slurp of my tea as she pushed a packet of custard creams towards me. "... of all the people hey? Suppose I should just accept it and be grateful."

She nodded sagely.

"It wasn't like that in my day Mave. Lost kids, shitty nappies and dog bites; that was all we dealt with on the Women's Section, not all these heroics that you girlies get up to now." She dunked her biscuit two seconds too long; lifting it up she inspected the missing bit and began to fish round with a spoon.

"It's 2008 Marion, things are different now, we've come a long way since then. Believe it or not they even let us drive fast cars and not just to the chippy!" I gave a dramatic bow.

She smirked and grabbed another biscuit. "What made you join Mave, can't have been easy, single mum, wrong side of thirty?"

I wasn't sure if that was a dig at my age, but decided to let it slide.

"It was an epiphany Marion, I had an epiphany." I looked out of the window, taking in the orange glow of the street lamps and my own reflection. "How long have you got?"

Marion touched my hand.

"As long as you want chick, as long as you want."

...

It was sometime during October 1988, whilst wearing a dreadful pair of dayglow pink legwarmers, kicking leaves and pushing Ella's tricycle as she skipped behind, that I suddenly decided I wanted to follow a lifelong ambition to join the police.

Just like that. My epiphany.

As I trampled through another pile of leaves, carefully avoiding a rather large doggie deposit but wheeling the bike through a smaller one, I excitedly began to plan my new career. After all, regardless of sex, status, quality or quantity of brain cells or even hair colour, this was supposed to be a time of equal opportunities. I had a passion, an idealistic idea to give something back, to make a difference.

I was quite good at making a difference; my Mum has always referred to me as being 'a bit different', maybe this was what she meant.

Maybe she knew I was destined for greater things.

I trundled the bike along an uneven bit of pavement, humming gently to myself. I have a rather lovely life. Okay I wasn't quite a merry divorcee, but I did smile a lot, I've got Ella, my beautiful but exasperating 7-year-old daughter, a cosy little seaside cottage to call home and a kitten, who was quite simply called Cat. What more could I want?

"Mum, Muuuum why aren't you listening to me? Can we jump puddles Mum, hey can we, can we?"

I turned to see Ella staring at me with her hands on her hips. "Sorry munchkin, I was just having a bit of a daydream, what's the matter?"

She looked up at me, eyes shining brightly as she wiped a rather large booger across the sleeve of her coat.

"Puddles Mum, can we jump puddles?"

Her excited chatter carried along with her as she started to run ahead. "Of course we can, but don't go too far ahead... and watch out for..." Too late.

As always Ella's knack for finding muck was a gift. Picking her up from the deep muddy puddle she had fallen hands and knees into, I allowed myself a wistful smile. Ella and muck always went hand-in-hand, just like I had been at her age, but mine was for mystery, wrongdoings, the Famous Five and excitement, which were actually my first forays into the realms of crime and detection. Grabbing a tissue from my pocket I wiped her face as she squirmed.

"Don't spit on it Mummy, that's so deeeegusting."

Laughing at her choice of word, I carefully inspected the tissue.

"Ella, how come you can always find muck and trouble? I despair, I really do." Pulling away, she skipped ahead, her childish laughter drifting on the breeze.

'I despair; I really do...'

I couldn't believe I'd just said that to my own daughter; I was turning into my Mum with her infuriatingly annoying expressions. I bit the inside of my lip as I remembered her berating me with the same words over the unfortunate incident with our rather odd next door neighbour when I was about Ella's age. Sitting down on a nearby bench where I could keep an eye on her as she played, I pulled my collar up and hunkered down with my hands in my pockets.

A solitary burnt orange leaf drifted slowly from a tree, finding rest in a small puddle. A sudden gust of wind scattered brown sycamore copters, picking them up and swirling them across the grass as I fondly remembered an age gone by, full of Enid Blyton, exciting adventures and red Clarks sandals.

DOGS, SOCKS & ENID BLYTON

Harold Kirby! Yes, that was his name. What a strange little man he had been.

Hunched and crumpled, with his grey hair and nobbled fingers and a dreadful taste in knitted cardigans. He must have been at least 102 if not more.

After reading The Famous Five Go to Smugglers Top, I'd suddenly decided that Harold was also a smuggler. Of what I had no idea, but it seemed incredibly exciting at the time and I just knew that dear old Enid would have agreed with me if she had seen him. On a nice, clean unrumpled page in my Investigations Diary, I'd diligently scribbled my first instruction. I, Mavis Jane Upton aged 7 ¾'s was going to help catch a notorious criminal, just like Enid did in her books.

'1) Deesguys as a tree; ingreediants: cardbord box, green crayon, gloo'

In hindsight, it had not really been one of my better ideas. Running around Harold's garden wearing a cardboard box childishly decorated with leaves had seriously upset Harold's dog, a rather large specimen called Biff. Lolloping over, slobber flailing from each side of his jowls, he had sniffed and then piddled on my stick thin legs that were protruding from the bottom of the box.

In utter panic I'd run away squealing, toes squelching in my wee-riddled plimsolls, only to crash head-on into the brick gatepost which in turn caused me to swivel and become wedged in the wooden gate. Much to my despair, this had allowed Biff a second attempt at relieving his bladder on my legs and for me to wish that I'd cut some eyeholes in the ruddy box.

I had stood in the kitchen with two grazed knees, Mum glaring down at me. *"Mavis, these are wet and smelly, what on earth have you been up to now?"* I grimaced as she swung two patchy yellow socks towards me.

"Sink now young lady, you can wash them yourself."

Standing on the stool, socks pinched between my fingers, nose wrinkled, I'd argued.

"... but Mum, I was only doing what Enid does, I'm a Detective, I investigate things, that's what Detectives do!"

Mum had squirted a dollop of Fairy washing up liquid into the bright red bowl and raised one eyebrow.

"Mavis this really has to stop; the neighbours think there is something seriously wrong with you child. I despair, I really do!"

Half-heartedly I'd rubbed my socks together, making little impact on the yellowing stain whilst looking at Mum's face which had turned several shades from pink to red and back to pink again.

"If you carry on like this Mavis your father will stop your pocket money."

I'd thought about this threat for all of ten seconds, scraping the toe of one sandal on the top of the other and counting the cut out flower petals. *"But Mum, he's...."*

She had waved her hand to cut me off mid-sentence.

"Mavis, I won't tell you again, do as you're told, I'm warning you, go to your room...now!"

Making a huge effort to stomp loudly on every stair to

show my bitter disappointment, I'd sloped off to sulk in my bedroom. Swinging my legs over the edge of the bunk bed whilst picking my nose, I'd considered my solitary confinement. There had to be other ways to carry on with my detective work. The Famous Five NEVER gave up. Slumping back onto my bed I made a hasty note in my investigation diary;

'Saturday 26th June 1965 – crimnal in garden hiding things. Rite letter to Enid Blyton to member eye holes for box and worn of dogs that wee on soks.'

The entry was finished off with a few hastily drawn flowers and a heart. Snapping my diary shut, I'd flopped back onto my pillow, pulled my pink 1960s quilted counterpane over me and reached for 'Five Go Off in a Caravan'.

Turning to Page 8, I had waited for the obligatory electric shocks from the bri-nylon sheets to abate before settling down to my favourite author.

THE DECISION

Reminiscing about bri-nylon sheets suddenly made the hairs on the back of my neck stand on end, bringing me swiftly back from my bittersweet memories to the reality of Ella, puddles and leaves, just as black clouds rolled in from the sea and drifted overhead. Large spots of rain plopped onto my face and trickled down my cheek. Pulling my hood up I quickened my pace.

"Toot Sweet Ella, let's get home before we're soaked. I think a mug of hot chocolate is in order don't you?"

Her eyes lit up as she nodded, twirled around and ran ahead.

Listening to her pink spotty wellingtons thud gently on the pavement as her pigtails bounced in time to her uneven gait, I felt a sudden twinge of sadness. Enid Blyton never did reply to my letter which had contained helpful hints and tips for her next book.

Maybe she already knew.

...

Sitting in the kitchen with my hands around a steaming mug of tea, a cottage pie in the oven, Ella engrossed in front of the television watching Teddy Ruxpin and an application form for the police in front of me, I weighed up my options.

a) Throw it in the bin
b) Fill it in and post it
c) Become a Nun

On second thoughts, even though Julie Andrews had looked pretty damned good in a habit and a pair of floral curtains, I couldn't see myself obeying a vow of silence for more than thirty seconds.

"Ella, Mummy's going to be a policewoman, what do you think of that?"

Barely dragging her eyes from the screen, she shrugged her shoulders and waved a half-eaten packet of crisps in the air.

"Will you be able to drive very, very fast in cars and send people to jail Mum?" She crunched another crisp and wiped the crumbs from her pyjama bottoms.

"Hopefully sweetheart. Now, did I ever tell you about Enid Blyton and how much I loved her books, I think that was where..."

The rest of my sentence tapered off into a muffled grunt as my head disappeared into the cupboard looking for a decent pen.

Sitting myself back down at the table I set about changing my life. I was going to be an Officer of the Law. A real life Cagney & Lacey; minus the handbag and gun of course.

Reading through the questions it was clear this was going to be a test in integrity, a lot of family history and a damned good memory. I was four mugs of tea and half-a-pack of digestive biscuits in before I'd even got to the second page. I chewed my pen and looked out of the window. It was still raining. I chewed my pen a bit more. Eventually I took the plunge and grabbed the telephone, taking another bite of biscuit I wiped the crumbs from my chin and dialled.

"Hi Nan, it's me Mavis."

"Yes dear, I realised that by the familiarity of your voice."

"Very funny Nan. Listen, I need you to think really, really carefully. Has anyone in the family ever been arrested, deported or suspected as a spy? It's very important."

She thought for a second, tutted and sighed heavily.

"Not that I'm aware of dear. Your Grandad did forget to pay for his paper once, walked out he did with it under his arm, but he wasn't arrested though; oh and your Aunt Eleanor worked in Lewis's haberdashery in the City centre."

I inspected my own bemused expression in the mirror that hung lopsidedly above the fire. "What on earth has that got to do with it Nan?"

There was a momentary pause for thought before she replied. "I don't know dear, but the money was good."

Twenty minutes later, and after much reminiscing, I had discovered that Martha Hindmarch, my Great, Great Grandmother had once suffered a total lapse of memory in the local Fishmongers shop in 1823, when she couldn't account for a large piece of haddock and a quart of shrimps tucked into her lace-edged bloomers. Although this had been our family shame, by a twist of fate and a few hours in the village stocks, the episode had brought her to the attention of one Horace Ignatius Upton, to whom I owe my existence and for which I suppose, I should be eternally grateful.

I was also relieved to know this didn't statistically count as an offence.

A further two mugs of tea and three Jaffa cakes saw the final flourish of the pen with my signature, promising on oath that everything contained therein was true. All I needed now was the obligatory passport sized photograph.

A quick glance in the mirror at my unruly mop of hair told me that would definitely have to wait until tomorrow.

THE PHOTOGRAPH

"Come on Ella, wakey, wakey!"

Her tousled hair appeared over the duvet as I began opening and closing the drawers to her wardrobe.

"Lots to do today so let's get a move on, it's not raining but welly boots just in case and don't forget to clean your teeth." I breezed out of her bedroom and jumped the stairs two at a time in excitement.

"Where are we going Mum?" Ella's voice echoed from the bathroom followed by the sound of several hundred sheets of toilet paper being unravelled from the holder.

"Asda, we're going to Asda, it's the only place that's got one of those photo thingummies."

A brief silence followed before a very uninspired "Ugh" drifted down the stairs.

...

"Muuuuum, what you doing in there, can I come in and see, please Mum, please?" I leant forward, coins in hand trying to find the slot.

"Not now, just wait by the curtain so I can see your legs underneath; I'll only be a few minutes."

Ella was undeterred. "Why my legs Mum, is that so you know I'm still here and not stolen, hey Mum?"

Exasperated, I pulled the curtain to one side. "Yes Ella, please this is important for me, I just need one good photograph."

She let out such a big sigh for a little girl. "Okay Mum."

I lined up the shot in the reflective glass, jiggled and wriggled to get my best angle, and then it happened…

…all in a split second.

As the first flash sent out a bright light and a resounding 'woompf' which caught me off guard, I struggled to regain my composure for the second shot as a small foot clad in a pink spotty wellington boot edged its way underneath the curtain and kicked down hard on the seat adjuster arm.

Flash… woompf…and the seat disappeared into the floor with me still on it.

"Ha-ha Mum that is soooo funny." Ella's voice giggled outside as I tried to extricate myself from the corner of the booth where I had become wedged.

Flash…woompf.

"Ella, for goodness sake, you silly girl!"

Good grief, I was starting to sound even more like my Mum. Flash…whoompf.

And then it was over.

As the booth spat out the photographs, I could only look down at the metal slot in horror whilst my ample boobs continued to wobble from the sudden impetus of the unexpected seat drop.

Photo No.1 gave a fabulous view of my head, proving that a trip to the hairdressers for my roots to be done was horrendously overdue. Photo No.2, slightly blurred by the motion of the seat disappearing into the depths of the floor, was a particularly startled, wide-eyed shot evidencing the force of gravity and its effect on rather large mammary glands. They were touching my chin and pointing in two different directions. Photo No.3 was a hand and partial gluteus maximus shot as I had tried to stand up. Photo No.4 showed me dishevelled, harassed and grinning like a lunatic on an uneven tilt to starboard.

I closed my eyes and took a deep breath.

"Well thanks to you Ella I've spent up, so this one will have to do. Just five minutes of peace, that was all I asked for!"

She kicked the toe of her boot into the side of the kerb, chewed her lip and let a giggle catch in her throat.

"I'm so sorry Mum, I was only trying to help." She checked the tip of her wellington and grinned at me.

Shaking my head, I clipped photo No.4 to the form with a warped paper clip I'd found after rummaging around in the bottom of my handbag. Trying not to laugh, and remembering my own escapades, I gave her a hug.

"Well, we'll just have to wait and see what they think then won't we?"

Trudging through the still falling leaves to the post box, watching Ella skipping and jumping puddles again, I hoped with all my heart that this would be the start of a better life for us. We needed a bit of luck.

Excitedly shoving my future through the slot in the red pillar box, I counted myself lucky that I hadn't missed the collection deadline, but my smugness was short lived when I realised that I hadn't missed a rather large doggie deposit piled up on the pavement either.

Walking the next 300 yards home, dragging and scraping one foot on the grass verge like a rabid Quasimodo in the now torrential rain was just too much for Ella. She collapsed with the giggles whilst holding her nose.

"Eeeww, that's so deegusting Mum."

She retched and stuck out her tongue as I threw my tainted boots into the porch.

Grabbing a few more logs from the basket, I stoked up the fire and looked over to the window. The rain had lessened a little, but was still leaving a pattern of sharp diagonal ticks across the glass as the wind whipped up from the beach.

Cuddling up on the sofa with Ella, I watched as the fire crackled and flared, bringing warmth into the room. Wriggling my big toe which had poked through a hole in my woolly sock, I began to wonder how on earth I would survive the wait to see if our postman would bring me exciting news of my new career.

THE BEGINNING

"Muuuuuuum I've run out of toilet roll. Muuuuuuum can you hear me, quick Mum, I need some more toilet roll."

Ella's voice echoed around the tiled bathroom, bounced off the small landing and travelled down the stairs.

I tentatively spread the margarine across the burnt piece of toast that was threatening to shatter into a thousand crispy black crumbs. I banged the top of the toaster, more in exasperation than anger. I desperately needed a new one but money was so tight lately.

Taking the stairs two at a time I pushed open the bathroom door. Ella, legs dangling above the mat, one shoe lace undone, grinned.

"Fanks Mum, thought you'd forgotten me."

She threw the empty cardboard tube onto the floor for Cat, who promptly sunk his teeth into it, skitted it with his paw and then disappeared out onto the landing.

"Don't forget to clean your teeth when you've finished, breakfast's nearly ready."

I picked up the damp towel from her bedroom floor and crammed it into the laundry basket and looked out of the window. My stomach gave a little flip, just as it did every morning when Frankie the Postman paused to check the bag on the front of his bicycle.

I watched him deftly flick through a large bunch of envelopes, held together with a thick elastic band. He pulled one out, checked it and reached for our gate. This had to be it.

I rushed downstairs and wrenched the front door open.

Banging the gate shut behind him, Frankie ambled down the path, pausing halfway to skip over next door's cat that had taken to lying prostrate in the watery sun. I was ready and waiting for him.

"Bloody hell Mavis, how much of my skin did you get with your nails!" he wailed rubbing the back of his hand with a grimace whilst I coveted the brown envelope he had been holding.

Ripping it open in excitement, I gave him an apologetic smile.

"Sorry Frankie, but this is so important to me." Quickly scanning the embossed letterhead, I read the words, over and over again.

'...to attend Police Headquarters on Thursday 24th November, 1988 at 10:30 a.m. for the Police Entrance Examination and Interview Panel'

My heart thudded and leapt. My dream hadn't been jeopardised by the pose in photograph No.4 or good old Martha's haddock and shrimps episode. I flung my arms out to give Frankie an excited hug, then thought better of it. Grinning, I slammed the front door behind me, leaving him standing bemused on the step. Dancing a little jig of happiness in the hallway, Ella watched from the stairs.

She rolled her eyes. "Do you know you wobble when you dance Mum?"

"No sweetheart I didn't, but thanks for telling me."

I hugged the envelope to my chest and carried on dancing.

···

As the big day loomed, I took the time to work on my interview techniques and to make some changes to my appearance to enhance my chances. Nothing spectacular, just subtle little flourishes.

Shampooing a Betty Blush No. 22 Light Brown with a Frisson of Caramel into my hair, I wiped an errant blob of foam from my eye and waited for the stinging to stop. Tomorrow was my big day; tomorrow could be a make or break day. Wrapping the towel around my head, I whispered 'Constable Mavis Upton' under my breath. It sounded just right.

I dried my hair, and piled it up in a rather messy topknot before taking Ella a mug of hot chocolate. She was curled up on the sofa reading Roald Dahl's Matilda.

"Ella, pass me Grandma's old spectacles will you?"

Grabbing the frayed blue pouch from the table she threw it across the room, Cat, thinking it was a game, made a vain attempt to catch it in his outstretched paws.

I popped them on my nose and looked in the mirror.

"Thought I'd look rather clever with dark hair and glasses, what do you think?" I stepped back to admire myself further.

"Mummy watch out!"

Amid the clattering of cups, saucers, scattered books and cushions I lay sprawled on the floor. Cat, half frightened to death by my huge posterior threatening to imminently end one of his remaining seven lives, had made the sensible decision to run and hide in the kitchen.

I rubbed the base of my back and looked at Ella for sympathy. None was forthcoming as she buried her face in her book to giggle.

THE INTERVIEW

"Jeez Mum it was an absolute nightmare; I've never sweated so much in all my life." I threw my bag onto the coffee table and flopped down onto the sofa next to her.

"It was when the one in the middle said *'Did you do any preparation for this interview Ms Upton'...*" I carefully mimicked the aloof voice of the interviewer, "...and I just froze, stuck to the leather chair by my clammy backside, gawping into space."

I wanted to cry but held back, only allowing my chin to wobble as Mum grabbed a tissue in anticipation of a waterfall. She looked at me with a modicum of empathy as she stubbed her cigarette out and blew the smoke sideways from her mouth. I watched it plume upwards towards the shaft of sun streaming through the window before it fanned out.

"So what did you reply, you must have said something Mavis, please don't tell me you just sat there?" She plumped the cushion behind her and leant back.

"No,. I didn't just sit there, wish I bloody had though. Instead I brightly informed them that I had and when they asked what, I told them I'd dyed my hair specially."

A hot flush crept over me as I relived the moment. The physical and medical tests had been bad enough, but my whole future now hinged on that one interview and three less than amused faces that had stared back at me when I had openly declared, like a lapsed member of Alcoholics

Anonymous, the use of Betty Blush No. 22 Light Brown with a frisson of Caramel.

Trying not to laugh, she patted my knee.

"Oh I wouldn't worry dear I'm sure they understood, everyone gets nervous in interviews."

I could see she was trying to make me feel better but it wasn't working. "Maybe, but not if you go on to provide them with the ruddy brand and shade number..." I grabbed the proffered tissue and blew my nose. "...I should've just carried on and discussed the difference in colour between my collar and cuffs for all the good it did me!"

I looked at her for more sympathy, only to be met with a frosty glare.

"Oh for goodness sake, you didn't wear an old blouse did you? I've told you before Mavis, there really is nothing worse than a grubby collar on a woman; whatever their age!"

I wanted to laugh at her naivety and my own attempt at sarcasm, but I was pretty sure I'd just spent the best part of a day watching my dream of a career in the police disappear down the Mersey.

•••

A few weeks later Frankie once again bounced down my path flicking elastic bands at next door's cat as it sat watching him from the fence. Digging into his bag, he brought out an envelope and began to wave it in the air as I hurried down to the gate to meet him.

"Is this what you're waiting for lovely?" He tantalisingly held it above his head.

"Ooh, yes, think so; this could be the start of my dreams Frankie."

I caught the envelope as he frisbee'd it towards me. Hugging it with folded arms, I turned to run back inside, eager to read its contents.

"Thought your dream was to marry Mel Gibson and live in a mansion Mave?" he teased.

I wrinkled my nose and winked. "Nope, that was last week, this week I want to fight crime."

Laughing, he flicked another elastic band at the cat who was attempting to escape over the fence. "Well as long as you don't wear your pants on the outside of your jeans you should be okay..." He closed the gate and pointed a finger, "... I would hate to see you get arrested."

Kicking the front door shut, I held the large brown envelope out in front of me, pausing for only a fraction of a second before hastily ripping it open. I quickly scanned the first page and turned over to the attachment. The last paragraph confirmed it.

Mavis Upton was going to be a Police Officer. I had been accepted.

Throwing another log on the fire, I adjusted the cushions on the sofa and settled myself down to read it properly. Excitement gnawed at my stomach making it flip rhythmically. Taking a big slurp of tea, I scanned the joining instructions and almost spat most of it on Cat who was curled up on my knee. It was there in black & white.

A hurdle.

I was going to hit my first little hurdle right at the beginning of my new adventure. Well if I'm being truthful, it was actually a bloody big hurdle.

The Police Training Centre was in Warrington, 40 miles away.

I had a car – check.

I knew how to fill it with petrol – check.

I held a full driving licence and insurance – check.

I had a map for Warrington – check.

Which left only one thing.

My nemesis; I had to get there on a motorway.

Now this would be an ordeal at the best of times, but for someone like me who burst into tears when the engine to my first car, a VW Beetle, went missing and was later 'found' in the boot by my next door neighbour after much sniggering, the word *ordeal* was something of an understatement. I had never driven on a motorway, and more to the point, I had never driven more than 3 miles from home – in any direction.

Picking up the telephone I quickly called Mum to impart my exciting news. She was delighted. I wasn't.

"... but Mum it's on the motorway what am I going to do?" I wailed. "I'll get lost, I know I will, they'll have to send out search parties and everything."

I heard her light up a cigarette and exhale.

"Mavis, Mavis calm down love, it's not that difficult, slipway, motorway and then off at the other end – simple," she soothed.

"Where at the other end Mum? London? Bristol? Scotland? It's no good, I just can't go."

Fear stabbed at the pit of my stomach. She exhaled again. I could imagine the smoke billowing upwards like steam from an old train.

"Yes you can. Look if it helps I'll take you the first time. Motorways are really easy once you get used to them."

I paused.

Yes, I liked the idea of that. Nice offer Mum...

...until I realised it would be a slightly embarrassing start to my police career to have my Mummy drop me off at the gates of the Regional Police Training Centre; with or without my thermal vest and bellybutton hugging knickers.

THE JOURNEY

Taking Ella's pink crayon that had been left on the kitchen counter, I crossed off Sunday 15th January on my wall calendar. Mel Gibson stared out at me with those beautiful blue eyes.

"See me and weep Mel, I'm no longer available. You missed your chance mate." I winked. Mel held his sexy smile but stayed silent.

Pulling up the bottoms of my fleecy PJ's that were threatening to end up around my ankles due to the perished elastic, I picked up Mum's old Road Atlas that had been festering on the coffee table. I had already meticulously planned and memorised my whole route to Warrington, via A roads and country lanes. No motorway for me, although it would probably take me the better part of four hours to get there.

Flicking through, its aged pages catching on ripped corners, a sequence of numbers embossed on the glossy front page caught my eye. Why hadn't I noticed them before? I wiped my hand across a large, still wet mug stain.

"Shit, shit, shit." Grabbing the telephone, fingers trembling, I dialled. It was answered on the third ring.

"Mum, it's me, where the hell did you get this Road Atlas from?" I spat. She gave a sharp intake of breath.

"Good God Mavis, do you know what time it is? It was your Great Grandfather's. Why?"

I couldn't contain my panic.

"Why Mum, why? I'll tell you why, it's the 1952 edition and the flaming route I've chosen was probably last walked on by the Romans. I don't think it exists anymore!" There was a minute's silence.

"Well if it was good enough for them AND your Great Grandfather Mavis, then it should be good enough for you too."

•••

Brushing my hair and tying it into a neat bun ready for the day ahead, I resigned myself to my worst nightmare.

Motorway driving.

I had hardly slept, my waking moments filled with dread and apprehension, my sleeping moments filled with nightmares. I wanted this so much, but couldn't shake off the feeling of child abandonment, a huge bout of separation anxiety and the fear of failure.

Nothing had prepared me for the guilt I was suffering in leaving Ella with Mum. I bent down to check my bag. Everything I needed for registration at the Centre was neatly folded inside a handwritten envelope. A large tear escaped, rolled down my cheek and plopped onto the manila paper, blurring the ink. I silently berated myself.

Come on Mavis old girl, stiff upper lip and all that.

Pasting on a smile, I began to load up the car with all my worldly goods, including an egg mayonnaise batch and a flask of tea courtesy of Mum.

"It's only forty minutes Mum, I'll be fine." I gave her a hug.

"You could be stuck in a traffic jam for hours, you'll thank me then," she quickly retorted whilst shoving a KitKat into my pocket.

Ella sidled up to me, her small hand dipping into the fabric to retrieve it just as quickly as Mum had put it in there.

"Come here sweetheart, give me the biggest cuddle you've got." I held out my arms to her.

She grinned whilst extricating a particularly large booger from her right nostril. "Love you Mummy; I'll write you a letter tomorrow."

Holding her tight, whilst avidly avoiding contact with what was hanging off her index finger, I breathed in the fresh smell of her hair. "I love you too sweetheart, be good for Nanny. I'll ring you every night I promise."

She nodded and smiled weakly, tears starting to brim. I quickly turned away and jumped into my car, fearful I would lose my resolve. How on earth would I cope in the months ahead only seeing her at weekends?

The engine revved into life. I took one last look in my rear view mirror before pulling away, watching as they both became just a distant blur, their silhouettes framed by the grandeur of Mum's old Georgian house.

Concentrating on the road ahead, I hit the little country lane that led to the motorway.

Down the slip road, mirror, signal, manoeuvre and bingo, I was on the motorway without having caused a multiple pile up. I gave myself a little mental pat on the back.

It actually wasn't as bad as I had anticipated as long as I didn't exceed the speed limit. I found that I was quite comfortable in my little Millie Metro doing a nice steady 45 mph on the M56. The constant beeping of other motorists' horns was a little bit of a distraction at first, but I just accepted that motorway drivers were probably very friendly folk and soon got into the spirit of things by giving them little toots or a friendly wave back.

Strangely enough, the closer I got to Warrington I began to notice a bit of a physical anomaly with the local drivers. When some of them waved they only had two fingers.

It didn't occur to me in the innocence that I was about to relinquish at the police training centre that it was an offensive gesture; rather than my first thoughts of an unfortunate industrial accident or a rather odd genetic trait.

After a few little unplanned detours, which resulted in a complete circuit of Stockton Heath, Thelwall Viaduct and Great Sankey, I excitedly arrived at the main gates of the Regional Police Training Centre, with egg mayonnaise batch and flask intact.

I had made it.

I felt a burst of complete and utter pride, not just for the journey, but for the start of my childhood dream. Taking a deep breath, heart pounding with anticipation, I waited as the security guard slid open the window of the gatehouse.

"Hi I'm Mavis Upt..."

He cut me off with a surly wave of his hand. Beckoning his fingers in a *'give me'* motion he took my paperwork in silence. The seconds ticked away before he eventually nodded, stamped the sheet in from of him and with a wry smile, lifted the barrier.

This was it, my gateway to another world. Life would never be the same again.

I put Millie Metro into first gear, slowly swept the clutch

and the accelerator in a beautifully precise undulating motion and sailed through the gates...

...only to smash straight into the first concrete bollard in the car park.

I jerked forward as Mum's flask and her precious egg mayonnaise butty flew off the seat, landing with a squishy thud in the foot well.

Oh shit, please not now; not today.

I looked around at the horrified faces of my soon-to-be-colleagues who had stopped unpacking their own cars to watch my dramatic entrance. Hastily throwing the gearstick into reverse, I managed an embarrassed smile and a little wave...

... and promptly stalled the engine.

As the security guard shook his head and closed the window, I knew with unreserved confidence and pride that Constable 1261 Mavis Upton had at last arrived.

NEW FRIENDS

At 9.00 a.m. on the dot, I came rampaging through the doors of the Training Centre full of enthusiasm and hope, dragging my suitcase behind me like a lost tourist.

Looking at everyone else gathered in the hall, I suddenly realised that being the wrong side of thirty was going to have its drawbacks. This lot looked like they'd been training for the Olympics, whereas my body could only boast an occasional shimmy round the front room to The Best of Spandau Ballet, wearing special edition 1980s leg warmers and a pea green Lycra leotard, whilst carefully avoiding the cat and the coffee table.

My half-hearted home fitness sessions had all taken place behind closed curtains after catching my neighbour Boris impaled on the Christmas holly bush under my window with his faded blue Y-fronts around his knees. Not surprisingly, my relationship with him had never been the same again.

Standing in line waiting for instructions and dorm numbers, Spandau Ballet a thing of the past, I was happy to see that I was not the only wide-eyed looking probationer.

"Upton, Mavis – Force Identity 1261."

Hearing my name resonate across the admissions foyer by the smartly uniformed Sergeant made my stomach plummet to somewhere near my knees. I dragged my suitcase, wonky wheels scraping on the woodblock floor towards him whilst attempting a bit of a military style march, hoping to impress.

Standing to attention, clipboard in hand, a hint of amusement drifted across his face.

"Save it for the parade ground Upton, 'J' block ground floor," he barked loudly.

Suitably humiliated, I grabbed the blue file held out in front of him, carefully tucked it under my arm and turned to leave.

"Yes Sir, Sarge err... Sergeant, thank you...err uhm Sir."

I cringed. I had sounded more like Barbara Windsor in a Carry On film than a grown woman embarking on a professional career. I could hear sniggering from the queue behind me as I trundled my suitcase, which had suddenly developed a definite squeak, towards the main doors.

"Upton...!"

I stopped in my tracks. "Err, yes Sergeant."

His eyes narrowed as he pointed towards my suitcase.

"I think you will find that's my case you're attempting to abscond with."

I didn't want to look down, in fact I didn't even want to acknowledge that twenty minutes into my time at the Training Centre I had already flattened a concrete bollard and potentially stolen this cheerful chappies luggage.

I sighed.

I bit my lip.

I looked around and finally plucked up the courage to look down.

The handle clenched in my hot, sweaty hand did indeed belong to a very masculine grey case and not the one with lilac and pink flowers I had moments earlier dragged from the back of my car.

He wasn't finished.

"Now unless you intend to spend the next ten weeks wearing my boxer shorts Upton, may I suggest you take your own bag..." He swung my raggedy girly case towards me whilst deftly retrieving his own, "...and as much as the rumours will tell you otherwise, I don't fancy wearing your knickers for ten weeks either."

Bumping and wobbling my suitcase out of reception onto what the sign post reliably informed me was Hadfield Way, the breeze cooling my embarrassment, I took a moment to take everything in. Large three storey muted brick accommodation blocks with a multitude of windows facing out from every side loomed over the narrow roads that were edged with grass and shrubs. Weeping willows, devoid of their summer finery stood to attention, framing a small pond leading to the drill square.

This was going to be my 'home' for the next fifteen weeks.

Locating 'J' Block and my room, I pushed the door open and looked around. Wash basin, wardrobe, bed, mirror, a small desk for studying and a plastic chair. I heaved my case onto the wooden framed single bed and began unpacking.

Pinning my picture of Ella onto the wardrobe, I bounced back down onto the bed and grabbed my folder. Unclipping the timetable, I quickly scanned the first few lines. My heart sank. There was an awful lot of jumping, jogging and physical exertion scheduled for the coming weeks. I folded it up and slipped it back inside my folder. Looking out of the window, across to the car park at the back of the accommodation blocks, I wistfully wondered if I would die in the first week or exceed expectations and expire during the second week.

A loud knocking was quickly followed by my room door bursting open. It slammed against the wall and bounced back into whoever was standing on the other side.

"Shit that bloody hurt!"

Silence followed as it slowly swung open again revealing a rather tall, gangly girl, all legs and arms.

"Hi Mavis, just thought I'd pop in and introduce myself, I've got the room next to yours. I'm Norma."

She flung out one hand whilst rubbing her now reddening nose with her other one. "Think we're going to get along great you and me. Now, we're all getting together in the bar tonight, no excuses, you're coming too, a few drinks, break the ice."

She swept her eyes around my room, giving me no chance to reply before she turned on her heels and disappeared back into the corridor. Her voice getting fainter.

"All work and no play makes Mavis a rather dull girly. See you later chick." And with that she was gone.

Smiling, I closed the door and carried on unpacking.

•••

"Hey up, here's the girl. Mavis Upton! Car crusher and suitcase stealer."

Laughter rippled around the bar as Melvyn Blake, a rather amicable looking lad from Yorkshire, his dark spikey hair sprouting in all directions, raised his pint in greeting as I walked in.

I blushed.

"Oh come on lads leave her alone. Blakey you can't talk – check your tax disc on that shitty banger of yours. Who

comes here on their first week committing an offence hey?"
Norma crossed her arms in triumph as Melvyn turned several
shades of pink.

"Aww come on I was only joking." He took a gulp from
his pint as Norma thrust a glass of white wine into my hand.

"Glad you made it chick, we all need a bit of recreation."
She tipped her glass towards me.

I took a sip from my glass. "Well I suppose if I spend all
my time learning offence definitions and swotting, I'm not
likely to make much of an impact on the social scene am I?"
I looked around for reassurance as several heads nodded in
agreement.

"Yep that's quite true Mave, quoting '*a person is guilty of
theft if he dishonestly appropriates property*' to a prospective
shag will bugger your chances of a second date by the time
you get to the offence of *Common Prostitute Loitering!*"

Norma laughed at her own comparison whilst I squirmed
in embarrassment.

"Oh come on Mave, you're not a prude are you? Tell
you what, fifteen weeks here will soon change all that!" she
snorted.

Now it was my turn to knock back my drink. I had a feeling
that Norma would prove to be right.

THE EARLY DAYS

I flung my hand out to hit the 'off' button on my alarm. Squinting I checked the time and groaned. 6:00 a.m.

Who in their right mind would get up at this time? Oh yes, sorry, that would be me.

I swung my legs out of the bed and grimaced as my feet touched the tacky carpet. Our first of many early morning shuttle runs. Glad that I had only indulged in one glass of wine the previous night, I splashed my face with cold water, brushed my teeth and squeezed into my tracksuit bottoms and a clean t-shirt. Lacing up my new trainers I had a sneaking suspicion that my previous claim to fame of tripping the light fantastic as a second rate dancer in my youth might not get me through what lay ahead on the fitness front.

By the time I reached the sports quadrangle Norma was already bouncing up and down on the spot whilst intermittently carrying out rather awkward star jumps. I joined in with some un-elegant ham string stretches.

"Nice trainers Mave...err they're very white though, not had much use then?" She added an extra star jump, puffed her cheeks and blew a section of hair that had escaped from her pony tail.

I looked down at my £2.99 budget trainers. Bugger, they were very white now I was outside in daylight. Not wanting to look like a novice, I carried on stretching and grunting.

"Oh these, my old ones had soooo much use they fell apart, I had to get myself a new pair." I over-emphasised the word 'so' for maximum effect. I had also lied. Norma shrugged her shoulders, grinned and gave another wobbly star jump for good measure.

"Right attention everyone, line up, set off in groups of six, full lengths of the football pitch until I say stop, then shower, breakfast and straight to class for 8:30 ladies and gents." Fitness Instructor, Sergeant Rob Dooley all muscles, slicked back hair and rather short shorts waved towards the field, counting us off as we started with little on the spot jogging steps waiting for our turn to move.

"Go... go...go...go..."

Norma was off like a racing cheetah, legs going east and west in a cumbersome gait, quickly followed by the rest of the class. I was stuck at the back with Marjorie, a rather plump, freckly girl with a mass of wonderful red hair. Marjorie was on an intake from Cheshire Constabulary.

"Steady does it Mavis, stick together, don't over exert," she wheezed. Over exert! Me? Not a chance, but I wasn't going to admit that.

I set a steady pace, bouncing along behind Melvyn. As I looked down I realised 'bouncing' was a bit of an understatement. I made a mental note to invest in a more supportive over-the-shoulder-boulder-holder on my next weekend off.

Reaching the end of the first straight I stumbled, knocking into Marj – my left trainer had suddenly decided to part company with the sole. Jeez, could there be anything else to single me out as a dork in my first week? I hadn't been able to afford anything more expensive, but I had at least expected more than a 50-yard sprint before they fell apart.

Marjorie caught my arm, howling with laughter she tried to catch her breath.

"It's talking to yer Mave, it's flapping like a prozzies leather skirt in a Dock Road breeze..." I stood mortified holding my foot up as she fussed.

"...here give it to me, always got a little something for everything."

Hobbling over to her kit bag she pulled out a reel of tape as she grabbed the offending trainer from my foot. I watched as she wound it round and round, binding the sole to the trainer.

"There you go, almost good as... what the feck is that?" She squealed as she dropped my trainer and began to inspect her left hand.

In blue letters, imprinted on her palm in reverse, was the word '*Reebok*'. Marj let out a loud snort as she waved her hand at me.

"Err Mave, I think you've been done here girl, it's drawn on in felt pen. You need to take 'em back to where you bought 'em from."

Mortally embarrassed, I feigned surprise.

"Oh my goodness, would you believe it! They're not Reeboks at all are they?"

Consoling me in my hour of need, she helped me hop back to the accommodation block with my hand clenched firmly around the offending trainer.

"Are you sure you're alright, I can sort out a spare pair for you if you want?" she soothed.

I almost choked. "No, no, you're okay, thanks anyway, I'll see you later."

Quickly shutting the door, I breathed a sigh of relief, glad to have a piece of wood between me, Marj, my pretend Reebok trainer and my guilty secret.

How terrible, fake trainers, whatever next?

Letting out a resigned sigh, I looked around my room, found the blue felt tip pen I had borrowed from Ella and chucked it in the bin with a clatter, which was closely followed by the gentle thudding of my trainers as they joined it.

•••

I could feel a tear slip slowly down my cheek.

Brushing it away with the back of my hand, I turned my back to the glass partition of the campus telephone kiosk. The queue outside was snaking towards the main doors of the entrance foyer. I didn't want anyone to see me cry.

"I miss you too Ella, very, very much." My voice broke.

"Mummy how much longer before you can come home for good? I love Nanny but I miss our cuddles."

Her voice faded to a small sob on the other end of the line.

"I know sweetheart, I miss our cuddles too, not much longer now, it'll go quick I promise. I'll see you on Friday to pick you up from school." I wound the cord of the telephone tightly around my finger.

Silence.

"Are you still there Ella?" I could hear her breath noisily rasping.

"Yes Mum, I've got snot from a cold and I've wiped it

on my dress, Nanny's just getting me a tissue. Bye, see you Friday."

   ...and with that she hung up!

PLAYING WITH FIRE

Spreading out my textbooks and homework diary on the bed, I'd just started to arrange them ready for an evening of study when my door opened and Melvyn popped his head in.

"Here you go Mave, you don't mind do you?" He thrust a particularly bleak looking pair of size 10 boots towards me that had been swinging from his hand.

"I'm going to start charging you Blakey, all this bulling boots for you lot whilst you prop up the bar! Go on, you owe me though, hope you've sprayed them first."

He grinned. "Of course, only the best for you, Paco Rabanne and here's some polish too."

Catching it mid-air, I popped open the tin. "It's dried up mate, I can't use this. Didn't you put the lid on properly?"

He stared at the ceiling. "Err, think I did, not sure. It's okay, just heat it up a bit, that always works."

He jerked a thumbs up and disappeared into the corridor.

I looked at his boots, sitting forlornly on the end of my bed, scuffed and daubed with mud. Bringing boot toecaps to a shine you can see your face in or whatever other dubious body parts you just might fancy dangling over them had become a bit of a forte of mine. I poked the end of my pen into the polish. Solid. I suppose warming it would be a better option, more hygienic than spitting in the tin to moisten it and with less chance of sending your false teeth shooting across the room and under the bed.

That's if I had false teeth, which I hasten to add, I don't.

Digging out my cigarette lighter, I sat with the flame under the tin, gently warming it to soften the mixture. As the tin got hotter, so did my fingers and it wasn't really making much impact on the dried up contents. Maybe if I put the flame directly onto the polish, after all, it wasn't flammable was it? Pleased with my eureka moment I bravely held the naked flame over the crusty, black contents.

Suddenly there was a little popping sound as the polish gave off a slight haze of fumes and then...

... poof!

The polish fizzed and caught fire.

In blind panic, I squealed and shoved the burning tin as far away from me as possible.

I watched in awe as it slid across the top of the cabinet coming to a halt underneath the curtains as the flames flicked higher and higher. There was a momentary pause and then woompf...

Oh shit.

The curtains burst into flames.

Gasping in horror, I desperately tried to fight the fire, but it was obvious that a career in the Police was preferable to one in the Fire Service as my extinguishing skills were proving to be quite pathetic. Coughing fit to burst, I flung my best knickers around, which due to their huge expanse of material seemed to fan the fire rather than assist in its extinction. I frantically looked around for something else to douse the flames with.

Suddenly the door burst open and Norma, throwing her gangly legs and arms in all directions, came rushing in from the corridor, fire extinguisher in hand.

"For fuck's sake Mave, what are you trying to do, kill us all?"

She began to spray anything and everything, apart from the damned curtains as I launched my mug of coffee at the flickering flames.

At last Norma found her target with the extinguisher and it was out.

We sat down on the bed, amid the smell of acrid smoke that was hanging in the air.

The curtains, or what was left of them, were swinging in the breeze of the window that Norma had managed to open once the flames had been doused.

"Think we've got off lightly there, don't you?" she giggled.

I caught my breath and shook my head. *Lightly!* This girl seriously wasn't right in the head.

We surveyed the scene.

I looked at Norma. The corners of her mouth twitched before she let out a huge snort of laughter that blew a bubble of snot from her left nostril. Swinging a melted bit of string over her head, she wiped her nose on her jumper, inspected it and grimaced.

"Well, all I can say is I don't think much of your M&S frillies, Mave. You won't be wearing these little beauts again," as she catapulted them into the bin.

The rest of the evening was spent trying to rectify the damage using a pair of plastic scissors and the smallest needle in the world whilst I considered my ignorance on the effects of flame on flammable material.

Poking the needle into the side of the cotton reel, I slumped back on the bed to survey my curtains that were now six inches shorter than everyone else's in the dorm and the rather large coffee stain on the wall from the mug I'd flung at it in sheer panic.

Fearing expulsion, or at the very least being back-classed, I quickly covered up the stain with a rather fetching picture of Norman Tebbit, torn from an old Sunday Supplement, until such time I could trundle around B&Q to find a paint that would match the rather fetching off-magnolia/nicotine hued walls.

TIM

"Right, going around the room, let's have a little bit of background to start the day off." Sergeant Bradshaw clasped his hands behind his head and leant back in his chair. "We're going to have a sort of Q&A familiarisation session so we can all learn a little bit about each other."

Carrying a hint of amusement on his face, he pointed in turn as he worked his way around the classroom. So far, so good, nothing out of the ordinary. Some of our previous jobs ranged from being a Paramedic to working the tills at Tesco. Chipping in with little snippets on our personal lives and our families, everything was going smoothly.

Until it came to Tim.

Tim was better known as 'Timothy Spalding from Yorkshire'. He was very much a loner and kept himself to himself. Invitations to class nights out and friendly banter in the first weeks had all been refused by him. He now sat rigid in the far corner. I was unsure if his bright red colouring was due to embarrassment or the fact he was sitting so close to the radiator. The Sarge zoned straight in on him.

"Right Tim, let's hear from you, speak up loud and clear son."

"Oh err, err, umm I...I'm twenty-three and err, err... oh..."

Tim's mouth became paper thin. A very palpable silence followed as a previously unnoticed nervous tic in his left eye began to rapidly pulsate.

"Come on Tim, anything about yourself. What job did

you have before joining the police?" Sergeant Bradshaw encouraged.

Still nothing from Tim, who sat open mouthed turning an attractive shade of pink.

The Sarge patiently tried again.

"Do you have siblings Tim?"

Tim's eyes widened in horror. He stared at the floor, the ceiling and then out of the window. Clearing his throat, he eventually broke the silence.

"Absolutely not Sergeant! I have never, ever had a sexual disease in my life; not any kind, not now, not ever...in fact I haven't even..."

We all burst out laughing as the Sarge frantically waved his hand to cut him short, but there had been no need for Tim to say anymore. We knew exactly what the next words out of his mouth were going to be. He had been just about to declare his long standing, yet to be lost virginity.

Poor Tim, the whole class continued to snort loudly with laughter, his eyebrows knitting together in confusion as he slumped further and further down in his chair.

...

"Did you see Tim this morning? Bleedin' hell, bet only his mother can love him, what a fuckwit."

Danny Hodges heaved his 6'8" frame from the sofa, ducking his head through the doorframe as he ambled out of the lounge and into the corridor.

Norma flicked the kettle on and clanked two mugs together. "It's a bit like being 5 years old and starting school all over again being here isn't it?"

I bent the corner of the page over and closed my book. "Yep, suppose you're right, apart from the fact we're supposed to be toilet trained and capable of eating with a knife and a fork at the same time."

Norma laughed and waved a spoon at me, probably to remind me there was a third utensil that often came in handy.

"Shit!"

We didn't bother turning around, we all knew the sound of head hitting wood and a curse meant that Danny had re-entered the room without ducking.

"He's just plain odd..." Danny rubbed his hand on his forehead and checked for blood. "...I still don't know how he got past the selection process."

We silently contemplated that statement.

Norma plonked a mug down in front of me and offered the biscuit box. "Penny for your thoughts Mave."

I picked a chocolate digestive, took a bite and then licked my fingers before replying. "I was just remembering Tim's virginity announcement; you've got to feel sorry for him."

She shrugged. "Suppose, but he's going to get eaten alive out there if he doesn't toughen up you know."

I took another bite. I felt pretty much the same for myself.

TOOLS OF THE TRADE

"For fuck's sake, these pants wouldn't fit one of my thighs let alone my whole body!"

Marj's face was turning three shades of red to almost match the colour of her hair as she struggled to breath in and zip up the boiler suit without ripping a large chunk of flesh from her stomach.

A disembodied voice from the other side of the locker broke through the sound of Marj's heavy breathing.

"Hey Mave this is more your size, it's an XXL, think your boobs will squeeze into that?" I ducked as a navy blue 'sack' like object, smelling of someone else's sweaty armpits masked by cheap perfume, came hurtling through the air of the changing room from Norma's direction.

Picking it up from the floor, I gave it a shake and held it up against me. It was huge but it would have to do. I folded the leg cuffs over a few times and tucked them into my boots as Norma gave me the thumbs up whilst Marj was still trying to zip up.

"Come on girls, it's not a fashion parade. One, two, one, two, let's see those legs moving." Dave Deacon, the Drill Sergeant was standing in the doorway, his Lancashire accent booming across the changing rooms, rattling and bouncing off the metal lockers. He was ex-army, a towering 6'6" tall and just as wide.

"Anyone left in 'ere in five seconds will have an extra ten laps of the footie field!"

That threat quickly spilled us out into the corridor where the lads were also emerging from their changing rooms. A rancid air of underarm sweat, manly farts and old socks breezed out with them.

"Bloody hell girls, witwoo get you," Melvyn leered.

"Oh sod off Blakey you perv..." Marj, hot, flustered and clearly disgruntled spat as she grabbed her belt and pulled it in two more notches. "...you're no sodding oil painting yourself."

Melvyn hadn't fared much better in his boiler suit either, two sizes too big with a rip in the knee, but somehow Danny had managed to find a decent off-the-peg number that accommodated his gargantuan height. Lacking any form of enthusiasm after checking each other out, we trundled out onto the Parade Ground.

"Feckin' hell, look at Lancs, are their's made-to-measure?"

We turned to where Danny was pointing to a rather smart looking posse of Lancashire recruits.

"They've got their names embroidered on them AND they've got proper zip-up pockets, not pretend ones AND they fit!" Norma jealously compared the drooping crotch on hers, giving it a hefty tug.

I checked the pockets in my boiler suit. "Blimey, your hands go straight through, there's nothing there, you can stroke your own thigh!" I wiggled my fingers under the fabric to prove my point just as Norma began squealing.

"Eeeew that is just so gross." She pointed animatedly at Melvyn who was standing by the edge of the field staring off into the distance, hand stuffed into his pretend pocket. "Melvyn Blake I know exactly what you're stroking you disgusting little sod!"

Hastily retracting his hand Melv stood open mouthed in surprise. "That's your dirty mind Norma, I was only checking the fit."

Curling her top lip Elvis style, she flicked her ponytail. "Exactly, hoping for room to grow knowing you."

She stomped off to join the line that was already forming at the edge of the football pitch as Dave Deacon's Lancashire Lilt carried on the breeze.

"Right you 'orrible lot, helmets on, visors down, shields up... go..."

•••

Very few of us made the campus bar that night. I don't think I've ever ached in so many different places, all at the same time.

Hearing Marj shuffling in her distinctive fluffy slippers along the dorm corridor just after 10pm, I switched off the bedside lamp, snuggled down and stretched my toes as my calf muscle went into cramp.

"Night girls, handcuffing tomorrow. Now that should be fun don't you think?" Silence followed as she waited for a response.

"Go to bed Marj..." Norma's disembodied voice drifted from the next room, ".... or I'll be bloody handcuffing you to the toilet in trap 3!"

Silence once again reigned, broken only momentarily by the sound of a loud fart from two rooms down.

I smiled and closed my eyes.

•••

"Okay lads and lasses, Handcuffing and Baton Techniques Level 1. No unauthorised swinging of batons, no handcuff use without keys being available, listen up at all times."

The ginger headed, portly Sergeant paused as he waited for his words to sink in, or at the very least to see some sort of acknowledgement from us. We all stood silent in eager anticipation of being taught the craft of defence, detention and restraint.

"Hey, bet you won't find these covered in pink fluffy feathers in an *Ann Summers Catalogue* will you?" Danny dangled the set of handcuffs between his fingers.

Norma snatched them from him, gave them a quick polish on her sleeve before inspecting them closely. We'd already had a full-on lecture on abuse of handcuff use, and that wasn't even on prisoners; that was on each other.

The previous week, Barry Ennis of Greater Manchester Police and Julie Goolie from 'M' Block had taken up a romantic night time liaison together under the guise of handcuff practice. Apparently after hours of foreplay, Barry had got bored and ambled off to the toilets before going back to his own dorm in 'K' Block, leaving poor Julie still handcuffed to her bedhead for Beryl the cleaner to discover the following morning.

Beryl had hoovered around the bed and polished the windowsill much to Julie's horror as she lay prostrate, arms stretched to their absolute limit.

"Listen ducks, you're not the first, won't be the last neither. You girls never learn..." Beryl had soothingly imparted her wisdom to Julie whilst giving one last sweep of the hoover under the bed. "... now if you ask me..."

Beryl had suddenly been cut off in her prime by a loud juddering, sucking noise coming from her hoover as Julie's hastily discarded knickers began their rapid ascent up the tube.

"Every year, every bloody year..." Beryl had sighed whilst struggling to turn the hoover off. "...I could open a lingerie shop with all the smalls you lot leave lying around."

If being left handcuffed to the bed wasn't bad enough, Julie had then endured the humiliation of knowing that her size 20 knickers had been paraded through campus, half-stuck in the tube, half dangling in the clear plastic dust canister whilst en-route to the janitor's office for repair.

I sniggered out loud at the thought of Julie, suitably chaste and once again single and Barry being put on report.

"Upton, less of the dreaming, eyes front. Right, where were we? Basic handcuffing. Now this is a form of restraint that..." and as the Sarge pointed out the do's and don'ts we nodded whilst feigning some form of understanding.

Emerging from the gym two hours later with swollen fingers, bent wrists, bruises and bits of each other's skin attached to our handcuffs, we waited to be dismissed.

"Okay class listen up, homework for tonight. Revise *'Use of Force and Recovery',* along with the basic handcuffing techniques you've done today."

He waited for a response, when none was forthcoming, he began to pack his kit away as we animatedly spilled out onto the quadrangle and the glorious sunshine that had broken through the clouds.

Revise and practice. Sounds simple doesn't it? Well that was unless you were Tim.

Nothing was ever simple if you were Tim.

"Tim, we're going for tea now and then a practice later in the common room, why don't you come too?"

Marj tucked her hair behind her ears and waited expectantly for his reply, but he shook his head and ambled off towards the dorm, handcuffs in hand, where he quietly disappeared through the swing doors.

"Well, you can't say I didn't try!" she puffed.

We all wondered how he was going to practice by himself until Norma shouted from the canteen window that Chicken Kiev's were on the menu and they were going fast.

Chicken Kiev's suddenly became more important than poor Tim as we stampeded towards the canteen.

AN UNUSUAL PREDICAMENT

Bright and early the following morning we sat in class awaiting the arrival of the Sarge to start the written part of the test. It was then that we saw Tim's desk and chair were noticeably vacant.

"I see there's one missing from class," the Sarge growled as he shut the door behind him. He counted heads. "Anyone seen Tim?"

We all shook our own heads in unison.

"I don't think he was at breakfast either Sarge," Norma helpfully offered whilst concealing a smirk.

He pushed the file he was carrying into the drawer of his desk, locked it and popped the key in his pocket.

"Okay, Hodges, Upton, come with me. The rest of you, heads down, revise page 113."

As the classroom door banged shut, sixteen bottoms shifted from their seats to bolt across the room so that thirty-two eyes could peer out of the window to watch as we disappeared into 'J' block.

"Here you go Sarge, this is Tim's room."

I stood to one side as Danny pushed open the door to its full extent. There was a brief silence before he spoke again.

"Oh crap, Tim what the hell have you done?"

I edged past Danny and the Sarge to see what was wrong.

Sitting on the floor, head in his one free hand, the other handcuffed to the radiator pipe was Tim, still dressed in his blue and white striped pyjamas. His haunted eyes stood out against the paleness of his skin.

"Oh bloody hell I can't believe I did this, please, please unlock me I really need the toilet!" he wailed.

He was holding his crotch so tightly I thought he was going to pass out.

The Sarge quickly fumbled in his pocket for his own handcuff key, whilst Tim, between sobs, carried on kneading his groin.

"I didn't have anyone to practice on, it was the only thing in here that was the right shape..." he heaved a huge sigh as a solitary tear ran down his cheek. "... I just forgot one thing, one small thing that's all and I've been stuck here for nearly ten miserable hours!"

I choked back a giggle.

Tim's 'one small thing' had been his own handcuff key, which he'd apparently left in the pocket of his uniform trousers.

"Where are your trousers now Tim?" I tried to sound sympathetic.

He grimaced and jerked his head to where they were hanging in all their glory from the hook on the back of the bedroom door. Unfortunately for Tim, being tidy and putting his clothes neatly away had its drawbacks, as the door was several feet away from where he was now crouched with a bladder fit to burst.

Unlocking the handcuffs, Sarge helped Tim to his feet whereupon he promptly bolted for the door. As he ran along the corridor towards the toilets, his pyjama bottoms started to rapidly lose their hold on his rear giving us a view we could have done without.

Clicking the handcuffs back into place, Sarge wistfully smiled.

"They never learn do they? First time it's been one on their own though," he winked as he left the room.

...

Unfortunately, poor Tim in his first three weeks had become a statistic in the Training Centre's *'Book of Legendary Fuck-ups'*.

He'd cut a solitary figure ambling around campus during the days that followed his most 'unfortunate incident'. Any enthusiasm he had carried, slowly dwindled away leaving a mere shell of a boy.

Standing in the gym hall, I considered our position.

"Look, we've got baton training this afternoon. It doesn't entail keys, virginity or siblings, so I'm sure if we try we can help Tim regain his confidence, what do you think?"

I gave an optimistic grin but there were no words of encouragement, just a murmur of barely supressed laughter.

Danny was swishing a substantial stout, long and glossy wooden truncheon with a short leather strap in front of him, he swaggered to the back of the hall.

He executed a figure of eight in the air. "It looks the part hey girls?"

"Yeah, yeah Danny boy, in your dreams matey, probably the first time you've held more than three inches in your hand!" Marj swivelled on her heels, rolled her eyes and winked.

Danny gave her a single middle finger salute.

"Come on girls, they're issuing ours now." Norma barged her way to the front of the queue.

As we stood excitedly in line, it was with bitter disappointment that we saw the gaping disparity between the sexes. Our truncheons were pathetically short and stumpy, held together with bits of old blue rope.

"You're having a laugh," snorted Phyllis, a rather stout girl from North Wales, who was sporting a masculine haircut and an even more masculine smattering of upper lip hair. "I've had bigger vibrators than this," she sneered whilst poking her tongue out in concentration, swishing the baton backwards and forwards.

I cringed and looked over at Norma who made a rabbit ears gesture behind Phyllis' back.

"Right ladies, handbags over here, one each." Melvyn randomly threw the cellophane covered packs towards us. "You should've been given these in your Force area before coming here, but stock's only just come in apparently." He carried on throwing the packs to each of us in line.

"Handbags, handbags!" squealed Marj as she inspected the rather fetching dull black plastic bag gracefully swinging from her arm. "They're not even Dolce & Gabbana, they're a ruddy job lot from the Docks market!"

The gym door suddenly banged shut forcing us into silence, Dave Deacons' voice boomed around the hall. All our complaints were temporarily forgotten.

"Right class, split into two groups, one each end of the hall, batons at the ready." We shuffled into position and waited.

"You've got your basic techniques; you know the rules so we're going to have a little practice."

An excited murmur rustled through the hall.

"I'm here not only to teach you, I'm here to ensure safety,

so no wild truncheon strikes, no pissing around, watch, listen and if you hear the whistle... STOP!"

Here we go again.

This was where Tim was to become the first casualty of the day courtesy of the biggest lad in the class called Brian. At 6'10" and 19 stone, affectionately known as The Wookie, he was a bruiser. A three tier baton charge was beautifully choreographed by the Sarge as he repeated the drill three times.

"Okay everyone, listen up. Do you understand your places, when to duck, strike or pivot and where you should be standing?"

Seventeen keen faces smiled, seventeen keen heads nodded, but face and head number eighteen, aka *Tim, Tim Nice but Dim* only managed a very slight wobble. Thinking about it now, maybe I could have done something to avoid what came next, but as they say, hindsight is a wonderful thing.

On the start of the whistle we were off and the first of ten fierce warriors charged from one end of the gym to the other. Baton swing, baton strike ...

... but Tim didn't duck and he certainly didn't pivot. In fact, he didn't do anything but stand there, frozen in time.

As the Sarge's whistle reached a crescendo, it was joined by the resounding thwack of wood on skull which brought a chill to the bone.

Tim smiled, or more aptly, grimaced, and promptly slid gently to the floor.

We all liked Tim very much.

We were sad to see him go.

KNOWLEDGE IS THE KEY TO ENLIGHTENMENT

"I'm actually doing quite well here, week 8 and I've not been sent home."

I looked over at Norma who was crashed out on the sofa in the communal lounge, one leg stretched across the faded teak coffee table, the other tucked under her.

"Sent home, why on earth would you be sent home?" she grinned.

"Don't look so surprised, I've never been away from home before and I... well, it just seems I've taken longer than everyone else to find my feet and then there's the little incident with the curtains and of course there was Tim..." I tailed off into an embarrassed silence as Norma jumped up, knocking a half drunk mug of tea from the table. She bent down to pick it up.

"Never been away from home? Oh come on, you're kidding me. How old are you?" I shifted uncomfortably in my chair.

"Well, I went on a Brownies camping trip once, but it was a disaster, I hated every minute of it."

I watched her scrub furiously at the wet patch on the carpet with a tea towel, pausing to wipe her nose with the back of her hand.

"Bet you were a right little goody two shoes for the Brown Owl, all sweetness and light, volunteering for everything, a little Water Sylph or Fairy Fire Lighter!" She began to snigger. "Yep Fairy Fire Lighter – you're good at that!"

I couldn't help but laugh, she was right.

"It was *because* of the volunteering Norma, that's where it went wrong." She looked at me quizzically, waiting for me to expound.

"We had to pick what chores we wanted to do, Pixie Cook, Elf Washer Up, Sprite Wood Collector, get the gist? They were all crap and boring and when Brown Owl said *'La Trine Duty'* I nearly fainted with unadulterated pleasure, it was so very French, couldn't help myself, I squealed, jiggled a bit and stuck my hand in the air shouting *me, me, me*."

A loud snort came from the chair behind me. I bit my lip, "Yeah, yeah Melvyn, how the hell was I supposed to know?"

He pulled a face, "French not your best subject at school then Mave?"

Norma hid behind her tattered edition of Cosmopolitan to laugh, but her shaking shoulders gave it away.

"Glad you both think it's funny, but can you imagine what it was like spending a whole week digging holes and emptying portable toilets filled with everyone's poo and wee AND about four ton of *San Izal* bog paper?"

Melvyn tried to reply, but could only manage a choked "San Izal?" before collapsing into a heap on Norma.

Realising they were probably too young to remember what it was, I tried to explain. "It was toilet paper, sometimes called *wet bum-shiny-surface* as it didn't actually soak anything up, just slid right across your nether regions wipe after wipe. It was ruddy useless!"

That just seemed to make things worse, Norma was hyperventilating and Melvyn had lost the power of speech.

Indignant, I picked up my book.

"It was a lesson learnt, what more can I say, it put me off anything remotely French – even Sacha Distel!"

They both stopped laughing, looked at each other and simultaneously shouted "Who?"

To be honest, I really couldn't be bothered explaining.

...

I shoved an errant turquoise sock into the drawer and slammed it shut. Socks, regardless of fancy colours, had no place for a night out in Town. I had the choice of a nice little polka dot dress, a woolly jumper with jeans or my dressing gown. I slumped back onto my bed and stared at the ceiling. Was I really ready for a drunken class night out? My horrendous relationship with intoxicating liquor was legendary, hence my preferences for orange juice or soda water.

I had a mathematical equation for this anomaly; Me + Alcohol + High heels = FLOOR

I could still remember the ensuing hangover when I was fifteen from a run-in with several bottles of Babycham at a family party. After several sausage rolls and a pork pie had failed to mop up the excess, I'd somehow managed after a bout of hiccups and a loud burp, to vacate my entire stomach contents into my Nan's handbag, destroying a packet of Embassy No. 6 cigarettes, a bingo pen, a pack of Fisherman's Friends and her pension book before staggering off to the toilet. Once inside the cubicle, my stiletto heels had failed to take purchase with the wet floor and I was a goner; wedged between the toilet seat and the wall.

This had been my very first indication that I was double

jointed and although not natural, my legs could go behind my head without really trying.

I shuddered at the thought of ever getting THAT drunk again as I zipped up my dress and checked the mirror. Smearing a good slick of Coral Blush lippy on, I smacked my lips together just as Marj knocked on the door.

"Ready Mave?"

...

"You're having a laugh girl, no alcohol on a night out!" Norma barked at me in utter disgust as she dragged her stool up to the bar.

"Oh come on, orange squash, you've got to be kidding?" Wrinkling up her nose, Marj raised her eyebrows.

Their derision was not hidden.

"Look girls, I don't drink, it sends me sort of funny, I like to have my wits about me." I took a swig of my OJ just to prove a point. Marj grabbed my hand and took the glass from me.

"Here, have a go at this." She shoved a pint of White Lightning Cider towards me and waited.

I tentatively took a sip. Mmmm not bad, it was like lemonade with a bit of a kick.

So here I am, six pints of White Lightning cider later, dancing on a nightclub table with Norma, Marj and the gang cheering me on. Amid screams of laughter, various insults and shouts of encouragement which include *Come on Mave, give it a bit of Tina Turner* to *Look at this lads, Mave the Rave's giving it some welly* all just audible above the persistent bass beat of the music. I gyrated, bounced and wobbled, my confidence soaring.

It was bound to end in tears.

Having not quite earned myself the bladder capacity of a two humped camel, I was taken short.

"Norma, I need a wee, look after my drink for me," and with that I staggered off to find the loos.

Once in the brightly tiled washroom I took my place in the queue, hanging on to a nearby door frame as nausea washed over me. I'd clearly overdone the pop again.

Whispering *never again* under my breath, the click of a door lock gave me an available cubicle and I disappeared behind the door.

Five minutes later I stood, or in reality, hung over the wash basin. Squinting through an alcoholic haze I fumbled around the low level basin for the hot tap, finding instead a rather squidgy bar of soap. Clasping it firmly in my hand, I pulled.

"Hey, what the hell do you think you're bloody playing at? Hands off!" Dropping the 'soap' I stumbled backwards.

"Jeez, you women round here have deep voices, must be all the pints you drink..." I wiped my hand on my dress. "... bet you've got a hairy chest too!"

I sniggered at my little joke.

Come to think of it, I had as much right to the soap as they did. Indignancy rising, I pointed my finger at the blurred silhouette with an exaggerated stabbing motion.

"Don't you dare mess with me little Miss Testosterone..." I let a hiccup escape but held back on the burp for fear of once again producing a technicolour yawn. "... I'm Ninja trained, so watch out!"

There, that'll teach her. I'd had six martial arts training sessions and was good to go.

I could take her on. The closeness of my adversary meant I got a rush of hot breath mixed with the smell of fresh lager as she spoke.

"Maybe if you were English language trained you might have read the sign on the door too, you stupid bint."

In the silence that followed I heard the sound of a trouser zip being hastily pulled up. Within seconds I was roughly removed from my hand washing duties by Security, who took great delight in marching me through the club and out through the double doors.

As the cold night air hit me, I suddenly became acutely aware that washing your hands in the Gents urinal is apparently not cricket in this neck of the woods, nor was insulting a grown man by comparing his Wang Doodle to a squidgy bar of soap.

Waking up the following day in my little room I had no recollection of how I had been returned to Campus. Taxi, bus, car, TNT Parcel Express or The Post Office. The absence of stamps, string or brown paper anywhere about my person led me to believe it most definitely wasn't the latter. I had retained all my clothing, including my shoes, which was a bonus and I was on my own.

That was not so much a bonus but more of a relief.

The whole unfortunate episode encouraged Norma to give me a new mathematical equation;

MAVIS + ALCOHOL + MENS TOILETS = DOOR

This was happily endorsed by Melvyn who, embarrassingly enough, had also been availing himself of the toilet facilities in the Gents at the time of my forced removal.

CAN YOU HEAR ME?

"Jeez, I know it's not all work and no play, but it's getting harder the closer we get to the end of training isn't it?"

I let out a long sigh which blew the sheet of paper I was reading across the desk.

I watched it as it swung in a slow sideways motion before it settled on the carpet of the classroom floor. I looked over to Norma who was twiddling a section of hair around her fingers, tongue hanging out in deep concentration, bent over her desk.

"Norma, it's getting harder isn't it?" She looked up bemused.

"I hope you're not talking about me, but if it's a compliment then I'll go with it." Melvyn interrupted. He laughed and checked the front of his trousers.

"You're nothing but a perv Blakey!" Marj threw a screwed up piece of paper at him, it bounced off his head and dropped to the floor.

Hour upon hour had been spent either in class, out on the parade ground, in the gymnasium, swimming pool or at the library study centre. Exams had been set every week and to fail meant being either back-classed or sent back to Force as unsuitable for progression.

I picked up my sheet of paper, smoothed it out on the desk with my hand and gazed out of the window. The daffodils were up around the pond, the trees gaining their leaves. Summer was just around the corner. I was missing Ella dreadfully and really looked forward to her weekly letters in which she told me of all the things Nanny would let her do that I wouldn't.

This letter was no different, in her best childish handwriting, she had brought me once again to the brink of tears and then left me with a smile.

7th April

Dear Mum,

Missing so you so much, is it nearly Friday yet? I'm doing good at school but Moey the goldfish had to go on holiday yesterday Nan said his water was a bit cold and he needed sunshine. Think I'm going to miss him but can I have a guinea pig instead.

The hamster escaped from his cage but Nan found him in the bath. I don't think he was dirty he might have been thirsty but he wasn't hungry because he ate Nan's soap.

We looked all over for him but we needn't have worried as he'd shat in the bath. Love you Mum, can't wait to see you

Love Ella xxx

Having had visions of a dead goldfish and Mum's bath being full of hamster poo, I was relieved to discover during last night's telephone call that although Moey truly was deceased, the hamster had actually been *sat in the bath* at the time of this particular crisis.

My reverie was broken by the Sarge's voice cutting through the silence.

"Okay Ladies and Gents, hand your papers in, ten-minute break and make your way over to the main hall for the First Aid Exam."

Groaning in unison, we filed quietly out of the room, only Brent Carlisle, super egghead and ex paramedic was looking forward to this one. We had spent weeks being rigorously trained to cope with every eventuality. If you were suffering a heart attack, asthma, head trauma, electrocution, gunshot wound, diabetes, Chicken Pox or a boil on your bum, then we were the right people to be first on scene to assist and treat you.

Hmmm.

I could just imagine the horror of some poor casualty seeing me bearing down on them, grinning inanely whilst screaming loudly in sheer panic "MY NAME IS MAVIS, I'M A POLICE OFFICER, CAN YOU HEAR ME?"

Up until now it had never crossed our minds that one day we just might be practicing these life-saving skills on real live, well almost live, human beings. Huddled together in the main hall waiting to go through for the exam, we patted each other on the back and threw around a few 'good lucks'.

"If they think I'm gonna give the kiss of life to some minger they can think again." Marj stuck out her tongue in exaggerated disgust.

I looped my arm through hers, "It'll be our job, you can't just pick and choose who you help."

She raised an eyebrow, tilting her head to one side.

"Well I'll tell you this Mave, if it stinks, has puke anywhere near it or doesn't have teeth, I'm not touching it!" Each descriptive was accented by her finger being jabbed into the air.

Sergeant Phillips stood in the doorway of the exam holding area, clipboard in hand. "Right everyone, listen in.

It's your job on entering each incident room to quickly assess and decide what you are faced with, be it accident, illness or disaster and deal with it appropriately, got it?"

Nodding in acknowledgement, we waited with baited breath, as he opened a large box.

"Each one of you will collect one of these. Wear it and use it during the scenarios and remember, although they are actors, you must treat them as proper casualties and don't forget to verbally explain your findings and actions."

Slapping an old issue BURNDEPT Radio into my hand he grinned. Phased in during the 1970s and phased out again just as quickly they were the size of a house brick, weighed about the same and had to be worn with a chest harness.

Chest harness, I ask you?

As if I didn't have enough trouble with what nature had gifted me hanging from my front without adding a ruddy great big brick to it. I fumbled with the straps, trying to figure out how it should fit. My humongous boobs weren't helping in the slightest and pushing them under my armpits made no difference whatsoever. Time was ticking away and Sarge was looking on impatiently.

"Upton, stop farting around and get a move on, you're next." Flustered, I resigned myself to compromise.

The top part was clearly meant to go around my neck so that the radio hung tantalisingly at the front, smack bang in the middle of my nellies. Dangling from the bottom were two extra straps, which try as I might, I couldn't figure out where they were supposed to go. Panic rising, I continued to fiddle with them.

"1261 Upton to Exam Station 2, Room 6" the distorted

voice boomed out from the nearby loudspeaker.

Shit, I wasn't ready, I still had hold of the two straps, where the bloody hell do they go. Giving up, I hastily shoved them down the front of my trousers hoping they would remain secure and wouldn't be obvious.

"Knock 'em dead Mave!" Danny thumped me on the arm to accompany his much needed verbal encouragement.

As I began the long walk along the corridor to Room 6, I suddenly had another one of my wonderful epiphany's where I was kicking leaves and avoiding doggie deposits without a care in the world; not trying to remember breaths to compressions ratio whilst smearing my favourite Coral Blush lipstick all over Resusci Annie's latex lips.

I entered the room and looked around. I had thirty seconds to survey the scene.

Sitting in the corner behind a desk, not in the least bit discreet, was the Examiner. A portly guy with two strands of remaining hair that were clinging on for dear life, brushed across his shiny head and a nasal wart of humongous proportions.

I took a deep breath, made a mental note not to stare at his wart, and began my assessment.

"Unconscious casualty, query fall due to overturned stepladder. There are no dangers to myself, casualty or others."

Way to go Mavis, I was on a roll.

All I needed to do now was to check the level of consciousness of the poor guy lying prone on the floor. I took a closer look. He was good, barely a flutter of an eyelash, real RADA type stuff. Right, this was it, time to show just how competent I really was. The culmination of hours of study. I could do this...

...and then it all went horribly wrong.

As I knelt down on one knee shouting 'Can you hear me?' I suddenly found out to my eternal horror what the two extra straps I had hastily shoved down the front of my pants were for.

As the impetus of my sudden descent challenged the laws of gravity, the untethered brick-like BURNDEPT radio swung from between my nellies and smacked my casualty with some considerable force...

...right in the face.

Bullseye!

Letting out a howl of pain, he sat bolt upright, blood trickling through his fingers. I looked around the room, absolutely mortified. In the silence that followed I could feel my life slipping away.

"Oh bugger, I'm so sorry, oh crap what have I done, oh bloody hell... shit, shit I can't believe I've just done that!"

A further terrible silence followed in which my casualty's face turned a mottled shade of purple splashed with crimson blood. I let out a nervous snigger before adding;

"I don't suppose you can either?"

The last thing I remember hearing before I was hastily removed from the room, was the Examiner's voice resonating from behind the desk in the corner.

"You wrap the two straps around your waist and tie them together at the back you absolute bloody moron..."

A NIGHT TO REMEMBER

"Grab the wine, I'll see you in Marj's. I've got crisps and a couple of bars of chocolate." I swung the carrier bag at Norma as she deftly hooked her fingers around it and shoved it into her sports bag.

I watched her, bottles clanking together as she ambled along the corridor towards Marj's room before taking the chance to look around my own room. Norman Tebbit, who I hadn't got around to replacing, stared forlornly back at me. He was all that now adorned my walls apart from the odd blob of Blu-tack. My suitcase sat half packed and ready to accept the rest of my belongings. These were our last days of training. Soon we would be scattered like cheap bird seed around the North of England as fully fledged Police Officers.

Closing the door behind me, I was almost knocked sideways by Phyllis, her Welsh lilt filling the corridor as she galloped towards the toilets in just a pair of knickers, gripping her stomach.

"Esgusodwch fi, esgusodwch fi, outta the way girlies green apple splatter coming through!"

As Phyllis and her rather wobbly Little Miss Bossy knickers disappeared from view I had a feeling the word *unleashed* was probably a better description.

•••

"Here you go, get that down you." Marj slopped another plastic beaker of wine at Norma.

Trying to wriggle my legs from underneath her, it was obvious that a single bed wasn't designed to accommodate all three of us, plus wine, plus crisps, plus chocolate.

"Right, *Truth or Dare*, you go first." Marj giggled as she brushed broken bits of crisps from her pyjama bottoms onto the duvet and pointed at Norma. "Okay, let me see, have you ever had wild sex outdoors?"

We burst out laughing as Norma thought for a second, hiccupped and burped loudly.

"Oooh no, but I did have my ears pinned back when I was younger, does that count?" she drained her beaker and held it out for more wine.

"What's your ears got to do with wild sex outdoors you dork?" I howled. Giving an enigmatic grin, she flicked her overly large ears for effect.

"These are all down to my last boyfriend." She took another slurp of wine and grimaced. "He was an Auriphiliac, always playing with me ears. Didn't do much for me like, but for him it was as good as playing with a set of Pamela Andersons baps!"

We almost rolled off the bed laughing.

"Seriously Norma, you're having us on, you must be!" Not bothering with her beaker, Marj took another swig of wine straight from the bottle.

"Nope, it's the truth. Two years playing with them every night as foreplay basically buggered all the work me plastic surgeon had done." She shrugged her shoulders in resignation.

"Auriphiliac! That's not even a proper word," Marj spat as she wiped her hand across her chin, smearing the wine she'd dribbled.

"I know it isn't, made it up myself so it sounded a bit respectable every time he fondled me ears in public." She let out another hiccup and a burp before continuing. "I used to look at him all pitied like and say to people *'he can't help it, he's an Auriphiliac'*, like he had diabetes or something."

We both tried to look empathetic to her plight, which was difficult as all we wanted to do was laugh.

"So you see, some of us have big boobs..." she looked accusingly at me, "... some of us have big bums..." she glared at Marj, "...and some of us have just got bloody big wombat ears."

As if to prove a point she gave them a hefty slap from the back with both hands, which set off another round of raucous laughter.

I was going to miss Norma. She had a light of her own that always made me smile.

•••

The screaming echoed down the dorm corridor from the direction of the communal shower room.

"Aww for eff's sake, look at the state of me bleedin' leg and it's the one where me dress splits too!"

A low moaning noise followed the sound of metal curtain rings being forcefully pushed back in temper. By the time I reached her, Norma was already out of the shower, towel wrapped loosely around her with the offending leg stretched out. Blood was dripped from a landing strip of missing skin on her shin.

"Aren't I going to be the bloody Belle of the Ball with THAT sticking out from under me frock?" She threw her trusty orange Bic razor into the nearby bin. It hit the side, clattered and dropped to the bottom.

I puffed out my cheeks, trying to think of a suitable reply.

"Oh it won't be that bad lovely, couple of sticking plasters and by the time every one's had a few drinks..."

She cut me short.

"Oh yeah, of course I can just see Brent running his hands up me leg and getting stuck on a *Mr Tickle* plaster. The whole night's going to be feckin' ruined." She winced as she wiped a ball of wet toilet paper along her shin.

We both looked at her half-shaved, outstretched leg and burst out laughing.

Dining-In Night was the one thing we'd all been looking forward to, almost as much as the Passing Out Parade the following day, hence Norma's decision to shave her extremely hairy legs. Tonight it was going to be frocks, frolicking and fun as we celebrated our final days at the training centre.

Leaving Norma to her leg mishap, I wandered outside and plonked myself down on the bench by the pond. Looking around at the buildings, the drill square, the quirky little roads where we had practiced our motoring offence skills, the main gates where it had begun all those weeks ago, I felt quite sad to be saying goodbye to it all. There had been friendships forged, lessons learnt and bodies pushed to their absolute limits. Some of us had been back classed through illness or injury, but in the main we had stuck together through thick and thin.

I threw a chunk of leftover bread from the canteen to the resident duck, who had splashed his way to the edge. Looking less than impressed, he fixed his shiny black eyes on me in anticipation of something a little tastier.

I showed him my empty hands, he fluffed himself up and swam away.

Lights were blazing from the window of the accommodation blocks as animated silhouettes primped, preened and sprayed. I stood up, eager to join them. We had a night of celebration ahead of us, where we would dine, drink and dance into the early hours.

Looking up towards the already darkening night sky I smiled at the thought of the Sarge's stark warning earlier in the day.

"Ladies and Gents, a gentle reminder, no handcuffs, truncheons or other dubious accessories tonight. As I'm sure you will all recall... they were the unfortunate downfall of Julie Goolie and her size 20 knickers!"

...

"Bloody hell Marj, you scrub up well for a Northern lass!" Melvyn's eyes were out on stalks as he offered her his hand.

She floated down the steps, her pink and silver evening gown billowing out behind her.

"Don't touch what you can't afford Melvyn Blake!"

She playfully slapped his hand away and that was when I saw it. A blush and a flutter of Rimmel false eyelashes from Marj and a hint of something more than just lust from Melv. "Come on you two, behave!" I teased, "Look, here's Norma now, right, big smiles for the birdie."

Flash, whoompf

And that was our memory for a lifetime, set in the colour of our gowns and our smiles, the tuxedo that didn't quite fit Danny to Norma's desperate attempt to hide her jug ears and savaged shin for the camera and Melvyn's hand that had sneaked around Marj's waist.

Friends ready to go their separate ways in the real world.

"Right, enjoy the evening but remember, it's going to be a hot one tomorrow, marching with a hangover in heat is not advisable so keep an eye on your alcohol consumption Ladies and Gents." Sergeant Deacon winked.

We gave a collective groan as he ushered us through the double doors, but judging by the look on Danny and Melvyn's face, it had already fallen on deaf ears. I was also pretty sure the Sarge had seen it all over the years, and probably been part of it himself in his younger days.

Laughing, we linked arms and stepped out in time, reminiscent of Dorothy, the lion, the scarecrow, the tin man and Toto as the doors closed behind us.

•••

Several hours later, after an evening filled with much merriment, laughter, outrageous antics, speeches and awards we emerged happy, bedraggled and a little bit tipsy into the cool night air. Even those who had been found prostrate in the bushes by the pond, fuelled by excesses and the odd one or two who had to be rescued from bedposts, trees or road signs after ignoring the no handcuffing rule, happily agreed it had been a night to remember.

"Hey Mave, Danny, anyone seen Marj?" I turned to see Norma emerging from behind the large willow tree near the pond, gown wafting in the gentle breeze as she animatedly swung her arms in exasperation.

"Nope, the last I saw of her she was flailed out on the dance floor doing *Oops Up Inside Your Head* with Melv stuck between her legs," Danny helpfully offered with a wink before adding, "Come to think of it, I haven't seen Melvyn either."

We gave each other knowing glances, just as a gentle voice, crooning a soft song, began to drift from one of the nearby benches. The words floated dreamily on the night air.

"... *Marjorie, Marj, my one and onleeeeeeeeeeeee, my truuuuuue lurrrrrrrve, forever mine...*"

Marjorie's dulcet tones followed up on the last note.

"Melvyn Blake, there's no such song, nobody in their right mind would write a song with the name Marjorie in it! It's a shit name, I've hated it all my life."

There was a momentary pause.

"You wanna try being a Melvyn with a 'Y' then, even my mother didn't know 'Y' she chose it, geddit?" he snorted in amusement.

Marj let out a long sigh.

"Melv, just shut up and kiss me!"

The campus lighting cast a glow across the bench, outlining the silhouette of Melvyn and Marjorie in a very intimate embrace, her head resting on his shoulder.

We silently watched as Melvyn took his first kiss, then we crept away to find somewhere where we could laugh out loud without disturbing them.

TIME TO SAY GOODBYE

"Where's my hat, anyone seen my hat?"

There was an air of excited chatter, doors slamming and half-dressed girls running up and down the dorm corridor.

"Here, one hat..." Marj flung the bowler towards Alison Bryant, who scowled, caught it and disappeared into her room. "... now anyone seen my hairbrush?"

Twenty minutes later we were ready. Giving each other air hugs so that we didn't dislodge hats, hair or tie pins, we lined up to begin our single file out onto the quadrangle. This was it, our long awaited day.

Our Passing Out Parade.

Family and friends seated, Dignitaries fawned over and poor Billy, the campus caretaker running around after the horses with a shovel and a large bucket.

"Oh jeez listen to that. I know I'm going to get it wrong, I always do, I'm sweatin' just thinking about it." Norma waved her white gloved hand towards the brass band as they kicked off with a rousing rendition of Colonel Bogey.

A snigger passed along the line as Brent cleared his throat and tipped his hat towards her.

"Just swing them hips Norma babe, just like you did last night!" He winked making her blush.

"I didn't swing anything Brent Carlisle, that's just me bad hip playing up." She shoulder-barged him in feigned annoyance.

So here we are, standing tall and proud, attired in our

smart dress uniforms, hats perfectly placed, Force badges dead centre of nose and the shiniest shoes and boots in the world, bulled to perfection and ready for inspection.

The anticipation was killing me.

I looked along the line to Norma. 6'1" tall, gangly legs, arms that reached below her knees, wombat ears, she struggled at the best of times to look smart. It wasn't that she didn't try, it was just everything conspired against her. She looked at me and smiled, tucking her blonde hair behind those very ears. Oh dear, those poor ears. They were enormous.

We'd spent several hours the previous day in a team effort, having steamed her hat and stitched the badge so it wouldn't move from centre and after pressing her uniform for the umpteenth time, we stuck it under Danny's mattress for him to sleep on.

Her boots had been another matter. It didn't matter how much spit and polish we had used; they just wouldn't shine. In sheer desperation we'd resorted to the unthinkable and sent Melvyn to the local supermarket to buy a KIWI Instant Shoe Shine sponge.

"Why me?" he'd whined. "It's banned, if I get caught it's my neck in the noose, I've cleaned mine properly so why do I have to go?" Unclipping his seat belt, he'd waited.

"Desperate times call for desperate measures Melv, just go." Danny had given him a hearty shove out of the car.

Later that afternoon Norma's boots were treated to several wipes of the glossy, sticky sponge until the sun had shone from the toecaps. We'd all slept better that night.

"Looking good Norma." Danny high fived Melvyn, "Worth the risk wasn't it?"

Melvyn shrugged whilst Norma fair glowed in the knowledge that for once she would pass muster. Drill Sergeant Deacon in his ceremonial uniform stood proud at the front and once satisfied with our formation, he began to pass along the lines, his eyes travelling from top to toe inspecting each Officer in turn.

One or two of us had allowed a little smirk to drift across our tense lips, but these were not to last as he dramatically stopped dead in his tracks in front of Norma.

Puffing out his chest to the point where I thought his shiny buttons would explode, his teeth bared, he went nose to nose with poor Norma who looked like a rabbit caught in headlights.

"Constable Bottomley, do NOT have the audacity to tell me that you have bulled those boots!" he roared.

In the flair of a synchronised swimming team, our heads individually bowed along the line to turn and stare at Norma, who all of a sudden began to wrinkle and crumple before our very eyes. She attempted to speak but only a squawk could be heard as she frantically nodded her head, vaguely resembling something that should be sitting on the parcel shelf of a Nissan Micra.

He pointed again at Norma's boots.

"Greasy, 'orrible, cheap, nasty shoe shine Bottomley?" The steely expression on his face was daring her to contradict his expert opinion.

Norma nodded, shook her head and half-nodded again, shifted from one foot to the other, squirmed and groaned.

Deacon was not going to let it rest.

"Before you commit yourself to a lie Bottomley, may I suggest you scrutinise the toe caps of your boots."

Eyes on stalks, he wiped the spittle from his mouth, expertly turned on his heels and walked on to the next class formation, leaving seventeen faces still staring at Norma and Norma carefully inspecting her boots.

A long silence followed, broken only by the brass band throwing a few oompah's out to end Colonel Bogey's jaunty march. The apprehension between us was almost palpable.

Norma suddenly became apoplectic, squealing fit to burst. "Oh my God, oh fuck, look..."

We all held our breath and stared at her boots as she carried on squealing. "...they're pubes... I've got feckin' pubes stuck to me boots!" she bellowed, loud enough for the whole quadrangle to hear.

Like children in a school playground, once the word '*pubes*' had been uttered, it was only natural that Marj would start a chain of uncontrollable giggling that passed rapidly along our line as Norma frantically tried to remove the offending hairs by wiping her boots across the back of her trousers.

"Why me? What have I ever done to deserve this?" she moaned.

Choking with laughter, we couldn't answer her as we watched several stray strands of her short and curlies quiver in the breeze, adhered for dear life to the toe caps of her boots by the glossy but very sticky Kiwi Instant Shoe Shine.

If this hadn't been bad enough, to her absolute horror, it was very obvious to all and sundry that she was not, and never had been, a natural blonde.

"Get it together lovely, we can laugh or cry about it all later, I promise, you can't lose it now." I gave her a sympathetic smile.

"Oh Mave, I'm so embarrassed; on my last day too..." she grimaced as she struck out on her first steps towards the Parade Ground, trying desperately to keep in step with the line in front of her. "...hopefully they'll blow off in the wind," she forlornly whispered.

"Oh shit, there's me Dad and he's wearing his funeral suit, jeez Dad." Melvyn's observation was a welcome distraction for Norma.

He straightened his tie and strained to get a better look at where all our families were sitting. "He either thinks this is a special occasion or me Nan's croaked it and he hasn't told me!" he joked.

Danny thumped him in the back, pushing him forward as our section moved off.

I could see Mum and Ella sitting on the front row, Ella wearing the straw hat with pink daisies she'd found in the attic. Mum gave me a little wave, her face beaming with pride.

The weather was gloriously sunny, if a little windy and those with hangovers were already starting to sway in time to the music as the Police horses trotted onto the drill square with us following behind.

Barely two seconds in, it all started to fall apart.

We marched out beautifully in step only for the first line to lose the momentum on the first turn of the Drill Square. What followed was a brilliant impression of Spotty Dog from *The Woodentops*.

"Oh for fuck's sake, we look like a gang of navvies out on the piss!" hissed Danny as Norma attempted to swing both arms in the same direction and Marj looked like she was dancing the military two-step.

Sniggers came from the row behind. I knew from experience that when one person loses their step, it would only a matter of time before it spread like a rabid attack of measles down each line. Six steps in and we were all marching like Spotty Dog. The only saving grace that I could see was that at least we were all synchronised. That was until Geordie Geoff decided to keel over because as previously warned, hangover, plus warm weather, uniforms and marching don't mix.

As he gracefully kissed the tarmac amid silently mouthed 'ooohs' and 'aaahs' from the audience, the brass band picked up the tempo. As much as Geoff was a popular young lad, we felt our best option was to step over his horizontal torso in turn, rather than completely lose momentum. I looked over to where Sergeant Deacon was stiffly standing, half hidden by one of the Ceremonial Horses from the Mounted Division, salute frozen in time along with a grimace he couldn't hide.

Our beloved families, safe in the ignorance that we had well and truly screwed up, looked on with pride, as Geoff was dragged by his ankles to be deposited behind the VIP stand until he regained consciousness.

An hour later, parade completed, awards handed out, speeches given and hats thrown into the air to signal the end, with hugs and promises to keep in touch, we all stood at the main gates. Euphoria tinged with a little sadness.

I watched Norma, all dangling arms and wombat ears, waving from the open window of her Mum and Dad's car as it slowly drove out of the campus gates.

"Bye Mave, good luck, keep in touch. Don't forget to always make sure your collar and cuffs match though!" She winked, laughed, slapped the back of her ears for one last time and was gone.

A tear trickled down my cheek. I would miss Norma most of all. Using the heel of my hand I wiped my face.

"Come here you daft mare, give us a hug." Melvyn wrapped his arms around me as I fought the huge lump that was threatening to choke me. Another tear escaped down my cheek.

"We can make a difference; you'll see Mave." He cocked his head to one side and grinned.

I ruffled his hair, "Thanks Melv, take care of yourself too, don't be getting into mischief out there and take care of Marj, she's a good kid." Our touching moment was quickly interrupted by a huge snort from Marj.

"I heard that Mavis Upton, praise indeed from you, but just so you know, I'm still not giving the kiss of life to anyone without feckin' teeth... ever!" she blew a kiss and jumped into her car.

"Mum..."

I turned to see Ella, her pretty pink summer dress picking up the colour of her cheeks. "... I've missed you so much, can you come home for good now?"

READY OR NOT... HERE I COME

"It's nice to have you home again, Ella has missed you."
Mum took a last drag on her cigarette and stubbed out the
remainder in the ashtray. The pale smoke curled up into her
nostrils as she tucked her bare feet under her and adjusted
the cushion on the sofa.

"I know, she's been such a good girl, it can't have been
easy for her." I angled my mug so it sat squarely on the coaster.

She looked knowingly at me. "It can't have been easy for
you either Mavis, I'm very proud of you, you know that don't
you?"

She patted my hand.

"I do Mum, and that means the world to me."

•••

"Oh gawd... Cat... get out of the way!"

Tripping over Cat I just caught myself before I went
headfirst into the kitchen door.

This is typically me, excited, panic struck and hyper – at
4:30 in the morning.

Cat looked at me in disgust. I had ruined his comfy
sleeping position on the third from bottom stair. Grabbing
my coat, I took a last gulp of the black coffee designed to
wake me up from Ella's pink sparkly mug. Dropping it into
the sink I made a mental note to at least start washing up
regularly or I'd be in danger of having my next coffee from
Cat's bowl.

"See you tonight Cat, but no more mousey gifts thank you very much." He stared, swished his tail and blinked as I shut the front door behind me.

The journey to work hadn't taken nearly as long as I thought it would. I sat in my car, drumming my fingers on the steering wheel and humming along to Rod Stewart watching the back door to Westbury police station.

This was where I had been posted to on patrol. It was an immense building, modern by today's standards, brick and concrete with a multitude of windows facing down onto the car park. To the left, a row of chequered concrete blocks with thick bullseye glass stood to attention along the wall, the low level lighting casting an amber glow from the first floor.

They were different from the rest, they had a feeling of Victorian dread to them. They were probably the Bridewell cells.

I shivered.

Turning the heating up a notch I waited. Timing wasn't my better point and terrified of being late on my first shift, I'd over calculated, hence killing time in the back car park as I was half an hour early. As the minutes ticked by boredom set in.

I sang along to Rod a bit more and then thought about playing a few of the car games Ella and I enjoyed on long journeys. Unfortunately, 'I Spy' on your own in a car park is not much fun, everything begins with 'C' and you always seem to guess it right first time. I fiddled with some buttons and knobs on the dashboard that I hadn't noticed before, pulled faces in the rear view mirror and watched the second hand tick round on my watch.

6:30 a.m.

Dragging my public order kit bag across the car park, I flung open the doors to the station and stood for a moment. Several cycles were wedged up against a large blue door that had an official sign ironically declaring "DO NOT OBSTRUCT" in large red letters, a mountain of cardboard boxes were stacked in the corner threatening to topple over, an old pair of boots hung from the radiator along with a rather battered custodian helmet.

Juggling my kit bag and butty box, I shoulder barged the door marked 'locker room'.

It suddenly opened, throwing me backwards to the floor.

The weather-worn guy in half blues standing over me tutted loudly. "Bloody hell girl, what d'yer think yer playing at?" He held out his hand to help me up whilst studying me. "Ah a new sprog, tell you what kid take my advice, turn around and go home, the job's fucked."

With that he snorted, belched, lit a cigarette and disappeared back into the locker room.

I stood staring as the door banged behind him. Jeez, what a welcome. "Thanks for that!" I shouted after him as the door bounced open, creaked and shut again.

Gathering my stuff together, I took the stairs to the first floor. I'd try the locker room later in the shift, I wasn't chancing bumping into him again. First off I needed to find the Sergeants office.

I hesitated, wondering which corridor to take, it was like a maze.

"Hey, sprog over here, drop your stuff I'll take you through.

I'm Don, Don Penny." He thrust out his hand as I juggled and fumbled with my butty box and kit bag.

"Ooh nice to meet you I'm..."

"Mavis, I know, we've been expecting you," he quickly interrupted. With a smirk he ambled off along the corridor ahead of me.

He seemed pleasant enough, not particularly tall, a little rotund around the middle with slicked back dark hair, swept to one side. He held open one of the doors further along and with a bow and a flick of his hand, he ushered me in.

A huge table was set dead centre of the room, around it a mass of faces all looking at me expectantly.

"Sarge, this is Mavis, fresh out the box. Mavis, this is your section." He jerked his thumb towards them and sat down on the chair nearest to the guy with the three stripes on his shoulders.

They stared.

I stared.

I swallowed.

They stared a bit more.

A rhythmic tapping of a chewed pen on a blue plastic clipboard was reminiscent of my nan's old grandfather clock and was the only thing that broke the palpable silence.

As my childish enthusiasm began to slowly drain away, I quickly reached the conclusion that this was going to be one very long day.

...

Don followed me into the night kitchen. My first task from my new Sergeant, Rob Carlton was to make the tea and coffee. As the Probationer, or 'sprog' on the Section, this was going to be one of my roles for the foreseeable.

"Look Mave, don't take it to heart, they'll weigh you up, see what you're made of, just give everyone time. It's pretty easy, avoid Kevin he's a cantankerous old bastard, no use until he's had his third mug of tea and a cigarette on the back step of the nick."

I nodded. I had a feeling he'd been my welcoming committee in the locker room. "Frank's okay but don't ever bend down anywhere near him, he's a bit of a perv and then you've got Bob, never get in the car first, he farts like a warthog when he gets in. Let the air clear first..."

I nodded again, making notes in my book.

"...and for Christ's sake put the flamin' book away, we don't need Adrian Mole's Diary on everyone's bad habits!"

I blushed and hastily stuffed the book into my shirt pocket.

"Right, straighten your tie, it's time you met the Chief Inspector, he has a hands on approach and wants to welcome you to the fold."

He breezed out of the room leaving me to trail behind whilst he carried on chatting as he led me along one corridor, through another door and into another corridor.

"His name is Ronnie McDonald but he prefers to be called Sir McDonald when being introduced for the first time."

I nodded tentatively, slightly less enthusiastically now as I feared any further shaking of my head would give me permanent whiplash. It had been a day of constant nodding so far.

"So don't forget, it's all about etiquette. I'm taking the time to help you, so make sure you follow my advice."

He condescendingly gave me a pat on the back as he stood outside the muddy brown painted door. I was sure I'd read somewhere that Police Officers can be knighted for services to the Queen. This must have happened to Chief Inspector McDonald. Thank God Don had taken me under his wing, it would be awful to look foolish or uneducated on my first day.

"Thanks Don, I really do appreciate your help."

Patting my tie straight, I tucked a stray piece of hair behind my ears and checked my boots, giving them a hasty wipe on the back of my pants as Don wandered off down the corridor and out of sight.

Clearing my throat, I knocked and waited.

"Enter."

The door swept open as I gave it a gentle push.

Behind the desk sat an imposing man with a shock of the reddest hair I had ever seen.

Standing up as I entered the room, he completely towered over me. "Ah Mavis, please take a seat."

His handshake was firm whereas mine was limp and sweaty with nerves. A knot tightened in my stomach. *Come on Mavis, say it with confidence.* I cleared my throat.

"Thank you Sir McDonald, it is a pleasure to meet you, Sir."

I added the extra 'Sir' just to show him how much I respected his title.

Yay, go me!

His eyes widened, he took a sharp intake of breath as the air went dramatically frosty and his body language stiffened.

"What was that?"

"Errr, ummm thank you... Sir...err...Sir McDonald."

The last word had a slight crescendo to it, as though it really shouldn't have been allowed out of my mouth, more of an exclamation than a statement.

"Yes, that's what I thought you said." He purposely strode around his desk and sat down.

His face had taken on a rather pink, rosy flush which complimented his red hair in a funny sort of way. I couldn't stop staring at it.

He looked me squarely in the eye, carefully placed his pen next to his diary, straightened the ink blotter and locked his fingers together in front of him.

"Thank you Constable Upton, but two facts you need to know..." pausing to draw breath, whilst I nodded like an idiot, he continued "... I don't eat hamburgers, wear silly outfits or blow up balloons for children on a Saturday and you..." pointing his manicured finger at me "... should not always believe what your colleagues tell you."

The rest of the meeting was rather strained as I squirmed in my chair and racked my brains. I couldn't imagine what I had said wrong to have deserved such a reaction, or what on earth hamburgers had to do with it.

As I left his Office the name plate on his door caught my eye. In huge letters it read:

CH. INSPECTOR R. BARNETT

...

"It's an initiation Mave, take in the spirit it's intended kid." Don wiped away the tears of laughter as he breezed into the canteen and sat next to me. "We all have to go through it."

I squeezed the teabag from my mug. "Yeah, thanks Don, I'll laugh later."

On my very first day I had earned the elite *'McDonalds Happy Meal'* badge and a rather special relationship with Chief Inspector Ronnie Barnett with the bright red hair...

.... also known as Ronald McDonald to his troops – but only behind his back!

And here ended lesson No. 1.

FINDING MY FEET

"See Mum, if you'd let me eat McDonalds stuff when I was a kid, I would've cottoned on sooner." I laughed and grabbed a handful of crisps from the bowl and sat down on the stool at the breakfast bar.

"Ah, so it's all my fault then..." she chuckled, "... I wonder what lifelong trauma's I've caused Michael and Connie then?" She carried on peeling the potato, cut it into four pieces and plopped them into the pan.

"Well I know Michael's got an aversion to wearing pink knitted loopy loo hats after your spate of using only hand-me-downs to save the pennies, regardless of who wore them, boy or girl, and Connie was distraught when you told her that Grandad would melt if he stayed out in the sun too long." I crammed another handful of crisps into my mouth.

"Oh Mavis, that's ridiculous, she never believed that... did she?"

"Yep, remember that day at the beach when she went hysterical and we couldn't calm her down, well that was because he'd got overheated and was wiping his forehead with his hankie, Connie had half expected him to turn into a gigantic puddle and dribble out to sea."

Mum stood open mouthed with the second, half peeled potato in her hand.

"Good grief, I didn't think I had that much of an effect on my children. I'm surprised you all made it into adulthood."

...

"Three sugars Mave and not too much milk."

Bob Cairns slid his grimy mug across the table in the night kitchen. Leaning back in his chair he picked at fluff mixed with toast crumbs from his blue NATO jumper.

I looked at the back of Bob's head for something to do whilst I was waiting for the kettle to boil. There was something about men who refused to acknowledge male pattern baldness and Bob was one of them. His three solitary strands of greying hair were draped across his shiny scalp and then carefully tucked under the left arm of his spectacles.

Don caught me looking. "He had four strands last week Mavis. didn't you Bob?"

Bob grunted, smoothed his hand across his head and threw a discarded tea bag at Don.

"That's enough you lot." Sergeant Carlton tapped his clipboard on the table. "Right, for once try to stick to your scoff times lads and keep safe out there."

To the sound of chairs being scraped on lino, we acknowledged the Sarge and vacated the night kitchen in favour of the main enquiry office for radio collection and overnight crime reports. Banter was excitedly being exchanged over the latest scandal involving some poor unfortunate on another Section. He'd been discovered in *flagrante delicto* with a wife that on closer inspection, wasn't actually his own. It was a good story and what wasn't known as fact was easily added to with a bit of imagination and a lot of invention.

The radio room was only second in size to one of the toilets cubicles, so it was inevitable that a back log of bodies would ensue as the gossip continued.

"...so she denies anything's going on, claims she's just delivering Tupperware or something in her underwear as you do..." Loud guffaws were interrupted by the crackle of the radio's being tested for battery life.

A sharp stab in my stomach followed by a deep rumbling reminded me that Mum's overcooked sprouts and cauliflower from last nights' dinner were starting to nicely ferment.

"Ooops watch out lads, Mave's having a grumble, clear the decks."

I glared at Don. I'd got used to one or two of them lifting a leg and letting rip in the morning, it seemed to be obligatory to let out at least one fart before and one after Parade.

"Not from me boys, I'm a lady."

As another wave crept over me, I took a deep breath and hung onto the desk, waiting for the feeling to pass.

Don chucked his briefcase down next to me, slumping back into the typists' chair. "Mave, you've gone purple, what's up love?"

"Nothing, nothing I'm fine, just a touch of tummy ache." Another, more intense wave stabbed at my lower stomach.

I wasn't going to be able to hold onto this one, I was in danger of blowing up and exploding like a budget balloon from the local Pound Shop. I simultaneously clenched and shuffled my way to radio room only to discover it was still very much occupied.

Shit.

I frantically looked around for somewhere I could let rip without being heard.

Spotting the door to the office across the corridor, I remembered that Bernie, our Intel officer was away on leave.

It would be empty.

Surreptitiously backing up towards the closed door, I waited for a lull in in the corridor, my hand clutching the handle behind me. Giving another quick glance to check the coast was clear, I opened the door and backed in, pointing my offending body part in the right direction. Whilst keeping watch along the corridor, I allowed Donald to get out and walk, so to speak.

To my horror it was louder than I'd expected.

The ill-timed cough designed to cover up my bout of flatulence was sadly suffocated by the sheer volume of it.

Past caring, I could only sigh with relief as I looked towards the Enquiry Office.

No one seemed any the wiser as they carried on with their allocated tasks, chatting and laughing to each other. Allowing myself a relieved smirk and an extra, less noisy little squeak, I turned to close the door to the office and in doing so, trap my indiscretions within its four walls.

Suddenly a distinctive voice, accompanied by the tapping of a pencil on a plastic filing tray filled the room behind me.

I froze.

"Good morning Mavis, I hadn't realised it was so windy today. It certainly wasn't forecast when I listened to the news this morning."

Slowly turning my head, I came face to face with Chief Inspector Ronnie Barnett sitting at Bernie's desk, paperwork scattered in front him, his red hair parted in the middle and standing on end. His face frozen and lips pursed as though he had been caught in a Force 12 Hurricane.

He sniffed and flicked out a perfectly ironed handkerchief,

dabbing it to his nose as his nostrils flared. "Please leave the door open to let the air circulate my dear, I have a feeling it will be slightly stuffy in here for a little while longer."

I wanted the grey tiled floor to open up and swallow me. I was supposed to be a lady.

Ladies categorically don't fart in mixed company, particularly the company of a senior officer.

Turning to slip away discreetly, I was confronted by Don, Bob and the rest of the section standing in the corridor. They were each holding up a numbered queue waiting card purloined from the public counter.

My fart had scored a rather impressive 20, 18, 22, 24 and 19 respectively.

A POLICEMAN'S LOT

"Mum have you seen my school bag?"

I stuck my head around the kitchen door in time to see Ella, head first in the coat cupboard, discarding various remnants of clothing behind her into the hallway. A pink spotty welly came hurtling out, thudded on the wall and dropped sideways onto the floor.

"Muuuuuuum...have you?" She brushed a long strand of stray hair away from her face, blowing air upwards from her lips so her fringe gently parted revealing two quizzical eyebrows.

"It couldn't be that brown leather thing that's hanging on the peg above your head would it Ella?"

Grabbing it, along with her coat, she smirked. "What would I do without you Mum?" Before I could answer the front door trembled under the weight of a loud knock.

"Uh-oh... Daddy's here, see you later." With a slam of the door she was gone.

I bent down and picked up the pink spotty welly. Ella would be lucky to get just her toes in it now. She had grown so much these last six months. Holding it close, I felt a stab of nostalgia. It was so true how quickly your children grow with independence.

I tucked the errant welly back into the shoe basket that was marked 'Ella'.

Maybe tomorrow I would have a sort out, but not today; today was not a day for relinquishing memories of bouncing pigtails and muddy puddles.

...

The smell of sweaty boots lingered in the locker room. I grabbed a can of deodorant from the top shelf and sprayed it copiously around the stacked aisles of grey metal upright lockers. It barely touched, it was now a heady smell of sweaty boots mixed with peach blossom and freesia. I baulked, slamming my locker door shut.

"You've got your new Tutor Con today haven't you Mave? She's going to have a shed load of fun with you," Bob grunted as he sucked in his ample belly trying desperately to accommodate his belt. Giving up, he resigned himself to letting it out another notch or two.

"I know, her reputation precedes her, hope to God I don't mess up." I clipped my tie into place whilst watching him slowly began to return to a more normal colour as the extra inches around his middle offered respite.

"You'd better get up there now then girl, the Sarge'll be waiting for you."

Running up the stairs to the first floor, I barged open the door and picked my seat on parade, notebook at the ready and waited.

"Mavis, you're with Shirley today. She's an experienced officer, work closely with her." Sarge checked his watch. "She's running a little late so have a brew and I'll see you in my office at the end of the shift."

Throwing me a packet of half-eaten biscuits, he disappeared into the corridor. I didn't have long to wait as suddenly the doors to the parade room burst open, startling me. I looked up astounded. There, framed in the doorway, ample red lips and a massive expanse of chest that probably encompassed the whole of the alphabet in cup size stood Shirley McCready. A sublime mix of Diana Dors and Jessica Rabbit in a uniform.

"Just put it there my boy, yes, there, right in front of me, any toast to go with it?" she purred.

The young lad holding the tea tray carefully positioned a bright pink mug and plate on the table and made a hasty exit. Plonking herself in the chair next to me she looked me up and down and took a bite from her toast.

"Right chick, first rule; you've got to work twice as hard as any man in this job to be seen to be half as good. Got that? Fab, then we'll begin." She grinned.

I sat in silence, mouth agape, overawed and overcome.

She stood, smoothed down her skirt and began to rummage in her handbag. A gentle click was followed by a long intake of breath with an even longer exhalation. Shirley turned to face me, waving one hand in the air holding a Berkley Menthol cigarette, the other hand on her hip.

"Right chick, GEO duties, front counter, public desk, whatever you want to call it. You'll do a stint this morning so we can see how you get on unsupervised." I inwardly groaned.

It was Saturday morning, common knowledge that every lunatic from miles around would call in as they had nothing better to do than make strange and bogus reports for us to wade through. I let a hint of a smile touch my lips.

"Fab, looking forward to it..." I lied as we wandered off to the GEO in a plume of cigarette smoke.

Two hours ticked by with Shirley showing me the ropes.

"Right, I'm going for a coffee, Mavis you do the desk, Don will keep on top of the telephones, any problems, just shout up." She lit another cigarette, puckered her ruby lips, blew a rather impressive smoke ring and breezed out of the office.

I busied myself at the enquiry counter with a fascinating array of incidents which included Mr Edgar White, a rather dapper man with a pork pie hat who was my first caller after coffee break.

"I'm sorry Sir, could you run it by me again?" I tried not to giggle as he glared at me.

"There should be twelve ginger nuts but there's only ten, no one's been in me house, so I know, I just know." He frowned as he shoved the open packet towards me dropping crumbs on the desk.

"Could you have eaten them Sir, they are very moreish aren't they?" My empathy seemed to fall short on Edgar.

"No I bloody haven't, I know, I've told you I know, it's aliens, they come in the night and eat me Ginger Nut biscuits!" He tapped his bony finger on the counter.

Jeez... but Edgar wasn't finished there.

"So, what are you going to do about it then, I pay me taxes you know, I'm not leaving until you find out what's happened to them."

Trying to retain my calm exterior, I ushered him to a seat in the reception area in the vain hope that after a while he would eat the remaining biscuits, forget why he was here and go home. I was getting to the point of despair waiting for a genuine crime to be reported when Mrs Ethel Higginbottom arrived to lodge a complaint.

I was optimistic. She had excitingly mentioned the word *theft*.

"Can we speak somewhere in private dear, it's a very delicate matter," she conspiratorially whispered.

Taking her into the side room, I sat her down.

"It's me *Marks & Spencer* knickers Officer. I bought a size 18 but when I got them home they were more like a size 14, I couldn't get them over me thighs." She folded her arms in a resolute gesture. "It's not right, it's like stealing material isn't it, you pay for it, so where does it go?"

I bit my lip and studied the size of her large posterior, her hips hanging down like a deflated balloon either side of the grey flocked chair.

"It might be a good idea to take them back to M&S Mrs Higginbottom. I'm sure they'll know what to do." I helpfully offered, before adding, "Have you considered the possibility that you might have put on some weight?"

This was clearly the wrong response.

She grunted, snatched the offending panties from the table and stormed out of the room into Reception. Knickers still in hand, she gave a coy smile to Edgar, who was standing by the door cossetting his open packet of ginger nuts.

Clicking the security lock, I watched them through the window, secretly wishing they could find romance over her M&S knickers and his Netto biscuits. On second thoughts, maybe they already knew each other. It would explain Edgar's missing biscuits and her too tight knickers.

Bouncing back into the office, I let the door slam behind me. Don, feet up on the desk, was startled from his momentary reverie.

"We get 'em all in here Mave, the odd, the strange, the mad and the numpties," he helpfully offered.

I shrugged and pushed his feet from the desk and sat down. "I'd already resigned myself to that matey, they're unbelievable, haven't they got homes to go to? Doesn't anyone ever report a proper crime round here? I know some are just lonely but the others..."

My observations on life were suddenly interrupted by shouting from the corridor.

"You feckin' idiot, what do you think you're playing at?" Kevin Bartlett's voice bounced off the pale plaster walls. We stuck our heads out of the office door to see what the commotion was.

"I'm so sorry, really I am." The tiny, frightened voice wavered.

"You will be son. What possessed you? If someone's reporting their back entry is blocked, it doesn't give you permission to give them advice on constipation. You made me look like a right knob!"

Spittle sprayed out of Kevin's mouth as Don and I started laughing.

"Think it's funny you two? You try being paired up with this feckin' buffoon. Here you go, meet Constable 1469 Petey Thackeray, expert on constipation and other matters of the arse end but knows absolutely nowt about vehicle obstruction and cobbled entries!"

Kevin turned on his heels and stormed off along the corridor, slamming the fire door after him.

We stood in silence as the door swung twice before settling in the frame. Petey looked crestfallen.

He couldn't have been more than 12-years old. The only thing his top lip was sporting was an abundance of perspiration as he nervously pushed his metal rimmed glasses back onto the bridge of his nose. He ran a hand across his head, flattening down the fringe of his wispy dark hair. The seconds ticked by before he spoke.

"It's my first day, I think I've made a bit of a mess of it really." He looked at us, either for reassurance or confirmation. I couldn't be sure.

Don resumed his position in the chair, feet up on the desk studiously filling in his pocket notebook whilst scraping wax out of his left ear with his car key. Holding it up he admired what was attached to the end, wiped it on his pants and turned to Petey.

"There happens to be quite a difference between Wilful Obstruction and having a bodily function that's stuck in neutral lad. Are you sure you didn't want to be a Doctor?"

IT'S A DOG'S LIFE

"I'm off for two days' mid-week Mum, do you fancy a day of retail therapy and a spot of lunch?"

She smiled whilst rummaging around in her handbag. "Yes, that would be nice love, I could do with a trip to town, you haven't got any cigarettes on you have you?"

"No I haven't, you know I gave up years ago, I really wish you would too." I hated to see the smoke pluming out from her mouth, filling the room.

As if to prove a point, she shouted *eureka* and held a squashed Embassy No. 6 in the air with a flourish before lighting it, which was quickly followed by a coughing fit.

"It's my small pleasure love, it's not doing me no harm."

I didn't answer as I opened the window to clear the air.

•••

"You did okay chick, still rough around the edges but it'll all come in time, I've signed you off, you're on your own now."

In a waft of Yves Saint Laurent and a puff of Berkley Menthol smoke, Shirley was gone.

"Bleedin' hell, they're letting Mave loose on the natives on her own, batten down the hatches!" Bob looked around for an ally.

I picked up a pencil, took aim and fired. It hit the middle strand of hair on his head, bounced off and spun across the table.

"She might be independent, but Mavis is needed to double

up with Jim Baldwin on the IR car, sorry Mavis, needs must." Sarge scribbled my number on the duty sheets next to the AR12 call sign. "He's waiting for you in the back yard."

I wasn't the least bit disappointed, a night in the IR car was every probationer's dream. It had been known for some to craft effigies whilst in the toilets of whoever was riding shotgun in one, hoping they would fall victim to illness, accident or bum boils to free up a space in the passenger seat on a dark, wet, windy night.

I skipped down the stairs dragging my coat and briefcase. Jim was leaning against the open driver's door, a cigarette dangling between his fingers. He was a nice affable, laid back sort of guy who swore like a trooper. It was hard to put an age on him but I guessed at around 40-ish.

"Jump in Mavis, call's just come out for burglary in progress." He pushed his key into the ignition and revved the engine.

Throwing my briefcase into the foot well, I'd barely clicked my seatbelt into place before he'd pressed his foot on the accelerator, narrowly missing the security barrier on its slow ascent.

"Doing a silent approach so we don't spook 'em," he puffed through a trail of smoke that curled up and out of the open car window. I excitedly nodded, gripping onto the dashboard as we rounded a bend on two wheels.

Within minutes we were driving through the gates of a huge property named Risers Forge. Situated on the edge of a coastal cliff overlooking the sea, its clapboard turrets silhouetted against the dark sky, fleetingly lit by the moon before it skipped behind clouds. I could see everyone spread out in the gardens making a cordon around the house. Seconds later our radios burst into life.

"Male detained, male detained..."

A furious barking was followed by a flurry of activity at the side of the house before a shadowy figure was dragged out of the darkness and pinned to the ground.

"Leave 'em to it Mave, give one more check of the grounds and then we'll go and speak to the occupier, see if we need to take a statement." Jim flicked on his torch and disappeared behind a bush.

I stomped around for a bit, climbing over rockery and tramping across the large lawn.

Sweeping my torch from side to side I picked up the silhouette of Conan, Steve Coombe's police dog having a dump. I sniggered. I was just about to make a second pass when I met the Sarge emerging from behind the Summerhouse.

"Occupier's waiting for you inside Mavis, up the stairs..." he thumbed towards the front door "...be warned though, she is very upset and, well, not particularly pleasant to be honest."

"No probs Sarge, everything seems in order here, I'll see what I can do." I started walking towards the front door, leaving him examining the jemmied window.

The Victorian lamp swung gently in the breeze, casting a glow over the front door. I pushed it open and walked into the entrance hall, where a vast central staircase, covered in the most luxurious red carpet, swept up and branched out onto a galleried landing. A large, round inlaid mahogany reception table took pride of place to the left, standing out on the black and white chequered tiles. The crystal chandelier tinkled as I shut the front door.

I was in awe.

I began to climb the stairs, mentally ticking off the number as my hand cosseted the carved bannister rail. Reaching the top and a count of thirty, I stood mesmerised by the view. No wonder the living space was upstairs. It was breath-taking. Looking out of the vast floor to ceiling window, across the sea to the lights of passing ships out on the horizon, I watched the moon once again dip in and out of the clouds.

The plush red carpet was laid across the immense landing and right through the upstairs too.

"Can I help you dear?"

Startled, I looked over to where the very plummy voice had come from.

"I'm Mrs Constance DeVere, the owner of Risers Forge." She held out a rather limp, perfectly manicured hand.

I didn't know if she expected me to kiss it or shake it.

It was decidedly difficult to place an age on her. I plumped for late sixties, maybe early seventies. Carefully coiffured grey hair in a neat, French pleat wearing a 1950s style oyster coloured silk pyjama suit and matching robe.

"Mrs DeVere we need a few details from you and a statement." Jim interrupted my musings, giving me an exasperated look. I'd been so busy admiring the furnishings and fittings, I hadn't heard him come up the stairs.

Mrs DeVere wrinkled her nose, sniffed the air and then held her index finger under her nostrils, a look of distaste passing across her face.

"Ah yes Officer, if you would like to come this way," she mumbled from behind her hand.

As her silk robe swished to one side giving off a gentle breeze, a rather unpleasant smell wafted up and met my nose too. I tried very hard not to snort and grimace as I looked at Jim, hoping against hope he hadn't farted.

Jim looked at me; I looked at Jim. Jim shook his head; I shook my head. We looked at Mrs DeVere.

Oh my goodness, surely she was too refined to have let one rip!

Jim looked down and it was then I saw an immediate change in his expression. "Err Mavis, perhaps you could check the gardens again but be careful where you TREAD out there."

The emphasis on the word *tread* made my heart sink. I looked down at my boots and my heart sank.

Jim quickly ushered Mrs DeVere away from me, almost pushing her across the landing as she tried vainly to retain some composure.

"Do something for God's sake!" he mouthed behind her back.

As the lounge door closed silently, I clung onto the bannister and lifted up my foot to check.

"Oh shit, shit, shit."

Which was actually very apt to be honest as I'd trodden in the biggest mound of dog poop whilst trampling across Mrs DeVere's vast garden. The disgusting mess was now squashed into the thick tractor-like treads on the sole of my right boot, curling up over the edges. I puffed out my cheeks, my shoulders sagging as I looked behind me.

Yep, no doubt about it. It was me.

Not content with treading in it, I had dragged it into her

house, tainting and smearing every one of those thirty, lushly carpeted stairs and then right across the landing to where I now stood.

"Thanks Conan, police dog, shit machine and crook catcher," I grimaced.

I frantically looked around to see if there was anything to wipe my boot on as I certainly didn't want to have to hop around like an old Irish clog dancer or even worse, put up my hand and shout *Oooh look Mrs DeVere I've just smeared shit on your shagpile!*

I spotted an old tatty, funny shaped multi-coloured brown rug by the telephone console table. It didn't look like an heirloom or an antique, in fact it looked quite out of place but it would have to do. Better an old rug than her beautiful red carpet.

With a hop, skip and a jump I struggled over. Slamming my boot down I began to wipe it vigorously backward and forwards along the middle of the rug.

I was on the fourth rigorous rub across the matted fibres when the most dreadful caterwauling noise screeched out from under my foot. The *rug* jumped up, somersaulted and shot down the thirty lushly carpeted stairs and straight out through the front door like one of Paul Daniels' errant toupees.

Mrs DeVere, alerted by the noise, appeared in the doorway.

Seeing the tail end of her cat disappear into the darkness, she began to shriek and swoon, whilst holding onto the bannister to support her attack of the vapours.

"Aramorph, Aramorph, come back my darling pussy don't be frightened, oh my God he's been traumatised by it all."

I stood there, wide eyed and open mouthed.

Traumatised! What about me being traumatised with the fear of what she would do when the huge, ragged, long-haired Aramorph the cat returned home with a great big stripe of dog poo down his back courtesy of me?

As my mind scrambled for an explanation, I plumped for a rather off the cuff response.

"It's okay Mrs DeVere I'm a trained Trauma Counsellor, I'll go and find him."

...and took the opportunity to hastily disappear into the night leaving poor Jim to explain.

DON'T MAKE ME LAUGH

"One of the things you'll discover about being a Probationer Mave, is that every shitty job everyone else avidly avoids, will either fall on your shoulders or kick you up the arse, fact of life girl I'm afraid." Don swilled his mug out in the sink.

I took a slurp of my tea and shoved the plate with a broken digestive biscuit towards Bob. He took it and lumbered out into the corridor.

I couldn't argue with Don, one glance at the overnight job sheets and I could tell straight away which would be mine. The ones that no one else would touch with a barge pole. I looked out of the window onto the car park, watching the trees sway in the summer breeze. It was going to be a hot one today.

"I know Don, but don't we all want the sharp end, cars that go fast with blue lights and wailing sirens, to be right in the middle of it all?" I waited for an answer.

He nodded sagely but didn't offer up any further conversation.

"Oh well, see you later, I'm off out to hit the town centre, wish me luck." Don curled his top lip, but he still didn't reply.

Standing in front of the mirror in the girls' loos, I checked the alignment of my hat and badge, gave my lips a smattering of coral blush lippy and straightened my tie. I was ready to go. My tummy gave a little flip.

The click of the door lock behind me as I left the station signalled the start of my first ever solo daytime beat. With the sun shining and clear blue skies, the day could only get better as I strolled into town occasionally checking my reflection in the large shop windows. I smiled at people, ruffled the hair of a little boy, patted a dog and kept watch on the queue of OAP's drawing on their pension at the Post Office.

This might not be the excitement of the IR car, but it was still good in my book.

Suddenly Heidi's distinctive tone trilled out over my radio. Heidi Rosenberg has a voice that borders on the soprano range, each word ending on a higher note than the last. She could make a report of a lost dog sound like a robbery in progress.

"1261, 1261 can you start making to Capstan Construction, Falkirk Road, they've had a burglary," she squealed.

In all the excitement I almost broke into a run, well a bit of a jog really, if I'm honest, until I realised the incident was three days old and that once again Heidi had done her usual trick and gone up several octaves.

The site was a pleasant ten-minute walk away, the entrance stood at the side of an old three-story red brick house, where once beautiful trees had been felled in order to give access to the builders.

"Yo...over here Miss..."

As I picked my way across the rubble and dust a figure approached, holding out his hand in greeting.

"Jeff Bingley, I'm the Construction Manager, they've screwed it over the weekend Miss, got the crews lined up to see if they can help you, been about six houses in total done."

"Oh it's not really necessary at this stage Sir, we..." I

stopped in my tracks as I scanned the line-up of workmen, hard hats, shirtless, bronzed muscles. These guys gave the Diet Coke advert a run for its money. Mmmm on second thoughts.

"... oh err, of course, yes, I can interview them in a minute, if you'd just like to remain boys."

Phew, I was starting to blush. How unprofessional of me!

Jeff nodded and continued. "So you see miss, we locked up Friday night, just after...it was six wasn't it Bazzer or was it earlier when you went for the donuts, or was it custard slices?"

He droned on and on. I was in danger of losing control of my very first solo investigation as I started to get very hot and very bothered. His reluctance to keep to the key points coupled with the blazing sunshine were not a good combination.

"Forget the custard slices Mr. Bingley, do you have on site security?"

"Well, that's the point you see, we did have, think it was last week, or it might have been the week before, but..."

I took off my hat to allow some of the cooling breeze to reach me whilst I carried on taking notes as Jeff rambled on and on.

And then nothing. Nothing but silence and the solitary song from a dunnock in a nearby tree.

He had finally shut up, but rather too abruptly for my liking.

I looked up, pen poised.

Jeff stared at me and began to snigger. I looked at the crew, they were staring at their boots and smirking too.

Was it my hair? It was hot after all. Maybe my fringe was sticking up at an odd angle.

"What? Is there something wrong?" I barked as my professionalism slowly slipped further away.

"You tell her Nige, I can't," Jeff snorted.

Smoothing his golden locks through his fingers, the muscles rippled through Nigel's tanned arm as he stepped forward.

"Err, if it helps Miss, we've got a khazi with a mirror over there, you might want to nip in and have a look."

What the hell could be so damned funny? Feeling quite indignant if somewhat annoyed, I stuck out my chin in a show of determined resolve.

"I don't suppose any one of you would care to enlighten me then?" The silence was akin to tumbleweeds rolling across a desert.

Turning on my heels, I made a mad scramble up the steps of the nearby portacabin.

Breathing heavily, I slammed the toilet door behind me and looked in the mirror. What stared back filled me with horror.

"You utter, utter bastards!"

I spoke as much to myself as to anyone else.

...

"If it wasn't bad enough having a fringe like Cameron Diaz in that *Something about Mary* film because of the sweat..." I threw my hat down on the night kitchen table in temper "... I then had to suffer the added humiliation of having a huge sodding penis in thick black marker pen tattooed smack bang in the middle of my forehead! What is it with you lot?"

I pressed my knuckles into the table and looked at Don and Bob daring them to answer.

"In front of a whole horde of men on a bloody building site, have you got any idea how that felt?"

Bob took a slurp from his Mr Grumpy mug and tried to look suitably chastised but failed miserably when he snorted the tea through his nose as he tried not to laugh. Don grabbed my hat and dutifully inspected the inside.

"Aww come on Mave, you've gotta see the funny side, how could we know you're a Sweaty Betty and it'd come off on yer skin?" He licked his finger and wiped it across the artwork drawn on the leather band lining the inside.

"But spikey hairs on each plump little testicle too, it's not exactly in the style of Picasso is it?" I was still furiously scrubbing at my forehead with a wet ball of toilet paper.

Regaining his composure, Bob wiped the tea drips from his nose with a yellowing cotton handkerchief hastily pulled from his trouser pocket. "The hairy bits were my idea; ace aren't they?"

I swiped him across the back of the head with the damp tea towel. "Just stick to cats and willies in pocket notebooks Bob, I'm just amazed you think this..." I shoved my hat under his nose, "...is what you consider to be an acceptable size for a man!"

"Well we can't all be big boys can we Mave?" he arrogantly winked as he chucked the marker pen in the bin on top of a half-eaten butty, some stale tea bags and an empty biscuit wrapper.

I flicked him again with the tea towel.

"No, and from what I can see matey, you certainly aren't one of them!"

FRISKY FIRST DATES

"I think it's the best decision I've ever made Mum, the job satisfaction is immense and I can provide so much more for Ella now."

She took a long drag on her cigarette. I watched as the tendrils of smoke blew from her lips, some snaking sneakily back up into her nose.

"It's not been a year yet Mavis, give it time, I'm sure the novelty will wear off soon enough."

Sliding her feet into the red leather sandals in front of her, she wriggled her toes until she was happy they were all comfortably ensconced in their rightful place before leaning over and picking up an envelope that had been slotted between two books in the book case. "Here, have a look at this, what do you think?"

Taking the already opened envelope from her, I pulled out the rigid invitation card and gave it a quick once over. "Oh my God Mum, you can't go to this, do you know what this is for?"

She took another puff, blew the smoke sideways from her mouth and jabbed her finger on the embossed heading. "Of course I do, it's just like those Tupperware parties we had in the 60s, see... it says here *we cater for your every need* and there look, *battery operated device demonstrations in the privacy of your own home.*"

She sat back looking very pleased with herself.

"Jeez Mum it's like Ann Summers stuff, you know... Ann

Summers!" She looked at me blankly.

"Mavis, I haven't got a clue what you're talking about love, but you know how much I struggle in the kitchen. I've got one electric socket, and the toaster and kettle are both plugged into it."

My eyes widened, wondering what was coming next. I held my breath as she continued.

"I've always wanted one of them coffee making things so, if they do a battery operated one of those..."

She paused for effect,

"...it solves my problem doesn't it?"

•••.

Cuddling up to Ella on the sofa, smelling the coconut shampoo in her freshly washed hair, I couldn't help but feel that life was just about perfect. I had even managed to point Mum in the right direction for a coffee maker and an extension lead, although I was still filled with horror at what battery operated device could have been left lying on the kitchen drainer if I hadn't.

Ella took my hand. "I do miss you though Mum, and I get scared when you're working in the dark at night when I'm asleep"

I hugged her closer. "Oh sweetheart, I'm always careful, I have lots of lovely people at work who look after me, there's no need to worry."

Nestling her head into my shoulder, she carried on watching Mary Poppins, as she crammed another handful of crisps into her mouth.

This was the downside.

I missed Ella so much when she was staying at Mum's, the shifts were long and my rest days seemed to vanish in a haze of washing, ironing, shopping and housework. I really did need to make sure that we had *Mum & Ella* time more often.

Tucking her into bed later that night, as I bent down to kiss her cheek, she held my face in her little hands and stared intently into my eyes. It was as though she was searching me for the truth.

"Promise you'll never, ever leave me, please don't die, please Mum, promise."

"I promise Ella, I promise." I stroked her face and kissed her forehead.

I clicked off her lamp and closed the bedroom door, leaving a small opening where the light on the landing could stream through, casting a glow on her hair spread across the pillow. It was just enough light to keep the bogeyman at bay.

I sat on the top stair of the landing. That had just felt like a kick in the stomach, where on earth had it come from? I had no intention of departing this life prematurely but clearly something was worrying her.

I shoved a fluffy pink sock that she had left on the floor into the wash basket, Ella's Promise weighing heavily on my mind.

...

Ambling into work the following morning, I chucked my butties in the fridge, popped the kettle on and set out several mugs. The City Half Marathon event was on and eight of us were being shipped out to help swell the numbers. Plonking the laden tea tray on the parade room table, Don was the first to grab his mug, followed by the rest of the section.

We sat in a silence that was broken only by the odd slurp of tea as the Sarge tapped his folder on the desk.

"Right, listen up, the Carrier will be picking up at the back door in twenty, be ready with full kit but remember, it's a fun day."

"Yeah right Sarge, fun for who?" Don took another swig of his tea whilst ticking off his kit list. "These two might enjoy it..." he jerked his head towards me and Petey, "...but the rest of us old farts?" He let that float in the ether as he closed his notebook and shoved it in the top pocket of his shirt.

I nodded but Petey was otherwise engaged trying to extricate his arm which had somehow become wedged between the wall and the radiator.

Half an hour later we were all squeezed into our seats, feet on kits bags, packets of Polo mints being passed between us as the Carrier manoeuvred out of the back yard on its way over to the City Centre. Watching the now dilapidated shops and buildings pass by, shutters warped, dented and graffiti laden I pondered the different styles of policing between one Division and another. If you stopped someone on this side of the water and asked their name, you more often than not got it, eventually. In the City it was akin to pulling back molars with a pair of eyebrow tweezers.

Stopping at traffic lights, I watched one of the locals animatedly engaged in conversation with his friend, chin jutting out, hands plunged down the front of his tracksuit bottoms, fumbling away. No matter which side of the water they were from, they all had that universal need to cosset their testicles whilst trying to think.

Hey, maybe men's brains really were in their trousers.

Pulling up in the yard of Mosely Hill nick, the carrier juddered to a halt as one by one we bailed out dragging our kits bags behind us to form an untidy queue at the door.

"Upton, 1261... right, there you are. You're with 6672 Cameron. Bruce take Mavis with you." The Event Sergeant threw a copy of the briefing sheet at the guy standing next to me. He caught it, folded it in half and flashed me a smile. "Righto Sarge."

I cringed as I gave him the once over. Tall, dark, quite good looking in a funny sort of way but he had a strip of hair nestled under each nostril and splayed out across his top lip.

There was something about facial hair that sent a gut wrenching wave through me, giving visions of congealed dinner scraps and boogers hidden amongst the wiry strands.

"Right Mave, it's okay to call you that isn't it?" he paused momentarily as I nodded and followed the line of his gaze. "A mile or so in that direction, we're on a static point."

Bruce's 'mile or so' turned out to be twenty-minutes of boot stomping, which by my junior school calculations well surpassed any mile I have ever walked.

For the next two hours we watched the runners pass through the nearby water stop, the crowd happily basking in the sun, cheering them on. Bruce's custodian helmet had adorned the head of every child within spitting distance, mine had stayed firmly on my head as Don's drawing, although slightly faded, could still be seen.

I had tried to change the testicles into Mickey Mouse's

ears but sadly Mickey didn't have a long nose, so that idea was doomed to failure. The last thing I wanted was for little Wendy from Wavertree to end up in tears after borrowing my hat.

"Right in for a brew, I think we deserve one." Bruce gave me a pat on the back and then knocked my hat off, laughing as it rolled across the pavement and shot under a parked car.

"You know if you got rid of that merkin on your top lip Bruce, you'd be a bit of alright!" I grunted as I leant under the rear wheel, fingers probing for my errant hat.

Grabbing it I stuffed it back on my head, tucking a section of hair that had escaped from a hairclip behind my ear.

"MERKIN, what the hell's one of them? There's nothing wrong with my exhibit of manliness Upton!" He stroked the corner hairs and gave them a twist.

I was mesmerised, half expecting a previously lost marrowfat pea to reveal itself.

"If you don't know by now you never will." I stifled a snigger "Come on, biscuits are on you."

...

I dropped down exhausted into the red plastic bucket seat in the station canteen as Bruce slid a chipped mug full of stewed tea in front of me.

"Fancy a garibaldi?" he winked as he held out two broken biscuits. Hungry, I stuffed them into my mouth and was just at the point of no return, chewing and wiping crumbs from my lips, when he pulled his chair closer.

"Erm, Mave, I've just been thinking, we got on okay today didn't we, so err... would you like to go out for dinner?"

The fear of spitting Garibaldi crumbs all over him gave me precious seconds to weigh up the situation. With my face resembling Ella's hamster at teatime, I stared into my mug.

Okay, so let's put this into perspective. He was tall. Tick. He was tanned. Tick. He was fairly good looking. Tick. ... with an 80s style moustache. I thought marrowfat peas again. Mixing career with pleasure had always been a complete no-no, so that was a huge factor to base my decision on. I swallowed the last mouthful of biscuit and flicked the crumbs from my shirt.

"Oh Bruce, that's so very kind of you... but nooo...err yes..."

I sat there stunned. Where the hell had that come from. How had my *No* become a *Yes*?

"That's great, no strings Mave, just a nice evening hey?" he looked behind him to the next table. Several surprised faces looked back at him and then just as quickly disappeared behind books, newspapers and magazines.

"Saturday it is then!"

I watched as he sauntered out of the canteen and disappeared through the double doors. Cramming the last Garibaldi into my mouth, I drained my mug, hopeful that at least I wouldn't be reciting offence definitions by the time I reached the pudding on this date.

"Hey, we've been wondering, has Brucie just asked you out?" Phil Evans, who double crewed with Bruce on their section, plonked himself down on the still warm chair Bruce had just vacated.

"Err, yes, why?"

Laughter drifted over from the next table as I caught Phil out of the corner of my eye giving the thumbs up sign to the rest of his section, who once again quickly disappeared behind their magazines.

He looked suitably embarrassed.

"Ah, we thought so..." he looked back again at the others "... listen, I hate to be the one to tell you, but you do know that he's gay don't you?"

I involuntarily jerked my head as my eyes snapped wide open. Gay!

Gay happy?

Gay prefers men?

Gay... well what other type of gay is there?

I swallowed hard. My tongue suddenly decided to stick to the roof of my mouth. "No, I've only just met him, he wouldn't ask me out if he only liked men would he?"

I waited for a response as my face flushed bright red.

"Oh, that's just Brucie, he loves the company of women, makes him feel comfortable, he's just getting in touch with his feminine side."

Phil patted me on the shoulder before walking back to his table, leaving me deflated and mortally embarrassed.

I was a woman who made gay men feel comfortable. How much worse could my love life get?

Packing up my stuff into the carrier half an hour later, I decided that regardless of his sexual orientation, he was a lovely guy, I enjoyed his company and he made me laugh.

I would keep the date.

"Penny for them Mave." Don winked at me as he heaved his bag in next to mine.

"Think they're worth more than a penny mate, my life is never straightforward," I sighed.

...

"Jeez Mum, what the hell do you wear for a date with a gay guy?"

I twirled around the bedroom in my current choice of outfit. I looked at her with an expectant expression. Sitting on my bed, glasses perched on the end of her nose, she made her usual clicking, humming and tutting noises.

Eventually she spoke.

"Well...to be quite honest love, I don't think he'll appreciate flashes of your froo-froo when he's more interested in Dorothy Gale's ruby slippers do you?"

"Mum!"

I stopped in my tracks and looked down at the rather nice figure hugging dress I was wearing. She was right. I wouldn't be able to move an inch without letting Bruce cop an eyeful of my heaving cleavage and wobbly thighs in this little number.

I tore through my wardrobe, pushing coat hanger after coat hanger to one side, whilst muttering under my breath.

"Short, skimpy, short, short, knicker skimmer, jeez where did I get that one from, it's just a belt, short, bap flasher, short, minute, bap flasher..." I flopped down on to the bed "...oh Mum what am I going to do?"

Unless I was going to wear an old evening dress that was crushed up against my Nan's ratty fur coat circa 1927 that smelled of mothballs, I was at a loss. Pointing at my boobs in an over-exaggerated fashion, I wailed. "These I can cover, but I can't make a dress longer can I?"

"The black one Mavis, it's short but at least you can lean forward in it without everything dropping out into the soup bowl," she helpfully offered.

I snatched at the pink hanger and held it up to the light. My old, tried and tested black Bardot style dress. Squeezing into it, I slipped my foot into a strappy stiletto, stood on one leg and checked the mirror.

"It'll have to do, he's gay for goodness sake, it's not as though he's a fashion icon himself." I pulled down on the hem and gave a jiggle just as the doorbell rang loudly.

Mum ushered me out of the bedroom.

"Don't keep him waiting Mavis, have a lovely time. Ella will be fine with me." I tottered down the stairs, pulling and yanking on the hem of my dress.

"Muuuum I can see your knickers; you are soooo embarrassing!" Ella was standing in the hall, hands over her eyes, peeping through her fingers.

I gave a defiant glance in the hall mirror. "They're clean and paid for sweetheart..." I gave her a kiss, which she immediately wiped off with the back of her hand, "... now be a good girl at Nanny's and I'll see you tomorrow."

I turned the lock and flung the front door open ready to greet my date.

Ella groaned in the background and I was almost sure I heard Mum laugh too. There was Bruce standing on my faded *Welcome* mat, wide eyed and wearing a shocking pink tailored shirt.

There you go, a bright pink shirt. What more could I say? I half expected him to start singing 'YMCA' with all the actions. I sighed loudly as I closed the front door behind me and tottered down the path for my date.

Bruce had booked a table at a restaurant overlooking the

Dee Estuary and Welsh Mountains, and although he started off being attentive and incredibly funny, this dwindled with each passing slug of red wine.

I spent most of the night writhing, jiggling and pulling the hem of my dress to a respectable level every time I stood up, only for it to spring back to thigh level again once I started walking. By my third trip to the ladies' powder room I'd almost given up trying to salvage any decorum I might have had.

I looked at Bruce as he absent-mindedly pushed a mushroom around his plate.

"Jeez Bruce, I can't apologise enough. I did try to find something that covered me up a bit better, because of... well, you know, but this was the best of a bad bunch to be honest." I quickly draped my serviette over my thighs.

He blushed and pulled at the collar of his shirt, sweat trickling down the side of his face.

"Errr, it's not a problem Mave, I mean, it's not as though... hold on, back in a minute." With that he got up from the table and rushed off to the Gents.

The date was panning out to be a disaster. He eventually emerged from the toilets, paid for the meal and drove me home in silence.

I snatched the odd glance at him as the lights from oncoming cars skimmed across his face. He was quite handsome and I found myself feeling a little disappointed to know his secret. As he pulled up outside my house, I consoled myself with the fact he was a safe date with no ulterior motives.

"Do you want a coffee before you drive home Bruce?"

I didn't hesitate to ask; after all you couldn't be safer in your own home than with a gay man now could you?

He nodded and turned off the engine, clearing his throat loudly his voice squeaked a response. "That would be very nice Mavis, thank you."

Positioning himself on the sofa, I left Cat watching him closely whilst I made him a coffee and helped myself to another wine. He looked decidedly uncomfortable, so choosing the armchair, careful not to invade his space, I expressed concern.

"Are you okay Bruce, you seem really on edge?"

He looked at the floor, pulling at the collar of his shirt again. "I'm fine Mavis, just a little bit, well you know..."

No, I most definitely didn't know.

I checked my hemline, nothing showing there and I knew I hadn't flashed anything else when handing him his coffee. Cat, who had now positioned himself on the back of my chair, began to scrutinise Bruce through his amber eyes. He was clearly not as impressed with him as I was. I watched his tail lazily swish from side to side, a sure sign of agitation for him, but quite hypnotic for me.

Suddenly, without any warning Bruce sprang up from the sofa, launched himself across the room and jumped on top of me, slobbering, drooling and panting.

"I've been wanting to do this all night baby, come here gorgeous."

Spitting the mouthful of red wine I'd just slurped all over him, I tried desperately to push him off me as Cat, startled by Bruce's sudden sexual advances, sprang into the air, landing heavily on his back, digging his claws through his lovely pink tailored shirt.

"Aaaarrrggghhh get this feckin' thing off me!" He frantically flailed his arms trying to extricate himself from one very wild and furious Cat.

Bruce howled.

I screamed.

Cat yowled...

...and Bruce staggered backwards still trying to pull Cat off him.

I watched in slow-motion as he landed with an almighty crash on top of my coffee table. The table legs splayed in four different directions taking Bruce with it.

As he lay panting on the floor, I frantically straightened my dress, which was now flashing the cheeks of my wobbly butt as I tottered around the lounge on one stiletto.

"You're supposed to be gay you absolute fuckwit what the hell are you playing at?" I screamed.

Groaning, Bruce rolled onto his knees and extricated a table leg from under his left armpit. Waving it in the air he took in huge gulps of breath. "Bastards, they've done it to me again, every bloody time they do this. I'm as straight as, well, as straight as this...this bloody table leg!"

Wielding one of the remaining table legs in a fighting stance, I watched as he limped away from my house muttering under his breath something about paying for the damage.

Slamming the door behind me, I collapsed on to the sofa.

Cat glared at me with an air of indifference as I kicked off my remaining shoe and inspected the damage. Picking up my glass, I took a large gulp of wine and quietly counted my blessings.

The most important one was that at least on this occasion,

the only legs Bruce had seen splayed were the ones on my £29.99 coffee table.

I SWEAR BY ALMIGHTY GOD...

Don spat half a chewed up chicken sandwich over his trousers.

"Gay! You're having me on Mave, you fell for that one?" He furiously rubbed at the greasy mayonnaise stain.

I carefully underlined the date in my notebook with the edge of someone's discarded cigarette packet. "Yep I sure did, chalk it up to experience I suppose. Mum thought it was hilarious, said my dad did the same to her, not the gay bit, but apparently he made a grab for her on their first date but my Nan hit him with the yard brush and sent him running down the back jigger."

I scribbled my patrol beat on the first line and looked up at Don, his head tilted to one side with a quizzical look on his face. "That's the first time I've heard you mention your dad, I thought maybe he was dead."

I shrugged.

"No, not dead, might as well be I suppose. He left when I was little, I don't even remember what he looked like. Mum got rid of all his photos, no family left on his side. I tried looking for him in my teens, but hit a brick wall. He just vanished."

"Ever thought of trying again?"

"Not really. If he had wanted to be part of my life, he would have looked for me. It's sad that Ella will never know her grandad, but then again, I never knew him as a father."

I suddenly felt an unusual stab of sadness but just as

quickly brushed it away. What you've never had, you never miss. Well, that wasn't entirely true but it worked for me as long as I believed it.

Don gave me a sympathetic glance as I clipped my utility belt into place, checking that I had at least two working pens stuck in the pocket of my shirt, I flicked the empty cigarette packet at him. "See you later... and keep your fingers out of the biscuit tin!"

He grinned, sticking out his tongue which held a large chunk of digestive just as Petey popped his head around the door. "Yo Mave, just chucked an envelope for you in the Parade Room, it's on the desk. Looks a bit important, oooh nasty dose of thrush Don?"

Don stuck his tongue out further, dropping a glob onto his trousers.

I grinned and threw Don the tea towel. "Thanks Petey, on my way there now. How are things going for you?"

One look at his face told me that they weren't going as well as expected.

"It's okay Mave, sort of still finding my feet – literally." He looked down and raised an eyebrow. My eyes followed to where his feet were sticking out from the bottom of his trousers.

"You've only got socks on!"

"Yeah, I know, can't find me boots, think someone's playing a trick on me, Sarge has grounded me until I find them." He gave a wry smile, shrugged his shoulders and disappeared into the mail room.

Plonking myself down at the parade table, I spun the orange envelope around a few times before opening it. Oh great, my very first Crown Court Warning.

"Face like a smacked trout Mave, what's up?" Jim ambled into the room.

"Thanks for the compliment mate, Crown Court, first time!" I dropped the envelope onto the table in front of me.

"You'll be fine, we've all had a first time haven't we lads?" a snigger ran around the table from the others on the section.

Jim pushed a mug along the table towards me. It juddered to a halt as it touched my prized envelope, slopping tea over it. I wiped my sleeve across the shiny surface, soaking up the drips. "How come you can make everything you say sound like an innuendo Jim?"

"Pure talent Mavis my love, pure talent!"

•••

"It'll be alright when you get there, you'll be fine." Mum licked the butter from her fingers and offered me the plate of crumpets. "Here have one of these, I brought them over specially."

I waved the plate away. The last thing my queasy stomach wanted was one of her offerings covered in two inches of Lurpak butter.

"I won't be fine Mum, it's taken me almost six weeks to learn the Brownie Guide Law to help Ella, I haven't got six hours let alone six weeks to get this right!" I ran my hand through my hair in frustration.

"There's a Judge and a Jury, it's not like Magistrates Court. No matter how many times I go over my evidence, as soon as it hits my brain it's lost."

Kissing Mum goodbye, I watched her grow smaller as

she ambled along the path towards her own house until she disappeared from view. Ten minutes later I was in my comfy bed, humming Doris Day's version of Que Sera Sera, which had sort of popped into my head as I was brushing my teeth.

The Brownie Guide Law I knew off by heart, why the hell couldn't I remember verbatim what someone had said without referring to my notebook.

I turned off the bedside lamp, pulled the duvet over my head and willed myself to dream of anything other than Judge's wigs chasing me around the kitchen like over excited miniature poodles.

...

"Court 3, top of the stairs and turn left." The Usher tapped his pen on the clipboard and placed a tick alongside my name. "Police Room's next floor up."

I nodded my thanks and hit the button on the lift to the 1st floor.

Sitting in the Police Room, repeatedly turning the pages of my notebook whilst murmuring like a good Catholic at confession, my heart thudded and quickened its pace.

Shit. I'd quoted my prisoners responses, word for word in the most colourful of language, which included several renditions of the *F-word*. Never in a million years did I ever think I'd have to repeat them, out loud, in public, in front of a Judge and Jury.

My legs started to jiggle furiously, a sure sign of my agitation. Jeez at this rate I'd be dancing the Fandango rather than addressing the Court. Mum would be horrified if she knew her eldest was uttering profanities to a packed audience. I could just hear her now *"...Mavis, I brought you up to be a lady..."*

I looked out of the window onto the Maritime Docklands and the rippling waters hoping for inspiration, instead whispered memories of one of my less notable youthful moments came flooding back;

"Mavis you'll be starting with Mrs Potter for elocution lessons, a good speaking voice will take you far when you get older...it is how real ladies are taught."

I remembered looking at Mum and thinking she had gone completely and absolutely off her trolley. Me... elocution lessons! I had begged her not to make me, but she had.

I had spent many miserable and deathly boring hours at Mrs Potters' home, which smelt of cat wee and Palma Violets, listening to how brown that ruddy cow had been, whilst staring out of the window onto the shiny wet cobbles of her back yard.

"Muuuum its awful, I bloody hate it!"

"It's for your own good Mavis and mark my words, if I catch you swearing ever again, I'll wash your mouth out with soap!"

Fearing the cheap carbolic, or even worse, the bar that my brother had inadvertently dropped down the toilet when playing submarines, not another swear word had ever passed my lips.

Well, not in front of Mum anyway.

Standing up, I grabbed my smart uniform tunic from the rail. It was now or never, I'd just have to suck it and see. Shrugging each arm in, straightening off the shoulders, I began to pull and tug at the sides, trying to make them meet.

Oh bloody hell, it didn't fit.

There was almost an inch gap between the shiny silver buttons and the button holes.

Why on earth hadn't I tried it on before today? This was all I needed. I breathed dramatically out, willing my ample nellies to reduce just a fraction, even a centimetre, so I could button it up.

Ten minutes later, pink and glowing with exertion the buttons eventually met, but only just. As I sat nervously jiggling my legs outside the courtroom, Shirley McCready's words echoed through my mind;

'Stand confident in the box, hold the Bible in your hand and repeat The Oath – do not look at the prompt card – I Swear by Almighty God that the evidence I shall give......'

My heart thudded, the Oath – I'd forgotten the Oath.

I racked my brains as panic set in. Oh come on brain for goodness sake. Got it! Hallelujah, there is a God after all.

The Courtroom doors suddenly opened, giving me no more time to think. "Constable Upton to Court 3, Constable Upton to Court 3."

Okey dokey Mave, this is it, head high girl you can do it.

I strode confidently into Court as the Usher indicated to the box where I should take my place.

So far so good.

The Court was awesome. Oak panelled, ornate carvings, deep blue velour upholstery and there at the front of the Court, dressed in his regal red robes and wig was the Judge.

The Bible was placed before me.

I took it in my hand.

I stood straight and true.

I faced the Jury and inhaled a deep breath ready to

promise my undying loyalty and honesty in the form of The Oath...

...and then it all went horribly wrong. Again.

The huge intake of breath swelled my chest by an extra four inches, this in turn stretched my already tight uniform tunic to new and unprecedented measurements.

The strain was just too much for the first two silver crested buttons. I watched in horror as they proceeded to ping and propel themselves forward ten feet across the Courtroom landing with a tinkering plop, plop on the oak bench of the Prosecution and Defence barristers.

One each. What a shot!

In the previously held reverential silence of the Court you could hear stifled sniggering drifting around the four corners of the room. The Judge stared at me, eyes wide, as I desperately tried to make the sides of my tunic meet once again, without success. I looked at the Usher, silently begging him for help. He held his professionalism.

"If you would like to continue Constable?"

I looked at the Judge, weakly smiled at the Jury and glared at the Defendant, wishing I could wipe the smirk off his weasely little face.

Leaving nature to take its course and allow my nellies to settle into their natural, untethered position, I quickly regained my composure and held the Bible high in my hand and began the Oath.

"I promise that I will do my best, to do my duty to God, to serve the Queen and help other people and keep the Brownie Guide la...oh shit..."

I stopped.

I looked at the sea of faces. I looked at the Judge. I looked at the prompt card in front of me.

"Oh bollocks it's the wrong one...!" my voice bounced off the walls as snorts, guffaws and sniggers came from the Jury. The Usher quickly called for order.

I stood in the box, eyes wide, every ounce of breath snatched away from me. The Judge leant forward and peered over his glasses.

"Constable, when you have quite finished with sharing your shiny buttons and the Brownie Guide Law, can we please proceed as directed?"

I squirmed in my highly polished shoes. "Of course Your Honour, I do apologise."

With the help of the prompt card, I swore out the true Oath and as an added bonus, remembered my own name too, much to the relief of the CPS Barrister who was by now frequently mopping his brow with a fancy blue, monogrammed handkerchief.

The Prosecution helpfully 'led' me through my evidence, more through fear of what I would say next than anything else and I was beginning to relax a little. That was until we arrived at the point I had been dreading. The verbal responses I had noted from the Defendant prior to and during his arrest.

"Constable Upton, if you would be so kind as to tell the Court, when you cautioned and informed the Defendant that he was under arrest, what was his reply?"

The Prosecutor turned and regally waved his arm to indicate His Honour and the Jury. Taking a shallow breath for safety, I began to repeat my well-rehearsed response.

Unfortunately, it didn't quite go according to plan.

I stuttered.

I stammered.

I looked around the Court. I looked at the Jury. I stared at my shoes.

I glared at the Prosecutor...

...and finally I watched the second hand on my watch tick by slowly.

How on earth could I say the *F-word* out loud to a roomful of people? Mum would kill me.

Every pair of eyes were on me.

Waiting.

That was it! In an instance I knew exactly what I had to do. I could just say it 'posh'.

It wouldn't sound so awful then would it? I could put those stupid elocution lessons into practice at last.

With an air of confidence that was growing greater by the second and with some satisfaction at my marvellous idea, I gave it my all in the best plummy voice I could muster.

"He replied *'you can faark off you faarking bitch, I'm not faarking getting locked up by youz, so you can faark off you faarking bint'*..."

I paused for dramatic effect before adding in respectful tones and with a very smug smile;

"...Your Honour."

I think His Honour greatly appreciated my good effort.

As he placed his head in his hands he seemed to smile to himself.

On second thoughts, maybe it was a grimace.

REVENGE IS SWEET

Within 24 hours, my indiscretions at Crown Court had made it back to the station, providing untold mirth for everyone and a new 'Mavism' was born.

The word *'faark'* was fondly accepted as an alternative to *'fuck'*, and even I had to admit it did actually sound a lot more genteel, although I still had absolutely no intentions of trying it out on Mum. She was now on to Imperial Leather soap and that tasted disgusting.

"Still can't believe you almost flashed your nellies to the Judge Mave." Bob boggled his eyes whilst at the same time making curved gestures with his hands in front of his chest.

"I didn't, you lot just like to make things up, it was only my jacket!"

"Still very funny Mavis..." the Sarge paused as he flicked through his folder "...you need to get yourself to stores and replace that tunic and anything else that's refusing to fit. Chief Super was amused but would prefer to know you're properly attired next time eh?"

"Yes Sarge, I'm due over next week, I'll sort it."

Wandering down the corridor into the night kitchen I curled my lip in anticipation of a trip to stores for anything uniform related. Everyone hated going there. Bert and George had exceptionally long memories and were renowned for holding grudges for all eternity and beyond. The smallest of female bottoms could be made to resemble the rear end of a rhino if you upset either of them and legend had it that

Bob once sang Soprano due to an overstitched crotch on his trousers after he'd swiped George's cheese and onion crisps from his butty box.

"Hey Don, you wouldn't go to stores and pick a tunic up for me would you?"

I gave my best pleading look. He glanced up from his book, sighed, bent over the top of the page as a marker and put it down on the table.

"Erm let me think about it – err nope! Anyway, you've got to go yourself remember, Queenie's coming for a Royal Visit next month, all the girls have to wear skirts for it."

I groaned. I'd forgotten, it was a full dress uniform order and very few of us had skirts anymore. We all wore trousers.

"'Bout time you showed a bit of leg Mave, you lot only wear kecks to be like us fellas."

He licked his lips and winked. I clipped the back of his head with my Points to Prove book.

"Didn't you know, it's really all about the psychological castration of sexist pigs like yourself."

He grinned and waved a middle finger at me.

"Great, suppose I'm going to have to face Bert sometime. I just hoped it wouldn't be this soon, there's no way he'll have forgotten." I screwed up my nose as Don raised his eyebrows at me.

"Only got yourself to blame kid, he doesn't take kindly to anyone pointing out his little problem."

I bristled with indignation.

"Jeez, I only said that his breath stunk, how was I to know that he was standing behind me?" I folded my arms in defiance.

"Bert's rabid halitosis is well documented Mave, we just don't mention it, he's an evil bastard if he wants to get his own back. You've got a lot to learn kidda!"

...

"He won't have forgotten Mave, he'll be waiting for you duh, duh, duh, duh." Carrying on with the theme tune from Jaws, Shirley swung off the bailing pole and jumped down the steps of the Carrier, followed by the rest of the girls.

Thirteen of us traipsed across the Stores car park and in through the main doors, taking up all the seats in the reception area. I nervously shuffled my feet on the threadbare carpet tiles. Two fitting rooms were in use. One for George, one for Bert. In between were rows of metal shelves containing just about every piece of kit you could imagine. From shin pads to ties, from helmets to flat caps...and eyes.

Eyes!

They were Bert's eyes, I'd recognise them anywhere, peering out between two boxes of jock straps.

He'd remembered; that one look said it all.

I shuffled along a couple of seats. Maybe if I was out of sequence Shirley would get him for her fitting. I checked the gap between the boxes. He was gone. Just the solitary jock straps and a battered old clipboard remained.

Shirley smirked.

"If you're marked chick, nothing and I mean *nothing* will save you now!" I gave her a sickly grin, crossed my fingers and sat on my hands.

Seconds ticked by until the door opened. There stood Bert

in all his glory, tape measure around his neck brandishing a large chunk of dressmaker's chalk and an evil glint in his eye.

"Upton, you're next."

A waft of garlic hit my nostrils as I inched past him, forcing me to inhale deeply and hold my breath.

Bert quickly worked his way around, measuring waist, hip and length. I watched in silence as he jotted down his requirements in his little red book.

"Err thanks Bert, much appreciated." I gave a wan smile and made towards the door for a quick exit.

"Not so fast girlie, tights or stockings?" he leered.

"Oh uhmm, stockings please."

I gave him my best happy smile in the hope that maybe he'd forgiven me, only to be met with a slight curling of his sweaty upper lip.

Bursting through the doors, I skipped across the car park back to the Carrier, glad to be away from the rancid odour of Bert and content in the knowledge that a tailored skirt and a box of stockings couldn't make me look like a hippo or sing in a high voice.

Jumping into the carrier I plonked myself down in the seat next to Shirley. "Phew that went well, he seemed okay and he didn't mention a thing."

She giggled, shaking her head. "You really think he's forgotten? You've gotta be kidding me. He still remembers something I did in 1979! Why do you think my shirts never fit? You're so naive at times Mave."

I wiped the flat of my hand across the steamed up window.

"Shirley, it's a skirt and a box of stockings, seriously, what could go wrong?" The silence that followed should have sent shivers down my spine.

•••

"Let's hope HRH doesn't have an aversion to pink tinted shirts."

Bob laughed as he nodded towards Petey, who was in the process of clipping his tie into place. I ran my hand over the sleeve of his shirt.

"Jeez Petey, what happened?"

He blushed almost the same colour as his shirt. "Err it was Betty, her knickers got mixed up in the wash but it'll hardly be noticed, will it?"

We said nothing, the knowing glances between us said it all. A rancid sock came hurtling through the air, landing to hang limply on the top of Don's locker door. This was followed by a loud fart from two lockers along.

"Martin Phillips if that was you, you'll be wearing your testicles as an ear muff you disgusting sod." Shirley breezed through carrying a large box from stores. "Didn't think they'd get these here on time you know, they only arrived last night. Here you go Mave, your skirt and erm, let's see."

Digging deep into the box she pulled out six pairs of black stockings and threw them at me.

"Cheers Shirl, I'll catch up with you in the briefing room in a minute, I've got a huge Jacobs' ladder in this pair."

Ten minutes later I was still struggling to get dressed. For some unknown reason the black stockings appeared to be terribly small. Sitting down on the bench, I gripped the top of one of them, trying hard not to tear it with my fingernails.

I huffed, puffed and pulled.

The harder I tried to get the top of the stocking to meet the suspender belt clip, the more I failed. The gap was closing, but my poor toes were curling up like a pair of Aladdin's carpet slippers. In sheer desperation I took them off and tied them round the door handle, yanking them backwards with all my weight. They started to stretch, fading from black to grey as the fibres gave way.

I rolled them back on.

There was a small advantage where they now met the clip but only just, the strain on the suspender belt was really starting to show. It began to slide slowly down over my hips as the fibres in the stockings tightened up again.

I rummaged around in my locker for a spare pair of tights, but could only find one sock with a hole in the heel. Grabbing my new skirt, I resigned myself to the ridiculous stockings that were now adorning my ankles. A hefty heave brought them back up to my thighs.

I pulled up the side zip of my skirt and smoothed it out checking in the mirror. "Oh for God's sake Bert, you absolute tw..." I was quickly interrupted by jeering from the bottom end of the room.

"Yo lads, Mavie here nearly used a naughty word," Don smugly imparted before he took a look at me. "Oh crap Mave it's a bloody mini skirt!"

"No shit Sherlock! I can't believe Bert has done this to me, what a bastard."

I was almost in tears. My skirt hem was at least an inch above my knees and there was absolutely nothing I could do as the Briefing was in five minutes. I wandered off cursing Bert under my breath, acutely aware that I had adopted quite an awkward looking bow legged amble to my stride as I hobbled off down the corridor to book out a radio.

Far from it being a day to remember for the right reasons, it became a day to remember for all the wrong ones.

I was given King Street for my point and could have kissed the Bronze Commander; it was one of the main sections for the procession. I would get to see HRH in all her glory. I took position, excited but on high alert for anything out of the ordinary, whilst watching the children waving their flags in eager anticipation of seeing a real Queen.

The moment was clearly having an effect. I was jiggling and tapping my feet to the beat of the nearby brass band when Bert's stockings suddenly decided to snake down my legs, pulling the suspender belt closer to the pavement with every passing second.

Panicking, I frantically hitched them up whilst tugging furiously at the sides of my skirt, praying they wouldn't part company and leave me doing a good impression of Nora Batty.

"Upton have you got worms or something, stop writhing around like a ruddy pole dancer."

I snapped my head around. Shit, that was all I needed, Inspector *Terry Tourette's* was towering over me.

"I'm sorry Sir, there seems to be a problem with my uniform."

He took all of two seconds to appraise me, utter several expletives, and remove me from my bird's eye view of Her Maj.

Distraught, I was ushered off to guard the industrial wheelie bins at the back of Woolworth's, which in turn gave me time to lament my loss whilst walking up and down like bloody Pinocchio as the stockings pulled each leg independently, twanged and snapped back ready for the next step.

After a long duty, we piled into the Carrier and drove back to the nick.

Landing heavily on the nearest bench in the locker room, a sense of relief washed over me as I peeled each stocking off.

"Jeez Shirl, look at this."

I lifted my skirt to reveal a serious case of chafing on my hips from the constant 'flossing' action from my suspender belt.

"Eeeww, it's raw Mave, they must have been shit quality to do that," she sympathetically crooned.

I sat rubbing my poor toes. They were bent double and curled up courtesy of Bert's ridiculous stockings. Shirley ambled over to the bin and rummage around. Howling with laughter, she waved an empty packet at me.

"No wonder you've been walking like a geriatric wearing an incontinence pad..." Pinched between her fingers was the wrapping from the stockings I had donned in haste that morning.

"...they're ruddy knee length POPSOCKS Mave, the bastard's had you away girl!"

Grabbing the wrapper, I clenched my teeth together and swore under my breath. I couldn't believe it, she was right.

I had been wearing a pair of 20 denier *Popsocks* with a suspender belt whilst looking after The Queen.

Shirley sat down next to me, draping an arm around my

shoulder. "Welcome to the club Mave, I think you've pissed old Bert off more than anyone else ever has. Gotta say, respect to you girl."

THE PRINCESS & THE TEDDY BEAR

Curled up with a mug of hot chocolate on Mum's oversized sofa with her tartan blanket wrapped around me, I regaled her with the day's story.

"Oh how funny, I hope you took it in good humour though?"

She leant forward and took a cigarette from the packet on the coffee table. The lighter sparked up and the amber glow grew brighter as she inhaled deeply.

"Of course I did, I'm learning all the time. At least it gives some respite from the horrible things we have to deal with, I love the job, but sometimes it's just so hard."

Pulling at some fluff on the sleeve of my jumper, I leant back against the cushion to stare at the ceiling. I'd come to understand all too soon that wearing a uniform was a bit like wearing armour. It gave you some protection from fear, instilled you with confidence and was a symbol of authority but what it didn't do was protect you from feeling the heartbreak of other people's suffering.

"It's like a loss of innocence, before I joined I saw only the good in others and life seemed to have been painted in all the beautiful colours of the rainbow with the odd little butterfly floating around."

She sat next to me and gave me a hug. I rested my head on her shoulder.

"If I go to the town centre, I don't see it the same any-more Mum. There's no pretty colours or butterflies, it's more like a box of horrible kids' games. All I see are *Spot the Shoppie, Hide The Cannabis, Tag The ankle* and *Pass the Wrap*."

She stubbed her cigarette out in the ashtray, which was in danger of overflowing. I hated her smoking and really wished she would pack them in.

"Mavis, life is all about losing aspects of innocence. Kids first lose their innocence once they find out that Father Christmas doesn't exist."

I gave a scream of exaggerated horror, cutting her short as I clenched my hand to my heart.

"Muuuum, please tell me that's not true, no Father Christmas! I don't believe you, you're fibbing."

We collapsed in a fit of the giggles.

"Mum."

"Yes sweetheart."

"I love you."

"I love you too Mavis."

...

I threw my kit into the patrol car, the knots in my stomach beginning to tighten. I clicked the button on my radio. Night shifts always seemed to bring child welfare jobs.

"Yep, go ahead with the details Heidi."

"Thanks Mave, it's a young child in a phone box, corner of Waverley Lane, her name's Amy, age given is six. She'll wait for you there."

"Roger."

Shirley revved the engine as I jumped in. The windscreen wipers clunked loudly as they rapidly swished from side to side clearing the torrential rain from the glass. Taking the shortest route, we arrived in just under three minutes.

"There she is by the phone box, oh god Shirl she's soaked to the skin, poor thing."

I grabbed my jacket from the back seat and stepped out into the rain. The sad little figure stood silent, caught in the beam of the headlights, her blonde hair flattened against her face, droplets of water dripping down onto her *Hello Kitty* slippers.

"Come here sweetheart, let's get you in the car." Wrapping my jacket around her, I bundled her into the back seat and sat next to her so I could rub some warmth back into her arms.

Wiping her face with her sleeve she bit her bottom lip as her chin wobbled.

"Me Mum's sick and I've got no nappies or milk for the baby, I didn't know what to do 'cept phone you." The tears began to flow again.

I looked at Shirley who was shaking her head as she leant forward to turn the dial on the dash. "Here you go poppet, I've put the heating up for you."

The warm air blasted out as I cuddled Amy closer to me. She had the lingering odour of dirt in her hair, on her skin and her clothes. It was 2:15 in the morning for God's sake; this poor kid had been wandering the streets in the pouring rain. "Where's your Mum now, is she still at home?" I gently coaxed.

She nodded and tucked a wet strand of hair behind her ear. "She's wiv me bruvvers and me baby sister."

"How old are they Amy?"

She thought for a moment. "I'm six, Jamie's four and

me younger bruvvers two, got a baby sister too. Annie was borned in June."

I counted off the months. That made the baby just five months old. "AM21, AM21 are you free to speak."

"Yep, go ahead Heidi."

My heart sank as Heidi continued.

"They've previously been on the At Risk register with Social Services, combination of alcohol and drug dependence with the mother and no father on the scene."

The radio fell silent.

"Think we'd better go pronto Mave, if the mother's sick the kids are on their own."

Shirley pulled away, tyres juddering to find purchase on the wet road as we sped towards the address.

It was a mid-terraced house, just like any normal house. A blue door, grey nets at the window, chalked graffiti on the red brick, which was pretty standard for the area.

As I pushed open the door, I quickly realised that nothing I had dealt with so far could prepare me for what was inside.

Climbing over discarded newspapers and black bin bags spilling rotten food onto the uncarpeted hall floor, I tried hard not to actually touch anything as the dried brown streaks smeared on the walls gave off the distinctive smell of excrement. The stench was unbearable; my boots stuck to something tacky on the floor.

Amy's mother was sprawled out on the sofa in the first room I came to. She wasn't sick; she was drugged up to the max. Used hypodermic needles were scattered nearby and empty bottles of cider littered the floor. I shook her awake.

"Uggh warra youse want? Just fuck off, piss off out me

'owse." She dropped her head back down onto the sofa, oblivious to anything else.

I needed to find the children.

Pushing open the second door in the hallway, in the dim light I could make out two little boys huddled together on a mattress on the floor, dressed in filthy soiled clothing. The baby was lying, eyes open but not moving in a battered old cot in the far corner. The silence from them was hauntingly cruel. No sobs, no cries, nothing. Just an eerie, dark undertone.

I brushed the baby's cheek with my finger looking for a response. She grabbed it and curled her own little fingers around it. Scooping her out of the cot, trying not to baulk from the smell of this tiny room, I pressed my radio.

"Heidi, get Supervision here urgently and Ambo for the kids, they seem okay, but they need checking.

All around the house was evidence that Amy had been trying so hard to look after her brothers and baby sister. She had positioned a chair by the cupboard and fridge so that she could reach them for food. This was so futile as they were empty, apart from two bottles of cider on the middle shelf of the fridge along with a small lump of fur-covered cheese, wedged in between.

This was wrong, so very wrong. Children were here to be loved, cherished and protected. I'd seen animals in better living conditions than this.

Leaning against the wall as I rocked Annie in my arms, I allowed a tear to escape and trickle down my cheek.

This is what I meant Mum, this is the reality. THIS is the loss of innocence.

These kids probably didn't even know that there should

be a Father Christmas, let alone know he didn't actually exist. My radio crackled into life.

"Mavis, Duty Inspector's on scene, he's coming in to see you." I clicked my radio and acknowledged Heidi.

Wiping the heel of my hand across my cheek, I clenched my teeth. It wouldn't do for anyone to see me like this.

...

Inspector Kellet slipped the signed paperwork into the red folder and handed it to me. "I've authorised an Emergency Protection Order Mavis, Social Services have been notified, we're just waiting on a crisis placement for the children." I tucked it under my arm.

"Thanks Sir, what's happening with the mother?"

"Don and Bob are taking care of that side of things, she's been arrested, she's on her way to the Bridewell now. Didn't go without a fight though."

I couldn't think of anything to say, I was struggling with a mixture of anger and despair. How, in this day and age, could this happen? They were babies, isn't it a mother's job to protect her babies?

A few hours later, in convoy, we took Amy, Jamie, Christopher and Annie from the hospital to their emergency foster home. They were bathed and given clean nightwear and the little ones were settled down to sleep. I held Amy's hand as she opened the door to her own bedroom. Bending down to her level, I took her dressing gown off.

"This is where you'll be staying Amy, you're only in the next room to the others so don't worry."

Eyes wide with wonder, she quickly scanned the room,

taking in the single bed, the pretty pink night lamp and framed pictures of Peter Rabbit on the walls. She put her little hands on the clean sheets of the bed, smiling as she bent down to smell them.

"It's flowers, it smells of flowers, can I really sleep here?"

Her bottom lip began to quiver. As I wrapped my arms around her and held her to me, she began to cry. Not big heaving sobs or noisy wails, but the most distressing cry of all. The silent cry, a cry that signals despair and defeat. She still loved and missed her Mummy, regardless of the obvious neglect, but she was torn with loyalty, fear and apprehension.

She snuggled into me, her head on my shoulder, leaving a wet trail of tears on my neck.

In the tiniest of voices, she whispered "Thank you, lady."

I felt a surge of anger mixed with an overwhelming desire to cry with her, but I was a Police Officer, I was here to make things right, to be strong.

We don't cry do we?

In reality I knew that I had separated an already fractured and damaged family and what lay ahead for Amy, her baby sister and two little brothers was now in the hands of the Courts and Social Services. We had done our duty, it was time for them to do theirs, to hopefully give one little girl and her family a safe and happy ending.

I tucked Amy into her bed and told her a magic story of Princesses and Castles, kings and Queens...

"...and they all lived happily ever after..."

With her eyes closed, her breathing gentle and rhythmic, I tiptoed out, closing the door behind me.

As I left the house I looked up at her bedroom window. *Please God take care of her.*

A slight movement from the curtains caught my attention, and there she was, waving to me, holding the teddy bear I had given her.

I blew a kiss, got into my car, closed the door and wept.

A DEAD END JOB

Six rest days off after nights signalled lots of Ella & me time. This was even more poignant as I kept returning to the incident with Amy and looking at comparisons between her and Ella. I knew it was going to be one of those jobs that would stay with me for my whole career.

"Right you little monkey, come and sit here for a cuddle, I've got crisps, Twiglets and Chocolate Buttons."

Ella's face lit up as she bounced on the sofa next to me. Clicking the video remote I started the film. Our favourite. *Mary Poppins*.

Ella crunched a Twiglet and pointed the remaining bit at me.

"Mum, have you ever seen a dead person yet, you know a real dead humung beening?"

I tried not to laugh.

"It's human being Ella, erm no, not yet but that's a strange thing to want to know." She shrugged her shoulders as her hand disappeared into the Twiglet bag.

"I just wondered if they had wings when you found them or do they come later?"

Jeez, questions on Theology, I could only spell the word, not have an in depth discussion on it.

"I'm not sure I get what you mean sweetheart."

"Oh nuffink' I just thought it would make it hard to get them out of the front door if they were dead AND had a huge pair of wings. Can I have another Twiglet?"

...and with that the conversation on dead people was over.

•••

"Neighbour from No. 32 is reporting he hasn't seen the old lady next door for several days Mavis; voters show an Alice Creighton, 87 years."

I groaned. Thanks Ella!

No sooner does she mention something, it happens. I'd avoided the optional Post Mortem visit during my early probation as I didn't quite fancy savouring my breakfast twice in one day. After all, I wasn't going to be the one that had to bloody dissect them. I just needed to know how to deal with finding them.

Standing in front of the dull black door to No. 34, the abode of the unseen Mrs Creighton my heart sank. The backlog of newspapers and milk bottles could mean only one thing.

Grimacing, my stomach did a huge flip in anticipation of finding someone just a little bit dead for the first time. To be honest, unless someone has ever taken the opportunity to actually keel over and expire in front of you, the chances of seeing a dead body are probably few and far between. I lifted the letterbox, had a discreet sniff and baulked. Yep, something smelt very dead inside the little terraced house.

"Here yer are love, it's her spare key, use this."

The kindly neighbour proffered the shiny bit of metal on a piece of string to me. I looked at it, looked at him and looked at the front door. It was at this exact moment I realised that I was the one wearing a uniform, and as such, I was probably expected to do something about the unseen Mrs Creighton.

Why couldn't I have worked at Sainsbury's, they never have to find dead people do they?

I let that thought hover in the air before slipping the key into the lock, tentatively turning it and stepping through the door. I glanced back to a sea of faces belonging to the concerned neighbours outside, watching in a medley of keen anticipation and sheer nosiness.

Just on the remote chance that there was anyone alive to hear it, although I did seriously doubt it judging by the smell, I loudly announced my arrival in a quivering voice.

"Mrs Creighton, Mrs Creighton, it's the Police Mrs Creighton."

No reply, nothing. Not even a whisper.

I carried on along the hallway, checking each room in turn. There was no sign Mrs Creighton but in the kitchen I found a pan of some awful smelling gunk on the old enamel gas stove. The furry growth on the top had been fermenting for some considerable time. I held my breath, this was going from bad to worse. I tried again.

"Mrs Creighton, don't panic, it's the Police, just need to know you're okay."

Silence.

I began to climb the staircase, picking my feet through the threadbare runner, sweeping my fingers along the dark brown bannister. I just knew I was going to find her rather deceased somewhere upstairs.

Oh please God don't let her be all horribly... well you know what I mean... just make her sort of fresh...ish...!

The first bedroom was empty apart from an old 1930s wardrobe, several dead flies on the ledge of the cast-iron fireplace and a commode. Motes of dust whipped up, catching in the muted sunlight from the window. Coughing I closed the door. Creeping out onto the landing, I put my very sweaty hand on the door handle to the second bedroom, pausing long enough to control my breathing as my heart threatened to explode through my shirt.

I turned and pushed.

The door creaked open...

... and there, lying in bed amongst her pink rayon sheets and green polyester quilt, mouth wide open and eyes hooded was Mrs Creighton.

Very grey, very still, very cold and very, very smelly...

...and in my expert opinion... just a little bit dead!

I froze.

Oh faark I've got a dead body. A real life dead body. My first.

Panic ensued. *Think Mavis, think, what did they teach you a Bruche?* For a split second I didn't care what they had told me at Police Training college, it didn't matter. All I wanted to do was get the hell out of there...

...and then I remembered. It all came flooding back, I knew exactly what I had to do.

My priority was to confirm that there was no output from Mrs Creighton, no breath, no pulse, nothing that could be resuscitated, no signs of life.

Way to go Mavis.

I held my breath and walked gingerly over to the bed, jumping as the floorboards creaked. Oh blimey, facial hair. Mrs Creighton has facial hair. I hesitated, wondering if she still had her false teeth in, which in turn reminded me of Marj at our first aid classes. A quick glance at the bedside cabinet confirmed that her teeth were accounted for, floating in a disgusting yellowy green glass of err, something. Fantastic that was all I needed. I'd never get a good seal around her mouth for CPR if it was caving in through lack of teeth. The thought of shiny gums and spit made me feel sick.

Taking hold of her limp wrist, I bent over her to check for any signs of life.

As I tentatively move closer to her face, I paused waiting to see if any air was being expelled from her nose. The hairs on her top lip remained static. Oh dear. I moved in closer, my own breath barely perceptible ... and suddenly her eyes shot wide open.

A low moan drifted from her mouth as she sat bolt upright in bed. Letting out an almighty screech akin to a banshee, she flailed her arms in the air.

"What the fuck are you doing in me bedroom?"

I screamed.

Mrs Creighton screamed...

...and I legged it out of the bedroom in sheer terror, flying down the stairs, missing several steps as I went.

The neighbours, fearful of my findings and the wailing from inside the house, crossed themselves in Godly reverence before disappearing back into their own houses as I fell over the door mat, landing sprawled out on the pavement.

Standing alone outside, I gathered what was left of my dignity and quietly meditated my predicament before forcing myself to return inside the House of Horrors.

I made Mrs Creighton a cup of tea, washed her dishes and contacted a relative to advise them she had been suffering from a rather awful bout of influenza, aggravated by a *Night Nurse* induced coma.

Plumping the pillow behind her, I folded back her quilt and handed her a bowl of chicken soup the next door neighbour had brought round.

"Here you go, that'll make you feel better Mrs Creighton."

She grumbled, sniffed, tasted the soup and let the spoon rattle back into the bowl. "D'ya know what would really make me feel better?"

I was mesmerised by the flake of chicken adhered to her top lip as her tongue snaked up trying to dislodge it.

"Anything, just say and I'll see if I can sort it for you," I gently crooned.

"I'd feel a whole lot better if you'd just fuck right off – and don't let the door smack you on the arse on the way out!"

...

Back at the nick I filled in my report on Mrs Creighton before going off duty, still stinging from her ingratitude and gobsmacked that an 87-year-old lady could actually know, let alone use, the *F-word*.

"There you go then Mave..." Bob dunked his biscuit in the chipped mug, brought it up to his mouth with seconds to spare before it drooped, "...it's the four **S**'s, you should've known that!"

I closed my notebook. "What on earth has sun, sea, sand and sex got to do with an ungrateful old biddy with Tourette's?"

He grinned, cramming the rest of his biscuit into his mouth. "Nope, it stands for not all **S**hitty **S**mells **S**niffed Are **S**tiffs...!"

A COUPON FOR
JAYNE MANSFIELD'S BRA

"I've been thinking lately...you know, about Dad. Have you really never heard from him since he left?" I curled a piece of hair nervously around my finger and stared intently at Mum.

I waited.

She picked up her oversized blue leather handbag from the side of the chair and using it as a distraction technique she began to rummage around in the bottom, almost disappearing from sight as her head plunged further into the depths.

"Mum!"

She looked up. Guilty? Chastised? Embarrassed? Hurt? Her face was trying to tell me something, but what it was I couldn't tell.

"It was a long time ago Mavis, you, Michael and Connie were just babies. He's never been a part of our lives and there's really no reason why he should be now."

Her lips were set in a thin line. Now that was one look I did recognise. I wondered if I should keep trying or let it slide. She was right, I knew that, but curiosity was getting the better of me, and for some strange reason, after all these years, I was beginning to feel a sense of loss. How could a man walk out on his wife and three young children and never look back?

"There's not much to tell, he got up one morning, went out to fetch the morning paper and that was it, he just didn't come home. He always had the wanderlust your Dad, he was a roamer before I met him, Merchant Navy did that to him. I was surprised that he actually wanted to settle down at all."

I moved to sit on the edge of the armchair as soon as I saw her blue eyes glisten with the onset of tears. Once again she delved into her handbag and pulled out her handkerchief with a flourish.

"Oh Mum, I didn't mean to upset you, I was just, well, curious. That's all." She dabbed her eyes.

"I was distraught Mavis, absolutely distraught. By the time I got over to Anselm's Newsagents later in the day, they'd sold out of the Daily Mirror, apparently your Dad bought the last one before he disappeared..."

She paused to light up a cigarette, blew the smoke upwards and closed the pack, letting it rest on her lap.

"... I just needed one more coupon for a moulded foam cup bra, all the way from America just like Jayne Mansfield wore, and that bastard took it with him!"

•••

4 a.m.

Fumbling around for the bedside clock, I turned it towards me as the red light flashed. I was in so much pain.

Within the hour I found myself counting spots that were rapidly appearing along my right leg, across my nellies and down my left arm. Joining up the spots I swore I could spell out several unusual words, although none of them were a match for Mrs Creighton's swear word the previous week.

"It's shingles Mavis, I'm afraid you've got shingles..." the Doctor began to write out a prescription for me. "... no work for at least a week or more. Wear cotton clothing, nothing too tight, plenty of fluids and absolutely no scratching."

I closed the surgery door behind me, sick note and prescription in hand.

Jeez, a pair of untethered baps would be fine in a foreign country where letting it all hang out was acceptable, but I wasn't somewhere hot and exotic. I was here in my little village, where in 1872 Agnes Billinge-Clarke of Lower Hoose had attended Church without wearing a hat which caused much consternation to her fellow villagers. Agnes was duly brought before the Village Council and was castigated and then banished from the Village for all eternity.

If Agnes had to face fire and brimstone for a missing hat, I bit my bottom lip wondering where on earth I would end up if I chanced out in public, bra-less and completely unholstered in the frozen foods aisle of the Co-op. Brazenly showing off nipples you could hang your coat on in the chiller section would definitely go down a storm.

My respite for peace, quiet and recuperation was to be short lived.

A flurry of cigarette smoke through my letterbox and a frantic banging on the door heralded the arrival of Shirley. She wasn't alone but I felt too rough to care.

"Right, kettle on let's have all the gossip, oh my goodness have we got you out of bed?"

I stood holding open the front door in my Minnie Mouse fleecy pyjamas with a serious case of bedhead hair and the creases from my pillow still ingrained on my left cheek.

"Oh dear, not looking your best Mave, oh well, a good brew will perk you up, oh by the way this is..."

She breezed past me, trailing off into a mumble, waffling on about work, her latest, very young male acquisition, chocolate and wine, whilst the poor guy with her just stood looking very bemused. I was pretty sure she'd introduced him as David.

"Tea or coffee David?" I busied myself in the kitchen throwing a couple of biscuits onto a plate, whilst kicking Cat's squeaky toy under the breakfast bar and simultaneously breathing into my hand and sniffing to check for any overnight dragon breath.

"Oh err tea will be fine, thank you. Shirley said you've had the jingles or something, I hope you're feeling better?"

He gave a cheeky smile, his brown eyes full of warmth. *Stop looking at the colour of his eyes you utter hussy and just make the tea!*

I looked out of the kitchen window as a distraction, Shirley's marked police car was causing some consternation amongst the neighbours. I had visions of Boris from next door setting fire to his dubious magazines in the back garden in sheer panic.

"Have you just transferred to our station David?"

I offered him the plate of biscuits. Mmmm, he did look rather good in his uniform. I checked his wedding ring finger, no ring and more importantly, no untanned strip. That was a good sign.

"Oh, I almost forgot, this is for you." He pushed an envelope and a bar of Toblerone across the coffee table. "It's just a little Get Well card, thought it might cheer you up."

was almost apoplectic with lust as she strained her head over the counter to catch a last glimpse of him as the door closed behind him. "I wouldn't complain if he wanted me to unwrap it for him."

I didn't so much blush as turn a violent shade of crimson. "It was a Toblerone Bev – and no it isn't a euphemism, it really was a chocolate bar!"

"Toblerone, Snicker, Marathon! Who cares when he's got a physique like that, I definitely wouldn't kick him out of my bed." She chewed on the end of her pen and winked.

"A few bites on a Toblerone doesn't always ruin a diet Mave, you really should give it a try sometime!"

I blushed.

"Well isn't that lovely Mave, how thoughtful, you don get many men these days that are that caring do you?"

Shirley winked as she took another bite from her biscuit and licked a crumb from her bottom lip.

"He's got a nickname Mavis, called The Bear aren't you my lovely?" She grabbed his muscular upper arm and gave it a squeeze. "Bet you don't have to be a genius to work out why, hey Mave?" she giggled like a schoolgirl.

I just wanted the ground to open up and swallow me. I could smell a set up and I didn't think David was in on it judging by the uncomfortable squirming he was currently engaging in on my armchair.

It quickly crosses my mind that he is probably thinking *'What the hell am I doing sitting here with a large Toblerone?'.*

And to be honest, I couldn't really answer that for him as I didn't know either.

...

A week later, partially recovered and back at work I fleetingly gave Dave the Toblerone a passing thought when I saw him in the Bridewell with his prisoner whilst I was dealing with mine.

No mention was made of his visit, the card or the Toblerone as he disappeared into one of the Interview rooms, leaving me slightly disappointed, but relieved.

Men equalled broken coffee tables, complications and heartache.

"Oh my God he's the one with the mahoosive Snic isn't he Mave?" Bev, the ample bosomed Custody Assi

A FINE ROMANCE

My much welcomed rest days started with a blur of activity.

A presentation assembly for Ella, who was now in her last year at Primary school, two horse riding classes in which she kept in the saddle for both, much to my relief, four loads of washing, three baskets of ironing and a rather unappealing chicken curry which actually didn't contain any chicken because through lack of sleep, I'd forgotten to put any in.

I reluctantly took to tackling the household chores that had become dreadfully neglected of late, as kicking bits of fluff and crunchy leaves under the rug in the hall had only been a temporary measure. Well as temporary as it could be until the mound had become a bit of a Health & Safety issue for visitors.

I loved my little house, it was such a happy home for us.

Crunching a bag of Wotsits and dancing to Spandau Ballet I flicked my duster around the room. I felt a sort of smugness as to how fab my life was, everything was perfect, there was nothing more I could possibly want.

I had Utopia right here within my four walls.

The trill ringing of the telephone interrupted my happy moment. "Hello."

"Oh err, hello Mavis? It's David."

"David who?"

"David, you know, David from work."

There was a hiatus from the other end, giving me time to think. I mentally ran several *David's* and *Dave's* through my brain.

"Oh gosh, yes, sorry David. How's the wife and kids?"

"Err no, not that one, I'm not married. I'm the one that came to your house."

Nope, it still wasn't ringing even the smallest bell. He tried again.

"I was the one that had a large Toblerone..."

Large Toblerone! My mouth went dry. Was this a secret code word for something else? It was said with an air of pride, oh God no, please don't tell me...

His gentle voice interrupted.

"...and a Get Well card, I came with Shirley."

Phew!

"I was just wondering if you fancied going out for lunch one day?"

I caught sight of myself in the nearby mirror, phone stuck to my ear, a look of utter horror on my face. I brushed my fringe to one side and could almost see my reply written across my forehead.

It's a no Mavis...a great big fat no. You don't need the complications.

A simple, polite 'no thank you' would suffice, but said nicely so as to not hurt his feelings. Been there, worn the T-shirt, dirtied it, washed it, shrunk it and thrown it in the bin. Me and romance were finished.

"Oh David, that's very kind of you, but nnnnnnnooooo... yes, that would be very nice."

I had done it again.

Against all sense and sensibility, I now had a date with Toblerone Dave.

•••

"Jeez what am I going to do, I can't believe I said yes."

As per normal I hoped Mum would help me with my ills, woes and need for advice. At times like this she would toast crumpets, drown them in Lurpak, offer me one, I would refuse and she would eat the lot whilst giving me her aged-worn words.

Today was no different.

"Well, all I can say Mavis is make sure your new coffee table isn't in the way this time."

The butter dripped from the half-eaten crumpet and landed on her blouse, the colour deepening as the grease soaked in. "Yes very funny."

"Are you sure you don't want a crumpet darling?"

"No Mum, I don't."

•••

Sitting in nervous anticipation, I watched the second hand jerk its way around the clock. Funny, I'd never noticed how loud the ticking actually was before. I'd dressed conservatively for my date with Toblerone Dave, a simple blouse and jeans and the biggest pair of knickers I could find. A sort of comfort pair.

I'd already pushed the coffee table out of the way and it now sat in awkward solitude in the corner by the television. I wasn't taking any chances. It was going to be lunch, quick chat and then home.

I watched David through the kitchen window as he struggled with the garden gate, Cat was hunched on the fence giving him the evil eye. Tentatively opening the front door before he had chance to knock, I was met with a huge grin.

"Hi Mave, are we ready then?" He jerked his head towards the road and a line of parked cars.

Swinging my bag over my shoulder, I gave him a rather wan smile and that was when I noticed what he was wearing.

I choked back a snigger as my eyes scanned him from head to foot, taking in his brown suede waistcoat, jeans and a blue checked shirt. I groaned, wondering if he had a ruddy horse tethered up outside ready for me to ride side saddle.

Jeez, I hope he isn't into line dancing and lassoing too – either as a pastime or a means of foreplay.

This was definitely going to be a first AND last date.

Escorting me to his waiting car, with not a horse or a donkey in sight, relief washed over me. A blue Mercedes, a very nice new Black Range Rover and a red BMW. I could forgive him for the waistcoat and the checked shirt if he drove one of these.

He led me past the Mercedes, paused by the BMW and then made towards the shiny black Range Rover, fumbling in the pocket of his jeans for the keys. I rushed excitedly ahead and stood by this dream car, a symbol of lushness and class. Hanging off the door handle, tongue sticking out, drooling in anticipation, I breathlessly waited to hear the central locking click so I could slide onto the sleek leather seats and...

"Here you go Mave, it's this one."

He jangled his car keys in my direction like they were a trophy. Tucked behind the Range Rover was...

... a little silver Fiat UNO.

With a flourish, he opened the passenger door, waved his hand to show me my seat and waited. Lowering myself in, I sat in embarrassed silence as I watched him squeeze all 6'3" of himself into the driver's seat, completely filling what little space remained inside.

David's left thigh was almost touching my right thigh and somewhere in between sat a gearstick and the handbrake. His bulk squashed me forward, so I was jammed up against the glove box. Struggling to breathe I tried to adjust my position, but with no room for manoeuvre my boobs became wedged upwards resembling a nifty budget airbag that had exploded from the dashboard.

He smirked and raised an eyebrow. "Right, off we go then, date day here we come."

I gave him a *'touch my thigh feel my fist'* sort of look and dared him to select first gear.

"Mavis, if we are going to spend the first thirty minutes of our date sitting outside the SPAR shop because I'm too terrified to pick a gear for fear of fondling your thigh, it's going to be a very disappointing day don't you think?"

I looked out of the window and feigned interest in a very boring leafy hedge whilst I reluctantly allowed him to brush his fingers ever so slightly across my right knee cap. He eventually found first gear.

"Hold on to your ...err..." taking in my hunched position, he changed to second gear and grinned. "...hat, hold onto your hat Mavis, we're off."

•••

Strolling along the river in Chester later that afternoon after a nice pub lunch, the fading sun casting dappled shadows across the water, I smiled with contentment. Against all odds, and regardless of waistcoats, checked shirts, Fiat Uno's and squished nellies, I'd actually had a lovely day with Toblerone Dave. We sat on a bench by the bandstand watching ducks and swans fight for chunks of bread thrown by day trippers.

"David."

"Yes my lovely Mavis."

"I've just been thinking how your name really, really suits you. *David*. It's sort of strong, masculine, biblical almost."

I sighed, dangerously close to becoming dreamy.

"It does sound rather potent doesn't it? Maybe it's because he was the one that defeated Goliath..."

His gentle brown eyes gave off that warmth again, slightly crinkled at the corners. I rested my head on his shoulder as he smiled and put his arm around me.

"...it's just a pity that I'm really called Joe!"

MAVIS HITS THE ROAD...
AND OTHER STATIONARY OBJECTS

Sergeant Carlton's head popped through the open door of the night kitchen. "Ah there you are Mavis, see me in my office after Parade."

"Err, yes Sarge, will do."

My first thought was *oh shit, what have I done now* as I watched him disappear down the corridor. Suddenly I didn't feel like eating the rest of my Hobnob.

"Ooooooh Mavie's been a naughty girl, lads, what you been up to then?"

Don dunked his biscuit into his mug, yanked it out and stared mournfully as the end broke off and splashed back into his tea. "Well that's the ruddy Hobnobs off the Ten Second Dunker list."

I smiled. All the time I'd been here and we'd still not managed to find the perfect dunking biscuit. I made a note in my scribble book to remind me Hobnobs had not made the grade for when it was my turn to buy the biscuits. I racked my brains. I couldn't think of anything I could be in trouble for. Well at least nothing to warrant a trip to the Sarge's office.

"Nothing, absolutely nothing! Well nothing that I can think of, unless it was Tyrone, but that was his own fault." I turned a lovely shade of pink.

When I'd been on a foot chase with Tyrone McCormack the previous day, he'd looked back to see how close I was behind him. Unfortunately, he'd failed to see the ornate Victorian signpost bearing down on him and had smacked his face, with some considerable force on the metal plate that simply stated in black and white "Cobblers Drift". Landing ungracefully on his back amid blood, snot and a burst bag of white powder hanging out of his pants, he threw his hands up in defeat.

Although I'd laughed, Tyrone himself had failed to see the funny side, even more so when he was given a strip search back at the Bridewell. Don found another bag of powder stuffed in Tyrone's boxers and wrapped around his testicles. Don's off the cuff comment of *'Dunno 'bout Cobblers Drift, think this is more of a Scrotum Skid'* went down like a lead balloon.

Not only did Tyrone forfeit his supply, he gained three stitches to his forehead, two black eyes, a fat lip, a strip search and would be standing in court, I looked at my watch... right about now.

Maybe he'd made a complaint. I knocked on the Sarge's office door and waited. "Ah, come in Mavis. I'd like you to meet Sergeant Beryl Scully, she's starting on the section tomorrow."

He waved towards Beryl who was sitting at the corner desk. Slim, dark curly hair, cut fashionably short and legs that seemed to go on forever. I couldn't help thinking that Bert would have a field day altering her trousers.

"Hello Mavis nice to meet you, good job with McCormack yesterday." She clicked the top of her pen and slotted it back into her pocket.

I felt a slow wave of relief. "Thanks Sarge."

"Right down to business, there's been a cancellation on

one of the advanced driving courses, so you're booked on it, start day after tomorrow. You've got an assessment drive this afternoon, take it that's okay?" Smiling, she closed her folder.

"Wow, are you kidding Sarge, I can't wait." I tried very hard not to jiggle on the spot with excitement.

"Great, go and find a copy of *Roadcraft* and have a bit of a refresher before this afternoon." I turned heel and was half way through the door. "Oh Mavis..."

"Yes Sarge."

"Tyrone says thanks for the lip enhancement!"

At 2pm sharp, Harry Wakelam the Force Driving Instructor pulled up outside the station in an unmarked Vauxhall Vectra for our first assessment drive. I stood in nervous anticipation with two other lads from A3 division, as Harry went through all the checks.

"Right, drive as you would, observe the rules of the road and..." he paused to wipe a large dollop of tomato ketchup from his tie "...keep your eye on the game."

•••

Two hours later we returned to the station and waited as Harry handed us each a report to be given to our respective Sergeants.

I made a quick detour to trap 3 in the ladies' loos to have a quick shifty at mine before handing it over. I was quietly confident. After all I'd learnt to conquer the M56 and a general panda beat, what more could they want. I began to read, my lips mouthing each word as my heart sank.

'Constable Upton drives everywhere at 40 mph, regardless of the dictated speed limit. This would not remain an issue

if she were using a road that has this limit in order to reach Sainsbury's to obtain her weekly shop. I believe she would also achieve a smoother drive if she occasionally selected fourth gear and tempered the need to 'bounce' on the clutch. Her parking skills leave a lot to be desired and it might be useful for Constable Upton to know that in the main, most roads have kerbs. There is much room for improvement."

So, there it was in black and white.

I drive like an OAP, shop at Sainsbury's and enjoy the occasional bit of kerb crunching. I folded it up, slipped it back into the envelope, waited until the Sarge's office was empty and discreetly left it on her desk.

•••

Harry dangled a set of keys in front of me as we stood on the abandoned airfield. "Right ladies and gents, this is where size really does matter." He grinned.

Starting to panic I looked pleadingly at Harry. The huge personnel carrier stood ominously in the middle of the flat concrete runway. A monster. The thing nightmares are made of.

Tufts of coarse grass shifted in the wind as I watched balls of dead bracken blow like tumbleweed from the surrounding fields. Four weeks in a variety of saloon cars, marked and unmarked learning to drive very fast in them was one thing, but this was on a whole new level.

"Harry purleese, can't I just miss this bit of the course out, I didn't have to do it for my Class 3?"

Harry gave me a sympathetic look. Hopefully he would be supportive and understand my fears. No such luck.

"Upton, get that fat arse of yours into the driver's seat and let's see some driving."

I reluctantly slid into the driver's seat, turned the ignition key and...

...completely and utterly amazed myself, my fellow students and Harry. I was a natural.

Snaking the huge beast of a vehicle through a slalom of cones, forwards, backwards, reverse parking into a restricted height, I ended my lesson with a wonderful piece of parallel parking between a myriad of cones.

"Well Mavis, I've never seen anyone handle the Carrier as superbly as that."

Harry seemed very surprised, but probably not half as surprised as I was. I had found something I was good at first time.

"Okay ladies and gents, enough of the vehicular choreography, it's time to see how you all fare on the open road. Mavis, you can go first."

The others jumped in the back whilst I confidently manoeuvred the Carrier along country lanes, through the town centre to the local industrial estate. Harry wanted to see how we would cope with varying lengths and widths of roads that held obstructions. I made a perfect left turn into a narrow road and using my wing mirrors to gauge distance I confidently increased my speed...

... only to hear *thud, thud, thud, thud* from both sides of the carrier as I drove along and Harry screaming at the top of his voice.

"Stop, stop, stop for fuck's sake Mavis stop the bloody van."

I was utterly shocked. I had never heard a grown man squeal in such a high pitched voice before, not unless he'd been kicked in the testicles.

With a sickening realisation, it began to dawn on me that only on an industrial estate would you find several parked transit vans and lorries that had, and *had* being the operative word here, wing mirrors the same height as the wing mirrors on a Police Carrier.

As we surveyed the scene, picking up various bits of plastic casings and glass, trying desperately to match them to their respective vehicles, Harry felt the need to offer me a little gem of advice.

"For Christ's sake Upton, if at any time in the future they need a Carrier driver on a public road for Gods' sake tell them you've got a bloody headache."

As I sat in bed that night reading my Roadcraft Manual and reciting the System of Car Control, I wondered if this little mishap would ruin my chances of passing this all important course. My final drive was in two days' time and I had to show my skills in Vehicle Pursuit with a Bandit vehicle, observation skills along with a Response drive and a general drive.

Drifting off into a troubled sleep I dreamt of kicking leaves and jumping puddles with Ella. The simple days when I didn't have a care in the world.

...

"I'm pleased to tell you it's a pass Constable Upton, well done."

I stood staring at the Examiner as he held out his hand to shake mine.

Mavis Upton who once upon a time couldn't drive three miles from home in any direction was now Mavis Upton, Advanced Police Driver, licenced to drive a jingly jangly, all singing, all dancing police car, very, very fast!

They'd even thrown in a Carrier Driver qualification. Now that did surprise me.

...

"Watch out lads, they're going to let Mavis loose in an IR car, it's all downhill from here."

Degsy faked a swoon, so I helped him out a bit and hit him over the back of the head with the Sarge's clipboard to make it a bit more realistic.

Derek 'Degsy' Legge was another transfer to our section. With ten years' service already under his belt, he was a welcome addition. He was also a Carrier driver, which was a relief as hopefully they'd call on him to drive it rather than me.

"Now, now children, that's enough!" Sergeant Scully wagged a finger and grabbed her clipboard back. "Here you go Mavis, congratulations, it might not be a Cav or one of the trial Peugeots, but it has got four wheels."

She threw a set of car keys at me. My ecstasy knew no bounds; I was going to be upgraded from a basic panda car. It also made me pretty much oblivious to the snorting and sniggering behind me.

I skipped out of the parade room and fair bounced down the back steps and out into the car park, stopping only to collect my briefcase, jacket and hat. I knew I could only covet the Cavaliers, as although my Driving Authority would allow me to drive one, I was so far down the pecking order it would take an Act of God for me to feel my curvy butt on a Cavalier's driving seat before the following Christmas.

By the time I got outside, the new Cavalier, the pride of the fleet, was exiting the car park, closely followed by two older Cavaliers and, as I counted them, one Peugeot, two Peugeots, three Peugeots.

Bemused I watched them disappear from view.

I looked down at the set of car keys clutched in my hand. That was all the cars accounted for, so where was my mine?

I surveyed the car park.

There in the last bay, stuffed behind the industrial wheelie bins and two broken chairs was a little battered ten-year-old Ford Fiesta with its blue and green stripes, Police crest on each of the two doors and a little round blue lamp in the middle of the roof.

It couldn't be, surely this wasn't my car? A wave of disappointment washed over me.

Checking the key fob against the number plate, my heart sank. This was definitely my 'response' vehicle.

My ecstasy had, in a matter of seconds, reached its limit and just as quickly, dropped through the floor.

I use the term 'response vehicle' very, very loosely.

The drivers' seat had obviously taken a bit of a hammering over the years as it had sunk and the springs were poking through the upholstery, hence a rather fetching shiny brown beaded shiatsu massage cover adorning it. The rear view mirror was thoughtfully stuck in place with an old bit of well-chewed gum and the gearstick had a yellow cue ball pinched from the snooker room drilled out and shoved on the end, which in turn sported a crusty blob which looked uncannily like something Bob had excavated from his left nostril.

Bloody hell, was I supposed to drive this heap of shi...

"Yo Mave, love yer wheels baby!"

Don carried out another circuit of the yard in his Cavalier, laughing fit to burst. I watched as the rear lights of his car disappeared from view, leaving me alone in the car park with my newly named...

Florence The Fiesta.

DEATH BECOMES HER

"See they're shafting us with Pete Thackeray, wonder how his back entry is doing!" Don slammed his locker door shut, jiggled his key and then gave the bottom a hefty kick.

Several loud groans echoed around the room, Degsy's moan being the loudest. He lobbed an old rolled up sock over to the bin, it missed, hit the wall, bounced and dropped in front of my locker. "Well I'm not feckin' working with him, I'll end up punching him."

Bob looked on in amusement. "I'm the senior Con, after Don of course, so I say Mave's the best one to have him."

I picked Degsy's sock up and threw it at Bob, hitting him square in the face. "Don't think so lads, I'm the youngest in service with the least experience, it'll definitely be one of you lot."

...

After parade, Sarge beckoned me into her office. Petey was perched on a chair opposite her.

"Mavis can you work with Petey, take him under your wing. Here's a list of offences that he needs some experience in."

She handed me a sheet of A4 paper whilst I tried to hide my bitter disappointment. As my eyes glanced over the list I caught sight of Bob, Degsy and Don in the corridor. Keeping out of sight of the Sarge they danced in circles, silently laughing and miming 'told you so' hand actions. I childishly stuck out my tongue and carried on reading.

From what I could see I was certainly going to have my work cut out. Apart from detaining someone for shoplifting four months ago, who Petey had subsequently let go, which had then resulted in a full-scale search until the offender was found still handcuffed and face down in a garden pond with ten packets of NETTO bacon down his tracky bottoms, he hadn't actually arrested anyone on his own.

Tucking the list into my pocket, I grabbed my hat and briefcase. "Come on Petey, things to do, places to go."

He silently trailed behind me as we loaded up the car and set off for what I hoped for his sake, was going to be a busy shift.

"Right, what type of offence do you want to look at, give me the definition and points to prove too?"

He suddenly became very animated. "POCD, I'd love to look at drugs, I haven't done that one yet."

He then went on to recite the offence definition word perfect, and I suddenly realised that this was why he was struggling. Petey was an academic and putting it into practice was where the problem lay.

It wasn't long before I spotted an opportunity for him in Edinburgh Road, a long street of red brick terraced houses. Swaggering along the pavement was one of our regulars.

"Look, there's Jason Ballard, CID want him for that burglary in Falkirk Road earlier."

No sooner had the words left my lips, with Petey looking in every direction apart from the one that Jason was in, then he was off like a whippet up the nearest back jigger.

I stopped long enough to chuck Petey out of the car.

"You follow him, I'll cut him off at the other end and shout up for the others to support us."

Sounds good on paper doesn't it?

Tyres squealing as I braked harshly at the other end of the jigger, I jumped out of the car just in time to see Jason emerging from the entry. Petey should have been seconds behind him, but there was no sign. Degsy and Bob were the next to arrive on scene as I made a grab for Jason, swinging him around onto the ground, pinning him down with one knee as Bob ran to help.

"I don't know what's so funny Jason; you didn't get very far did you?"

He was puffing and wheezing, still sniggering, with his nose squashed into the cobbles. "Nah miss, don't fink yer mate did neever!"

Petey still hadn't emerged from the jigger and I was starting to get worried, after all, he was my responsibility. Handing Jason over to Degsy and Bob, I ran back to search for him.

"Oh shit, he's okay lads but you've got to see this!" I stood in disbelief in the back jigger.

Petey was hanging from the arched metal railings on top of a wall, held only by the back of his jumper, six feet off the ground with an upturned wheelie bin under his dangling and kicking feet.

"Bleedin' hell Petey, how the faark did you get stuck up there?"

He didn't reply, he just groaned.

Righting the wheelie bin I managed to unhook him from

his predicament and with him miserably dragging his feet along the cobbles whilst pulling at his overstretched jumper, I walked him back to where I had left the boys with Jason.

"I tried Mave, I really did. I nearly had him too, but he just..." waving his arms in exasperation, Petey let out a long, disappointed sigh.

"No time for that now, you know your stop and search powers, this one's yours mate, make it count." Giving him an encouraging smile and a pat on the back, I waited.

Petey took a deep breath. "Err right Ballard, you've been detained for the purpose of a stop/search, a copy of which will be held..."

He droned on and on, doing a cursory search of Jason as he spoke, whilst Degsy and Bob looked on in amusement.

Rummaging around in the top pocket of Jason's denim jacket, Petey became very animated, quickly withdrawing his hand, palm up, with a flourish to show several broken pieces of what looked like cannabis resin. He could hardly contain himself.

He had found drugs, his dream arrest.

With unexpected confidence Petey swung round to face Jason, shoving his still outstretched palm right under his nose.

"Well, well and what have we got here then Ballard?" Petey smirked. I cringed.

Jason squirmed, his eyes darting backwards and forwards.

He rolled his eyes, shifted from one foot to the other, examined what lay in Petey's palm, licked his lips, took a deep breath and before anyone could stop him, he exhaled loudly, blowing the little nuggets in all directions to the ground.

"What? I don't see nuffink do you?" he laughed.

Petey let out a feral wail of despair as he fell to the ground, scrabbling around on all fours with his torch, trying to recover his all-important evidence. Simultaneously, Jason was trying to make a break for freedom, managing a 200-yard sprint until Degsy executed a superb swallow dive, taking him down into a nearby gorse bush.

Seconds later Petey emerged from the gutter triumphant, holding two small pieces of cannabis, three stones, a chunk of grit and a blob of chewing gum, totally oblivious to the events that had unfolded around him. "No worries folks, I think I've...oooh Degsy what're you doing in the bushes?"

Degsy stood up, pulling bits of gorse from his jumper, examining a graze to his hand as Bob clicked the handcuffs on Jason.

"Don't even go there sunshine," he snarled "I've never had the opportunity to strangle a Petey before!"

•••

"Guess what lads, I've got the Oakland's Estate, Sarge says it's just right for me." I poured milk into one mug and two sugars into another, played 'mother' and stirred the teapot. I looked up.

Silence.

"I've got the Oakland's; you know that big estate off the County Road," I repeated. Still silence.

Looking at Degsy, Bob, Don and the others, I waited for a response. Nothing. No reaction at all, apart from the odd smirk between them. I was finding all this smirking rather tiresome.

Degsy draped his arm around my shoulders and patted my head. "Honestly Mave, there's nothing to worry about, you'll enjoy it – eventually."

Unimpressed with their lack of interest, I grabbed my stuff, picked my keys up, gave a test call on my radio and left them to it.

Brooding over Degsy's reaction at 03:30 in the morning is not conducive to a good night shift; my senses were telling me that maybe my enthusiasm for my new beat was a little premature. Unfortunately, it was all too obvious that it was going to have to be a suck it and see learning curve. I'd been to the odd one or two jobs on there before and it hadn't been that bad.

It was 'Q' for the first seven hours of the night and we had spent most of it bumping into each other as we trawled the same streets and back jiggers actively looking for anyone who fancied being naughty.

It's a little superstition of all the emergency services that as soon as the word *quiet* leaves the lips of the speaker, all hell usually breaks loose, so 'Q' is used in the hope it doesn't tempt fate. Petey had clearly not heard of this, or if he had he had either forgotten that he'd heard it or was just being plain stupid as usual. No sooner had he uttered the immortal words *'Blimey it's quiet tonight'* and before Degsy could smack him around the back of the head with his A to Z, three different immediate response jobs came through, a burglary in progress, a violent domestic and a concern for safety.

"Take one each, whoever clears first backs the others up as needed." Degsy quickly shoved his A to Z in the door pocket. "Mave if you take the concern for safety, stand off if it needs back up though."

Nodding in agreement, we starburst in opposite directions as Heidi gave me an update on my job.

"Female threatening to kill herself Mave, no address; history coming up for it though."

I arrived at the little mid-terraced house within minutes. Hearing crashing noises and crying coming from inside, I suddenly became little Miss Valiant even though my insides where churning like a navvy's cement mixer. No way was I going to stand off, she might be seriously hurt. I shouted up telling Heidi I was going in.

Bursting through the front door I came face to face with Frankie Elizabeth McDonald, 28 years old, single, the proud owner of several body piercings, eight tattoos and a huge kitchen knife.

Knife! Oh shit.

An even bigger *oh shit* was the sudden realisation that I'd left my body armour in the boot of my car.

"Frankie come on love, put down the knife, we can talk about this can't we?"

I could feel an adrenalin surge. Frankie had already slashed one wrist and was spraying blood everywhere. Her wet hair was sticking to her face, spittle foamed on her lips.

"Just fuck off, it's all shit, all of it, come any closer I'll cut my fucking throat." Raising the knife to her throat she pressed down, the blade making an indentation on the skin of her neck.

My opening gambit of sympathy and understanding had failed, and with it any hope of avoiding direct conflict. This wasn't an idle threat, an attention seeking episode; this was real.

I had to do something.

Crap, do what? What am I supposed to do? I should wait for back up. No, no I can't do that, it'll be too late.

It was now or never.

As Frankie sliced the blade across her neck, I made a grab for her and the knife. I lunged.

She moved...

... and drawing her arm back she furiously stabbed the knife at me.

Air was knocked out of my lungs as a sharp, hard blow hit my ribs. Falling backwards, I landed against a battered old arm chair, instinctively holding my hand to my side where I could feel pain and a warm, sticky wetness on my shirt. Bringing my hand up to my face, I turned it palm up. It glistened in the light of the lamp.

Blood.

The charming Frankie Elizabeth McDonald – 28 years' old, with several piercings and eight tattoos – had stabbed me.

Oh shit, what the hell was I going to tell Mum. She would be so cross with me for getting stabbed.

Then fight or flight took hold. I chose to fight. I wasn't going down like a wimp, I struggled to my feet. Frankie had also been thrown off balance and was stumbling around the small living room. I made a move to snatch the knife from her, grabbing her arm, I pulled down with all my strength and we both fell over, hitting the coffee table on the way down.

Perversely it crossed my mind that this was starting to be

a bit of a habit with me and broken coffee tables, but at least with this one, Bruce wasn't lying on top of it.

Rolling her face down, I swept my arm around her neck, pressing my bodyweight down on top of her, pinning her arms.

"I'll fucking kill you, get the fuck off me you bitch." Screaming, she bucked and fought beneath me. I tightened my grip. The knife had been knocked under the chair, so as long as Frankie couldn't reach it, I was safe.

It seemed like forever, but was only seconds before I heard the sound of heavy boots on the uncarpeted hallway echoing to the backdrop of Frankie's continued screaming. My back up had arrived. Bob was the first to kneel down beside me as Frankie was restrained, allowing me to let go.

"Oh faark Bob, I think I'm a little bit hurt."

I held my blood soaked hands out in front of me in a state of shock.

"It's okay kid, I'm here, we're all here, you'll be okay, just hang in there, don't you dare piss off to one of your airy fairy clouds girl," he soothed.

I was fading fast.

I could see *The Light* as I lay stretchered out in the ambulance, flickering, beckoning me. There was so much blood, I knew death was imminent. What a way to go, I hadn't even had time to slap on some of my famous Coral Blush lippy.

Pulling Bob close to me I dramatically whispered with what felt like my last breath. "Promise me you'll tell Ella and Mum I love them, tell them to live every day as though it's their last... I think this is mine... Bob..."

Bob nodded and brushed his hand across my cheek, wiping away my tears. "You silly, silly girl Mave, was your life worth so much less than hers?"

I couldn't answer that.

Bob moved aside as the paramedics began to assess my injury. As they cut through my shirt I frantically tried to remember which bra I'd chosen when I'd got dressed earlier, was it one of my old fade-to-grey ones? Oh gawd, why hadn't I been shopping for something decent. I didn't want to die wearing shabby grey underwear.

I closed my eyes waiting for the inevitable.

"Bloody hell, look at this, would you believe it, someone's looking down on you young lady."

My eyes shot open as the paramedic carried on with his examination. I looked down past the huge bumpy hill of my fade-to-grey bra towards my left side. I had to blink several times to take it all in.

There wasn't a mark on me.

The blade of the knife had gone right through the front of my shirt, skimmed across my side and emerged through the back of the shirt.

"... but I'm bleeding, I've got blood everywhere, I'm dying..." I wailed to the paramedic.

"No you're not love, the blood's Frankie's and apart from some bruises and what I suspect is a cracked rib, you're actually in quite rude health."

Mortally embarrassed I winced as I sat up, pulling the cut ends of my shirt together. "... but I can still see *the light* Bob."

"Think you'll find that's my Maglite torch kid," he sniggered, flicking the torch on and off. "You bloody daft bint. I love you to bits but don't ever do that to me again!"

Leaning back, he grinned, wiping his hand across his forehead, "Oh and by the way Mave, I've now seen your humongous nellies!"

A hot flush crept across my face. "They're not humongous Bob..." I indignantly wailed, "...they're just sort of ... err... big-ish."

For once in my life I had to thank nature for giving me such massive baps, which in turn meant I had to wear extra-large shirts to accommodate them comfortably. Billowing like a three-man tent once tucked into my trousers, it had given ample room for the knife to pass safely through.

So there you go. Big boobs had saved my life.

Hallelujah!

A PRIMARK THONG

"I've decided I'm going to try and find my dad again."

Bob, Degsy and Don stopped mid mouthful, causing Degsy to lose the chunk of cod that had been clinging to the end of his fork. It hit his tie before landing on his leg.

Don wiped his mouth with the paper serviette and swallowed. "Bit of a bombshell Mave, why now?"

I thought for a moment, trying to pick the right words. To be honest I wasn't really sure why myself. It was just something I felt I had to do.

"There's a void in my life, like something's missing. I know I've always said it didn't matter, but looking at Ella, it does. He's part of me but he's also part of Ella." I shuffled a couple of peas around my plate. "Not in an emotional way, purely genetic but I do wonder where he is, or even if he's still alive."

That had just suddenly come to me. It hadn't really entered my head that he might already be dead.

"I think what happened with Frankie McDonald made me think about how precious family is too. If I had died, I would have gone without ever knowing my dad." I pensively stabbed at a chip, dunked it in the ketchup, popped it in my mouth and got up to make a cup of tea.

"I can see the light… it's getting closer… oh I'm fading fast." Bob swiped his hand over his forehead dramatically feigning a swoon.

"Very funny, you wouldn't be laughing if it had happened

to you..." I slammed the kettle down, slopping water over the sides. "...it was a near death experience, a real proper one, I thought I was going to die. I was distraught!"

I gave him my best hurt feelings look, hoping to elicit at least some sympathy.

"It was your disgustingly shabby underwear that gave the paramedics the best laugh Mave..." he spat crumbs across the table as he waved his bacon batch at me. "...were they actually grey when you bought them?"

Blushing, I peered down the front of my shirt. He had a point, my bra had definitely seen better days. The underwire was poking through the middle and a runner on one strap had broken giving a rather quirky lopsided look to my nellies. I couldn't even begin to imagine how my knickers had stayed in place as the elastic had started to perish on them weeks ago.

"Oh all hail Bob, the expert on women's lingerie," I snapped, more from embarrassment than anger.

"Ah you may jest my little plum pudding." He wiped his chin with the back of his hand. "Now take for example Primark knickers. They're always at least one size smaller than it says on the label AND they shrink in the wash too. Now I have it on good authority..."

I quickly cut him off mid-sentence, dreading what was going to come next. "Jeez you perv, what the hell do you get up to on your days off?"

Smirking, with one hand on his hip, he sashayed around the table before ending with an over-exaggerated pout and a subtle slut drop.

"You'd be amazed at what some of us wear under our combat pants on a night shift darling!"

...

I ran my fingers along the rail, watching the bright colours sway on the hangers.

I was braving the Lingerie Department in Primark. Knickers, G-strings, thongs and tiny shorts littered the floor where excitable teenagers had stretched lace and elastic for fit, admired, coveted and then discarded them before moving on to the Nightwear section for all-day pyjamas.

Holding a nice size 10-12 thong up to the light I could see I was going to have to bow down to Bob's superior knowledge of women's underwear.

It was absolutely miniscule.

I held it against me, pulling the elastic to its full extent as I caught a fleeting glimpse of my own rear end in a nearby mirror. It certainly wouldn't take a genius to know it definitely wouldn't fit my curvy butt. Well, not without an awful lot of huffing and puffing and several indentations left on my thighs at the end of the night. There was also the distinct possibility that a pair of scissors would be needed to remove them at bedtime.

Size 14-16 wasn't much better, in fact it looked pretty much the same as the 10-12's. I furtively looked around before allowing my fingers to settle on a hanger which bore a label that screamed size **'18-20'**. Sneaking them down in front of me to check for fit, I began to realise with unfolding horror that these not so small beauties would be the only ones that could respectfully accommodate my very ample posterior, survive a bit of shrinkage in a 40-degree wash and not give me a deep vein thrombosis in one or both legs.

Peering over the rails, I checked to make sure no one could see me before surreptitiously stuffing several pairs into my basket before wandering off to join the checkout queue.

Absent-mindedly turning each pair over, I folded them so the size labels couldn't be seen. I couldn't believe I'd been reduced to buying knickers that resembled a deflated parachute. The only thing worse than the paramedics seeing my shabby faded grey undies would be for them to know I was wearing size 20s to cover my hippo ass.

I inwardly cringed imagining them laughing over a mug of tea and a garibaldi biscuit.

The label on the top pair refused to be hidden, peeping out from behind the lace edging, mocking me; and that's when I had another one of my wonderful epiphanies.

I'd cut the labels off when I got home then even if I had another near death experience, no one would ever be any the wiser as to what size grundies I was currently clad in.

Mentally patting myself on the back for such a stonkingly good idea, I was in the process of allowing myself a smug moment, when my thoughts were suddenly broken by the dulcet tones of the cashier.

"Next. Drag yer basket down 'ere will yer."

Now it was at this point I suddenly got a tremendous urge to explain to *Miss Cashier No.3* why I had seven pairs of lacy black thongs in my basket and an even bigger urge to explain away their size.

As I shoved the basket onto the counter, and before I could even concoct a plausible explanation, I watched *Miss Cashier No.3* pick up the first pair from the basket and check the label. Scratching at a rather large, make-up encrusted spot on her chin, she inspected her fingernail, stretched her arm out to its full extent and swung my black lace, size 18-20 thong around her head. In a voice that was loud enough to wake the dead, she bellowed across the store:

"Code 2, Code 2 Maureen...how much fer polyester thongs size **TWENTY**..."

Every head in the queue seemed to swivel towards me. One or two ladies looked me up and down and tutted loudly, either in disgust that I was big enough to wear a size 20 or because I was going to wear something that looked like the gusset from a pair of tights with the legs cut off.

The only guy in the queue, who was proudly holding a T-shirt with the slogan *Cool Dude* emblazoned on the front, began to tremble and clack his false teeth whilst wiping sweat from his top lip with a crusty, creased handkerchief. I watched in utter embarrassment as his beady eyes went from the thong, which was still being ceremoniously waved in the air, to me, back to the thong and then back to me.

My eyes darted back and forth between the thong, the cashier and the queue, before I indignantly announced in my best plummy stage voice:

"Actually they're for my Nan, you can hang suet balls for the birds from them you know, it was in the Homes & Garden magazine."

Miss Cashier No.3 was by now stuck in a mannequin pose, thong still pinched firmly between her fingers with a look of absolute disbelief on her orange tanned face. I knew I would have to expound as she definitely wasn't going for it.

"Don't you see, if they're massive you can fit bigger balls in them; lots of balls, the more balls the merrier." I waited for her to give a nod of understanding.

Nothing was forthcoming, just a slight twitch of one of her pencilled in eyebrows.

Oh shit. I can't believe I've just said that.

What a pathetic excuse for wanting to purchase seven humongous pairs of black lace thongs. What was more, her loud announcement had revealed to all and sundry that they weren't even pure lace, they were the dreaded sweaty-gusset-polyester type. As I rummaged in my purse, I had to quietly concede that for fifty pence a pair there must be some trade off on quality somewhere along the line.

I grabbed my carrier bag and turned to leave, only to find *Mr Cool Dude* waiting for me. He licked his lips and made a final defiant clack of his false teeth as he leered out of the corner of his mouth. "Tell yer what love, it'd be more than balls for the birds hanging off them if it were me."

Recoiling in horror, I had a sudden mental image of a set of dentures hanging from the gusset of my newly acquired knickers. Hastily sidestepping *Mr Cool Dude,* I burst through the doors and out onto the street, my Primark bag slapping wildly against my left thigh as I ran to the car park.

Sitting in my car I had another little peek at my spoils. Huge they may be, but they were rather pretty and VPL's in my combats would definitely be a thing of the past. But more importantly, I could have as many near-death experiences as I wanted now. If I had to almost die, I would at least be wearing a decent set of frillies.

I just hoped Joe liked them as much as I did.

PETEY and the SEVEN DWARFS

"I really like him Mum, Joe makes me laugh."

"I'm sure he does sweetheart, but a word of caution. Your Uncle Percy made Auntie Doris laugh and look what happened to her."

I screwed my nose up and tried to think. "What?"

"She got pregnant Mavis, that's what happened, she got pregnant!"

The last three words were emphasised in the fashion of our local vicar at his Sunday morning sermon. I quietly waited for hell and damnation to follow.

"Jeez, I'm sure there was a bit more to it than that."

"I'm being serious Mavis, it only takes one giggle and that's it. Your Nan was the same; ten giggles led to ten children. You could hardly move in our house for babies, poo and nappies."

Surprised that a marriage in the 1930s would only allow a roll on the horse hair mattress for the sake of pregnancy, I mentally counted up my Aunts and Uncles versus Mum's calculation of giggles to babies ratio.

"She must have had a freebie giggle then Mum."

She dropped her glasses to the end of her nose and stared at me. "What do you mean by a freebie?"

"Twins Mum...one of those giggles produced twins!"

•••

Bob pushed a sheet of paper towards me and waited.

Picking it up, I quickly scanned the contents that were scrawled in his distinctive handwriting. "Salvation Army family tracing service?"

He looked a little uncomfortable, pulled at his tie and shifted in his seat so he was facing me.

"They might be able to help Mave, it's worth a shot if you're really serious about looking for your dad. Even if they do find him, wouldn't necessarily follow he'll want to get in touch, but you never know."

I didn't know what to say or how to react. This made it more than a thought, this could make it a reality.

"Thanks Bob, I'll think about it." I stuffed the sheet into my briefcase.

"You never did say what your dad name was, we've all been taking bets. Rupert or Henry are the forerunners at the moment."

I laughed. "Actually it's Arthur. Arthur Albert Upton and he'd probably be about seventy now."

Don punched the air. "I had Albert, does that count, must be entitled to at least half of the pot for that?"

Before anyone had chance to reply to Don's earnest plea for half of 87 pence, a button, a tap washer and a handful of M&M's that had been thrown into the pot, Sergeant Scully brought the parade to attention.

"Right listen up, Intel's had a tip off on naughty vids and pirate stock being bought and sold down at the Sunday Car Boot. Quite serious stuff so I want two of you to bring a set of plain clothes in with you this Sunday." She pointed to Petey.

With a flourish she signed off on the paperwork and handed me a copy. "You too Mavis, they need a female on the team, but more importantly someone to keep an eye on you know who!"

...

Sunday morning came around far too quickly, leaving me half asleep in the briefing room, staring out across the car park of the nick as the wind rattled the trees. They were already shedding their leaves, but with each gust, more fluttered down.

"Right team, I know it's ridiculously early, I know it's Sunday and I know it's miserable out there but listen in."

Ben Sherlock the Detective Sergeant on the Op shuffled a couple of A4 size folders in front of him and then spread them out on the desk.

"Your brief is to work independently of each other, target potential offenders and make a test purchase. Once you've got it, take it to the covert van and the lads will run it on the video set up. If it doesn't pass muster with content or the Trading Standards, then we're on a winner."

I looked over at Petey who was listening intently, chewing the end of his pen. "Mavis, Petey you'll be the customers, Don, Martin, Degsy take the covert vans for transportation of any physical exhibits, I'll liaise with Trading Standards. That's it folks, let's get out there and get it done."

Class dismissed, we trooped out of the Briefing, chattering like a horde of school kids, Petey trailing behind still making notes in his little book.

By 8:15 a.m. we were all in place. The test van was parked on the far side of the field, blending in with the other vans belonging to the buyers and sellers. I hadn't seen Petey since the briefing, when we'd both been in uniform, so I was horrified to see him now, striding out across the grass in the middle of the field, weaving in and out between the cars.

"Jeez Petey, which bit of plain clothes didn't you quite grasp?"

He almost did a pirouette.

Clad in a pair of yellow and green checked trousers with a purple shirt and a yellow jumper, he would have looked more at home wandering around Disneyland in 80-degree sunshine sporting a pair of Mickey Mouse ears and carrying a bunch of balloons.

"My Mum got me the jumper for Christmas, said it suited my skin tone," he proudly announced.

"You'll stick out like a sore thumb, go and get a jacket or something. You take the top end of the field, I'll cover this section and we'll meet up later okay?"

He nodded and skipped off eagerly in a flash of yellow, green and purple.

It wasn't long before I found my Target. He was even wearing the same grubby jacket that I'd seen on the Custody Photo of him at the Briefing.

Standing by his red Mark 3 Cortina, boot open and an extensive collection of videos carefully arranged along the wooden table in from of him, he had already drawn a crowd of sordid looking men cossetting plastic carrier bags and smelling of pungent body odour.

I grimaced. It hadn't taken me long to find this gathering of Percy Perv's. Their attendance was a pretty good indication that although the boxes and colourful features on the video's ranged from 'Mr Motivators Muscle Burn' to 'In the Oven with

The Galloping Gourmet' the actual contents would have very little to do with keeping fit and cooking.

I discreetly watched them one by one, with their videos clutched in hot hands or swinging in carrier bags, as they scuttled off with their spoils. Once the crowd had thinned out a little, I made my move and began to sift through the video boxes laid enticingly across a stained red and white checked table cloth. It was like a greasy spoon café for Leg Tremblers and Keyhole Peepers.

I picked two that looked to be rather interesting, *'Woodwork for Beginners – Spindles, Shafts & Screws'* and *'Cooking with Plums by Jenni Taylor'*. As I paid for them, my Target grinned through misshapen, yellowing teeth and offered a leery wink, almost stroking my hand as he swept the money from me.

"Nice choice Madam, that's one of my favourites too."

Shuddering, I glanced at my watch, made a quick mental note of the purchase time for my evidence and casually made my way to the covert van so they could be logged and viewed.

Twenty minutes later Ben's voice came over my earpiece.

"It's good to go Mavis, these are over and above obscene, bring him in."

Gerald Pinfold looked suitably shocked as we converged on his table. He began to loudly protest his innocence whilst trying to leap the nearby barbed wire fence in a flurry of discarded videos and five pound notes.

Running after him, I watched as he sailed over the fence with his right leg but failed miserably to make it with his left leg. There was a momentary pause before he suddenly tipped forward landing testicles down on the spikey bits.

A loud *oomph* burst from his pursed lips, followed by a string of expletives and a scream as I caught up with him. He was in too much pain to protest further as Don handcuffed him and pulled him to his feet.

Checking the ripped crotch of his pants, I couldn't help but laugh. "Bet he won't be cooking with plums for quite some time judging by the state of those."

Don grimaced, and as men do, made a quick check of his own crown jewels for peace of mind.

Once Gerald's videos had been seized, he was bundled into the prisoner van. We split into two groups and left a small team of two and the covert van for Petey. He was yet to find his Target and was still mooching around the various stalls.

Two hours later Petey returned to the station with a prisoner and twenty-four boxes full to the brim with videos, which the lads were currently bringing into the Briefing room in relay. As the boxes were stacked in front of us, Petey, who was by now beside himself with excitement, couldn't wait to tell us his news.

"I've seized over a hundred videos Mave, it's in my little yellow book, the Obscene Publications Act 1959, I know it inside out... I can recite it if you want."

The looks that passed between us said it all. Based on his past results, we were all starting to feel a little bit uneasy. The Detective Inspector stood up, walked to the boxes, pulled a video out and looked at the cover.

"How serious is the content of these Thackeray?"

"C-c-c-c-content Sir? I haven't watched them yet; was I supposed to?" We groaned in unison.

At the behest of the D.I. we sat down to view Petey's haul so they could be assessed for genre, level of obscenity and then be admitted for evidence and potential charges.

Six hours...

Forty-three mugs of tea...

Five packets of digestive biscuits...

Twenty-eight trips to the toilet...

...and 6 pairs of bloodshot eyes later...

.... we could categorically confirm that we had 175 videos that contained scenes from just about every Disney film ever made, *Bambi, Jungle Book, Peter Pan, Snow White and the Seven Dwarfs*, a whole collection of *Carry On* films and one complete series of *Morecambe & Wise*.

Livid, the D.I summoned Petey to his Office.

"Constable Thackeray would you care to impart to me which bit of the briefing did you not understand this morning eh?" He slammed a copy of the briefing sheet down on his desk. "How difficult can it be you blundering bloody idiot? Observe – target –purchase – test."

There was a distinct absence of any sounds from Petey at this point.

The D.I continued. "In Gods' name tell me what, in your little world, is bloody obscene about these?"

We heard the clattering of video boxes being thrown across the desk and a muffled sob coming from Petey. An overwhelming touch of sympathy momentarily washed over us, but it was very quickly replaced by smirks and sniggers as we held our noses to stop snorts of laughter revealing our spying position.

"Well, I'm waiting for an answer."

In a very high pitched voice that was breaking up like a 13-year-old in the local church choir, Petey's voice squeaked out from behind the partially closed door.

"I err, um, oh, well if you think about it S-s-sir, S-s-s-snow White was sharing a bedroom with s-s-seven men. Now surely that's not right now is it S-s-sir?"

Even the D.I couldn't think of an answer to that.

A FINE ROMANCE Part II

"Bye Mum, see you tomorrow."

The front door banged shut as Ella disappeared in a swathe of carrier bags, books and a multi pack of crisps to stay with her Dad overnight. I watched her head bob over the top of the hedge until she was gone.

Crumbling an Oxo cube into the pan, whilst at the same time kicking the fridge door shut with one foot and taking a large swig of Merlot from my glass, I secretly thanked Mum for teaching me how to multi-task. Shoving the lasagne into the oven, I took another large gulp of wine, topped up my glass and checked my watch.

6:45 pm.

Plenty of time to get myself ready before Joe arrived. Popping a cherry tomato from the salad bowl into my mouth, I happily gave myself a little twirl out of the kitchen and into the hallway. *Right Mavis, bath, hair and glad rags on.*

Joe and I had met up quite a few times since our first date in Chester. After having come to terms with him not being the *Dave* I thought he was but in fact a very nice *Joe*, we had skirted round the issue of getting too romantically involved. So far our dates had consisted of dinners, walks along the promenade and local National Trust land with a genteel kiss at the end of the night.

As I ran the Bic razor along my shin, being careful not to shred my skin in the process, I glowed in the hope that tonight would be the night to move our relationship on from cheek pecks and awkward fumbles.

An hour later I was ready. Hair beautifully swept to curl just below my shoulders, new lingerie, NOT from Primark I hasten to add, and a lovely little black dress. Slapping on a slick of lipstick, I made a quick check in the mirror and gave my reflection a word of encouragement.

Not too bad for an old bird Mavis my girl, not bad at all.

I felt that that observation warranted another glass of wine. I'm sure by now you're starting to get the picture.

After every event of the evening, no matter how minor, from Joe's arrival, to feeding Cat, to finding the pepper pot to heating up the custard...

...I celebrated by having another glass of wine.

It is now 11:30 pm.

Joe and I have enjoyed a really lovely meal, as long as you don't count the soup. The soup had taken on a life of its own and ended up in Joe's lap, across the table and splattered on Cat.

Joe blamed the excess consumption of wine. I emphatically denied it.

Leaving him to finish off what little was left of the third bottle of Merlot, I staggered off to the kitchen. This wasn't going the way I had planned. Throwing soup at him, getting drunk and then forgetting to defrost the pudding, were actions hardly conducive to an evening hinged on romance and sexual magnetism.

I know, maybe another glass of wine would help.

Fumbling in the fridge I found a rather nice bottle of Shiraz, but no glass. What the hell, it couldn't get any worse could it? Leaning over the kitchen sink to steady myself, I took a long swig directly from the bottle, which in hindsight, wasn't the cleverest thing I could have done.

It wasn't very ladylike either.

Oh sod it, I'll just ask him outright.

Another swig.

Not many men refuse an offer like that do they?

Staggering out of the kitchen, bottle in hand, with a new found confidence, I suddenly caught a glimpse of myself in the hall mirror. What stared back at me was unrecognisable from the 'me' of a few hours earlier.

I couldn't find one redeeming feature. I was just plain drunk.

Weeeeeeee, I was as drunk as... a...as a skunk. I swung round on the coat stand, sending it crashing to the floor, just missing Cat by centimetres.

Piddled as a newt.

I skipped two steps along the hallway and paused.

Flicking back my hair, I raised the bottle and gave a sultry look to the mirror. A little practice wouldn't go amiss would it?

"Hey big boy – how about a..."

Oooh no, that was anticipating too much. What if he wasn't a big boy and got all offended. I could end up making him feel dreadfully inadequate.

Oh sod it Mavis, just go for it.

Flinging open the lounge door I clung on to the handle, wiggled my hips, closed my eyes and dipped at the knees, not so much of a slut drop, more of a geriatric knee bend.

"I've heard sex is a killer; would you like to die happy Joe?" Silence.

Complete and utter silence.

Slowly opening my eyes, I blinked rapidly to clear the heady haze created by excess alcohol and my fringe. There was no sign of Joe.

The sofa stood alone with just an indent on the cushion where he had been, the table with its remnants of soup had taken on an eerie resemblance to Miss Havisham's wedding banquet, minus the cobwebs. I'd frightened him off and my own Great Expectations had gone with him.

Poor Joe.

He must have had visions of a rampant, alcoholic, mid-30-something female ready to jump all over him and he'd done a runner. I slumped in the chair holding my head in my hands. More wine, I needed more wine. I grabbed a glass from the coffee table and watched the ruby red liquid spin round, fill up and splash over the rim. I would apologise for being such an intoxicated, over familiar lush tomorrow.

Staggering back into the hallway, I turned off the lights and made my way upstairs to bed alone, nursing a heavy heart and a two steps forward, three steps back swaying motion. Wine bottle in one hand, half-full glass in the other, I pirouetted into the bedroom and began to drunkenly remove my knickers by scraping one foot down my leg, hooking my stiletto heel though the gusset.

Way to go Mave, you've still got the moves girl.

Err no, actually I hadn't.

With my £3.99 black silk knickers caught on one ankle, I stumbled and landed face down, butt-up on the carpet.

Hauling myself up, I quietly congratulated myself on my exceptional juggling skills.

Having executed a forward somersault with a slide landing, not a drop of wine had been spilt. Crawling along on my elbows and knees, giggling incessantly still with wine bottle in one hand, glass in the other, I looked up.

There was Joe, my lovely, darling Joe sitting on my bed, grinning like a Cheshire Cat. "Bloody hell Mave, I'll give you a nine out of ten for that one!"

Hanging onto the edge of the bed, still on my knees, I raised my glass in a toast to him and my gymnastic skills, whilst frantically trying to kick off my knickers that were now hooked on the heel of my left shoe. Giving him a come-hither look I pouted.

"Oooh Joe... did you know that my legs can go behind my head without me really trying?"

Taking me in his arms he nuzzled into my neck, brushing his lips down the front of my throat whilst dropping one shoulder of my dress, his tongue barely touching my skin.

"No I didn't," he whispered "but I've got a feeling you're going to show me."

...

Lying there in the afterglow, with Joe holding me tenderly, I had another one of my wonderful epiphanies.

I had fallen in love.

I was in love with Joseph Stephen Blackwell and I didn't have a clue how it had happened.

"Hey, I've just had a really weird thought."

He pulled his head away from my shoulder so that he could look at me. "And what really weird thought would that be my little dumpling?"

I lay back on my pillow and swept a strand of hair away from my eyes. "Well, you know how we've just done what we've just done."

"Errr yep, I really dread to think where this is going Mave."

"No Joe, just listen to me, it's such an intimate thing isn't it, very sort of personal?"

"I'll give you that, yes it's very intimate, unless you're a swinger..." he paused and pulled a face of horrified expectation. "You're not are you Mave?"

I was exasperated and gave him a playful slap on the arm.

"No I'm not, look what I'm trying to say is, look what we've just done and we haven't even tooted in front of each other yet. Don't you find that funny?"

He burst out laughing. "Tooted! What the bloody hell is *tooted*, you don't play the trumpet at weekends do you?"

I collapsed into a spasm of uncontrollable giggling...

...and the inevitable happened. I farted.

Joe grimaced in disgust as he inhaled deeply. "Christ Mavis I'm dying."

I quickly pulled the duvet cover up to my chin, blushing furiously.

"Oh don't be so dramatic, you wanted to know what a toot was so I've obliged. It's not that bad...is it?" I covered my nose with my hand.

"Well," he grunted "if you stopped breathing through your mouth and used your nose instead, you'd know!"

Letting out an embarrassed snort, I curled up against him. Relishing his gentle breath as it brushed across my neck, I closed my eyes.

I was happy, content and very, very sleepy.

...

"Jeez, what the hell was that?"

I was awoken with a start by a loud hammering on the front door. A quick glance at the bedside clock told me it was 8:15 a.m. Hurtling out of bed, I opened the window, dragged the curtain around me as a modesty wrap and looked out on to the path below.

Ella! Oh shit it was Ella.

"Hi Mum I've forgotten my geography book for school, Dad's waiting for me in the car.

Grabbing the clothes that we had discarded on the floor in our moment of passion, I flung them at Joe.

"Get up, quick, it's Ella, just put anything on and hide." I couldn't let Ella know that Joe had stayed the night, it was far too soon.

Our clothes flew through the air, backwards and forwards between each other. Joe got my thong, I got his boxer shorts and T-shirt. He refused to wear the thong and threw it back at me.

"Just hide Joe, in the wardrobe, the bloody toilet; anywhere, just don't let her see you."

I legged it downstairs, hopping the last three steps as I shoved my left leg into my pants. Pulling the cord tight, I paused behind the door, took a deep breath and opened it.

Ella breezed in, stopping only to kiss me on the cheek. "Sorry Mum, hope you weren't having a lie in or something."

Before I could say anything, she ran upstairs leaving me standing in the hall having palpitations. Coming to my senses, I quickly bounded upstairs after her.

Opening the door to her bedroom, she let out a very audible gasp and stood frozen to the spot. I craned my neck around her to see.

Standing there in his jeans and a pair of socks with what looked like a very, very tight black t-shirt was Joe; balanced on a chair. Ella froze in the doorway as he pretended not to see her. Whistling, he carried on inspecting the wall by her bed whilst waving a tape measure around.

"What's HE doing in my bedroom Mum?"

Oh bugger.

Joe casually looked up.

"Morning Ella, didn't see you there, thought I'd pop round early to measure up for that shelf that you wanted."

She started to frown at him and then just as quickly changed it to a half smile. Picking up her book from the end of her bed, she turned and skipped out of the door and down the stairs.

"Thanks Joe," she shouted.

Dumfounded I looked at Joe who in turn looked at me. I waited for the front door to bang shut before I spoke. "Blimey that was close." I looked him up and down. "Thanks for wrecking my clothes too you idiot."

Joe shrugged.

Stretched beyond recognition over his 19" biceps, was not a T-shirt as I had first thought, but my lovely little black dress.

He wriggled and pulled it up over his head. "Needs must Dumpling, needs must."

"Less of the Dumpling or I'll be getting a complex. Suppose it's shopping for shelves then is it?"

He nodded.

So instead of our lovely planned day out in Chester walking by the riverbank, holding hands and feeding the swans, we spent the best part of two hours trawling the aisles in B&Q quickly followed by the hasty installation of two floating shelves, all before a certain Ella Upton came home from school and sussed our guilty secret.

On a more positive note, whilst getting to know each other better, we had discovered two things about each other.
1) I couldn't laugh AND hold my farts in at the same time.
2) Joe definitely wore my dresses better than I did.

UNCLE FESTER, THE GODFATHER, JACKSON & ME

"You have haven't you?"

"Have what Mum?"

"You know, giggled, you've giggled with Joe haven't you?"

I looked at her, horrified. "Muuuuuuum, I'm over thirty, surely I don't have to account for EVERYTHING I do in my private life?"

"It's a mothers' prerogative to be concerned Mavis, besides it's written all over your face."

She took a long drag on her cigarette, flicked the ash into her favourite Theakston's black ashtray and sipped her tea whilst I casually checked my face in the mirror.

I half expected to see the words *I've just had a bonk* etched in raised pink flesh across my forehead, Exorcist fashion. I could see Mum's smile reflected behind me in the mirror as she continued with her Gypsy Rose Lee act.

"The day I stop worrying love is the day I'm no longer here."

•••

"Right, I've got the Alpha Mike 31 the Oakland's Estate beat car, it's free for the next few weeks, any takers?"

Swirling her pen in her hand, Sergeant Scully scanned her rota. I was busy underlining the date in my pocket notebook with the assistance of a half-chewed tea coaster in the absence of a ruler and when I looked up it was just in time to see the back of Degsy, Martin, Don and Bob disappearing from the parade room into the kitchen.

"Mave, hands up if you want a coffee!" Bob shouted as he pushed past Don. I threw my hand up. "Thanks Bob, no sugar."

My eyes widened as I suddenly had a fleeting memory of my volunteering escapade at Brownie Guide Camp.

Too late.

"Ah Mavis, thank you, at least someone's volunteered; never a popular beat this one but it'll give you experience before you take over the area permanently next month." She smiled and threw me the car keys for AM13.

Sighing, I took them from her, hopefully there wouldn't be a chemical toilet or roll of SAN IZAL in sight. On the upside, these weren't the keys to Florence the Fiesta as I'd been upgraded to a Peugeot a few months ago.

Skipping each stair down to the car park, I loaded up and started off for my first shift on the Oakland's. Having a permanent beat might actually be a good idea, something to get my teeth into. I could show everyone what I was capable of. I was starting to like this idea a lot.

...

Twenty-eight minutes later I found myself back at the station preparing a ten-page report to the Chief Superintendent explaining how I had just managed to set a new world record of how to wreck a patrol car in the shortest amount of time.

"I'm going to get eaten alive on that Estate Bob, I know

I will. Do you know I hadn't even made it to a job or got out of my car?" I shook my head resignedly and ticked the box marked *yes* on the vehicle job sheet.

My welcome to the Oakland's had been so warm the locals had kindly decided to give me a present as I drove past The Sandpiper pub. A house brick, disappointingly not gift wrapped, had hurtled through the air and bounced off the windscreen of my patrol car causing a nice little web pattern to starburst, which in turn caused me to shout *shit, shit, shit* several times as I tried to regain control of the errant Peugeot.

Poor AM13 had taken a direct hit.

Bob looked up from his own paperwork with a rather sage look on his face. "You have to make a stand Mave, let them know whose boss, take control. Brendan Carmichael is the one you need to get alongside; he's run that Estate for years."

I poked my tongue out between my lips in concentration, nodded and began to write the name in my notebook.

"Mave...love, you won't need to write that down believe me, you'll know when you see him. In fact, he'll probably find you."

Those last words from Bob were still running around my head later that night when I found sleep impossible. *Take control - let them know whose boss, he'll find you...*

Bloody hell, was I dreading work tomorrow.

•••

"For goodness sake Mavis, please try to return it in one complete, intact and undamaged piece, we've only got two other cars left on the road." Sergeant Scully sighed as she handed me the keys to a pool patrol car which was covering for the damaged one.

"I will Sarge, I've been up half the night deciding on how I'm going to handle the estate. Am I still going to be permanently posted there, it's just that Bob said..."

She quickly interrupted. "Shall we just see how we get on today hey? Let's try walking before you run."

With her experienced advice still ringing in my ears, I set off for the Estate.

As I trundled down the main Twickendale Road towards The Sandpiper pub, keeping my eye out for stray bricks, I had a bit of a déjà vu moment. All the ingredients from the previous day were there.

Bare chests, tattoo's, Lacoste tracksuits and baseball hats, hoodies and Adidas trainers, all enjoying the afternoon sun and several pints. I had done my research; this was where Brendan Carmichael, along with his boys spent their afternoons. These were the ones I had to speak to.

No way was I going to wait for Carmichael to find me; I was on a mission to find him and then Mavis Upton was going to lay down some ground rules.

Oh yeah, halleluiah, praise the Lord and all that jazz.

Pulling up outside I had the distinct feeling that maybe I'd bitten off more than I could chew. The beautiful weather had brought them all out. They were crammed together outside the pub, even spilling out onto the pavement, pints in one hand, ciggies in the other. I prayed there would be no errant bits of debris coming my way as I straightened my tie and slapped on a bit of Coral Blush lippy for maximum effect.

Crossing the road, head high with an air of false

confidence, I could already see the look of consternation mixed with annoyance on their faces as slowly a large group started to form, headed by the man himself.

Brendan Carmichael, the 'Godfather' of The Oakland's.

My heart pounds and a trickle of sweat slowly meanders down my back.

Looking at him I realise that I am very much in danger of losing my lunch as my stomach churns itself into knots. Brendan is a rather large chappie at 6' 4", who according to the lads on the Section, eats granite for breakfast and subsequently shits out trendy kitchen worktops for B&Q. Although he's in his 40s, he still holds the respect and fear of anyone who knows him, either in person or just by virtue of name; and at this moment in time his face tells me he isn't a very happy man.

Okay, Mave girl, keep it cool.

Fumbling in my pocket for my lippy, I quickly gave my lips another liberal smear, smacked them together and strode purposefully towards him.

A deathly silence fell over the entire crowd as Carmichael pointed at me. "We don't need no bizzies here, you should know that girl."

Under the thickness of my combat pants my knees are desperately trying to knock together but failing miserably because of my chunky thighs. I swallowed hard.

Oh come on Mavis, for feck's sake, this is ridiculous, you're a police officer, start acting like one.

The little voice in my head was almost screaming at me in frustration.

I'm scared, but I'm not going to show it, not to Brendan Carmichael, not to anyone.

This was my beat and I'll work it my way with or without their co-operation and deep adoring love. They merely had to get to know what my way was.

Simples really.

I stuck my chin out and looked Brendan defiantly in the eye. "I'm not just any old bizzie Brendan, I'm Mavis, pleased to meet you."

I stuck out my hand. Brendan looked at me, looked at my hand, threw out his own chin and puffed up his torso to double his size.

Oh shit, I've misjudged this.

He stared at me, snorted and spat on the pavement beside him, then after a wait that seemed like an eternity, he stretched out his hand, and albeit reluctantly, shook mine.

I took a deep breath, ready to impart my next line.

"Look Mr Carmichael, can we just get something straight? I've been posted down here to this Estate; I don't have a choice, if I don't have a choice, then neither do you."

He looked bemused, but I ploughed on.

"What you see is what you get, you're all just going to have to get used to it. I'm here to stay whether you like it or not."

I sounded more confident than I actually felt, my heart was still pounding and my palms were distinctly sweaty.

Carmichael still didn't say anything, he just continued to stare at me. I wasn't giving up.

"Now if you don't do anything wrong, I won't hassle you, but if you do something wrong, I will lock you up." I paused to let that sink in before I continued. "I will treat you or anyone else fairly and with respect but I will expect that respect back, understand?"

Still no reaction, this wasn't looking good. I had visions of hospital food for a few weeks, but in for a penny, in for a pound. Humour, that's what I needed, it had worked for me before.

"So, here's the deal. There are three things you don't do to me." I began to count them off on my fingers.

"Don't smudge my lipstick, don't mess my hair up and don't make me run because if you do and I catch you, I will slap the back of your legs very, very hard. Okay?"

By now they must have pigeon-holed me as a lunatic, but they hadn't killed me or strung me up on the nearby lamp post yet which had to be a bonus.

I stood there daring him to speak.

Nothing. I was half expecting the proverbial tumbleweed to blow across the car park. I swallowed hard, eying up how far it was to my car and debating how quickly I could get to it and lock the doors.

Just as a flow of adrenalin started to kick me in the calf muscles, Carmichael started laughing.

"You've got balls girl; I'll give yer that." Turning to the crowd behind him he nodded. "She works round here – got it?"

I gave a tacit nod of acknowledgement, turned on my heels and walked back to the car, which I was more than happy to report was completely undamaged, still had all four wheels, a klaxon on the roof and absolutely no gobs of spit anywhere about the bodywork or windows.

I had done it. I had shown them who was boss, taken

control, I'd told them how it was going to be.

Hadn't I?

Back at the station over a cup of coffee, I began to tell Sgt Scully how my afternoon had panned out and how confident I now felt working the Estate on my own without much trouble. Beryl, being longer in service and an awful lot wiser wasn't completely convinced.

"Well, that's as maybe Mavis, but this is not up for negotiation. I've got a warrant here on your beat; the lad's got form for kicking off so I'll be coming with you."

One look from Beryl told me that regardless of how successful I thought I had been, it would be futile to disagree.

...

"Right, Jackson Paul Kenwright's 23 years old with a long list of previous convictions for commercial robbery."

She handed me the briefing sheet and warrant details. I quickly scanned it. On this occasion he was wanted for a burglary at the home of an 82-year-old widow and had a failed to appear in Court for a previous theft, hence the warrant. He'd been lying low for a few weeks and not just from us. There were certain offences that Carmichael wouldn't tolerate, thieving from the elderly and vulnerable was one of them. Subsequently Carmichael's crew were also looking for him according to our intelligence.

"Hand your car over to the night section Mavis, we're one down because of the smashed one, we'll take Florence." She threw the car keys to me. I was amazed that good old Florence the Fiesta was still going strong.

Jackson lived in a ground floor flat in a small block on

the Twickendale Road and half an hour later we were parked up outside. Beryl, was squeezed into the front passenger seat, the gracefully long legs of her 6'1" frame finding slim purchase wedged under the glove box.

Popping a tab of chewing gum into her mouth, she opened the door and unravelled her legs onto the pavement, reminding me of one of those ridiculous clown dolls that have excessively long striped legs that you could roll up and flick back out again.

"Bloody hell Mavis, now I know why I prefer to walk! Right, no messing, if he's going to kick off, shout it up and we'll back off."

I nodded. I'd had dealings with Jackson before, and he hadn't given me any problems, but I suppose there's always a first time.

The blue door to Jackson's flat had seen better days. Peeling paint, deep gouges in the wood that looked suspiciously like axe indents adorned the door frame. The number 2 wobbled precariously and tilted to the left as I banged on the door.

"He's in Sarge, I can hear someone breathing behind the door."

Beryl drew her truncheon, keeping it dropped along the length of her leg, just out of sight in anticipation of any trouble.

The door creaked open to reveal Jackson, in his best tracky bottoms and hoodie, bouncing from one foot to the other, arms out in front of him, wrists held together.

"Here you go Miss, handcuff me, I'm not going to cause you no trouble, promise," he grinned.

I clicked the first cuff into place. "I'm starting to think you actually like wearing these Jackson."

His grin got even bigger, spreading right across his unshaven face. "Rather youse than Brendan's boys Miss. If you've got me, I'm safe."

I placed the second cuff on Jackson, and it suddenly started to go very, very wrong.

Hearing a noise from inside Jackson's flat, I turned just in time to see something that resembled Uncle Fester from the Addams Family bearing down on me, roaring like a bull, shiny bald head down and going full throttle along the length of the hallway, arms waving manically in the air.

"Aaaaarrrrrrgggghhhh death to the infidels... I am immortal... I live to kill."

Frozen to the spot by the shock of this rampaging vision, I started to laugh. Beryl, being one step ahead of me, had already run into the foyer, making for the front door of the flats and to my surprise Jackson started to run as well, dragging me along behind him as I had hold of the handcuffs. I was still laughing as we burst out into the fresh air.

"I've got the keys; I'll drive!" shouted Beryl who was already half way down the path.

"For fuck's sake get a move on, it's me mate and he's coked out. I can't handle 'im, he'll kill yer if he gets his hands on yer!" jabbered Jackson in genuine terror.

Not wanting to be in a position to doubt his first-hand knowledge of his idiot friend, I bowed to his superiority as he dragged me towards the car. I couldn't believe that I was actually running full pelt to keep up with my own prisoner, who just happened to be haring ahead of me to seek safety in *my* police car with *my* Sergeant.

As we reached the car I looked behind me. Fester was charging through the main doors to the flats, literally, as wood and glass fragments splintered across the pathway. He clearly hadn't felt the need to open the door before he went through it.

Unfortunately, this was where our problems more than doubled. The Fiesta only had two doors.

So here we are, trying to squeeze Jackson into the back of the car in a panic, no easy task as he isn't exactly a lightweight. With a bit of a shove he went in headfirst and ended up wedged behind the passenger seat with his backside stuck in the air. His legs were still hanging outside the car.

"Just bloody jump on him Mavis, anything, just get him in and shut the door." Beryl was sitting in the driver's seat jangling the keys in the ignition.

Closing my eyes and asking for forgiveness I got both of my hands, one on each of Jacksons' buttocks and gave another almighty shove which sent him lurching forward into the foot well behind the driver's seat. Hearing the roar of Fester getting closer, I glanced up to see him just a few feet away and gaining on us.

Jackson was squealing like a stuffed pig from the floor at the back. "If he catches up we're fucking dead; he'll tear us apart, he's a madman."

Screaming at Beryl to get a move on, all the niceties and acknowledgement of rank forgotten, I threw myself into the passenger seat and slammed the door shut.

"He didn't use the door Beryl... he just went straight

through it…, we're absolutely faarked if he gets hold of us." My brain was working ten to the dozen trying to think of a way out of the mess we'd just got ourselves into. "1261, 1261 urgent assistance, Twickendale Road heading towards Arno Road."

Banging the gearstick into first and foot on the accelerator, Beryl roared off along Twickendale Road in a cloud of smoke. I had almost let out a sigh of relief when I looked back and was horrified to see Fester attached to the boot of the Fiesta, slamming one fist repeatedly on the rear window.

Beryl slammed the brakes on in an attempt to dislodge him. He slid upwards so that we were treated to glimpse of his hairy white belly squashed against the glass as his pants began a slow descent. The momentum of Beryl's sudden braking continued, carrying him further upwards as he disappeared over the roof of the car only to slide slowly down the windscreen on the other side. At this point we were treated to a little more of his manly, but very small meat and two veg as it slithered down the windscreen before he rolled off the bonnet and out of sight.

In the stillness that followed, I looked at Beryl. Beryl looked at me. Neither one of us wanted to get out and see if he was still alive. Suddenly a faint disembodied voice drifted up from the floor behind her seat.

"Hey Miss, just wonderin', what's the chance of me gettin' bail after all this?"

Beryl's face was a picture. "Jackson, I hardly think this is the time or the place to discuss that burning issue do you?" she snarled just as Fester's huge face appeared at her side window pulling on the door handle, screaming obscenities with his eyes popping out on stalks as the sweat and spittle splattered the window.

Shrieking, Beryl slammed her foot down on the accelerator again and we shot off leaving him standing in the road, jumping up and down like a demented Tigger. The car engine was squealing fit to burn, still in first gear, even though we had cleared well over a mile. Only then did I allow myself to turn and look at Beryl.

Contorted behind the steering wheel and showing signs of acute embarrassment, she glared at me.

"Don't even go there Mavis... I'm warning you!"

With Jackson stuffed behind the driver's seat, which had been set to my vertically challenged height, poor Beryl had not had the time or room to make any adjustments to suit her stature in the earlier panic.

Her legs had nowhere to go so her knees had ended up hugging her ears like a set of Canadian earmuffs, making it impossible for her to reach the gearstick.

"Jeez Sarge, always knew your gear changes were a bit suspect, but this?" I wiped away a tear of laughter from the corner of my eye.

Beryl let out a nervous giggle "Well if you weren't such a dwarf Mavis my dear, we wouldn't be in this bloody predicament now would we?"

Before I could retort, a muffled voice from the back cut in.

"... well if I'm not getting bail, any chance of stopping at the chippy for a special fried rice before you take me in 'cos youse lot have made me miss me tea!"

I looked over into the back seat to see Jackson still wedged in the foot well.

"It'll be a Bridewell butty and a mug of tea Jackson, like it or leave it." I winked at Beryl.

"I'd shake on it Miss if I wasn't feckin' handcuffed," he grinned.

Once at a safe distance and with other patrols on route, we stopped to compose ourselves. After much huffing and puffing we managed to re-adjust Jackson to a more comfortable position, Beryl changed places with me and then the three of us collapsed with an attack of the giggles, fuelled partly from fright and partly from the ridiculous positions we had got ourselves into.

Fester was located still sitting in the middle of the road with a serious case of metal chaffing and testicular bruising where Florence's blue roof lamp had potted him like a snooker cue to a billiard ball. He was promptly arrested for an outstanding warrant, obstruction and criminal damage to the police car.

Once Jackson was lodged in custody, we sat back with a mug of tea and a couple of chocolate digestives in the night kitchen to debrief our little episode.

Beryl swore never to drive Florence the Fiesta ever again, I had another ten-page report to the Chief Superintendent to explain the snapped rear wipers, smashed blue lamp and dent to the bonnet of Florence along with a slimy streak of unmentionable bodily fluid on the windscreen...

... and Jackson Paul Kenwright stated during his interview that it was the most fun he'd had in years.

IS THERE ANYBODY THERE?

"Honestly Mum, I should've been scared, but I was too busy laughing." I slurped my tea, spilling a dribble down my t-shirt.

Mum passed me the box of budget tissues she kept down the side of the sofa.

"I know you keep telling me you can look after yourself Mavis, but really, sometimes I wonder which side of the family you get your ginger ho attitude from." She shook her head in exasperation. "Here, give it to me you've missed a bit."

Snatching the tissue from me she spat on it and began to vigorously wipe my chin, reminiscent of my childhood days. Only then it was chocolate not Typhoo tea.

"Ginger ho! I hope you're not being defamatory against redheaded Ladies of the Night?" I giggled uncontrollably at my own joke. "It's gung-ho, a gung-ho attitude."

She checked the tissue, rolled it in a ball and threw it into the wastepaper bin. "Whatever, you know what I mean Mavis."

"Now that's what really scares me Mum, I always do!"

...

Returning to work after having a fun filled couple of rest days with Ella and Joe, I swung my car into the much-coveted parking space next to the industrial wheelie bins, two broken chairs and a bike minus its saddle, when I spotted Petey.

He was obviously having a bad start to his night as I

watched him grapple with his rucksack, which had become firmly wedged in his car door.

"Evening Mave, hhrrmff, I erm...is the grrrmff...is the new lad starting tonight, do you know, hey?" Looking at me expectantly as he pulled and tugged on the unyielding bit of khaki canvas, he grinned and winked.

He was so desperate to have someone else who would run the gauntlet of pranks, jokes and general teasing, the prospect of another one on the section had sent him into raptures. No matter how good natured the teasing was, Petey had decided he'd enjoyed his fair share and how wanted to be one of the ones that was playing the games rather than being the butt of them.

"Yes Petey, he's with us from tonight but..."

A loud ripping sound interrupted me as he gave one almighty tug and catapulted himself across two parking bays, landing on his back, as the material on his rucksack gave way scattering a cheese and ham sandwich, two packets of smokey bacon crisps and a strawberry Telly Tubby fromage frais across the tarmac.

Hastily picking himself up to retrieve his goodies, he continued to mumble to himself. "Super, oh super so what have we got planned for him hey? Can we do the wet weather bike test Mavis? I could do the hosepipe bit, that'll be such a laugh."

Shaking my head and smiling to myself, I headed off to the locker room, leaving him muttering away in childish excitement as he disappeared under a car to grab a packet of Iced Gem fancies from behind the rear tyre.

To the rhythmic banging of locker doors as we gathered

our kit for Parade, Bob shouted across the din. "Yo Mave, all set for later, can't wait to see his face. Promise it will defo be the last time. Let's call this one for old times' sake eh?" He winked with an impish grin as he clipped his tie into place.

Shoving an avalanche of old sweaters, mismatched slash-proof gloves and half a box of 70 denier black tights circa 1989 back onto the shelf, I gave him the thumbs up and slammed my locker door shut. "Just don't go too far Bob, he's quite a sensitive soul really."

All through Parade Petey jiggled and wriggled in his seat in unbridled excitement at what the night was to hold, whilst keeping a watchful eye on our newest member, Constable 5682 Shaun Lovell. Now, contrary to what Petey believed, although Shaun was new to our Section, he'd already served six months in a neighbouring Division so wasn't as wet behind the ears as Petey thought. Looking from Petey to Shaun and then to Bob and then to our helping extra hand, Adrian Weldon from B Block, I felt a bit guilty knowing what I knew.

Getting Petey on his own after Parade, I ran through our plan of action.

"We're not doing the wet weather prank, mainly because it's raining which defeats the object, so you with a hosepipe wouldn't be very funny would it?"

Petey took a minute to digest this snippet of information, chewed his lip and nodded.

I ploughed on. "So we're going to do the old body in the mortuary one, okay? It's not been done for a while so it should be good."

He grinned in approval, happy to be part of the planning.

Final preparations in place, our little prank was all set for scoff break at 2 a.m, dead of night. The bewitching hour. Petey was doubled up with me again and as I tested the lights and klaxons and checked the vehicle log book, he sat in the passenger seat rubbing his hands together in glee.

"Right Mave, can I just run through it again. I get on the slab and then when Shaun comes along I jump up and shout Aaaaarrrrrrggggghhhh…"

I closed the book, started the engine and ran through it with him again. "No Petey, once in the mortuary you go to the cold storage section, get on one of the empty trays and cover yourself in a sheet, I'll slide the tray back in, close the door and you just wait in there. Got it so far?"

He chewed the end of his pencil and then stuck it in his left ear, giving it a robust jiggle. "Yep, yep got that Mave."

"Right, okay. You don't move, you don't say anything until the tray is pulled out again by Shaun. He'll have been sent to check a tag on what he thinks is a John Doe. Still with me?"

Inspecting the end of the pen he gave a nod as he vigorously wiped it on the sleeve of his jumper. I grimaced.

"So that's when you sit up and start groaning, still with the sheet on but for God's sake watch your head on the tray above."

He nodded with a vague look of understanding on his face. "Yep, yep, got that." He paused for a moment and added "Err Mave, what's a John Doe?"

"Bloody hell Petey, we're in a mortuary, what do you think a John Doe is? There's going to be at least six other dead bodies in there with you, are you sure you want to do this?"

As Petey chewed his bottom lip in silence, I stifled a

giggle. What neither Petey or Shaun knew was that the mortuary was closed and empty of any residents as a new chiller was being installed the following day. For the price of two packets of digestive biscuits and a Cadbury's fruit & nut bar, we had endeared ourselves to one of the mortuary assistants and had secured thirty minutes of uninterrupted time in the existing chillers before they were removed.

The early part of the night shift passed quickly with only one drink driver and two minor scuffles outside Ali's AbraKEBABra shop.

Indian Joe and his lovely girlfriend Liberty Lil had objected to the lack of chilli sauce with their kebabs. Subsequently Ali had objected to Lil ripping off her rather rancid, crusty fishnet tights to use as a duster to wipe the word 'Chilli' from his window display whilst advising him on the Trade Descriptions Act.

At 3 a.m. prompt, Petey was ensconced on tray 5 in the mortuary, covered head to toe in a white sheet after having climbed between two shroud covered bodies who were the residents of trays 4 and 6 in the stacked chiller cabinet. As much as the excitement of getting one over on Shaun had thrilled him, he clearly hadn't been thrilled at the prospect of being in such close proximity to dead people, but his desire to be one of the lads was stronger than his fear of a corpse.

Sitting up on the tray, with his eyes as wide as saucers he pointed to the shrouded bodies above and below him. "Oh God Mavis, do you know what they died of, it's not catching is it?"

Lying him back down on the tray and covering him again with the sheet I reassured him. "Petey, the dead can't hurt you, they're dead, gone, deceased, not of this world. Look, if you don't want to do this..."

He let out a long sigh before putting on his best stiff upper lip. Resigned to playing his part he leant back in repose whilst I pushed his tray back into place. As I slammed the door shut I could hear him giving a very muffled and quivering rendition of '*Jesus Wants Me for A Sunbeam*' from inside.

At 3:10 a.m. on the dot, Shaun, after receiving a radio message to attend the mortuary, was preparing to open the huge stainless steel door which housed trays 4, 5, and 6, which in turn contained the two unidentified bodies and sandwiched in the middle of them, our very own shivering Petey. As Petey held his breath in eager anticipation of playing a rather good jape on Shaun, he suddenly heard a groan emanating from Tray 4 above him.

"Oooh it's a bit bloody parky in 'ere innit?" wailed a ghostly voice.

Poor Petey froze in horror as a second voice moaned from Tray 6 below him.

"Yeah, no shit you can say that again. I popped me clogs in me underpants on the way to the bog, I'm feckin' freezing me nuts off in here."

A brief silence followed before the occupant of Tray 4 sighed.

"Hey, you in No. 5... what did you die of then?"

Petey, suddenly remembering that he was the occupier of tray 5, let out a scream of utter terror whilst banging his head on the bottom of Tray 4. The realisation that his two neighbouring dead bodies had just spoken to him was too much for him, finally tipping him over the edge...

... just as Shaun opened the door and started to pull out the tray containing the screaming Petey.

Seeing the shroud covered vision screaming and flailing in front of him, Shaun howled, Petey screamed again, the residents of Trays 4 and 6 screamed and wailed and Shaun turned on his heels and legged it through the doors into the night air, closely followed by Petey with his sheet attached to his trousers, billowing in the wind.

As the mortuary doors slammed shut, in the eerie silence that followed, I came out of hiding to see Bob and Adrian swinging their legs over the side of trays 4 and 6, completely helpless with laughter as they flung off their sheets, waving their arms in ghostly fashion.

"Woooooo that was bloody epic Mave, a two-fer-one. Did you see them go?" Bob wheezed with laughter sending him into a coughing fit. "... Ade, when have you ever worn gandipants mate?"

Adrian was lost for words.

I had a horrible feeling that wherever they were by now, Petey and Shaun would be very grateful for clean underpants, any style, any colour or any brand.

LOOKING FOR ARTHUR

"Police Officer of the Year, it's a huge honour just to be nominated, and you'll never guess what? If I win it, I get to go to London. London Mum, can you believe it?"

I could hardly contain my excitement. I'd never been to London; it had been my dream since I was a little girl. I had naively believed because Enid Blyton's books were published in London, that she actually lived in the offices of *Hodder & Stoughton* having a grand old time there solving mysteries, and I had so wanted to meet her.

Mum sat pondering my news and the prospect that Mrs Upton's daughter could get to meet famous people. She half smiled, but there was a definite look of concern on her face.

"That's lovely Mavis, but if you do win and you get to flit off to London just make sure you don't get Thailanded and end up dancing in one of those strip clubs." She slapped a large blob of Lurpak on her over-toasted crumpet.

"Thailanded Mum? What on earth has Thailand got to do with it, it's London?"

She took a bite of the crumpet and licked her fingers before throwing the butter knife into the sink.

"You know, when they drug you, or hit you over the head, force you to do things you don't want to do, that sort of stuff – Thailanded. It's serious stuff Mavis, they'll have you dancing *The Flamingo* on tables with no clothes on."

I thought for a minute, putting into practice years of experience with her malapropisms.

"It's shanghaied Mum, that's the word you're looking for..." I pinched a bite from her crumpet and reached for my mug of tea. "...and I really can't imagine me or anyone else dancing The Flamenco in the buff can you?"

•••

"I'll vote for yer Mave, after all, you make a cracking cup of tea." Bob laughed and snorted tea through his nose, which in turn made Don baulk.

I slid my notebook into my top pocket along with two well chewed pens before sitting down between them. "I haven't got a chance, there's so many nominated for it, but it would have been lovely to make Mum really proud of me and of course..." I suddenly thought of Dad again.

I had spoken to the family tracing unit at the Salvation Army, filled in the questionnaire and sent it back with my registration fee. So far, apart from their updates over the months that had followed, nothing had come back for him.

Don read my thoughts.

"Maybe he doesn't want to be found, have you thought of that? Your mum still lives in the same house; he could have made contact any number of times over the years but he hasn't Mave."

I breathed in sharply. "I know, but maybe he's ashamed, or scared. He might want to see me but not Mum, after all he did run off with the last coupon for her Jayne Mansfield bra," I laughed.

I looked up to see them both exchange a leery look.

"That's it Mave, maybe yer dad ran away to be a Drag

Queen!" Bob almost choked on the mouthful of tea he'd just swigged.

"Oooh Arthurilla Queen of the Desert..." Don slapped the table with his hand making the milk bottle shake, "...actually that's a thought, he might not even be in this country anymore, he could have gone abroad and made his fortune, you could be the daughter of a multi-millionaire."

I blew on my tea to cool it before taking a sip. "I'd rather be the daughter of a dad that actually wanted to have a daughter to love, not abandon."

A silence blanketed the table, neither Bob or Don felt it appropriate to add to my observation.

10 DOWNING STREET

I came hurtling through the front door, slamming it shut behind me.

"Mum, Mum... I did it! I got it, I'm Police Officer of the Year, Mum!" Throwing the front room door open, it bounced off the side of the sofa, almost knocking me senseless on the backward swing. "I'm getting a trophy and a Commendation certificate and stuff like that AND I get to meet the Chief Constable for butties and cake..."

I knew I sounded like a small child who had just won the three-legged race at the school sports day, but I just couldn't contain myself, I wanted to cry with excitement.

"Oh Mavis, I knew you would, well done I'm so proud of you." She wrapped her arms around me and gave me the type of huge hug that only a Mum can give.

"...and guess what else?" I excitedly breathed.

She paused to spark up a cigarette in celebration, puffed until the end glowed, blew a straight stream which plumed out and billowed into the shaft of sunlight streaming through the window. "What? More excitement? Never!" her eyes twinkled as she teased me.

"I'm going to Downing Street Mum, I'm going to meet the Prime Minister..." I flopped on the sofa beside her, "...and you can come too."

...

I gently thumbed the embossed invitation bearing the

Downing Street crest and placed it on the mantelpiece, leaning it at a perfect angle against the wooden candle holder so that I could continue to admire it.

It *requested the pleasure of the company of* one *Mavis Upton* to share in an evening of jollification and other exciting adventures with the Prime Minister himself, Tony Blair. Dress uniform was obligatory. Placing my bulled shoes in the bottom of the suit carrier, I gave a last-minute check of my uniform for any stray unmentionables like poor Norma's, zipped it up, folded it and carefully pressed it down on top of the neatly ironed clothes already packed into my case.

"Taxi's here Mavis, you'd better get a move on." Mum's high pitched excitable voice was reduced to a muffle as she dragged her own suitcase down the path to the waiting car.

I grabbed my invitation, admired it one more time before stuffing it in my handbag.

"Oh the picnic, don't forget the picnic, it's in the kitchen, those *bouffant* things on trains are far too expensive so I've done my own." Satisfied she had everything, she disappeared into the back of the car whilst I went back for her picnic.

The white plastic CO-OP bag had seen better days and the flask peeking out of the top was missing a crucial component – the cup, but bless her, she had gone to town with ham sandwiches, scotch eggs and enough crisps to feed the local Scout group for a month.

Buckling my seat belt for the journey to the train station a warm glow swept over me, which incidentally had nothing to do with the now leaking flask of tea.

Scotch eggs, crisps and my mum, what more could a girl want for the start of an awfully big adventure?

...

Dragging my borrowed suitcase along the platform at Euston, we emerged outside into the sunshine, 3 hours, 11 minutes and 22 seconds after the train had rumbled its way out of Lime Street station.

I stared, open mouthed at the hustle and bustle going on around me. Huge hoardings advertised Chicago as the *must see* revival musical at The Adelphi Theatre, a young girl breezed along, her bleached white hair splayed out like a halo, the laced red platform boots striking the ground in rhythm. A smartly dressed man with a burgundy silk scarf draped around his neck, paused to check his watch and then quickly carried on, sidestepping a middle-aged woman who almost spilled her take-out coffee in the unexpected dance with him.

This was London.

I had arrived.

Not as an excitable child to see good old Enid Blyton at Hodder & Stoughton's offices; but as plain Mavis Upton, lover of Primark thongs and the wonderful Joe, covered in scotch egg crumbs and broken crisps.

Booking into our hotel, I left Mum admiring the streak-free mirrors and fancy pop up ashtray, which in turn left the Concierge perplexed as he intently watched her pressing the gold button several times, fascinated by its swirling action as it threw up clouds of ash.

"Come on Mum, lets unpack and have a nice cup of tea in our room." I waved the key card at her. She was desperately trying to wipe the offending ash from the arm of the leather sofa.

"Gosh, I didn't expect that to happen, did you Mavis?" she rubbed her hands together as the lift juddered to a halt bringing us to our floor.

"I don't think the Concierge did either, I thought he was going to throw you out!"

Crinkling her nose, she shrugged, twirled her suitcase by the handle and strode out into the thickly carpeted corridor.

I opened the door to our suite and stood back.

"Here you go, home for the next two days...and nights!"

Dropping her case in the doorway, she glided into the room. A few *oohs* and *aaahs* told me she was in seventh heaven.

"Wow Mavis, have a sit on this bed...and look at the curtains...and the view." She bounced twice, stood up and disappeared into the en-suite.

"Oh my goodness, you even get little bars of soap and a flannel, look at the towel, it's a...well I don't know what it is... is it a duck Mavis?"

I listened to her happy voice echoing from the bathroom, followed by the shower being turned on and the toilet seat being dropped.

"Oh my, it's a silent flush too, how very exciting!"

...

"Mum, can you check my cap badge, make sure it's in the middle, it's got to be dead centre."

As she obliged I had a quick peek through the ornate metal gates of Downing Street and checked my watch.

5:50 p.m.

Another nine minutes and I'd be allowed through that famous door along with all the booted and suited police officers from other Forces who were starting to arrive. Brushing the sleeve of my jacket to dislodge any imaginary bits of fluff, dandruff or crisp crumbs, I glanced down to give the shiny toes of my shoes another once over for anything curly that shouldn't be there. I certainly didn't want the Prime Minister or his staff to be left wondering if I was a natural blonde or not. Mum straightened my tie and checked the pewter tie pin that proudly announced my Force around the crest.

I excitedly squeezed her hand. "I'm so sorry you can't come in too, but I'll tell you every little detail when I come out, promise."

She gave me a gentle kiss on the cheek and a thumbs up, brushing away a sneaky tear with her fingers, that unexpectedly slipped from her eye.

5:58 p.m.

I handed my invitation to the Officer on the security checkpoint and walked through the gates, pausing to give her a little wave.

"Mavis, don't forget to check your teeth before you go in," she yelled giving another thumbs up.

I was mortified, unsure if I should explain to the gathered crowd alongside her, her obsession with having bits of food stuck in your front teeth when you smiled, but decided to let it ride. I was far too excited to be embarrassed for too long.

Standing in front of the famous black door, I closed my

eyes and inhaled deeply, trying to quell my nerves. When I opened them again I came face to face with my own reflection in the highly glossed paintwork, which gave me the opportunity to check my hat and slap on a bit more lipstick.

The door opened to reveal the entrance hall. I paused in awe, my breath momentarily stilled.

An expanse of black and white chequered floor tiles led to a beautifully ornate iron staircase that swept upwards into a curve. The yellow painted walls were adorned with black framed portraits hung with precision along the length of the staircase depicting past Prime Ministers.

A feeling of complete reverence swept over me. The history contained in this magnificent place was almost tangible.

"If you would care to follow me Ladies and Gentlemen." The Staff Officer began to climb the staircase, myself and several others in line behind him. He opened the door to a large reception room. "The Prime Minister will be with you shortly, please take advantage of the refreshments that are being served." He bowed his head, and left the room backwards, closing the doors behind him.

There was in excess of hundred and fifty guests and the room quickly filled with a selection of Sergeants, Inspectors, Chief Inspectors, Chief Superintendents and a couple of Assistant Chief Constables.

Blimey, you're a bit out of your depth here, Mavis old girl.

Sipping a small glass of orange juice, I gave the finger buffet a swerve. I was so nervous I couldn't entertain eating. It was also slightly daunting to note that I seemed to be the only lowly Constable amid this select gathering.

Catching the eye of a dark haired smiley sort of guy was enough to give him the opportunity to sidle over to me, plate in hand. His badge announced him as Chief Inspector Giles Gilhouley from Norfolk Constabulary. He checked out my name badge, shoved a cocktail sausage into his mouth, chewed it vigorously and dropped the stick onto his plate where it joined a gathering pile of other little sticks.

"Have you tried one of these Mavis, they're quite delicious." He held up a half-eaten sandwich.

I dodged an errant chunk of egg white that flew from his mouth, it skipped across my sleeve and landed on the carpet. "Err not quite, but I'm getting plenty of yours on my tunic every time you speak though!"

He wiped his mouth with a serviette and grinned, revealing little bits of green cress embedded in his teeth. I grimaced. Now I knew why Mum had such an obsession with teeth checking.

He looked furtively around the room, before stuffing his serviette into his pocket. "Here, take these for me and get rid..." his sleight of hand was impressive as he shoved a bundle of cocktail sticks into my own hand, "... we certainly don't want them knowing it was me who ate all their little sausages do we?"

He patted the pocket of his own tunic, gave me a knowing wink, tapped the side of his nose and sauntered off leaving me with a large handful of No.10's finest cocktail sticks.

When my search for a bin failed, I quickly shoved them into my tunic pocket, hoping to get rid of them at some point during the evening.

Continuing to mingle with the other guests, I felt quite

proud that I was at least holding my own and being a bit of a chatter-box, I wasn't lost for conversation either.

I looked over to the far side of the room where the PM's wife, Cherie Blair, was carrying out her duties, breezing amongst each little group, smiling graciously offering warm greetings and snippets of personal information she had been briefed with prior to our arrival.

Keeping my fingers crossed, I hoped against hope that she wouldn't speak to me. I mean, what did I, Mavis Jane Upton have in common with the Prime Minister's wife? I could hardly discuss crisps, big knickers or Primark thongs, one woman to another could I?

I watched as she moved effortlessly between groups, her cream chiffon jacket pristine against the dark serge uniforms of those gathered. I turned my back for all of two seconds, just enough time to grab one cocktail sausage from the buffet table and pop it into my mouth, which was unfortunately also just long enough for Cherie to cover the whole length of the room so that when I turned back, I came face to face with her. My cheek bulged like a hamster's as my throat constricted, making it impossible to swallow.

Looking at my name badge, she leant forward with her famous grin. "Ah Mavis, yes I read about you, well done. Do you find it difficult to manage such a demanding career as a single parent?"

I could feel my eyes getting wider as my brain scrambled for a sensible, intelligent answer. I stood looking at her, mouth full, with a what I knew was an embarrassingly vacant expression.

I eventually managed to swallow.

I went to open my mouth but my brain just didn't want to play, there was no connection. The seconds ticked by.

I looked out of the window, I looked back at Cherie, a little bead of sweat began to work its way down from under my fringe.

Come on Mavis, think, there must be something you can say.

"Oh gosh yes and spaghetti hoops are so expensive too..."

Spaghetti hoops! Had I just said spaghetti hoops to the Prime Minister's wife? Where the feck had that come from? The perspiration went from a trickle to a stream.

Plunging my hand into my jacket pocket I pulled out my hanky, along with what seemed to my over-active imagination, a hundred and one Downing Street cocktail sticks. They proceeded to flick and soar through the air in slow motion whilst I could only look on in horror as they bounced off Cherie's beautiful jacket, before settling, scattered on the expensive carpet.

I choked back a nervous snigger.

"Oh, I see you have taken rather a liking to our cocktail sausages Mavis..." Cherie smiled in a sort of *'spider catches the fly'* way. "... they are rather popular with our guests."

With that, she smiled again and floated on to the next group.

I just wanted to curl up and die on the spot. I also wanted to kill Inspector Giles Gilhouley.

The ensuing perspiration from my failed meet and greet with Cherie had made my freshly pressed shirt stick along the entire length of my back. Knocking back my third large orange juice, I could feel my body temperature starting to settle at a more normal level, but I was now regretting my over indulgence.

I desperately needed the toilet.

Renowned for having a bladder the size of a peanut at the best of times, I checked my watch. Confident I had plenty of time for a visit to powder my nose before the Prime Minister would make his entrance, I wandered off to find the loos.

Pushing open the relevant door I let out a gasp. It was the height of luxury; even the toilet roll was amazing. I was in seventh heaven; just wait until I tell Mum. I tore off sheet after sheet, I was so impressed. None of your budget stuff here, you'd never poke your fingers through something this thick even on the most vigorous of wipes.

I spent a good ten minutes trying out the soap, hand creams and sniffing the bowls of potpourri, running my fingertips across the curve of the gold-plated taps. It was all very sumptuous and elegant. Checking my watch, I started to make my way back to the reception room.

Drenched in Lavender & Rose mist I stood in the middle of the room and looked around. Not to state the obvious, but there was something very much amiss.

It was empty.

I was in Number Ten.

In an empty room. Alone.

All by myself. Solo.

How the hell could over a hundred and fifty people just disappear?

Resisting the urge to start looking behind the curtains and drapes, I stood there feeling like an extra from the Twilight Zone.

The overwhelming silence was suddenly broken by a ripple of applause coming from behind a set of large double doors behind me. Opening them quietly, I took a peek into the next room. With their backs towards me, were all my fellow guests.

They were facing another door on the far side of the room, which I could just about see over their heads. I dragged a little footstool from under the window and stood on it. My view wasn't much better, I could only see the top portion of the door above an ocean of various colours, textures and styles of hair.

As the applause died down, the top of the door opened, there was a brief pause before it was closed again with an audible click, leaving just the steady hum of conversation from those gathered to bounce musically off the walls.

I flopped down on a nearby chair.

With an awful, gut wrenching stab of disappointment and embarrassment, the realisation hit me that in my haste to check out the bogs at Number 10 Downing Street, the Prime Minister had been and gone...

... and I had missed him. I wanted to cry.

Nice one Mavis you absolute bloody twonk.

•••

I emerged from 10 Downing Street some two hours later and stood with my new found friend, Giles Gilhouley; who had since apologised for his cocktail sticks, and a rather short, tubby Chief Superintendent from some strange sounding place in London.

Whilst having the obligatory photographs taken with

that famous shiny black door behind us, my stomach was in knots wondering what I would tell Mum. She was excitedly waiting by the gates to hear of my wonderful adventure in every detail.

I felt such a failure.

Mavis Upton had come to London all expenses paid to see the Prime Minister, a once in a lifetime opportunity and all because of a bladder the size of a peanut coupled with my curiosity to check out the toilets and feel the thickness of his bog roll, I had missed him.

I had not even seen a hair of his head above the crowd.

Nothing.

Zilch. Zero. Nada.

Diddly squat.

I couldn't even use the term 'not a sausage' as that brought back too many awful memories thanks to Giles and his bloody cocktail sticks.

After saying my farewells to everyone; that is everyone who HAD got to see the Prime Minister, not that I was bitter or anything, I sloped off along the pavement towards the gates where I could see Mum waving frantically with her head forced between two railings.

Hugging me furiously, knocking my hat off, she could hardly contain her excitement.

Her eyes were shining with tears as she took my hand.

"Oh Mavis, I have always been proud of you, but never more so than I am now, how wonderful, someone from our family with the Prime Minister. Go on then, what did he look like?"

Silence.

You know sometimes how you just have that sort of moment when your heart rules your head, where you know what you should say, but you also know that if you tell the truth it will let someone down?

Well I was having one of those moments now.

I looked at her face, I looked at the anticipation and pride, I looked back at Downing Street, I looked at my feet and I did the only thing that I could have done under the circumstances.

I lied.

"Oh Mum he was lovely, much taller in real life, and quite handsome in a funny sort of way. We talked for ages, it was fantastic and yes, he was very nice."

There, I'd done it.

I had lied to my Mum, something I hadn't done since I was 15 years old when I had vehemently denied biting a large chunk out of her special cheese in the fridge. I had only confessed when she had threatened to send it for dental impressions along with a missing alert on her silk French Knickers which had mysteriously disappeared around the same time. I had lied then too, blaming my brother for the known whereabouts of those little frillies, which was something I don't think he has ever forgiven me for.

I stood looking at her face and felt absolutely dreadful. It was a vision of pure, unadulterated happiness as she looked from me to Downing Street and back to me again. I had to believe that just a small lie was justified.

On the train home my conscience was in ruins as I struggled with the onslaught from her wanting more and more detail of my meeting with Mr. Blair.

"So, come on Mavis, what was he wearing? Did Cherie have on that dreadful red lipstick? Oh I would have given her a little woman-to-woman advice about that." She sighed wistfully looked through the window at the passing countryside.

Now, there is one very important fact that you need to know about lying, to be successful at it you must have a good memory. I was lucky if I could remember what I'd gone into the toilet for, let alone a string of untruths, deceit and downright lies. By the time we had reached Liverpool Tony Blair had been wearing a rather fetching suit from Marks & Spencer's in charcoal grey with a pink shirt and matching tie.

Why pink I have no idea, but it seemed to make her smile. We had intelligently discussed the Country's economy and the vision for the Police Service and he had thanked me for my contribution. I should really have stopped there, but I was on a roll, so what the hell.

"...and you never guess what Mum, Mr. Blair loves cheese on toast, but detests liver and onion dinners. He sleeps for eight hours a night without fail and always has Shredded Wheat for breakfast and he confided in me that Cherie snores incessantly."

I know, I know, that was one too many, but I couldn't resist and it made her laugh. I had achieved what I had set out to do, to make her proud and I had made her laugh and be happy too, that had to be a bonus.

Waving goodbye to her at her front door later that night, I silently vowed that I would never, ever let her know the truth.

She deserved her dreams as much as anyone.

THE UNFORTUNATE DEMISE OF MR BARTHOLOMEW BLYTHE

Petey was sitting in the Enquiry Office finishing off his notebook when I bounced into the radio room after having regaled Bob, Don and the rest of the Section with my Tales from Downing Street. Clicking my radio into the harness, I initialled the sign-out book, picked up the car keys and made my way into the corridor.

"Petey, have you picked up the overnight crime reports? Oh and don't forget a new log book for the car and your butty box. I'm not stopping anywhere Maccy D's for you today, you're starting to look like a bloody cheeseburger."

Rolling his eyes and groaning, he stood up, tipped his flat cap at an angle and began to chew on an imaginary piece of gum. "Yeah Mave, you got it."

As we rounded the corner, Petey trailing behind with his hands in his pockets, I spotted the first of many posters, stuck to the wall and swaying in the gentle breeze drifting in from the open back door to the nick. Petey's face was super-imposed over the head of a rather comical and bedraggled donkey, wearing a seaside straw hat.

Petey's face dropped. "Oh bloody hell Mavis, why me, it's always me, how the hell was I supposed to know they were doing a raid?"

I screwed up my nose and bit down on my bottom lip trying not to laugh.

Petey had been hauled before the Section Inspector

to discuss his 'poor performance' on his beat area. He had apparently failed to tackle a parking problem caused by visitors to a local house of ill-repute which had been causing much consternation to local residents. Very few customers took the bus to avail themselves of the 5 star services offered inside by Madam Penelope Perfection, preferring their fancy cars and the ability to park on the pavements and obstruct driveways in order to leg it to the front door to be first in the queue.

Complaint after complaint had been lodged but Petey had so far not issued one Fixed Penalty Notice. Consequently, this lack of action had proved to be a stroke of bad luck for Mr Bartholomew Blythe, a 68-year-old retired bank manager.

Mr Blythe's desire to beat a younger, more agile customer to the front door of *The Little House of Raptures* had caused him to park his shiny Mercedes into, over and on top of a nearby wheelie bin, wedging it firmly under the front end of his prized car. Spilling out of the driver's seat to make the rest of the way on foot, Mr Blythe had negotiated a street lamp, two further wheelie bins and a skip, and had breathlessly made it to the front door first.

Displaying a particularly smug smirk, he'd been welcomed personally by Penelope Perfection herself and had disappeared inside, leaving the younger customer at the gate.

Sadly, if Mr Blythe had taken the time to scrutinise his adversary in his mad dash for a knee tremble, he might have noticed the ear-piece he was wearing which was connected to a police issue radio, which was attached to the belt that held a Casco extendable baton and a pair of handcuffs under his denim jacket.

Alas these little appendages were not extras for an anticipated tryst of hot and steamy sexual encounters within the walls of 23 Worcester Close but standard issue for all police officers.

Much to the surprise of all who surveyed the rapidly developing scene, the young man who Mr Blythe had left at the gate, suddenly started to run up the driveway shouting *"Go, go, go."* as the front door to the *Little House of Raptures* was trashed by Constable Dexter Collins of the Rapid Entry Team with his bright red metal enforcer.

As Mr Blythe was led away, flushed and excitable, the realisation hit him that if he had taken the time to park properly, he would have been behind our fresh faced plain clothes detective, Ian Cottrell, rather than in front, and as such would not now have the honour of being front page news of the local Gazette whilst attired in his best Marks & Sparks 100% cotton red striped boxer shorts and a pair of gaiters holding up his socks.

After the successful closure of the Little House of Raptures was concluded with eight arrests and a large quantity of Class A controlled drugs seized, the search logs, warrant and paperwork signed off, all involved returned to their respective unmarked police vehicles that had hastily been abandoned at various locations in the road.

Their elation was short lived as each of the six vehicles, as owned by the Chief Constable, now sported a Fixed Penalty Notice slapped on the windscreens for parking contraventions.

Each ticket was proudly signed with a flourish:

Constable 1469 Peter Thackeray A1 Division

Petey had done it again. He had provided his now completely exasperated Inspector with a result but had coupled it with an awful lot of extra paperwork to the Chief Constable explaining why the Police Finance Department would be billed for parking offences on their own vehicles.

Looking at him standing in the corridor shaking his head at the posters, I couldn't help but feel some sympathy for him. He tried hard but always seemed to bugger everything up. I had to try something to build his confidence.

Jumping in the patrol car, I decided to give him a little pep talk as I drove out of the station yard.

"Look Petey, it's just a case of thinking before you act, a few seconds delay can mean the difference in getting it right. It's lateral thinking mate, just think things through."

He had mused this for a few seconds before opening his mouth to respond but was cut short by the radio.

"Alpha Romeo 21, can you make to a report of a Sudden Death, details to follow when you're ready. Discovered by the deceased G.P."

Arriving at the white picture postcard cottage, the Doctor led us in single file upstairs. Opening the bathroom door, we were greeted by a vision of none other but Mr. Bartholomew Blythe himself, ensconced on the soft close seat of his avocado low level flush toilet, paisley pyjamas around his ankles, The Sun newspaper on his lap, bent forward with his nose stuck firmly to page 3.

Mr Blythe had sadly breathed his last whilst performing his bedtime ablutions and enjoying the charms of a particularly well-endowed young lady courtesy of the tabloid newspaper.

Petey let out a nervous snort. "Oh shit Mave, he's really

dead!" He quickly clamped his hand over his mouth.

The doctor gave me an incredulous look, I returned it with an apologetic grin.

"No suspicious circumstances Mavis, he's had heart surgery and has been living on borrowed time for years." The doctor flipped the lock on his bag and straightened his tie. "There'll still need to be a PM though."

"Thanks Doc." I took the paperwork from him. "Petey, if you're going to barf, go outside or at the very least use the sink."

Petey's gag reflex was working overtime, I could hear him heaving outside on the landing.

Waiting for the undertaker to arrive to transport Mr Blythe to the mortuary, I began to check around for anything that would point to a next of kin. Twenty minutes later, after a chat with his next door neighbour, I'd ascertained that he'd been an eternal bachelor with no family. I found it all quite sad really, a man alone in the world. Apart from his little visits to Madam Penelope Perfection, which we had put a stop to the previous week, he had nothing. That was what probably made him resort to The Sun newspaper.

Jeez, that reeked of desperation in my book.

Giving a last glance at his neat little sitting room, I ran back upstairs to check on Petey, who had gone unnervingly quiet. I pushed open the bathroom door and there he was, sitting on the edge of the bath, mouth wide open, gazing at poor Mr Blythe. He barely dragged his eyes away from the rigid corpse before he spoke.

"You know Mave, we shouldn't really leave him here you know. It's so... you know, undignified. Can't we just move him to the bedroom?"

Now this is where alarm bells should have rung loud and clear. This is Petey; the sort of guy where his Fairy Godmother would tap him on the shoulder with her magic wand and shout *'Turn to shit'* because invariably with him, everything did.

Sighing, which was all I ever seemed to do when I was with him, I began to wonder why I wasn't listening to my inner voice as I started to help move the unfortunate Mr. Blythe. With Petey on one side, me on the other, I tried to lift him off the toilet whilst Petey pulled up his pyjama bottoms.

As Mr. Blythe had been there for in excess of twelve hours, rigor mortis had already set in and The Sun newspaper was firmly clenched in his hands, proof that even in death he was not going to relinquish his page 3. Having covered his modesty, we started the task of getting him from the bathroom to the bedroom. Mr Blythe was currently holding his 'sitting position' quite rigidly and as we tried to negotiate the narrow bathroom door onto the tiny landing, I realised that he was now completely the wrong shape to angle around and fit through the door. We tried anyway but his knees became wedged on the door frame and no amount of wriggling would free him.

"Petey, go back a bit, lean over towards the bannister. That's it...bit more, bit more...oh bloody hell grab his pants, they're dropping down."

By now Mr Blythe had twisted round and Petey, finding the weight was getting a little too much for him, started to sag putting him in a position where his face was inches short of Mr Blythe's posterior. As luck would have it, this was the exact same moment that the build-up of gasses contained within Mr Blythe decided to seek an escape route.

A resounding '*paaarrrrp*' bounced off the walls of the narrow landing.

"He's farted Mavis, oh God he's only gone and farted in my face!" Squealing, Petey wrinkled up his nose and let go of Mr Blythe in order to take the opportunity to wave his hands manically in the air, sticking out his tongue whilst displaying a very girly fit of pique, leaving me to prop Mr Blythe up on my right knee whilst holding him under his armpits.

"Bloody hell Petey for God's sake, grab hold of his legs or I'm going to drop him."

"... but Mave, he farted; I think I'm going to be sick."

"Believe me sunshine, you'll be more than sick if I get my hands around your throat – just pick up his bloody legs!" I roared.

Reluctantly he grabbed hold, but not before he had turned seven shades of purple through holding his breath.

After much huffing, puffing and trying to remember how I had moved my awkward two seater sofa from one room to another the previous month, we began to work on the old adage that where there's a will, there's a way and eventually managed to get poor Mr Blythe into his bedroom and onto his bed.

Standing back, we surveyed the scene.

"Aww, we can't just leave him like that, it's just not right, you've got to do something, please Mave."

I stood and looked at Mr Bartholomew Blythe, retired banker, valued client of *The Little House of Raptures*, long term subscriber to Men Only and shook my head.

He was now lying on his back, legs bent at a right angle, knees almost to his chest with The Sun newspaper still firmly clutched in his hands, as though he was sitting on an invisible bog.

I glared at Petey whilst I prised the paper from Mr Blythe's clenched hands.

Looking around the room I found an old copy of The Guardian on his bedside cabinet.

Opening it at the Stocks & Shares, I placed it between his nose and his knees, sat him up, plumped up his pillows and brushed his hair into a side parting.

"Oh that's so much better Mavis, thank you. You know, he could almost be waiting for a bacon butty and a cup of tea in bed instead of being...well...you know...sort of dead!"

No Petey, I really didn't sort of know...

...but it was most definitely a better class of newspaper.

A FINE ROMANCE PART III

"I do get a bit fed up Mum, we're on completely different shift patterns, working out of different nicks, we hardly get to see each other."

I gave a petulant pout as she emptied her Theakston's ashtray into the bin, wiped around it with a tissue and plonked it back on the coffee table ready for the next cigarette butt.

"Sometimes that's the best way Mavis, absence makes the heart grow fonder."

"I know, but I think Joe's getting a little impatient, maybe he's getting bored with me." I twisted my watch round so the face was sitting centre of my wrist.

She sat herself down into her chair, curled her feet up underneath her. "I don't think so sweetheart, you're far too erotic for him to get bored, being different only excites men, believe me."

"Jeez Mum I hope you don't go around telling people I'm like that; they'll think I'm sex mad!"

The confusion on her face was a picture. "What's sex got to do with being stressed out and unpredictable Mavis?"

I gave a sigh of relief and a snigger.

"Neurotic Mum, I think the word you're looking for is neurotic!"

•••

After one of my little chats with Mum I normally felt better about whatever in life was troubling me. This time, although it had been funny, I still had a sick underlying feeling that Joe and I were in trouble.

Bloody relationships, just how difficult can they can be, you'd think I'd be old enough to know better. On second thoughts, maybe I did. If I moved in with Joe, which was what he wanted, I just knew it wouldn't be long before the fairy dust would lose its sparkle.

I ran a little scenario through my head whilst drying the dishes, the typical day to day living with someone, once the first flush of love had faded.

He'd wake up, fart, shove me out of bed to put the kettle on. Livid, I'd stomp across the bedroom, fall over his shoes, get my foot hooked in his boxer shorts on the landing, fail dismally to regain my balance and head-butt the nearest wall.

His glossy April issue of GOLFER'S MONTHLY magazine would be left on the third to last step of the stairs which would then give me the added impetus when I trod on it to skid sideways into the kitchen tearing pages 2, 3 and 6 whilst completely shredding the 'Win My Balls' Competition page sponsored by Tiger Woods.

I shuddered at the thought.

It actually wouldn't surprise me if Joe ended up like Degsy Fairburn. On a drunken night out, Degsy's wife Lillian, had thrown back a couple of gins, her screaming laughter filling the small pub.

"That bastard over there blows into the palm of his hand and then sniffs it before a bonk, don't you Degsy my little love bug, just to see if it's worth brushing his teeth first."

Degsy had squirmed whilst Bob, Martin and Don almost choked on their pints as the girls grimaced. Unfortunately,

Lillian wasn't finished. "I'm telling you girls just you wait until they wobble their fat backsides to the bathroom..." She had paused to prod a finger into Degsy's overhanging gut. "... they always feel the need to piss their initials in the bog and leave a permanent puddle on the floor which guarantees you'll find it with your bare feet when it's your turn to pee."

Degsy had got to the point where he couldn't take anymore. Downing the last of his pint, he had stood up, wiped his mouth and loudly announced before departing the pub:

"Ladies and Gents... that ain't no lady... that's my wife."

I dropped the last spoon into the cutlery drawer and hung the damp tea towel over the radiator. Regardless of Golfers Monthly, Tiger Woods or artistic weeing in initials, was I really ready for everything living together would entail?

...

Valentine's Day arrived and so did a huge bouquet of red roses with a note from Joe to be ready for dinner at 7 p.m. Ella had packed her overnight bag and was excitedly staying the night at Mum's. I had on my new LBD and for one night only, I went a little more up-market at Primark.

Instead of paying fifty pence for a thong I splashed out and bought one for ninety pence.

This one had a little red bow on the front. I felt Joe was worth the extra forty pence.

He arrived on time smelling of Paco Rabanne and Imperial Leather soap. I stood on tiptoe to give him a kiss...and missed. If I hadn't known better, I could have sworn he'd sidestepped me.

Feeling a little embarrassed, I jumped into his car, making sure I was sitting 'side saddle' so my big curvy butt and thighs didn't interfere with his gear changes. The time we'd been together had taught Joe how to find the handbrake without committing an act of indecency on me, which in turn negated the need for me to punch him on the nose.

The restaurant he'd booked was part of a beautiful old Manor House, set in the most breathtakingly landscaped gardens. As his little car swept along the driveway I knew I should feel happy, but Joe seemed very tense and distracted and I began to wonder if I should have gone the extra mile and bought Primark's exclusive range knickers at £1.50 a pair just to cheer him up.

"This is so lovely Joe, very romantic," I gushed. We were sitting at a table overlooking the gardens, the trees lit with twinkling lights, the moon dipping in and out of the clouds.

Silence.

"Joe, I'm talking to you, it's very romantic isn't it?"

"Oh umm yep, it is that." He looked uncomfortable and went back to swirling his spoon in his gooseberry coulis.

"Would Sir and Madam prefer coffee in the lounge?" I looked up to see the Maître d', tray in hand, waiting for an answer. Joe went a very strange colour, patted his jacket pocket, took a deep breath, stood up, sat down again and began to fold his napkin.

"Sir?"

"Oh umm yes, yes thank you...the lounge..."

As the Maître d' weaved his way through the tables, Joe stood rooted to the spot. "Mavis, I...err...I oh dear, I don't know how to say this but ...." he tailed off.

My heart sank, hitting the bottom of my stomach like a stone.

I'd been here before.

Looking at Joe with mournful eyes, I shook my head. Not waiting to hear anymore, I fled to the powder room. He was going to dump me; I just knew it. That was why he was so uptight and it was all down to my reluctance to make a commitment. Typical, what a time and a place to pick, bloody Valentines night of all nights. He was probably only doing it here because he knew I was too much of a lady to go all dramatic and tearful in public and throw a hissy girly fit.

Locking the door shut behind me, I sat on the toilet and wept, yanking streams of paper from the roll to wipe the mascara that was streaming down my face.

Hold on a minute!

I could feel my indignation rising.

I wasn't going to be discarded like a... like a... I looked at the cardboard roll I was holding... *like a used sheet of bog paper. Oh no, I was worth so much more than that.*

Unlocking the door, I checked myself in the mirror, blew my nose, wiped my mascara streaked face and nipped back into the toilet for a quick wee. Sitting on that renovated 1920s chain flush bog, swinging my legs whilst unravelling the fresh loo roll, I decided that I would show Joseph Stephen Blackwell exactly what he would be missing.

Emerging from the loos, head held high with lipstick and mascara freshly applied, I prowled back into the lounge. Well, sort of half prowled with a bit of a stagger thrown in for good measure. I clung to the doorframe to steady myself.

Oooh careful my girl. Several glasses of red wine with the meal were definitely starting to have an impact.

I grabbed a large glass of wine from the tray being proudly held by the poor bemused waiter standing by the door. Taking a genteel ladylike sip, I followed up with a large slug and then several more gulps for good measure, until I had drained the glass. Slamming it dramatically back down on the tray, I fixed Joe in my sights as I tottered over to him.

I could see looks of admiration from the other men in the room who were smiling at me, so executing what I thought was a very sexy wiggle, I sashayed for the last few feet until I reached him.

Standing in front of him I bent forward and winked. Joe's eyes were as wide as saucers and he was flushed pink.

Way to go Mavis, just like Marilyn Monroe would do it. I was sizzling.

Leaning forward I slurred into his ear, as breathless and sexy as I could under the circumstances.

"I know what you're thinking and I know what you're going to say. I sure as hell won't give you the satisfaction and go all weepy on you, but just look at what you'll be giving up."

...and with that I spiralled around in an elegant pirouette so that he could see all my facets – or should I say, my assets.

"See it and weep Joe, see it and weep," I purred.

I was just about to launch into another slurred onslaught, when, flustered and red, he quickly interrupted.

"Mavis Jane Upton, for once in your life just shut up for one bloody minute so that I can ask you something."

Taking a deep breath, he dropped to one knee and with a flourish produced a little red velvet box. He fumbled trying to open it whilst I could only stand, my mouth wide open in shock.

Oh jeez, what have I done?

I wanted the ground to open up and swallow me. I caught sight of my reflection in the huge wall to wall mirror. Marilyn Monroe had been replaced with a fair impression of Phyllis Diller. This wasn't how I was meant to look, what on earth had happened between the toilets and here?

"Mave, will you marry me?"

I was stunned.

Nodding like an idiot I squealed *Yes, yes, yes* over and over again, but unlike Sally when she met Harry, I didn't have a table close enough to bang on in sublime ecstasy.

Joe slipped the ring on my finger.

"You have just made me the happiest man alive but can you please, please just sort yourself out Mavis, everyone is looking at your knickers."

Reaching my hand behind me, which was now adorned with a sparkly engagement ring, I could feel the reason for the manly stares of admiration, ensuing silence and the sniggering.

If it wasn't bad enough to discover that my beautiful dress was tucked firmly into my ninety pence thong allowing my cheeks to glisten in the candlelight, when I swept my hand further round, I could also feel several sheets of quilted toilet paper firmly adhered to my bum, hanging down and wafting in the breeze.

Jeez, you just can't buy class, can you?

LETTERS FROM THE PAST

"I think you just might have been slightly erotic to get that Mavis." Mum winked as she paid close scrutiny to the diamond as I waved my fingers in front of her. "Congratulations to you both, I'm glad you're going to make an honest woman of her Joe."

Joe actually blushed. "I'll look after her Mrs Upton; and of course Ella too, they both mean the world to me."

"Err, actually on that note." I felt uncomfortable; this was going to be the difficult bit.

Mum looked at me, lit a cigarette and tapped her lighter on the coffee table as she blew a wisp of smoke from the corner of her mouth. "She's awake Mavis, I swear that child's got second sight, she knows something's going on, she's been up since the crack of dawn."

Joe and I exchanged glances.

"I've bought her a little signet ring so she won't feel left out; I thought it would soften the blow when we tell her." Joe looked to Mum for reassurance.

She shrugged her shoulders. "Well there's no time like the present, you'd better go and get it over and done with but just be warned."

Joe started the ascent of the sweeping staircase with me clinging onto the back of his shirt, our trepidation making us giggle like a couple of school kids.

"What's so funny?"

Arms folded in front of her in a fighting stance, Ella stood at the top of the stairs still in her pyjamas.

"Come on sweetheart let's get your slippers, your feet are going to get cold." I patted her on the bottom and ushered her back into her bedroom, Joe remained on the landing, sitting like a garden gnome on Mum's carved monks bench.

Ella jumped on the bed and hung one slipper on the end of her foot, tongue out in concentration. I took a deep breath.

"Ella, Joe has given me a beautiful ring, he's asked me to marry him and I've said yes."

Her face fell. "Well, you can marry him but he's not living in our house, he's a man and he smells...and he doesn't like our cat... he's deegusting...he's... he's..."

At this point she ran out of derogatory descriptives for Joe as a flush of pink swept over her face and her eyes welled up, tears threatening to spill on to her cheeks.

A soft knocking stopped her in her tracks. Joe stuck his head around the door. "Ella, I've bought you a pretty ring too, so you can be like your Mum." He held out the box towards her.

Ella gave him a glacial stare that would have frozen the testicles off a polar bear.

Snatching the box, she took out the ring, placed it on her finger, momentarily admired it and then snapped the box shut.

"I hate you, you've ruined my whole, complete and entire life; I am distraught!" She angrily pulled the duvet over her head and disappeared under it.

I looked at Joe; Joe looked at me. He shrugged and let out a sigh as we closed the door behind us.

"Hmmmm, I'd say that went rather well wouldn't you?"

Err, no Joe, I don't think it did.

In fact, I thought he had just been damned to hell for all eternity.

···

Bouncing into work after my rest days and flashing my engagement ring for all to see, I didn't think my life could get any better.

Ella had recovered from her ruined life, which was now only very slightly destroyed and tattered and her melodramatic outbursts had lessened as the days progressed.

"Very flashy Mave but don't be showing it to Lillian, sure as hell I won't be forking out for something like that for her birthday; no matter what little extra's she promises." Degsy guffawed at his own joke.

Bob groaned and smacked him over the back of the head with his newspaper.

I smiled. "What little extra's would that be Degsy? Judging by your ever-expanding waistline it's got to be something to do with food!" I waved my butty box, wafting the aroma of my cheese and onion sandwiches towards him.

Degsy gave me the one finger salute as he crammed in another mouthful of pork pie.

"Heard anything more about your dad?"

I flicked off the bits of pork and flaky pastry that he'd just sprayed onto my sleeve. "Not from the Sally Army, but one of Mum's neighbours thinks she's got a lead, I just haven't got around to speaking to her yet."

Another one of those typical silences hung over the room, making me look up just in time to catch Degsy and Bob exchange glances.

"What? Why are you looking at each like that for?"

My face flushed. I hated it when they did that, it was as though they knew something I didn't.

Bob shifted uneasily in his chair, went to straighten his tie and then realised he wasn't wearing it. Unsure what to do with his nervous fingers, he plunged the index one up his left nostril and gave it a jiggle. It was Degsy who answered.

"Do you really want to find him Mave? It's just if you were that serious you'd have been standing on her doorstep the next morning to find out what she knew."

I broke my sandwich in half, went to take a bite and then changed my mind, suddenly I wasn't hungry anymore. "Maybe it's just better left as it is."

Bob ran his mug under the tap and dropped it down on the stainless steel draining board with a clatter. "In other words you're scared."

For once I had to admit he was right.

•••

"It's Arthur you're looking for isn't it?"

Mabel Clitheroe stood on her red painted concrete doorstep, the black front door behind her emphasising her large, well-padded frame. She unfolded her arms, smoothed down her green paisley housecoat, and shoved her hands into the pockets.

I nodded. "Do you know where he is Mrs Clitheroe?"

She jerked her head towards the small hallway, wiping her burgundy cord slippers on the mat just inside. "You'd better come in love, can't stand out here gossiping now can we?"

I followed her into the small kitchen and watched as she

carefully set out china tea cups on a warped and stained wooden tray. Her movements were measured. She filled the copper kettle and set it on the gas stove, using a spill to light the gas ring underneath. It was just like stepping back fifty years, but as quaint as it all was, I just wanted her to get to the point.

"My dad Mrs Clitheroe, where is he?" I waved away her offer of a stale looking biscuit.

She shuffled over to the sideboard, opened one of the cupboards and brought out a battered old blue tin that had *Jacob & Co.'s High Class Biscuits* still visible on the lid. Placing it carefully on the table she opened it and took out a small bundle of envelopes, tied together with string. Her fingers deftly parted them until she found what she was looking for.

"This is for you Mavis, he wanted you to have it, but only when you were ready." She pushed it across the tablecloth towards me.

My fingertips brushed across the aged paper of the envelope. I studied the handwriting. In dark blue ink it simply said;

FOR MAVIS

Mrs Clitheroe started to speak, but the high-pitched whistle from the ready kettle overwhelmed her words.

...

21st June, 1964
My Dearest Mavis,

It breaks my heart to write this letter to you, and only God himself knows when, if ever, you will read it. It is a very difficult letter to write, but I owe you the truth.

I have been away from your mum and all of you for almost a year now. Please understand it was not her fault, this was all about me. I am the one to blame. They call it an illness but for me it is and always will be a curse.

It was the drink, too many years at sea, too many long nights to fill, too many bars in too many ports, it haunts us in large numbers and it is our families that suffer because of it.

I watched your mum become a shadow of herself because of my drinking and how I treated her. I tried to change, but it was not to be. For everyone's sake, it was best that I went away to allow you all to have a better life without me.

Please believe me, it was a decision that was not taken lightly.

Let your mum know that it was because I loved her that I went, not for any other reason.

Yours always

Dad x

Mrs Clitheroe's hand gently patted my arm as a solitary tear slipped down my cheek and plopped onto the tablecloth. I folded the letter along the ready-made creases and went to put it back inside the envelope. It stuck halfway.

Peering inside I shook it and out fluttered a yellowing Daily Mirror Coupon advertising a moulded foam cup bra all the way from the USA...

... just like Jayne Mansfield wore.

CAPTAIN CORELLI'S UKULELE

I watched Joe prod the glossy brochure with his sticky finger, smearing jam over a particularly skimpy bikini clad female wallowing in a hot tub. "Greece Mave, how do you fancy Greece?"

I leant over his shoulder to have a proper look and recoiled in horror. Joe had hairy ears. *Eeeew, why hadn't I noticed that before?* I made a mental note to consider a pair of ear and nose clippers for his birthday.

"It looks lovely, just so long as it's hot and there's safe swimming for Ella, I'm happy if you are."

Joe frantically scrubbed at the jam smear, clearing just enough from the top half of her body to check out her, quite unnatural in my opinion, assets.

"Kefalonia it is then." He decisively circled the travel agent's number and then poked the end of the pen in his ear.

I dunked my digestive in my mug and watched as it slowly drooped, bent and dropped off onto my leg. Kefalonia, sun, sand, sea and Joe's newly discovered hairy ears.

What more could I want?

•••

For once, Ella was mildly excited.

"Muuuum, will this fit in your suitcase?" She swung her Pooh Bear onto the bed where it landed bottom up.

I checked my case. Eight full length dresses, five short

dresses, six pairs of shorts, four bikinis, nine pairs of shoes and fourteen strappy tops.

Mmmm, maybe I'd been a little excessive.

Throwing a handful of clothes out, I made a niche for Pooh, nestled him in comfortably, closed the lid, locked it, strapped it up and dragged it downstairs, bumping each step as I went.

"Joe's here Mum, I'll let him in."

Listening to Ella's excited chatter as she answered the door to him, I ran back upstairs to make a last-minute check around the bedrooms. Breezing into the spare room I groaned.

Ten pairs of newly purchased Primark thongs, in various colours, lay neatly on the bed.

Oh bugger, how could I have missed packing them?

"Car's loaded up Mave, we're ready to hit the road, Ella's got..." Joe's voice tailed off as my head disappeared into the wardrobe. Grabbing an oversized handbag from the shelf, I stuffed my Primark fineries inside along with a lipstick, a sticky packet of half-eaten Polo mints, tissues, a pen, two hair clips, passports and my purse. I gave the room another once over and ran downstairs to meet Joe.

"Hello gorgeous." Planting a rather passionate kiss on my neck, he patted my bottom and gave it a squeeze.

"Err, can we just be a little careful," I admonished, "we've got Ella to think of, you're going to have to rein it in a bit."

He looked crestfallen.

An hour later we were checked in at the airport with all three of us very much in the holiday spirit. Joe took Ella to buy a magazine and some sweets for the flight whilst I pounced on the opportunity to have a little shop in the duty free.

I sampled a nice little bottle of an unpronounceable, but very heady perfume from sales assistant Tiffany, her plastic name tag reflected brightly from the florescent overhead lights in the bustling shop. I couldn't help but notice how her vivid red lip gloss complimented the sliver of lunchtime tuna that was stuck between her front teeth.

Trying to break my gaze from the errant piece of fish, I turned my attention to the shimmering blue bottle she'd handed me with a flourish. Giving myself a liberal spray, I inhaled deeply. It was reminiscent of the musky *Midnight in Bootle* perfume, manufactured for the discerning 16 year olds of Liverpool during the 70s. It would sit on their dressing tables alongside the obligatory Charlie Body Mist spray.

I involuntarily smirked. There used to be nothing more enjoyable than asking a guy if he fancied a sniff of your Charlie and then watching the disappointed look on his face as you whipped out a small aerosol from your patchwork tasselled shoulder bag.

Waving my boarding pass with a flourish, I paid Tiffany for my beautifully wrapped gift, subconsciously poking my tongue between my front teeth in the hope it would encourage her to do the same and dislodge the unfortunate flake of tuna, before breezing back through the shop and out into the busy concourse. Joe was waiting at a table with a couple of coffees as I weaved my way through the crowd.

"Err excuse me, I think you dropped these." A young guy, sporting a smirk across his fresh face, was brandishing at arm's length a rather fetching turquoise thong between his two fingers.

I looked at him puzzled and shook my head.

"...these, they're definitely yours," he persisted, waving them vigorously towards me.

Jeez, what was it with me and knickers? They did look like mine, maybe I'd dropped them in the duty free when I got my purse out.

I quickly looked over at Joe. He shrugged and hid behind Ella's colouring book. I brazened it out. Hell would freeze over before I would admit they were mine. A quick mental calculation and I came to the decision that I would simply make do with being one pair down. I had at least nine other pairs still shoved in my handbag, ten if you counted the pair I was currently wearing.

"Sorry, you must be mistaken, they're not mine but thank you anyway."

Not daring to make eye contact with him, I swivelled on my heels and quickened my pace, desperate to reach Joe.

"Right, if that's the case you won't need these then either!" he shouted after me.

Glancing back, I was met by a rainbow of lace and cheap polyester as he swung several pairs in assorted colours from his fingers. A tropical heat of epic proportions quickly flushed from my toes to my face as I checked my bag again.

There was only one pair remaining, dangling tentatively from the half-open zip.

Shit, shit, shit.

Oh, well, there was only one thing for it if I wasn't going

to claim my colourful butt holders. I would just have to go commando in Kefalonia.

Now there was a thought as I disappeared into the crowd.

•••

"Oh Joe it's beautiful, what an amazing view."

I let out a small sigh of happiness. We were nestled between two coves with a view out to the ocean. It was idyllic.

"Mum, Mum, look it's got two pools and a waterfall, can I go and have a swim now? Please Mum, purleeeeeeese."

I smiled at Joe as Ella ran into her room to get her swimsuit. Maybe this holiday was just what we needed to help her accept our relationship. Reading my mind, Joe winked.

"I do hope we're going to get a little bit of 'us' time too Mave?"

I playfully thumped him on the arm. "The walls are paper thin, I could hear Ella unzipping her suitcase from our room, I think we might have to curb our enthusiasm or better still, wait until we get home."

Joe grimaced and looked at his watch. "A whole week Mave! Bloody hell. Can't we just whisper... or better still, lip sync whilst we're doing it?"

I thumped him again.

•••

By the third day of our holiday, I was happy, relaxed and starting to show a decent suntan. Ella had made friends with another little girl called Millie, and Joe, although not happy about it, was sort of getting used to my nookie ban. I admired his tenacity, but I wasn't budging from my decision.

He had been sulking by the swimming pool all afternoon, spasmodically coming up with all sorts of ideas to get around it.

"Oh for God's sake Joe, it's a week, just give it a rest...no means no!" I disappeared back behind my book.

He swung his legs over the sun lounger and stood up. "Coffee then? I suppose the amazingly chaste Mavis can indulge in a coffee?"

Stomping off like a petulant child, I couldn't help but laugh. I looked over to the pool where Ella was splashing around in her flippers, snorkel and mask with Millie. She was really enjoying herself and as an added bonus, she was starting to accept Joe too. I wasn't going to let anything spoil that.

"Mave, Mave."

I looked up to see Joe with his ruffled hair and obligatory ridiculous shorts, strolling back from the bar with a coffee in each hand.

"Hey guess what? Millie's mum has just said she'll watch Ella if we want five minutes to ourselves, you know, wink, wink!"

I sighed, exasperated at his persistence. "No Joe, how many times do I have to say it?" I rolled my eyes at Millie's mum who was following behind Joe.

She laughed. "Oh go on Mavis, she'll be fine with me for half-an-hour."

They'd worn me down and to be quite honest, I felt a little cuddle wouldn't go amiss. Joe grabbed my hand and like two giggling school kids, we disappeared along the path to our apartment.

Slamming the door shut behind him, I ran ahead into the bedroom. Peeping through the curtains I could see Ella happily playing in the pool as Millie's mum gave a cheery wave.

"Come here my elusive little Dumpling." Grabbing me, Joe threw me onto the bed, almost bouncing me off the other side.

"Joe, those shorts, please, they've got to go, they really are a passion killer."

He grinned. "Your wish is my command."

He gave a little dance around the bedroom as his shorts were whipped off and thrown in the air. They disappeared over his head, landing on top of the wardrobe.

Now in the time that it took to remove a sarong, a pair of bikini bottoms and Joe's shorts, and just as we were about to embark on a frisson of foreplay, I heard a rather strange noise passing the bedroom window and onto the terrace.

Flip, flop, flap, slap...flip, flop, flap, slap.

We froze in an entangled embrace. *Flip, flop, flap, slap... flip, flop.* Silence.

...and then a tap, tap, tap on the window.

Launching myself off the bed and grabbing my sarong I pulled back the curtain only to be greeted by a dripping wet vision of Ella in flippers and mask. I slid back the patio door.

"Hmmmppppffff, pheeeeet... I've been... pheeeeeeet... looking for you... Phhhharp... everywhere Mum... phffffffttttt... hmmmm-pppffftt..."

As her muffled voice radiated from behind the mask and snorkel, amid more snorts, squeaks and rasps, I tried to keep a straight face.

"Ella what on earth are you doing?" I held my hands up in exasperation waiting for a reply but before she could answer, I caught sight of Joe behind her.

He had wisely taken the opportunity to quickly vacate the apartment via the front door and was now running hell-for-leather across the grass towards the swimming pool.

My eyes widened in disbelief as I watched Millie's mum look on in horror, whilst Spiros the waiter juggled a tray of drinks in utter astonishment as Joe cut a dash through the sun loungers. I clasped my hand over my mouth just as a loud, very unladylike snort escaped.

Clearly Joe hadn't had time to retrieve his ridiculous shorts from the top of the wardrobe to wear for his marathon sprint...

...because his ample hairy backside was now tightly encased in my cerise pink, polka-dot, testicle-crushing bikini bottoms that had ridden up with each stride, giving him a rather unattractive wedgie.

JUST AN ORDINARY DAY

"It was wonderful Mum, Ella had such a great time, she was as good as gold and really took to Joe, it was probably the best thing we could have done to be honest."

She smiled. I was waiting for the ceremonial lighting of a cigarette, but it didn't happen. It struck me that she looked a bit tired.

"It's good to get away together love, I do hope you behaved though."

I choked back a snigger.

"Well..." I paused and gave her a wry smile. "... Joe had been looking forward to nookie but..."

"Newquay...!" Mum interrupted. "... I thought you said you went to Greece?"

•••

Later that night, sitting cuddled up to Joe, chewing the side of my mouth, I couldn't shake off a feeling of dread that had been creeping over me since I'd left Mum's. Something was wrong. The more I thought about it, the more my gut instinct told me to go back and speak to her, not to waste any more time.

In my hurried and busy life, I just always expected her to be there, to be...well, just Mum. Eating Lurpak soaked crumpets and smoking her Embassy No.6, wiping her Theakston's ashtray with a tissue, giving me advice, listening to my trials and tribulations.

These were the things that meant normal to me. This didn't feel normal.

"I don't think Mum's well Joe, she's been hiding something from me for weeks, even before we went away, I just didn't realise it, I've been so wrapped up with trying to find my dad and then our holiday..."

Joe hugged me closer, which only made the lump in my throat grow bigger. "She's a big girl Mavis, I'm sure if she was ill she would have been to see the doctor."

I pulled away from him, searching his eyes. "You've seen it too haven't you?"

That sounded more like an accusation than a question.

"Look, everyone gets older Mave and when they do, they start to look tired sometimes. That's just life."

A sudden surge of anger rose up. "No Joe, it's not *just* life, it's my mum we're talking about here!"

I couldn't take it in. Why hadn't I noticed her growing old and tired. To me she had always been young, fun, loving and vibrant.

She was the one who crawled around on all fours in the back garden trying to hold down a home-made banner she had painted for Ella's Blue Peter sale. Living by the beach the wind was so high it almost took Mum, the paste board and Ella's treasures out to sea, but she'd bravely held on, sitting underneath the paste board like a garden gnome with her silly knitted woolly hat and a bubble jacket.

She had the constitution of an ox and could drink anyone under the table, normally me. It didn't matter how hard I tried, I just couldn't compete. Where Mum clinked glasses until past the midnight hour, I had already succumbed by 9.00 p.m. slowly hiccupping and sliding down my chair to find solace by wrapping myself around the table leg.

She could be found many a night barefoot, singing and skipping from gutter to pavement, swinging her shoes in her hand, happily making her way home.

A woman who is funny, warm, kind, brave and like me, an occasional lush. She wasn't some decrepit, tired old woman that Joe was trying to make her out to be.

"It's no good Joe, I'm going round to see her." I disappeared into the closet for my coat. Joe followed me into the hallway.

"Do you really think it's a good idea at this time of night? She's probably in bed, or at the very least settled for the night watching the television."

I felt the words catch in my throat. "Yes, yes I do."

...

I knocked gently on Mum's front door. No reply

Light was casting a faint glow around the corners of the curtains in the window of the lounge. She was still up, unless she'd fallen asleep on the sofa.

I bent down to the letterbox. "Mum, it's me Mavis."

I waited.

No reply.

I used my key to open the door.

"It's only me, don't want to frighten the life out of you."

Pushing open the door to the lounge I saw her sitting on the sofa, feet curled up underneath her. Her beloved Theakston's ashtray on the coffee table in front of her, overflowing with cigarette stubs, a half-drunk bottle of brandy...

...and silence.

No television, no music, nothing. Just the rhythmic ticking of the old clock on the mantelpiece and Mum silhouetted against the orange glow of the fire.

She looked up at me, her eyes red from crying. "Oh Mum, what it is? What's happened?"

I studied every line and crease on her face and saw the world-weary tiredness in her eyes, and then a glimpse of something else.

Pain.

No words were spoken as I took her in my arms and I cuddled her as she used to cuddle me as a child.

As though there were no tomorrows.

...

"I'm so sorry Mrs Upton, the results are quite definite on the diagnosis."

A stunned silence hovered over the small consulting room, broken only by Mum as she caught her breath, taking in the consultant's words.

I felt sick.

"There must be something you can do, there's always something you can do. You can't just tell my mum something like this and then just say you're sorry, that's just not good enough."

I wanted to cry, no I actually wanted to shout, scream, anything... anything other than this awful heaviness I was feeling, the hopelessness and finality of it all.

"It's okay Mavis, Mr Chamberlain has done the best he can. I suspected it would be something like this for quite a while now."

She patted him on the knee, as though he were the needy child that needed comforting. Without saying another word, she stood up, smiled at him and walked out of the room.

Running after her I could only watch as the smallest and loneliest figure I have ever seen disappeared along the corridor, through the doors and outside into the sunshine.

I caught up with her.

"Don't tell me sweetheart, I don't want to know how long I've got. It's my life and if I want to laugh, smile and enjoy it, I'll do all of those things – but my way, it's the only bit of control I'll have left. Please understand that."

We sat in silence together on the bench, feeling the weak warmth of the sun on our faces. She smiled, held my hand, and then spat on her tissue and wiped away my tears, just like she always did when I was a little girl.

"Just promise me love, when it's time, will you stay with me, I don't want to die on my own..."

I nodded. There were no words to speak, there was nothing in this world that I could say or do that would make things better. She looked off into the distance, lost in her own thoughts.

"... oh and I don't want soggy butties and people weeping and wailing at my funeral. I want a party, a damned good knees up so I can say goodbye to the ones I love and a bloody big sod off to those who got right up my nose over the years."

She grinned, flicking her famous two finger salute, the wrong way round, she pursed her lips and made a '*phhttt*' sound.

"Is that a deal?"

...

"Right, stick the kettle on and let's get our heads round this."

Mum threw her handbag onto the sofa and rummaged around inside. Out came the packet of Embassy No. 6, her lighter, a notebook and pen. Dragging the ashtray towards her, she lit up.

Standing in the kitchen willing the kettle to boil faster as I didn't want to waste a second of being with her, I checked the calendar on the wall.

Six months.

Six poxy months. With luck she would have another Christmas with us, another birthday with me, but that would be it. No spring, no summer.

I couldn't imagine my life without her.

It was like drawing an imaginary circle around one day; I flicked the calendar over and counted.

March.

It would be like living up to that day and then what? Nothing. Would I cease to exist too? That was how it felt. I was going to lose her and in doing so, I would lose myself.

"Mavis, where's that cup of tea, I'm spitting feathers here, there's a couple of crumpets in the fridge they'll go down nicely too."

Jeez, Mum and her ruddy crumpets!

Pen in one hand, cigarette in the other, she was busy scribbling away when I returned with the tray of tea and of course, her butter-laden crumpets.

"I've made a note of a few funny little anecdotes that you might want to use, you know, for my sending off."

"Bloody hell Mum, I can't do this right now, it's not right. We've got to be positive, you sound like you're giving up." Tears started to sting my eyes. I fought them back.

"Now, now don't be silly, I've got cancer, there's nothing they can do, there's nothing anyone can do. The facts speak for themselves. We need to remember the good times sweetheart and there's plenty of them."

I opened my mouth to answer her, but she quickly cut me off.

"I've just been thinking about that Christmas with Geraldine, I don't think I've ever laughed so much as I did that day." She smiled wistfully.

I did remember, in fact how could I ever forget?

Getting fourteen of us around the table for Christmas dinner had been a feat on its own, and throwing 98-year-old Great-Grandma Lucy into the mix had caused a few raised eyebrows when my cousin Geraldine, after several pints of Foster's lager, announced to the gathered revellers that she was gay. She assured us all it had absolutely nothing to do with the fact she was also a vegan or because she had short hair and liked drinking pints.

Great-Grandma had been beside herself with happiness and had fully supported Geraldine by replying; *'That's nice dear we should all be very happy and very gay, after all it is Christmas!'* The whole table had dissolved into laughter, leaving a rather baffled Great-Grandma to raise her glass in toast to Geraldine being *'gay'* and very happy.

"I think it was the beer Mum, she had been knocking them back a bit."

She waved her hand at me as she took another sip of her tea, clattering the cup back onto the saucer. "She didn't drink Mavis; she was teetotal."

"No, not Great Grandma, I mean Geraldine. I think

I'd known for years Mum, but what a time and a place to announce it though."

Mum laughed, spurting tea onto the coffee table. "Couldn't believe how quiet it went around the table could you Mavis? I mean to say, it's a generation thing really, who'd have thought Geraldine would have had the nerve to announce to everyone she was living over a bush!"

She tapped a cigarette out of the packet. I almost choked.

"Muuuum, it's living over the brush... b-r-u-s-h... brush!"

"I know Mavis, but I thought bush was more fitting under the circumstances!"

We both burst out laughing.

She patted my hand. "So as you can see Mavis, there is ALWAYS something to put a smile on your face. You just keep remembering that, no matter what happens."

Tired from laughing, she leant back on the cushion and closed her eyes. I drew the throw around her, took off her glasses and placed them on the coffee table as her rhythmic breathing gently slowed.

I looked out of the Georgian window, watching the rain pool along the neat wooden squares before dripping onto the window ledge, catching the half-light from the street lamp. A young girl hurried past, huddled underneath her bright orange umbrella, keen to get home to shelter and warmth.

Life carrying on as normal.

ONCE SEEN, NEVER FORGOTTEN

"I'm so sorry love, if there's anything I... or any of us can do, just give a shout, we're always here for you." Bob looked as distraught as I felt.

Degsy and Don nodded in unison.

"Thanks boys, I'm still trying to get my head around it, I'm not ready to give up just yet, miracles do happen." I felt another lump gathering in my throat. These lumps were starting to become a bit of a regular visitor in my life. Every time I thought about what lay ahead Lenny the Lump would come out in force, almost choking me. I seemed to be on the verge of tears every five minutes. I finished making a brew and plonked myself down at the table.

Bob refilled his mug and grabbed another biscuit from the tin. Squeezing himself into a nearby chair he unclipped his tie, dunked his biscuit and surveyed the room.

"Here yer are, this'll cheer you up, did you hear about Petey's latest escapade with Betty? I swear that lad was at the back of the queue when they were handing out brains."

I shook my head and carried on rifling the tin for a decent biscuit that Bob hadn't taken a bite out of.

"Well he took time due from work to surprise Betty and get home early, you'd been giving him a few tips of the art of seduction hadn't you Derek?"

Degsy nodded and smirked.

"So he goes home and Betty, all surprised like, answers the door in some red lace number. Petey gets frisky and tries his hand but she looks horrified and says she'd rather have a glass of wine and watch a bit of telly..."

We hung on every word as Bob shifted his position on the chair and stretched his legs out.

"...so he points out that she looks like she's ready for bed anyway, gives her a hefty slap on the bum and chases her upstairs."

Apart from the slurping of tea and the odd 'oh faark' when a soggy biscuit, dipped too long, dropped into someone's mug as we still hadn't found the perfect dunker, you could have heard a pin drop.

Bob paused for effect.

"Well, half way up the stairs Betty starts talking dead loud like, making such a rumpus, half the neighbourhood would have heard her. Tumbling onto the bed with her, Petey hears a loud bang from the en-suite; so it's a bit of coitus interruptus like. He only goes and grabs Betty's best bristle hairbrush and runs into the bathroom like a hero..."

He paused again waiting for a response.

"Bloody hell Bob, come on!" Degsy was getting impatient.

"Hold on I'm getting there, so he comes into work the next day, all innocent like and tells us all this whilst we're trying not to laugh, I mean come on?"

The upshot of Bob's story was that poor Petey had imparted to half his section the story of Betty, her red lace Ann Summers finery and the intruder.

Bob continued, mimicking Petey's high pitched voice to perfection. "So he does no more than blurt it all out on parade, like this '...*bit of a bugger really lads, the shower had been leaking for weeks and Betty had only gone and managed*

*to get this guy to come and have a look at it. Really good of him
to be honest, it was late at night and he was still working on
it AND he didn't charge her anything. Can you believe that?'*

Apparently they didn't.

I was still giggling to myself over what had been dubbed
Betty's Secret Shag and the naivety of poor Petey, when the
Sarge called me in.

•••

Groaning at the prospect of a whole night shift with the
frustratingly dense at times, but nonetheless sweet Petey, I
shoved my kit into the boot of the car and jumped into the
driver's seat. I couldn't understand why it was me again. In
my book it had been Bob's turn, but the Sarge felt that Petey
needed a gentle approach and that I was perfect for the job. I
had a hunch that under the circumstances it was because she
didn't want me working on my own whilst I was fretting over
Mum, idle hands and all that.

I was just envisaging the prospect of a very long night
when the radio burst into life with Heidi's high-pitched
squeal. Petey hastily recovered his slouched position in the
passenger seat, eyes wide in anticipation, clutching a scrap
of paper and his trusty Bic biro poised in his hand.

"Oooh, it's a job Mave, hope it's on us, me bum's numb
with all this sitting."

I glanced out of the corner of my eye to look at him.
Ignoring the fact he was doubled crewed with me in a nice
warm patrol car, he'd still spent the better part of twenty
minutes in the locker room preparing himself for a foray into
the tempestuous imaginary storms he believed would strike

at some point during the night.

Woolly jumper, body armour, functional jacket topped off with his quilt-lined florescent coat, all strung together with his utility belt clipped on the outside and pulled together so tightly he could hardly breathe.

He now resembled a brightly coloured, double sided pan scourer. I smirked as he struggled to fasten the seat belt around him.

"AM21, AM21 can you start making to a Grade 1, possible Burglary in progress, neighbours report hearing unusual noises from The Harringby Chase, Dawsett Drive."

The area was the higher end of the market with large detached houses in extensive grounds. The last job I'd been to around there had ended with me chasing a Billy Burglar through a Greek Mythology designed garden hosting several half-dressed statues. I'd lost count of how many times I'd grabbed hold of a rather large manly appendage to stop myself from falling over. In hindsight, even Shirley couldn't boast to having clutched that many.

Putting my foot down on the accelerator, blues flashing in the descending dusk, Petey excitedly acknowledged the call. Heidi marked us down as responding.

"Bob's backing you up with Martin, they'll make the rear of the property on a silent approach."

We arrived at the huge mock-Georgian house in less than four minutes, Bob was just swinging his car into the cul-de-sac that ran behind the house. He disappeared out of sight.

A few seconds ticked by, broken by Martin's voice over the radio on talk-through. "Mave, we're in position at the rear, there's banging and shouting coming from the first floor."

Petey was fair straining at the leash in rising excitement. He could hardly contain himself, flicking one handcuff round and round in its holder. As he shuffled his boots in the foot well, I placed a restraining hand on his arm.

"Don't slam the car door when you get out, Martin thinks there's definitely someone in there, just stay calm, okay?"

He paused and exhaled loudly. "Okay Mave, but stay with me won't you, don't leave me on my own, it's dead dark out there..."

I gave him a sideways glance. At least he had the decency to blush.

"... it's just so I can look after you, that's what I meant really." He waited for some sort of acknowledgement but I was already thinking two steps ahead.

"Right, we'll go on the count of three, Bob will be in position by then."

With his hand on the door handle, he nodded enthusiastically as I began to count. "Okay...one, two... three."

I jumped out of the car and keeping to the shadows, ran through the gates and up the driveway towards the front door. I knew Bob and Martin would be doing exactly the same at the back of the house. Worryingly, although I was pleased not to hear Petey slam his car door, I didn't hear his usual gasps of exertion coming from behind me either, but I did hear a sort of muffled *thwuuuump* followed by a loud groan, gravel being kicked and a breathless voice rasping from the darkness.

"Oh shit, oh bugger, Mavis they've got me... I'm a man down Mave..."

My heart thudded in my chest. Skidding to a halt, churning

up gravel and dust, I turned and ran hell for leather back to where I had left him. Sweeping the beam from my Maglite torch around the nearside of the car, it caught Petey slumped against the open door, wedged between the grass verge and the gutter, rubbing the back of his head.

"Mave, I've been ambushed, I've been hit from behind, they've taken me by surprise."

I knelt down to check on him as his muffled wails tapered off. Apart from a huge bump to the back of his head, he was fine.

"Look at this you ruddy idiot?" I pointed to his handcuffs. "You've only gone and handcuffed yourself to the bloody seat belt when you were messing with them before."

Fumbling in my pocket for the keys, I ran the scene through my mind. As he'd tried to gather pace to follow me, digging his feet into the grass verge Usain Bolt style, ready for a quick take-off, the utility belt around his waist which held the handcuffs had refused to succumb to the strain. Even as the seat belt reached its full extension, the handcuff holder had held its own, yanking Petey backwards onto his butt whilst slamming his head against the side of the car.

"You absolute bloody muppet Petey..." I quickly unlocked the handcuffs. "Ambush, man down! Where the feck did you get that from? Come on, quickly the lads will be in there by now." Helping him to his feet, I shoved him in front of me, and started back up to the house.

Bob, who had already gained entry, was waiting for us in front of the open front door.

He had a huge smirk on his face. "You know how you've always said that nothing would surprise you any more Mave?

Well you've just gotta come and take a look at this."

With Petey in tow still rubbing the back of his head, I followed Bob up the winding central staircase to the first floor. Turning the handle of the second door along the corridor, Bob beckoned us forward.

Standing to one side, he opened the door with a flourish...

...and there in all his glory was the owner of Harringby Chase himself.

The Right Honourable Rupert Monroe Carrington-Browne, tied tightly by each wrist and ankle of his lightly tanned limbs to the four-poster bed by an oyster pink, fine-grade, woven silk rope.

If this vision wasn't bad enough, Rupert had embarrassingly chosen to attire himself in clothes from the Burlesque period and was currently sporting fishnet stockings, a red lace midi-basque with matching thong, a rather fetching pair of red spiked stiletto heels and a set of bronze nipple tassels that were now hanging limply down, somewhat tantalisingly, under each of his hairy armpits.

Sitting next to him on the king-sized bed was the delicious *Lorretta LoveHoney*, half deflated, slumped to one side, still rapidly losing air via a soft, gentle hissing that was coming from under her left vinyl buttock. She was frozen in time, her ruby red mouth mocking the unfortunate and very miserable Rupert.

Eyes wide in embarrassed horror, Rupert began to mumble. "She only went to make a cup of tea, but I think she forgot to come back."

I picked up an empty monogrammed leather wallet that had been carelessly thrown on the bedside cabinet alongside a glossy call card that announced *'Mademoiselle Femme Fantasie'*.

"Would this be the lady in question?" I held up the card.

He nodded and looked wistfully towards the window. "She wasn't cheap either," he whispered.

It quickly became apparent that Rupert, after paying for the procurement of her services, had allowed himself to be ensconced in his current predicament, whereupon she had quickly done a runner with a substantial amount of his cash.

Trying to show a concerned face of utmost discretion so as not to compound The Right Honourable Carrington-Browne's embarrassment, I choked back a snort of laughter and turned to look at Petey, who at this point was standing, open mouthed and glued to the spot.

I threw a blue silk dressing gown at him that had been draped over a nearby chaise lounge. "Petey, untie Mr. Carrington-Browne and help him to get dressed will you, I'll be back in a minute."

He caught the dressing gown and gave me a look of complete and utter confusion, as though he didn't know where to start.

I took him to one side.

"Just get him dressed mate, and for God's sake be discreet. We can't all have the same sexual preferences, don't make him feel even worse than he already does."

As I reached the bedroom door I heard Petey sigh loudly. "... but Mave."

I turned and gave him a withering look, just as Rupert chose that moment to disappear under *Lorretta LoveHoney's* left buttock in a futile attempt to slow her deflation with more air. Petey stood, transfixed.

Emerging onto the landing, I came face to face with Bob and Martin who had been using Rupert's quilted bog paper to wipe away their tears of laughter. Not being so lucky I had to resort to wiping my now streaming nose and eyes on the sleeve of my jumper.

"Tell you what Mave..." Bob collapsed again into a further fit of the giggles, spluttering over his words as Martin held onto the bannister rail.

"...it certainly brings a new meaning to the phrase 'blow job' doesn't it?"

"Bob, trust you! You know who he is though don't you?" I paused, waiting for some sort of recognition. After all, Rupert's face was currently splashed all over the newspapers due to his high-flying political career. Before anyone could answer the bedroom door slowly creaked open to reveal Petey sitting on the bed, with the newly released Mr. Carrington-Browne on one side of him and *Lorretta LoveHoney* on the other, with a bronze tassel clutched in each of his hands.

To the faint hissing of the doll as it continued to crumple to one side like a weekend drunk, Petey swung the tassels from side to side.

"...to be quite honest Sir, I don't think red is really your colour, or even bronze for that matter..."

Rupert, holding his head in hands looked pleadingly at me as Petey continued to offer his worldly advice.

".... and if you shaved your legs, the hairs wouldn't poke through the fishnets so much, it really does ruin the full effect you know Sir."

THE LAST CHRISTMAS

"I don't think there is anything in my life that I could regret. There's a few things I would've liked to have done but I suppose it's a bit late now."

I looked up from my book. "Oh I don't know Mum; I think you've set the world on fire a few times over the years."

She thought for a moment. "I suppose I did, didn't I? It seems such a long time ago now."

Slotting the bookmark into the page I was still reading, I closed it and placed it on the coffee table. She had been reminiscing a lot these past few days. Sometimes it lifted her spirits, other times, like tonight, it weighed heavy upon her.

"Tell you what, how about a take-out? Come on, you love Chinese. What do you fancy?"

She leant back on her pillow and closed her eyes.

"You know what Mavis; I've always wanted to try that automatic duck thing they do with the pancakes. Yes, I think I'll have some of that."

My eyes stung a little and Larry the Lump made another appearance in my throat, but I still managed a smile.

"Righto Mum, one order of Aromatic Duck on its way."

•••

Pointing one foot out from underneath the duvet, I tentatively tested the air. Cold. In fact it was very cold, which could only mean one thing, the central heating timer had failed – again.

Swinging my legs over the side of the bed, I gave Joe an

accidental dig in the ribs. He promptly repaid me with a loud fart.

"Happy Christmas my little pudding." He gave the duvet a Mexican wave and grinned. "Bacon butties and then presents or presents and then bacon butties?"

His head disappeared back under the duvet before I had chance to reply. Leaving him to an extra five-minutes of slumber, I pulled my thick fleecy dressing gown on, shuffled my feet into the dreadful rabbit slippers that Connie had bought me, and made my way downstairs.

Connie was already up, cupping a steaming mug of tea in her hands as she sat hunched up on the sofa. Michael was in the spare room in Mum's attic and was probably still asleep, too many stairs meant that neither of us would be venturing up there with a morning coffee for him.

It was the first time in a long time that we had all been together under one roof. With heavy hearts we had arranged our last Christmas with Mum, inviting everyone from Nanny Flo – Mum's Mum – through to cousin Geraldine and assorted Aunts, Uncles and their offspring. Ella was very excited to have relatives to play charades with after dinner and I was not so excited to be left in charge of the gravy. I had yet to make a batch that couldn't have served a better purpose as Polyfilla.

"Mum's still asleep, thought I'd let her have a little longer, she's getter weaker and weaker by the day Mave."

I caught a glimpse of fear in her eyes. The mammoth task of setting up a bedroom in the morning room for Mum as the stairs had become increasingly more difficult for her, had just taken the best part of two days. Dragging furniture out and rearranging familiar things in there for her had become a priority. I plonked myself down next to Connie and gave her a hug.

"We can do this together, we can get through it, don't give up yet, she hasn't given up, she's still so full of..." I paused. Was the word *life* the right one to use, it seemed horribly ironic, to be so full of life when that same life was slowly ebbing away.

Connie picked up her rucksack, rummaged around in the bottom and pulled out a faded sepia photograph. She laid it on the coffee table, using her palm to smooth it out.

"It's Dad. Dad with Mum, you, me and Michael... before he left."

I stared at it.

A smiling man, dark hair gelled to one side, with one unruly curl hanging down over his forehead. Although it was black and white, I just knew that his eyes were green, vibrant green. Mum, so young, was sitting next to him, her floral swing dress revealing a net petticoat underneath, legs crossed at the ankles with baby Connie on her knee, I was standing next to her, leaning my head against her arm. Michael was in Dad's arms, his mischievous smile almost obscured by the aged crease that ran across the paper.

I looked at Connie, surprised. "How...err when, gosh, how long have you had this?"

"Since we cleared out the other day, I found it at the back of the welsh dresser when I moved it ready for Joe and Michael to take. Mave, I know."

"Know what?"

"I know you're looking for Dad. Have you told Mum?"

I sighed, staring at the photograph for longer than I should.

"No Connie and I'm not going to, it's all on hold now and don't tell Michael either. It's got to be our secret."

...

"It was an epilator Mum, I ask you, a bloody epilator; and he looked suspiciously at my top lip as he handed to me!" I gave the gravy a stir and looked at her for a bit of girly support. She smiled as she frisbee'd a Tupperware lid at me from the other side of the kitchen. She sat down on the breakfast bar stool.

"So, romance is not dead yet then?" she laughed.

I squished a lump under the spoon and watched the brown liquid bubble. "Dead! It's buried under the wrapping paper, along with Joe." I sighed and hammered down another gravy lump, this time a little more aggressively. "Please tell me I haven't got a hairy top lip?"

Slamming the kitchen cupboard at the side of her, she paused for effect before wagging her finger at me. "No love you haven't, but you could try it out on that awful hairy big toe of yours."

She turned around to see if everyone was seated at the table ready for the commencement of the Upton family Christmas dinner; or as Michael so succinctly put it, the *Upton Trough and Trotter Convention.*

Joe held the carving plate high, the turkey for fourteen of us precariously balanced as he edged his way past Nanny Flo's chair, accidentally knocking Connie's reindeer ears off her head and into her glass. Crimson splashes spotted the white tablecloth.

"Hey up Connie, you've spilled a bit there, not like you to lose a drop of the old red."

Connie glared at him. "Very funny Joe, I'm actually pacing myself this year..." she hesitated and looked at Nan who was sitting next to her. "... think you should do the same Flo, that's the third glass of sherry you've had already. It's not good for you."

Nan pushed her bottom set of false teeth out, wiggled them and just as quickly sucked them back into her mouth. "Says who? A little bit of what you fancy never done me any harm before and I'm almost 87!"

She defiantly gulped down the remains from her glass and held it out to me for a refill. I looked at Mum for approval whilst Ella buried her face in her serviette, desperately trying not to retch at the sight of Nan's dentures at the dinner table.

"It's Christmas Mavis, but no whisky, just make sure she sticks to the sherry." Mum plopped a stuffing ball on Connie's plate. Connie held up three fingers, indicating she could manage more than just the one that had been offered.

"Frisky.." Nan almost spat her top set of dentures out to join her bottom ones. "... I haven't been ruddy frisky since 1957!"

...

"Anyone seen Nan?" Connie's voice was temporarily muffled by a huge mouthful of Black Forest Gateau.

Joe scraped the remains of his Christmas pudding into the bin and flicked a lump of bread sauce from his finger.

"The last time I saw her she was bouncing off the walls in

the hallway on her way to the loo. The two helpings of pud, God knows how many mince pies and all that sherry was too much for her, think she's asleep in the front room now." He let out a snigger.

Mum wasn't impressed. "How long ago was that? Can someone go and check on her?" She dried her hands on her apron and looked at me to oblige.

"She'll be fine Mum." I took my paper hat off, crumpled it into a ball and bounced it off Joe's head.

"I'll come too..." Connie jumped up from her chair, almost tripping over her own discarded shoes, before whispering in my ear "... we could have some fun here."

Linking her arm through mine, just as we always did when we were little, she dragged me along the hallway and into the main hall. We stood outside the door and waited.

"Look, I got this from your cracker." She held out her hand. Nestled in the palm was a black plastic moustache. "I'll position Nan; you can take the photos." She held back a giggle, which only served to make her snort loudly. She wiped her nose on her sleeve.

The lounge door swung open, quietly rubbing against the carpet as we stood in silence watching Nan, mouth open, slumped in the overstuffed armchair by the Christmas tree. The excess wine and brandy that we had drunk with our dinner seemed to fuel our mischievous mood. As Connie carefully shoved the moustache up Nan's nose, I pranced around doing a wonderful David Bailey impression, snapping one photo after another whilst Connie manoeuvred Nan's arms and legs into an array of poses.

"Oh Mave, this is bloody brilliant." Connie took the

camera from me, checking the remaining shots.

I took another look at Nan, sprawled out with her beautifully coiffured white hair, best frock, pearls and her black plastic moustache. The photos would really cheer Mum up. I had to admit, she did look absolutely hilarious... well, that was until I suddenly realised that she hadn't actually moved on her own accord for some considerable time.

My heart missed a beat. Actually several beats if I'm honest.

"Connie, Connie... I think there's something wrong with her." I tentatively touched her arm, whilst Connie, still in the rapturous throes of laughter, was verging on a Tena Lady moment.

"Connie, I'm serious, I can't find a pulse!" I was now frantically trying to find some sign of life in Nan's wrist as sheer panic began to set in.

Connie stopped laughing, the colour draining from her face.

"Oh crap ..." she exhaled loudly and ran from the lounge slamming the door back heavily so that it hit the arm of the sofa. "... Mum, Mum..."

I could hear Mum's voice drifting from the hallway. "What is it Connie, calm down love."

Connie's voice caught in a sob. "I think Nan might be a little bit dead Mum..."

...

Twenty minutes later we stood on the doorstep, watching Nan lying prone on a stretcher being carted off to the ambulance, still sporting her black plastic moustache, which was now unfortunately wedged underneath her oxygen mask, quivering with each strained intake of breath.

I closed the front door and looked at Connie.

"Shit, that didn't quite go according to plan did it?" she smirked. I put my arm around her and shook my head.

...and it was at that exact moment I knew next year's family Christmas card wouldn't depict Tootles, Nan's bulbous eyed Chihuahua under the tree wearing a stupid Santa hat, but Nan herself...

... resplendent in a diabetic coma, with a plastic cracker moustache shoved up her nostrils and a tantalising glimpse of her fuchsia pink bloomers.

THE EDGE OF NORMALITY

"Sorry Mave, short straw I'm afraid, not the best thing to come back to after Christmas." Beryl crossed my collar number from the duties sheet, "Bob and Petey are off sick and we're running on empty, I'll get you relieved as soon as I can."

My heart sank. There was nothing worse than the dreaded hospital duty, everyone avoided it like the plague. I caught Don exchanging a sly smirk with Martin.

"So how come you didn't get it?" I threw the tea bag from my mug towards the bin. It missed, splatted against the magnolia painted wall and dropped to the floor.

"Quick on me feet my little chicken, quick on me feet, told Beryl I'd got a full file to do for CPS and it's got to be in by tomorrow." As if to prove a point he did a soft shoe shuffle around the kitchen in his grubby SWAT boots. "It won't be too bad, well not as bad as a late shift is, it'll just be the overnight assaults that are still in A&E, quick crime reports for them and Bob's your Uncle."

I shoved my paperwork into my briefcase, checked my radio battery and grabbed a set of car keys from the table.

There was no such thing as a 'quick crime report', experience had taught me that and anyway, my uncle was called Ernest.

···

All walks of life.

That descriptive was running through my mind as

I doodled on my clipboard. Four hours in and all I had to show for it was a numb bum, a bladder fit to burst from all the black coffee I'd been drinking, one crime report and numerous interventions. I'd been making random notes on the ones I'd been watching and dealing with, more for my own amusement and to pass the time, than anything else.

Brittany had strolled into A&E a little after 10.30 a.m. A rather loud little girl, no more than 18, shouting and squealing like a 12-year-old. At just over 5' tall, wearing fake beige Ugg boots, trodden down on the outside of both heels, she resembled a Hobbit.

Dragging her Uggs to the vending machine, she snagged her fingers in her bleached blonde hair. "Hey Chantelle, d'yer wanna can of Coke?"

Chantelle shrugged and carried on biting the skin around her fingernails. I stare intently at Brittany's roots thinking maybe she should let Chantelle loose with a toothbrush and a 30-volume mix of peroxide to sort them out. She has a flower tattooed on her shoulder with carefully scripted words underneath that say *Sweet Pee*. Spelling obviously wasn't the tattooists best subject at school.

Overhearing the conversation between Brittney and the triage nurse, I learn that she's attended A&E because Chantelle's superglued the fingers to her bottom lip whilst trying to fix her false nails on. Chewing them at the same time the glue was drying apparently hadn't been one of her smartest moves.

She plonked herself down next to Dwayne, a 22-year old testosterone fuelled, shaven-headed muppet who has been wandering around A&E all night. I'd already given him two warnings in the last hour.

This fine model of manhood needs stitches to a gaping wound on his forehead and another at the back of his protruding Neanderthal skull. From what I can gather from the grunts he's exchanged with his equally muppet-like mate, he attempted to head-butt an unsuspecting victim who was leaning against a lamppost waiting for a bus. The potential victim had seen the rapid jerk of Dwayne's head and had quickly sidestepped it.

Dwayne had subsequently head-butted the lamppost with such force he had bounced backwards into the path of an oncoming milk float.

I couldn't wait to get back to the nick to tell the lads about that one. I shoved the remainder of the Kit-Kat into my mouth and absentmindedly wiped my hand along the side of my trouser leg.

"Connor you little shit, put that down now...!"

I looked over to where that particular screech came from. Connor's mummy, having said her piece, had gone back to reading her magazine, leaving Connor to sit by the toy box, stuffing spilling out onto the grey tiled floor, as he held a headless Peppa Pig up in triumph.

After kicking Peppa's head around for a few minutes, he clambered onto one of the plastic bucket chairs, swinging his feet backwards and forwards whilst wiping great big strings of green snot from his left nostril all over the wall with his index finger. I watched as he began to kick the rather large buttocks of the woman in front, that were protruding through the back of her seat. Mummy is totally oblivious to Connor's unacceptable behaviour because she is still far too busy reading her dog-eared issue of Take A Break.

Poor Connor can only obtain snot from his left nostril as, alarmingly, he has a Tampax Tampon stuffed high up his right nostril, leaving a dangly bit of string swaying in the breeze in front of his mouth. I'm assuming this is the reason he's here in A&E.

Then again, this is the human race, so I could be wrong.

A delicate looking lady called Doris, probably mid-eighties, lilac-silver rinsed hair, rose print frock and a cream patent leather handbag, is sitting quietly in the corner, immersed in a book. She looks very churchy with her matching cream patent leather shoes.

The title of her book throws me a curved ball, *Seduction of a Highland Lass.*

Somehow I don't think this page turner is about haggis and hairy bullocks, but then again, you never know.

I couldn't actually see what was wrong with Doris. Scanning her from head to toe, she seemed perfect. Her composure was such that she didn't appear to be in any pain. I underlined her short entry on my pad. She was giving nothing away.

"Mrs Doris Thorpe-Smyth, Mrs. Doris Thorpe-Smyth to clinic 2." The plummy voice announced over the tannoy.

Ooh, I might get a bit more on her now.

I sat with my pen at the ready, not even remotely embarrassed that my stint in A&E had lowered me to this level.

She carefully closed her book, placed it in her cream patent leather handbag on the chair beside her, rose elegantly, straightened her frock, picked up her handbag and gracefully made her way through the double doors that bore the sign *Genitourinary Unit – Sexual Health & GUM Clinic.*

I definitely didn't see that coming, I almost choked trying not to giggle.

Dwayne looked over and was still trying to mouth the spelling of the first word on the sign as Mrs. Thorpe-Smyth disappeared through the doors. His mouth moving silently, eyes squinted, he was clearly very confused.

"Fookin' 'ell, look at that, they give yer free chewy in here," he snorted.

He blew a bubble, strung out his own chunk of gum, wound it round his finger and shoved it back in his mouth.

"I could do with some of dat. Wiv all this hanging round, the flavour on mine's gone a bit shit."

•••

"Can you just move the pillow for me a bit, love? I don't normally like to end up on the floor unless I've had a few brandies." Mum smiled, pointing to the V-shaped pillow behind her.

Plumping it up, I jiggled it around so it sat straight against the headboard.

"There you go, no sliding out of bed now, I know you, anything to escape." Tucking the duvet around her, I picked up the newspaper and placed it on the table next to her. "Nothing to stop you from having as many brandies as you want Mum, just say the word, I'll send Joe to the off-licence, in fact you can have anything you want."

"Oh I think I'd like a bit more than a Brandy Mave, I've

always wanted one of those *Squiffy* things, but you'd arrest me wouldn't you?" She laughed, which in turn set off a coughing fit.

Waiting for her to stop heaving, I mentally went through every malapropism I could think of that could be linked to me arresting my own mother.

"Squiffy? Do you mean spliff Mum, a joint of cannabis?" I didn't know if I should stand back in admiration or be shocked.

She mimicked smoking, bringing her hand to her lips and pretending to blow out. "Yep, that's it, a Squiffy, I'd like a Squiffy Mavis."

I shook my head.

"Ah, no you can't go back on your word, you said anything I wanted I could have." She gave an impish grin.

Jeez she was right, I had said that, but my Mum wanting to take a toke on a doobie full of marijuana filled me with horror, and more to the point, she was expecting me to get it for her.

DEAL OR NO DEAL

"How's your mum, Mave?" Beryl closed the duties folder and shoved it in the bottom tray of the green wire filing basket on her desk.

"Not good Sarge, but she's hanging on, I've never known anyone so determined. She's got a bucket list so she's carefully working her way through the ones she can still do, even though she's rarely out of bed now." I felt a twinge of guilt.

I'd lost count of the number of times Mum had so far mentioned her *Squiffy*. It was a combination of it being on her list of exciting and naughty things to do before the inevitable and because she'd heard it was good for pain relief. She was quietly hoping that being in my position, I'd be able to help her, when in fact it was quite the opposite.

I would lose my job if I was caught even thinking about scoring an eighth for her. I tried to put it down to the morphine clouding her judgement.

"Penny for them Mave, or are they worth a lot more than that?"

I shrugged my shoulders. "Thanks Sarge, you're probably right, they could cost me a lot more than money."

I left her sorting out the duties for the following night and made my way down the corridor to the radio room. I couldn't wait to get out on patrol.

A busy night shift would keep my mind occupied. I checked my mobile, no missed calls, no messages. That was good. Connie was covering whilst I was working. Between us we had worked out a system that meant we could each carry on with our respective jobs, whilst utilising our days off to care for Mum. Luckily my shifts gave me greater flexibility and Michael was coming up at the weekend too, so that would be a huge help.

I clipped my radio onto my shirt tab and picked up my keys.

"Just so you know troops, Sally McAllen has been circulated as wanted on a no bail warrant, chocolate éclair to the one who brings her in." Beryl wafted the white bakery box in front of Bob, who, by some miracle, had fully recovered from his 24-hour man-flu, along with his appetite.

He prodded his finger in an eclair and grinned. "Right, you're on!"

...

I shifted down a gear and turned into Belvedere Street, and from there onto Corporation Road, a familiar haunt with our Ladies of the Night. I'd give it half an hour having a mooch for Sally and if no joy, I could move on to the Oakland's Estate, see if there was anything going on down there.

Sally wouldn't be hard to miss if she was out tonight, she was never short of clients being a big girl, if you get my drift and her speciality was oral sex...

...without her false teeth in.

The last time I'd locked her up, she'd told me it was because it gave a great vacuum seal and in turn a better suck. So as far as she was concerned, the better the service, the more she could charge.

I shuddered at the thought. I'd tried to help her over the years, but she'd steadfastly refused to consider a change in career.

"Eh Miss Mavis, if you worked at Mackie D's and yer loved burgers and chips, would you wanna change yer job and go work for Weight Watchers, you wouldn't would yer?"

I hadn't been able to think of an answer at the time and had to admit defeat. We'd since maintained a guarded mutual respect with each other. Sally knew I would lock her up but she also knew I would treat her fairly.

I drove slowly along Corporation Road, glancing down the back jiggers, without any luck. No punters out and no Sally. I was nearing the last of the cobbled entries that stood rigid behind the terraced houses and factories, when I spotted her.

As expected, she was on her knees in the process of entertaining and Sally, being Sally, didn't even bother to stand up when I turned on the high beam side light from the roof bar of the patrol car.

Her client on the other hand took great exception to being lit up like the Saturday night star turn at the local Social Club. He stopped mid-thrust, the light catching the whites of his eyes as he immediately lost whatever momentum, growth and rigidity he had managed to produce prior to my arrival. This left Sally in the unenviable position of having her mouth full and being unable to do anything with it.

As their shadow cast a comical outline on the wall behind them, she managed a half-hearted wave. Pushing her client away, she scrambled to her feet, fished around in her coat pocket, produced a set of dentures with a flourish, and popped them back in her mouth.

"That's better, I don't feckin' whistle as much now." She wiped her mouth with the back of her hand.

"Come on Sal, jump in, no point in wasting time with the niceties." I pointed back to where my car was parked. "At least you'll get a decent breakfast in the morning."

She didn't look impressed.

"Arr hey Miss, he's given me a fiver, can't I just finish him off before youse take me in like?" she grinned.

I laughed, it was hard not to. "Absolutely no chance, I'm not standing around waiting for you to finish your services before I lock you up. Now be a good girl and let him sort his pants and tackle out, he's looking a little uncomfortable over there."

She folded her coat around her and opened the back door to the car herself. "Take it I don't get to sit at the front then?"

My steely expression gave her the answer. She quietly slid herself across the back seat, took her dentures out, checked them under the interior light and put them back in her coat pocket. "Don't wanna wear 'em out, they come in useful sometimes when the punters don't wanna pay."

Closing the car door, I turned to have words with her gentleman friend, but as expected, he'd taken the opportunity with me being otherwise engaged, to execute a disappearing act. I could only watch as he stumbled and tripped over his trousers that were still draped around his ankles, as he legged it up the street, vanishing into the night.

Sally wound the window down and stuck her head out. "Loves Mick Jagger 'im, makes me laugh that, speshully as he's the one gone home with no feckin' satisfaction and I've still got his bloody fiver!" she snorted.

I settled myself back into my seat and adjusted the rear view mirror. "Right Sal, you know it's the warrant don't you? Take it you haven't got anything on you that you shouldn't have before we go any further?"

She shook her head. "Nah miss not this time, but I'll tell yer what though, got ripped off to the tune of a tenner this morning. Some cheeky twat, not giving no names like, sold me a bag of feckin' *Oreogami* shit instead of weed."

I watched her shaking her head in disgust at her own stupidity, whilst at the same time I was nurturing the most marvellously wicked idea and as an added bonus, courtesy of Sally, I had a chocolate éclair to look forward to.

AND THE WORLD KEEPS TURNING

"You can't do that Mave, I mean, can you even smoke it? It could make her sick, even kill her!"

Connie's face fell as she realised what she had just said. I wasn't sure if I should feel sad, horrified or laugh. "That's the point Connie, she's dying, she's not going to miraculously get better, she's going through her bucket list, can't you see that?"

"Of course I can..." she snapped "... but smoking oregano, is that the best you can come up with?"

That stung.

"For the time being, yes. I'm torn between doing every last little thing she wants and getting myself in the shit at work. It won't kill her; she just might get a bit of a headache that's all."

She hesitated, looking at the small wrap of dried herbs I'd packaged up. "Okay, let's go for it, but if Mum pukes, you're cleaning it up!"

...

"Ten out of ten for ingenuity Mave, wouldn't want to have been in that position myself." Bob swept his hand over his remaining two strands of hair. "Did she actually smoke it?"

I wondered where the third strand had gone, probably blown away during the high winds we'd had the week before. He gave me a look that dared me to mention his missing tendril. I chose discretion.

"Only a few puffs but it was enough for her to believe she'd had a Squiffy, so it was another one crossed of her list and she was so happy..." I pushed the opened packet of biscuits towards him. "... hated lying to her though."

Don quickly intercepted the packet and grabbed three from the top and crammed a whole one into his mouth. "Sometimes we don't have a choice do we? Don't beat yourself up over it love."

I smiled, brushed off the crumbs Don had spat all over my jumper and got up to look out of the window. "Thanks lads, it does mean a lot having you around, don't know what I'd do without you."

Larry the Lump was making another appearance so my voice wobbled and my eyes had started to sting as I fiercely tried to stop myself from crying.

I knew they were watching me and probably giving each other knowing glances behind my back. Grey clouds were starting to roll in, enveloping what could have been quite a pretty wintry sunset. I checked my watch. 5.21 p.m. Just under seven hours left of this shift then home to take over from Connie.

Half of me couldn't wait to spend every available minute with Mum, the other half just wanted to run away.

"Mavis."

Beryl's gentle voice cut through the silence.

"Your sister's just been on the phone, you need to go home."

•••

The ten-minute drive seemed to take a lifetime.

Hitting a set of red traffic lights, I sat there with a sick bottomless feeling in my stomach. The end had come all too quickly. I wasn't ready.

The first drops of rain hit my windscreen. Turning the wipers on, a smeared arc of water gave the headlights of the car on the opposite side of the road a bright halo. As the lights changed from red, to amber and then to green, I lost my resolve. The hard exterior I had so carefully created, dissolved.

I began to cry.

Pulling up outside Mum's, the ornate carriage lamp hanging outside casting an inviting glow over the front door, I sat watching the rain splash on the windscreen for a little while longer. The wipers continued to smooth an arch across the glass, pausing only long enough to allow new spots to settle.

I wondered if I just stayed where I was, if I didn't go in, would that stop the inevitable?

There was still so much that I needed to tell her. This was so unfair. I choked back a sob.

Why is this happening to us?

The ensuing silence told me there were no answers.

Between heavy bursts of rain, I ran inside, throwing my coat over the bannister.

Checking myself in the hall mirror, I took a deep breath to calm down and pushed open the door to the morning room.

"Oh Mavis, you're home early, help yourself to one of these, I don't think I feel like eating today I've been a little under the weather." She held out a plate containing a rather large bacon butty that Connie had made her.

"It's okay Mum, I ate at work, come on let's get you comfortable." I plumped up her pillow, an action I did more from habit than because it needed doing. She had hardly eaten anything in days. Even against the pure white sheets, she looked pale.

"It's just a little setback, now don't you be worrying yourself." she scolded.

As much as she wanted us to believe there was normality in the chaos, she also desperately wanted to believe in it too. I sat on the edge of the bed so I could hold her hand. The syringe driver, giving her continuous morphine, was inserted in her chest, the cannula attached to a unit which was hooked on the bedhead.

I looked up at Connie. She slowly shook her head, her face etched with defeat as she closed her eyes. That action spoke volumes.

"Tell you what, why don't I make us all something lovely for supper, I'm sure that'll help your appetite Mum." Connie looked at me pleadingly, desperate that I should agree. "Mave, you'll be hungry too, won't you?"

Mum rolled her eyes at me. Connie didn't do tins, packets or ready meals.

Connie did from scratch.

As the clock slowly ticked away the minutes and then the hours, to the backdrop of clattering pans, wooden spoon banging and the scraping of metal on metal, we waited.

Mum was getting slightly impatient.

"Bloody hell Connie, if God had given you the job of feeding the five thousand, they would have died of starvation by now!" She winked, gave a little giggle and sighed. "I know

I said I didn't want you to tell me how long I've got left Mavis, but do you think I'll still be alive by the time she's dished it up?"

I roared with laughter and then it hit me.

My beautiful, bright enigmatic Mum, was reduced to a fading shadow. I just couldn't comprehend how something unseen for so long could so quickly take away her light. My eyes began to fill with tears as I fought hard to stay in control. I needed her, I wasn't ready to let her go.

"Oh for goodness sake Mavis, if you are going to fart, please kindly leave the room, I can tell by the look on your face." She winked and gave me one of her cheeky, knowing smiles that gave me a flash of her former self.

A deftly executed diversion. Not a tear fell in sadness, only in laughter.

Dimming the lights down low later that night, I smoothed the duvet around her, pulled the armchair close to the bed and opened her book, *Fried Green Tomatoes at the Whistle Stop Cafe.* I would read to her for a while until she fell asleep.

"It's funny, when you're a child you think time will never go by, but when you hit about twenty, time passes like you're on the fast train to Memphis. I guess life just slips up on everybody. It sure did on me..."

She reached out to touch my hand.

"Mavis, stay with me, I don't want to be on my own tonight."

I swept my fingers across her forehead, pushing the wispy strands of blonde hair from her eyes. "I've got my blanket, my fluffy Primark Slippers and my PJ's Mum, I'm not going anywhere except this chair okay?"

Even though her eyes were closed, she still let a trace of a smile touch her lips. "Thank you sweetheart, have I ever told you how much I love you?"

"Yes Mum... always..."

...

In the early hours of the morning, just as the sun was appearing over the trees to shine through the window, throwing dappled patterns across the wall, I held Mum gently in my arms. Her breathing laboured, I kissed her and told her that it was time.

Time to say our goodbyes. Time for her to let go.

With a small sigh she peacefully slipped away to a place without pain, without sadness and without fear.

...

Sitting outside on the garden wall, I imagined that I was still a child.

I wished with all my heart that I could have my time with her all over again. To smell her perfume, to have her dry my tears and tell me everything would be grand.

Normality continued around me as I felt my heart being torn from me. The birds warbled their songs, people passed by on their way to work, to school, to the shops; laughing, chattering. Daffodils were trying to open, wet with raindrops.

I was crying like I have never cried before, silent heaving sobs for a loss that I couldn't comprehend.

I wanted the world to stop.

How could life just continue for everyone as though nothing had happened? Didn't they know that the world was now a much lonelier, darker place without her?

But it does. This is Life.

With happiness, laughter, joy and hope there is a balance that gives heartache, tears, sadness and despair and with it all there is the realisation that nothing lives for ever, not even my beautiful, wonderful Mum.

The world was carrying on regardless, ignorant to our loss, unaffected by her death. As I wandered back inside, closing the front door behind me I stood and looked at Mum's sofa. The cushions still held her imprint, her Theakston's ashtray sat clean and untouched alongside a packet of Embassy No.6 cigarettes and a cheap red plastic lighter.

I knew then, I would never be the same again.

SUNSHINE AFTER THE RAIN

The following months after Mum's passing were times filled with some recriminations and what-if's, laughter at remembering the good times, sadness in knowing that no new memories would ever be created with her again and an emptiness that was indescribable.

"It's hard love, but it does get easier, I promise. I was like that after my Dad died, didn't know which way to turn."

I chewed the end of my pen, breaking my gaze from the window to look at Degsy.

"I know Degs, but it's in here..." I held my hand to my heart "... there's such an emptiness, it's like having permanent butterflies in my chest and it's making me very bitter."

"In what way kid?"

"Oh I don't know, say like yesterday. I brought Carlisle in for burglary of an old dear's house. I just stood looking at him thinking he was a piece of shit and why couldn't he have cancer and die, he would deserve it." I could feel my anger rising again. "I've lost my mum, Ella's lost her nan, who incidentally was more like a second mum to her. It's just not fair."

"Life isn't fair Mave, but don't let it eat you up, if you do it means it's claimed two lives and your mum wouldn't have wanted that. She'll be up there watching you, wagging her finger."

I stared out of the window again, watching the dark clouds being pushed by the wind across the rain leaden sky. "I think she'll be more than wagging her finger Degs, if there is an afterlife she'll be waiting to smack my legs because by now she'll know I lied about the Prime Minister!"

Degsy feigned a look of horror, which made me laugh.

"Right troops, enough joviality let's get this show on the road." Beryl spun a set of keys across the desk towards me. "No fag ash on the carpet, crisp crumbs on the seat and definitely nothing slimy stuck to the underside of the steering wheel, capiche?" She glared at Bob who at least had the decency to squirm, if only a little.

His nose picking antics on long nights were legendary.

I jumped up and looked out of the window onto the car park to get my first glimpse of the brand new, fully liveried Vauxhall Astra patrol car. Sporty, flash and pristine. As Bob and Martin jostled for space beside me, I was pretty sure it wouldn't stay in that condition for very long, once it had a few thousand miles under the bonnet and the weight of Bob's backside in the seat after several shifts.

•••

"You'd better make sure you don't have any girly bumps in this beauty," murmured Bob as he lovingly stroked the bonnet. "It's my turn tomorrow and I don't want to be wiping globs of your lippy off the windscreen." He sniggered as he swept his hand across the dashboard.

"Crikey Bob, look at the size of them melons." Martin pointed animatedly at my chest. "Somehow I don't think it'll be her lips hitting the windscreen first. She's got her own built-in air bags!"

Suddenly getting an overwhelming desire to kick him in

the testicles, or at the very least give him a dead leg, I waved the keys at him.

"Alright lads, very funny, jealously is a very unattractive trait in men..." I watched them slope off towards the back door of the nick, Bob hitching his belt up in the vain hope his trousers wouldn't end up around his ankles. "... oh, and can you tell Petey to get a move on too?"

With the keys safely clutched in my hand, I threw my briefcase, hat and jacket on the passenger seat, gave the exterior a once over and excitedly jumped in, only to find myself lying almost horizontal in the back seat. Staring at the upholstered roof, I contemplated my current predicament as I fumbled around at the side of the seat for anything that even remotely resembled a lever. Finding various handles, gadgets and buttons, I pressed, pulled, pushed and rattled them in turn. This only served to help the seat suddenly adopt a will of its own as it slammed me forwards in one sweeping motion and then alternatively jerked me backwards and forwards in seven different stages, giving me a serious case of motion sickness.

I sat in silence, not daring to touch another button.

It didn't matter how many times I jiggled, wriggled, wangled or manoeuvred, my curvy butt just sank back down between the bottom and the back of the bucket seat. I was shoved so far down the only thing driving the car other than my hands were my nellies, which amazingly enough, were now hooked over the top of the steering wheel.

Jeez, give me Florence the Fiesta any day.

"Here you go lovely, try this." Geoff the civvy driver threw a rather fetching tea stained, grey velour cushion through the open window. "Shove it down the back and sit on it. Got that given to me when old Inspector Bertie Bollocks retired a few years back, it's done me well."

He gave me a wink, leaving me wondering if Bollocks had been poor Bertie's real name.

Geoff's cushion did the trick. Tucking my nellies safely back into their rightful place, or as rightful as a Gossard Wonderbra would allow, I was ready to go as the radio crackled into life.

"Quick jump in, violent domestic in progress," I hollered to Petey as he galloped like a three-legged gazelle across the car park. Blues and twos on I swept through as the barrier lifted giving a squeal of tyres as I sped onto the main road. Fingers crossed the cushion would remain where I'd stuffed it, the prospect of it sliding into the foot well taking me with it as I hit the Leverhulme Hairpin filled me with horror.

Four minutes ten seconds later, we arrived at the scene, cushion intact. Flinging the door open, I jumped out closely followed by Petey. Frantic screaming and shouting reverberated from the mid-terraced house, increasing in volume the closer we got to the already open front door. With no time to lose, I ran inside.

"Oh bloody hell Mave, don't go in there yet, you've got..." but the rest of Petey's warning was drowned out by a scream that would have woken the dead. Making my way along the darkened corridor and through the nearest door on the left where the shouting was coming from, I paused long enough for Petey to forget his brakes and slam into the back of me.

There in all their glory was Indian Joe, a regular heavy partaker of alcoholic beverages, his girlfriend Liberty Lil with the off-set eye, and PJ Pops, a man who favorited any charity shop that could accommodate his desire for striped pyjamas, worn day and night.

All three were the best customers the local off-licence had.

Indian Joe kept ferrets in the house, several of them were currently scampering across the mattress that was dumped in the corner where Liberty Lil was now reclined in her best modelling pose. She winked at Petey, who recoiled in sheer panic.

Lil was attired as usual in her favourite fur coat, which she wore day in and day out, regardless of which season we were in. This wasn't too much of a problem in the winter, but in summer, Lil took liberties where her personal hygiene was concerned, hence her nickname. The heat, coupled with Lil's reluctance to shower, bathe or even stand outside in the rain, along with the fur coat, was at times too much to bear.

If your hand was forced and you had to lock her up in the summer, you always ensured a prisoner van was available to transport her in the rear cage which was at least a decent distance from your nostrils. Failing that you could almost feel yourself contemplating handcuffing her to the rear bumper of the police car and driving into the Custody Suite at a steady 5mph whilst she aired in the wind.

On this occasion, Lil was draped across the mattress, fur coat pulled around her, which was making it increasingly difficult to make out what bits were actually her and what bits were the numerous ferrets scampering across her.

I looked over at Petey who was standing with his jaw almost hitting the floor.

Tugging at his sleeve and hissing for him to get a move

on, I suddenly came eye to crotch with what he was looking at. Liberty Lil, not known for her graceful, ladylike posture was treating him to a complete, full-on eyeful of her ladygarden, minus her knickers.

Giving him a hard dig in the ribs I shouted at Lil. "Oh for God's sake put it away woman, we don't want it snapping this poor innocent boy's head off now do we?" I waited for a response.

She shrugged her shoulders and spat on the floorboards. "I like's 'em innocent, doesn't I Pops?"

She smirked as she slowly moved herself around so that PJ Pops who was sitting on a mangy two-seater sofa got the eyeful instead. He was clearly not impressed in the slightest as he carried on rolling a cigarette, whilst sniffing up a rather disgusting string of mucus that had been draped across his top lip.

Indian Joe, wearing a stetson and with his two-string guitar flung around his neck, was clearly agitated and even more clearly intoxicated.

I stood in front of him, breaking his gaze from Lil. "What's been going on Joe, this is the third call this week, can't you three either get on with each other or one of you move out?"

Joe snorted, rolled his eyes and leant forward, elbows on his knees. "It's like this Miss, me and Lil, well we're an item like, Lil was giving me some favours like, when Pops comes in and sez we need more tinnies..." pausing to wipe spittle and drool from the corners of his mouth with the back of his hand, he continued. "... I'm his mate like, so I tells Lil to keep it warm for me whilst I goes down the offie for him and when I comes back Lil's not only keeping it warm, she's doing the feckin" favours with Pops." He jerked his head to where Lil was still lying in repose.

I tried not to laugh as a mental image began to form.

The gist of the story was that incensed by this betrayal, Indian Joe had completely lost it and had whacked Pops around the bare backside several times with his guitar which had subsequently made Lil cry out in short lived pleasure before Coitus Interruptus was induced. He had then smacked Pops on the back of the head twice with a six pack of Stella lager he'd just purloined from the off-licence.

Neither Pops, Liberty Lil or Indian Joe were bothered about any injuries sustained during the fracas, it had only kicked off when the cheap cans had exploded on impact and the realisation had hit them that they didn't have the money to buy any more, or the energy to steal them.

I looked over as Pops smirked and Lil winked; well she tried to make a fair effort at a wink, but the false eyelash on her off-set eye had come partially unglued and was now sweeping her left nostril. Licking her top lip, she slid her hand across Pops' thigh, gently fondling the stripes of his blue Sue Ryder Charity PJ's, and that was when I realised, albeit too late to do anything about it, that Indian Joe had seen the exchange between them.

Snarling and spitting whilst swinging his guitar he vaulted the sofa knocking a half-drunk can of Stella and Pops to the floor. Clearly terrified, Pops jumped up and scrambled for the door scattering several ferrets in all directions as Joe grabbed the back of his pyjama bottoms, dragging them down to his ankles.

Chaos then ensued as Petey sprang into action and flew

through the air to rugby tackle Joe. Joe sidestepped just as Pops tripped over his pants and fell to the floor, leaving Petey impaled headfirst between Pops' legs and a rather over-exposed pair of buttocks.

Lil, never one to miss an opportunity, liberated the half-drunk can of lager that had been rolling around on the floor just as I grappled Joe and handcuffed him. Dragging him outside to the police car I looked back to see Petey yanking the front of his jumper up, frantically scrubbing at his face.

"I smelt his butt, Jesus Mave I smelt his butt, it was disgusting," he sobbed.

As I shoved Indian Joe into the back of the police car, he started to laugh, spraying stale lager-smelling spit in my direction as he animatedly pointed at my back.

"Feckin' hell miss, have your got them 'emerroyds or sumat?"

Turning round to look, I was mortified to see swinging next to my handcuff holder, Swiss Army Multi-tool and my baton, was Geoff's beautiful velour cushion which was stuck fast to the velcro tab of my first aid pouch.

"Oh faarking hell Petey, thanks for nothing mate." I was horrified and couldn't work out why he hadn't warned me that I'd been inadvertently sporting a tatty piece of soft furnishings, which was now overhanging my curvy butt like a crappy Christmas bauble.

I jumped into the car, glad to be able to park my cushioned derriere into the driver's seat. Petey, who was still scrubbing his face with his jumper, sniffed and shook his head.

"I did try to tell you Mavis, but nobody ever listens to me..." he looked wistfully out of the car window with a resigned sadness to his eyes, "... do you know, it's the story of my life..."

Quick as a flash Indian Joe piped up from the back.

"I've not got me geetar, but if you hum it boy... I'll sing it."

•••

"I couldn't believe it Mum it was so funny, Petey was mortified. He even used a whole bottle of Hibiscrub on his face and then had to see the doctor because he got a reaction."

I giggled to myself.

"Ella's doing really well at school. Her report was amazing, straight A's in every subject, except maths though..."

I thought for a minute.

"... think she's going to take after me, bit of a dunce on the old maths." I took a sip from my mug of tea.

"Joe and I are planning our wedding. I've seen the most fabulous dress; I'm having white lilies for my bouquet. I'm not sure about a veil though. What do you think, do you think it'll be a bit silly at my age?"

I nibbled my biscuit.

"I'm looking for Dad too. I'm so sorry Mum, but I need to know where he is, or even how he is."

I waited.

I didn't expect a response; I just wasn't ready to give up our little chats yet. I closed my eyes and sighed, hoping she could still hear me.

Plumping up the cushion on the sofa, I moved the clean ashtray to the centre of the coffee table and looked around. The room that had once been warm and cosy now stood empty, cold and quiet, the silence broken only by the ticking of the old clock on the mantelpiece.

"Night Mum, speak to you tomorrow."
I closed the door.

A YEAR LATER...

"Muuuum... can you come upstairs, I need you?"

Ella's dulcet tones resonated down to the kitchen where I was desperately trying to sieve the huge, jelly-like lumps out of my gravy. I slammed the pan down on the chopping board, which in turn knocked the wooden spoon so that a large glob of gravy splattered across the wall tiles.

"What's the matter, I'm just doing the tea, can't it wait a minute?" Exasperated I poured the mixture down the sink, stamped the lumps down the drain with the spoon and reached for the Bisto instant gravy mix from the cupboard. Defeat accepted.

"I can't do my zip up and Luke's due any minute, and my hair's gone to the dogs too." She slammed her wardrobe door for the full effect.

Nothing beats having a petulant 17-year-old in the house. Some days I nostalgically wished for my petulant 7-year-old to be miraculously returned to me, at least then I wouldn't have to fight for the mirror and wonder where all my deodorant had gone.

"Come down here and I'll have a look at it and if you go in my bedroom there's some hair stuff that you spray on, it might work." Ella had inherited my unruly hair, no matter how much you tweaked or teased it, it wouldn't hold a curl.

She flounced into the kitchen, flushed pink and smelling of sweet chocolate, her new perfume from someone called Theory Muggles, or something like that. I suppose if you don't mind attracting Willy Wonka as a date, then you're onto a winner. She held up her long hair with both hands so I could see where the zip had jammed at the back of her dress.

"Mum, remember when you made me that promise?"

"What promise was that, think I've made a few over the years sweetheart?" I gave a sheepish grin and carried on fiddling with the zip until it released itself and moved smoothly along the metal teeth.

"The one where you said you'd always come home from work safely, that you'd never leave me, remember?"

I thought for a minute, grateful that it wasn't one of my good old 'mummy' promises, you know, the ones we all create at some time to get our children to do something they don't want to do and then hope they forget what bargain we made in the process.

"Oh that one, yes I do. I kept it too, didn't I?"

"Do you wish your own dad had promised that?" She dropped her hair and turned to face me.

I looked into her green eyes, the same eyes I had imaged over and over again that my dad would have, unsure how I felt. If he had stayed, would I be the same woman I am now, I had never known anything other than what it was. I had a dad, albeit an absent one. Would his presence have made any difference to my life?

I didn't know.

"Sometimes I suppose, but from what little I do know about him, I doubt he would ever have been able to keep a promise Ella. To do that sweetheart you have to experience love and loyalty. I don't think he was capable of either."

Wrapping her arms around me, she nestled into me,

holding me tight. I stroked her hair, just as I had when she was a child.

"You've always got me Mum, I'll never leave you, I promise."

The emotion of this unexpectedly tender moment left me fragile. I knew if I tried to speak, I would cry. The sing-song ring on the doorbell broke the emotional silence. Ella gasped in excitement.

"He's here Mum, Luke's here, gotta go." She grabbed her coat from the hallstand and disappeared.

As the front door slammed shut, I stood alone in the kitchen, valiantly holding the wooden spoon that still sported the congealed remains of another of my failed gravy attempts.

I couldn't help but laugh at the irony of her short-lived promise.

•••

My curvy butt had only just touched the battered old sofa in the rest room when Heidi's excitable tones barked out over the radio; just as I was about to take my first bite from a rather attractive looking BLT butty.

"Sorry about this Mave, it's probably a crock but can you start making to Morrisons, we've had reports of a disturbance in progress, no further details."

I threw my sandwich back in the budget cardboard carton that I had ripped apart in my haste to taste food after almost nine hours on duty, and chucked it in the bin. An errant piece of tomato slapped against the side and slid slowly to the bottom.

Heidi continued. "Apparently it's getting out of hand, so it's an immediate response, Grade one..."

Clicking my utility belt into place, I hoisted up my combat pants and grabbed my jacket. "Okay Heidi, show me responding."

Jumping the back stairs, two at a time, I made it down into the yard and into my car in record time, pausing momentarily to allow the security barrier to lift. Running the gauntlet of drivers who suddenly found the ability to complete a full slalom in and out of parked cars in sheer panic at not knowing where the sirens were coming from, I arrived at Morrisons, proud in the knowledge that I had only shouted *bugger*, *faark* and *twat* an average of three times each and one resounding *bollocks*, throughout my whole journey.

Clearly I had still maintained a small frisson of ladylike refinement about me after all these years in the job.

Based on previous calls to this store, I was half expecting to find a shoplifter embedded head first in the Organic Cabbage and Cauliflower display after a futile attempt at escape from the store security guards.

I wasn't completely off the mark, I just had the wrong location.

Brian and Stan where wrestling with a wiry little man in the middle of the foyer. Smashed bottles of whisky lay on the tiles, the strong-smelling amber liquid pooling out towards the sliding doors. The regular OAP shoppers were almost having the vapours as he spat out choice obscenities.

"Gerroff me yer shower of bastards..."

Stan had him in a rather nifty headlock, Brian was sitting on his legs which made handcuffing him an easier task than

I had at first envisaged as we fought to restrain him whilst actively avoiding the shards of glass nearby. Clicking them into place, I double locked them, and with their help, got him into a sitting position.

He absolutely reeked. I was surprised to see that he wasn't as young as I had first thought he was. Grey hair, uncut and greasy, grime ingrained under the fingernails of his large, calloused hands, shabby, dirty jeans and an old jacket that was at least three times too big for him, with the complexion of a hardened drinker. Difficult to put an age on him, but he had to be in his early 70s.

"Caught 'im red handed with two bottles of *Johnny Walker* shoved inside his jacket miss." Stan pointed to where the smashed bottles lay. "He put up quite a fight he did for an auld bugger."

"Take it the store's making a complaint Brian?"

Brian nodded as he straightened his tie and smoothed his hair back into place. "This isn't the first time; we've given him chances 'cos we felt sorry for him. He was in yesterday, got the stuff back and barred him, and then the cheeky bastard comes back in today."

He handed me a copy of the Banning Order they'd served him with, scant details, no full name or date of birth, just the words *Frank the Tramp* and a brief description.

"Right, okay Frank, you heard what's been said you're under arrest for theft, do you understand that?"

Frank shrugged, clearly not bothered one way or the other.

I brought him to his feet, which meant I was unlucky enough to get another nauseous wave of his body odour. Decision made, I shouted up.

"I've got a male under arrest at Morrisons Heidi, he's a bit stinky and volatile, is the van available for transport?"

Frank grunted and spat on the floor beside him. "I'd rather smell like shit than be a dirty bizzy, bet your family's so feckin' proud of you, hey?"

I glared at him. I was used to being called everything under the sun, day in and day out, it was normally water off a duck's back, but that really riled me.

"Prouder than your family probably are of you sunshine!" I spat back.

ANOTHER EPIPHANY

"Sarge, this male's been arrested for Theft Shop; the circumstances are that at 16:35 hours..."

I carried on giving the circs of Frank's arrest to Rob, the Custody Sergeant, whilst Bob and Martin carried out a gloved search of him, their screwed up faces indicative of the mixed aromas Frank was still giving off.

Bev breezed in with her marker pen ready to put his name up on the board. "Drunk tank 1 for him Mave?"

I nodded as she began spraying copious amounts of air freshener around, trying but failing, to sweeten the air. She stood behind Frank, held her nose and wafted her hand. I tried not to laugh. Martin, not known for his cast iron constitution suddenly went into overdrive and began baulking, which in turn made Bob retch too.

Frank, oblivious to our discomfort, was happily regaling Rob with tales of his many years at sea, the excitement of foreign lands and lovely ladies, gun-running and times spent on the floor of various bars and hostelries. I rolled my eyes at Bob and Martin, personally I didn't think he'd actually been out of Westbury, let alone the country, it was quite sad really, a sort of Walter Mitty.

Rob leant forward on the booking-in desk. "Right Frank, let's have all your details then we can get your fingerprinted, something hot to eat and get you bedded down okay?"

Frank shifted from one foot to another.

"Actually boss, me name's not Frank, if you want me full

title it's Able Seaman Arthur Albert Upton, date of birth 24th April, 1937, Sir!" He threw a salute for the full effect.

I could feel my eyes widen so much they were in danger of falling out of their sockets. Had I heard right? I felt sick, the colour drained from my face, my heart thumped against my ribs.

It was seconds that felt like hours before I found adequate breath to be able to speak as I grabbed hold of Bob's arm.

"Oh shit Bob... that's my dad...

... I've only gone and arrested my own feckin' dad!"

2008

Marion, her mouth wide open in shock, a crumb of digestive biscuit tantalisingly hanging from her bottom lip, put her mug down.

"You're having a laugh Mave, never, your own Dad?" She was incredulous. "That's worse than having Moggie Benson save your life!"

"Yep, I'm afraid so." I stood up from the table and waved my empty mug at her. "Another brew lovely?"

She nodded. "So what happened, did you let on to him?"

Flicking the kettle on, I smiled, more to myself than Marion. "That's another story Marion, another story entirely..."

The End

~

(or is it?)

ACKNOWLEDGEMENTS

After reading various blogs, self-help manuals, Facebook & Twitter links, I thought I knew a little bit about the do's and don'ts of writing a book. I don't think I've ever been more wrong in my entire life!

Writing it was the easy part. Submissions and rejections were to follow leaving me tearfully scrambling for the gin like a manic Miss Hannigan from Annie... until I suddenly remembered that I don't actually drink and alcohol apparently never solved anything anyway.

Never one to follow the rules, once I'd extricated my head from our low-level, silent flush loo the following morning, after producing various technicolor yawns brought on by the aforementioned gin, I brushed down my big-girl pants and tried again, and this is where my thank-you's begin.

To the person who has made it all possible, the man who read about Mavis, loved her as much as I did, and sent me that wonderful email whilst I was on holiday. Matthew Smith, my Publisher. (I've always wanted to say that!)

Matthew, thank you for believing in me and thank you for giving Mavis her moment. I am indebted to you.

Two very special people who have put up with my incessant writing based questions over a prolonged period of time are Luca Veste and David Jackson. I can happily call one my nephew and the other my neighbour. Luca your guidance and experience was invaluable, your kindness so warmly received. I didn't just gain a husband when I married your Uncle John, I inherited a fabulous family too. Dave, from the first writing class to panic struck visits to your house, bless you. You are not just my neighbour you are my mentor and friend.

To another member of the police 'family' and successful author, Matt Johnson. Your email on that chilly March morning in 2013 meant the world to me. I called you a saint; you denied it, but I still think you are! You took the time and trouble to encourage, help and guide me Matt, thank you from the bottom of my heart.

For the lovely, approachable John McDonald who helped me see that Mavis should be doing something a little more dramatic in the first chapter than cleaning her teeth! Well, she wasn't really but she might as well have been. That one chapter changed everything.

Nikki Bywater, Gill Beavon, Sharon Parr, Samantha Magson, Fyona Riozzi, Nita De-Asha, what would I have done without you all? You have endured endless read-throughs of various drafts, culminating in the finished product. Your opinions and reviews helped me to know I was on the right track. To the fabulous Pelsall Pair, Angela Collings and Dawn Hamblett, you'll never know how much your messages and giggles kept me going, the day we finally met will go down in history, including the dangling Sale price tag hanging from my cardigan! You just can't beat class can you? For the amazingly talented actor Lynne Fitzgerald, better known as Bunty The Bouncer, Desperate Scousewives etc., I couldn't think of anyone who could bring Mavis to life like you can. Thank you for loving her as much as I do.

Social media, from Twitter to Facebook is a godsend.

What is even more of a gift is the people you meet through them. Their encouragement and support is what every writer treasures. There are too many to mention individually, but for the lovely Anne Coates, Tracey Snelling, Carol & Kevin Maddox, Angie Wren, Diane Buckley, Eileen Streets, Karen Littler, Ron & Ann Cashin and Boff Moatman, bless you for the RT's, shares, messages, butt-kicking and interviews.

Many years ago there was a great guy who starred in an iconic Liverpool based soap. I used to sit glued to the screen for every episode never dreaming that one day he would so actively encourage me in my dream. Louis Emerick you are a star and a gentleman, thank you from the bottom of my heart, I sincerely hope you and Lisa enjoy Mavis.

Now to a truly fabulous friend, a completely off-the-wall, zany lady who makes me howl with laughter, Julie Ellsmoor. You have been with Mavis from the very first chapter and I know I've told you many times how much I treasure and value you, not just as a friend but also as a brilliant critic (I'll drop the case of Merlot at your house later). Thank you for being there.

For Emma, my beautiful daughter and Olivia and Annie my adorable granddaughters, thank you for being you, thank you for the days of distraction playing Crocodiles when the words refused to come, visits to the zoo, cuddles and kisses – and for telling Nanny that she could do it. I am so incredibly proud of you all. To my step-son Jonathon, in fear of your wicked, wicked step-mother, you suffered the pains of proof reading my bloopers, howlers and poor punctuation. In my defence it was predictive text to blame, well that's my excuse and I'm sticking to it!

Keeping it in the family, a special mention to my cousin. He is Derek when he wears trousers and Pound Shop Princess, Beverly Macca when he dons the leopard print frock and tights. Sharing your limelight with Mavis has helped her (and me) enormously, I mean come on, a retweet from the fabulous Fern Britton, Mavis was beside herself! To the very special Audrey Scally, or better remembered by us all as Sergeant 8247 'Auntie Aud'. Your kindness, friendship and laughter meant the world to me, we had so much fun working together. Sergeant Beryl Scally is my tribute to you, a little bit of immortality. I miss you every day Audrey. With fond memories until we meet again.

To my old colleagues and friends of Merseyside Police past and present and to 'the job' itself. I have loved every minute, I have shared laughter, tears, high jinx, heartbreak, fear and smudged lipstick with you throughout my career, and without you, there would be no Mavis and no stories to tell. Thank you. Stay safe, keep trying for the perfect biscuit dunker and I'll leave you to decide who is based on who – all very loosely of course!

And last, but definitely not least, to my husband John. This wonderful man has patiently endured various chapters being shoved under his nose to proof-read whilst trying to eat his dinner, and then had the horror of discovering his side of the bed had been drastically reduced in size to accommodate my burgeoning backside, wholly caused by my excessive consumption of biscuits whilst writing.

John you are my rock, this would never have happened for me without your love and encouragement. Courtesy of custard creams and digestives, I can truly say 'all my love from your Wide'!

Finally, I have a confession to make. My diligently scribbled list of people to thank and acknowledge over the last two years, which I placed in a very, very safe place, has been mislaid..err lost... err maybe stolen....okay, okay, hands up, I've completely forgotten where I put it. I hope I haven't missed anyone out, but if I have, please know it wasn't intentional, I appreciate every one of you, it's just down to me being scatty.

Gina

Gina was born during the not-so-swinging 50s to a mum who frequently abandoned her in a pram outside Woolworths and a dad who, after two pints of beer, could play a mean Boogie Woogie on the piano in the front room of their 3-bed semi on the Wirral. Being the less adventurous of three children, she remains there to this day – apart from a long weekend in Bognor Regis in 1982.

Her teenage years were filled with angst, a CSE in Arithmetic, pimples, PLJ juice, Barry White and rather large knickers until she suddenly and mysteriously slimmed down in her twenties. Marriage and motherhood ensued, quickly followed by divorce in her early thirties and a desperate need for a career and some form of financial support for herself and her daughter.

Trundling a bicycle along a leafy path one wintry day, a lifelong passion to be a police officer gave her simultaneously an epiphany and fond memories of her favourite author Enid Blyton and moments of solving mysteries. And thus began an enjoyable and fulfilling career with Merseyside Police. On reaching an age most women lie about, she quickly adapted to retirement by utilising her policing skills to chase after two granddaughters, two dogs and one previously used, but still in excellent condition, husband.

Having said goodbye to what had been a huge part of her life, she suddenly had another wonderful epiphany. This time it was to put pen to paper to write a book based on her experiences as a police officer. Lying in bed one night staring at the ceiling and contemplating life as she knew it, Gina's alter-ego, Mavis Upton was born, ready to star in a humorous and sometimes poignant look at the life, loves and career of an everyday girl who followed a dream and embarked upon a search for the missing piece of her childhood.